I0653779

# THE ARGENTINA RHODOCHROSITE

*An Ainsley Walker Gemstone Travel Mystery*

## J.A. JERNAY

"Soccer is a long series of frustrations leading up to near certain heartbreak. It rewards neurotic creativity. Many of the greatest players have been marginally insane. They respond to unfolding situations in unpredictable ways.

"It's also a game that teaches you that life is unfair. Superior performance does not often translate into victory. It reflects a tragic view of the universe."

—David Brooks, *The New York Times*

# CHAPTER ONE

Ainsley Walker was stirring cream into her coffee when she noticed the businessman making a kissyface at her.

At first, she hadn't even been sure that she was the intended target. She'd turned around to see which unfortunate soul was the recipient of this stranger's love.

But there was nobody behind her. Ainsley herself was the mark.

She was in the cafeteria aboard the Buquebus, a large, modern hydrofoil with comfortable seating for five hundred, though there weren't even a fraction that many on this weekday morning.

They had just left the country of Uruguay. Their destination lay three hours across the wide brown waters of the Rio de la Plata estuary.

Buenos Aires. The capital of Argentina.

The night before, her Uruguayan friend Sofia had warned her about Argentine men, about their masculinity, their forwardness, their presumptuousness. Ainsley had believed her, but she hadn't expected the come-ons to start quite so quickly. The hydrofoil wasn't even ten minutes out of the port.

Ainsley placed a lid onto her coffee and walked back to her seat. She could feel the businessman's eyes burning a hole in the back of her pants. In her seat, she hazarded a glance at him.

Bad move. He had been waiting for eye contact. Now he was coming over.

Ainsley swore under her breath, zipped her jacket up to her chin, and crossed her legs. She'd been hoping for a quiet ride. The last two weeks in Uruguay had been a real eye-opener, both exhilarating and exhausting. She'd been hoping for an anonymous arrival, unknown, undisturbed, unmolested.

After all, she had zero knowledge of what lay in store in the new country, beyond the fact that a driver would be picking her up at the terminal when she arrived. And that her new employer was apparently a famous person. Other than Evita, the scandalous first lady who had died fifty years ago, Ainsley didn't really know any Argentine celebrities.

In the meantime, she'd have to hoist up her armor to fend off this suitor. Of course she'd chosen a seat in a row that ended against the window. There was no escape. She'd sealed her own doom.

Ainsley looked at the pack of cigarettes in her purse. She'd picked up this habit again this year after her husband, a man she only referred to as the Legal Weasel, had left her. A smoke would really help the anxiety right now, but the Buquebus didn't allow it.

The lecherous businessman swung himself into her row, choosing a nearby seat. Ainsley began to study her passport. It had suddenly become an incredibly fascinating document.

"Do you have Spanish?" the businessman asked in Spanish.

Ainsley ignored him.

"I think that you do," he said, "so allow me to tell you something. Uruguay has a serious problem at immigration."

Ainsley's heart skipped a beat. She thought of all the misunderstandings that had occurred on her last gemstone adventure, the murder of José Ignacio Tabarez, her charcoal drawing splashed across the media, the last week she spent hiding inside Sofia's apartment. The moment at the immigration counter, just before the official had stamped the passport and waved her through, ranked as one of the most suspenseful of her life.

She decided to bite. "What do you mean?" she said.

The businessman became deadly serious. "Because they let a woman as beautiful as you leave the country." His eyes carried the look of a true romantic.

"Don't even try it," she said.

Then his eyes glanced at her figure. "Right now it feels like a small miracle that you walk upon this earth."

"It's a miracle that I've allowed to you stay in that seat," she said.

"Of course you are hostile," he said. "It's natural. Like the cactus grows the needles to protect its sweet core."

"You're a terrible poet."

"Maybe you're right, but I have the wallet of a businessman. Come have a coffee with me."

"Never."

"Just one cup."

"Only if you like it poured onto your head."

He sighed. "You are such a piece of beef. I wish I was an egg, so that I could lay down alongside you on a plate."

Ainsley had to laugh at that one. Her suitor took the opening and reached out to touch her hand. She knocked it away. "Take yourself somewhere else," she said, "I'm not interested."

The businessman shrugged. "Okay," he said.

He didn't seem wounded, or angry, or pensive. Instead, he took it as though he'd just learned that next weekend's weather wouldn't cooperate with his plans. He would change his plans, because there would be other weekends, just like there would be other women.

He stood up and walked away. Ainsley grudgingly admired his confidence.

She twisted around in her seat to verify that he had indeed left. Then she settled back again and stared out the window, out into the grayness and fog of the open river. She couldn't see water, land, or anything else.

There was a similar fog in her head.

The only things Ainsley associated with Argentina were steak and tango. One food, one dance. She suspected, however, that neither one truly described the country, in the same way that hamburgers and country-line dancing don't truly describe America, or the way that tins of beef and ball-room dance don't truly describe England.

She felt someone sit down next to her. It was the businessman.

Ainsley sighed out loud. "Wasn't I clear? You don't interest me."

"This is no longer a romantic conversation," he said.

"It never was."

"I would like to give you a piece of advice."

"Really."

"Yes. I was trying to tell you that you are a beautiful woman."

"You tried very hard."

"Don't you think it is better to appreciate the compliment than to become angry?"

"I wasn't angry."

"You were defensive. You still are."

"But—"

He cut her off. "Stop, please. I come to you with humble appreciation of your natural gifts."

"That's not how I interpreted it."

The businessman leaned forward. "But that's how the game is played. And I didn't invent the game. I'm only a player. We men are all players."

The businessman let the comment sink in. Then he patted Ainsley's knee.

"Welcome to Argentina," he said.

BUENOS
AIRES

# CHAPTER TWO

An hour later, the hydrofoil had been moored to the dock, the wide steel gangplank had been dropped with a terrifying clang, and a flood of humans stepped off the boat into the Buquebus terminal.

The human tide carried Ainsley down a carpeted hallway, around several tight bends, across an upstairs balcony, and finally down a set of stairs, where she was disgorged into a vast lobby. Yellow globes dangled from the ceiling over the heads of people lined up at three different windows to purchase tickets going the opposite way.

Argentina. This was its welcome mat for those entering by sea.

Ainsley strode across the arrivals lobby with her white purse slung comfortably across her shoulder, and a small duffle bag dangling from her hand. It'd been an impromptu parting gift from Sofia, her new friend back in Uruguay, before she'd left.

Standing near the exit was a black-suited driver holding a plastic-sheeted sign. On one of the signs the name WALKER was spelled in red marker.

She approached the man and said, "That's me."

"Identification," he said. She handed over her passport. He checked it, nodded, then handed it back. "This way."

She followed him out of the terminal. The light blinded her as she stepped outside.

The vehicle, a black Mercedes, waited a few meters away. The driver approached the car confidently, nearly strutting, his body moving side-to-side. He opened the door with a muscular flourish.

Ainsley didn't look at him as she slid into the back seat. The interior was upholstered in soft leather. Several magazines were stuffed into the netting in the back of the seats. There was bottled water and cans of juice and soda.

Far more interesting, however, were the sights outside her window.

The streets of Buenos Aires.

The Mercedes entered the stream of traffic. The cars were small and fast, darting around each other with no turn signals. Her driver accelerated between two slower taxis, splitting the lanes. Ainsley held her breath; her fingers curled around the bar above the doors.

Through the windshield she watched the cars squeezing, braking, swerving, zipping, zooming. They darted into any open space available. Lane markers were like donation boxes. Mere suggestions.

The imposing facades of several government buildings passed by her window. Then the Mercedes looped around a large structure that was half pink, half unpainted. Ainsley vaguely recognized it: Casa Rosada, the Argentine capitol. Madonna had sung the famous elegy from its balcony.

But Ainsley didn't want to think about Andrew Lloyd Webber right now. She was marvelling instead at the business district that they'd passed into, whose sidewalks were overflowing with people bundled in dark, stylish clothing. There was energy here, an excitement in the air that had been utterly absent from the sleepy backwater ambience she'd felt in Montevideo. This city felt like it was *going* somewhere.

"Señor," she said in Spanish, "where are we right now?"

"El Microcentro," he replied.

She was relieved to hear him using the same dialect, Rioplatense, that had been used in Uruguay. Ainsley didn't want to try to learn yet another variety of Spanish right now.

The Mercedes turned right onto a behemoth of a street. It was literally twenty lanes wide, striped with at least three medians. Through the windshield, Ainsley spotted what seemed to be a replica of the Washington Monument, a white obelisk roughly a hundred meters high, springing out of a roundabout.

This was the Obelisco, the undeniable center of Buenos Aires, like an enormous thumbtack pinning down this bustling city.

The driver turned into a leafy neighborhood, down residential streets lined with three- and four-story apartment buildings, all protected with security gates or thick doors.

"Where are we now?" Ainsley asked.

"This is Boedo, another barrio," he said. "Those houses are *chorizo* cottages." The name was appropriate. The homes were shaped like tall, thin sausages.

Soon the car passed into a different commercial district, less dense than the Microcentro had been, but equally interesting.

With little warning, the driver stopped the car in front of a sleek new two-story office building. The facade was pure white. The front door a sky blue-and-white fractal pattern, the type that is meant to indicate that incomprehensible modern work occurs within. There was no sign.

"We are here," he said.

He pulled himself out of the car in a single fluid motion

and yanked open her door, the practiced move of a professional. Ainsley hesitantly stepped out of the car.

"I don't have an address," she said. "Is that the building? All I know is to ask for Gabriel."

"We are here," said the driver, startled. "And if you're asking for Gabriel, it means you're working for Nadia."

"Who is Nadia?"

"She is a manager."

"Is she a criminal? Or a liar?"

It was an odd question, and he wisely dodged it. "It's hard to say."

Ainsley felt twinges of anxiety wiggling in her belly. "I just finished a very intense assignment in Uruguay where I found out that my employer had been lying to me. I want to make sure that that doesn't happen again."

He smiled as he hauled her luggage from the trunk. "I don't think Nadia will be your biggest problem."

The guy was diplomatic if nothing else. Ainsley had to respect that. She bent slightly at the knees to adjust her lipstick in the reflection of the Mercedes window. When she looked up, he was watching her.

"Beautiful," he said. He made a lewd kissyface.

She remembered the advice from the businessman on the Buquebus. This was just how it worked for women here. Femininity was a virtue.

"Thank you," she said.

"Please enter," he replied, "I will follow behind you."

Of course he would follow behind her. That much she was sure of, which is why she put a little bit of extra sauce in her hips as she approached the front door.

# CHAPTER THREE

When Ainsley opened the door, she found herself face-to-face with a dark young man, early twenties, dressed in a natty suit. Inside, he'd reached for the door at the same time.

"That's an excellent sign," he said. "We are on the same wavelength. My mother would approve." A couple days of stubble sprouted from his face, and a smile cracked the corners of his mouth. He was short and slight and seemed absolutely harmless.

"I'm already taken," she lied.

"So am I," he replied, "by my mother." He stuck out his hand. "I'm called Gabriel. *Mucho gusto.*"

She returned the handshake. "Ainsley Walker. *Igualmente.*"

He kissed her cheek in the customary way. "You are the person I was looking for. Please, enter. We have no time to waste."

He strode across the minimalist lobby and beckoned over his shoulder. Ainsley followed him. Several assistants were sitting at chic, colorless workspaces, wearing headsets, typing on laptops.

Gabriel ushered her into a conference room, which was

dominated by a glass-topped table and black Aeron swivel chairs. It made Ainsley think of every conference room she'd ever been bored to death in, back in the States. Every job that'd ever frustrated, infuriated, or dismissed her.

"You can wait here for Nadia," he said. "Can I get you something to drink?"

"Sure," she said.

"What would you like?"

"Get me your favorite."

While he was gone, Ainsley looked around. On one wall were several broadsheets advertising musical theater performances, each featuring a lineup of heavily caricatured actors. On another wall were colorful photos of Argentine singers performing in concert, striking Christ-like poses under dramatic lighting.

Gabriel returned with a Perrier. He noticed Ainsley studying the photos.

"What do you think?"

"These performers all look so confident," she replied.

"Is it your first time to this country?"

"Yes."

"Then you should know our most popular joke. How does an Argentine commit suicide?"

"How?"

"He jumps off his own ego."

Ainsley laughed. "That can't be true."

He suddenly became very serious. "Oh, that is our character. Believe me, you will see." He handed the green bottle. "Nadia said she prefers to meet in her office. Are you ready?"

"Absolutely."

"Then, as my mother says, it's time for us to eat our vegetables."

"I don't quite understand that," she said.

A grimace passed over her face. "Me neither. I also don't understand why I'm twenty-five and still living with her."

Gabriel shook off the thought and led Ainsley further into the office. Ainsley glimpsed executive offices through open doorways, all of them expansive and airy. In one, a male executive chatted on a headset while steepling his fingers. Another had propper his feet on his desk. A third winked at her.

Minus the flirting, these people didn't look too different from the people in most professional, high-stakes offices back in the States.

A single door waited at the end of the hall. It didn't look forbidding as much as neglected.

Gabriel knocked and pressed his ear to the wood. "She's ready," he said. He held the door open.

Inside, this office was as clean, smooth, and colorless as the others. However, it was quite a bit smaller than the others. And there was a woman sitting in it.

This was Nadia.

She was in her mid-forties. She stood up, came around the desk, and shook hands vigorously. Ainsley immediately noted her broad shoulders, thrusting jaw. She was probably a former athlete. Heavy testosterone. The type of woman who could hold her own in a boisterous male environment.

"*Señorita* Walker, thank you for coming on such short notice." Her voice was professional and strong.

"My pleasure."

"I am Nadia, you already met Gabriel."

"Yes."

She offered the only other chair in the room, and Ainsley took it. Nadia closed the door firmly, locking it, and returned to sit behind her desk.

"Our custom is to relax before starting business, to chat a bit. But unfortunately we don't have that kind of time."

She paused. "You were recommended to me by Bernabé Gradin."

Ainsley couldn't help smiling. Her friend, the old gemologist in Montevideo, bless his heart, was giving himself as a reference.

"He's quite a character," she replied.

"That's what I hear," said Nadia, "but I only know his reputation. It's a pity he refuses to come to Argentina."

Ainsley smiled inwardly at this bit of provincial rivalry. "I agree," she said.

"He also tells me that your tenacity in finding lost gemstones was remarkable."

"That's very kind of him."

"He said that you were born to do this job."

Ainsley's heart leaped at that. Until this moment, she had been steeling herself for an eventual return to the States, to a flat and featureless future as a wage slave, maybe an unhappy second marriage someday, a couple of kids dutifully birthed and tended to, followed by another divorce, a decade of aimless wandering and an ugly, impoverished demise. But Bernabé had validated her decision to find another way.

"Finding gemstones is more than a job," said Ainsley, "it's a calling." These words came out more easily in a foreign language than they did in English. It was as though she were opening a new personality.

"Have you ever been to Argentina before?" Nadia said.

"Never."

"What do you know about our country?"

"Only the stereotypes."

"Steak and tango."

"And Evita."

Nadia nodded. "I'm sure you are sophisticated enough to know that we have much more than that."

"I'm sure. What kind of company is this?"

"We are a management company. We control celebrities' careers. In exchange, we get a percentage."

Ainsley felt a little piqued. She wasn't an idiot, she knew what a manager was. "What kind of celebrities do you represent?"

"Mostly performers. Actors, singers, athletes, magicians. Even a couple of writers."

Ainsley noticed a picture on her wall. A soccer player, dark haired and well-muscled, was hanging like a monkey from the crossbar of a soccer goal. His mouth was wide open, his incisors unsheathed, like an ape screaming from a newly-conquered tree in enemy territory. Behind him, a wall of fans were on their feet, arms thrust into the air, screaming with him.

"That guy seems like he has a big personality," Ainsley said.

"Ah, you noticed him," said Nadia. There was a secret behind her smile. "He is a very special individual."

"Who is he?"

"Ovidio Angeletti. He is Argentina's most famous soccer player. And he is my biggest client."

"I've never heard of him."

"That's too bad," said Nadia.

"Why?"

Nadia caught her eyes and held the gaze. Suddenly Ainsley knew what was coming next.

"Because you're working for him."

# CHAPTER FOUR

Ainsley blanched at the news. She'd never really been interested in the upper reaches of society. The tabloid headlines at the grocery store checkout lines, the glossy gossips on the entertainment channels—all of it made her feel dirty somehow. In her opinion, the upper crust was nothing but a bunch of crumbs held together by dough.

But she wasn't going to lose this opportunity. "Tell me more," she said.

"Are you a soccer fan?" asked Nadia.

"Not really," Ainsley replied.

"Good. It's easier that way." As Nadia began to talk, Ainsley watched her fingers absently use a ballpoint pen to draw perpendicular shapes on a pad of paper.

"Ovidio is thirty-five years old," she said. "When he was younger, he played for a team called the Argentinos, until Europe discovered him. So he went to England for six years, where his team won the Premier League twice. Then his big mouth destroyed his success. He badmouthed the owner of his team. In public."

Ainsley nodded.

"He got fired. His management dumped him. So he hired us. Nobody here wanted to work with him. He was known to be absolutely impossible."

"Is he?"

"Of course. But I was the new girl around here"—she twirled her pen in the air—"so I couldn't say no. Since then, I have worked night and day to resuscitate his career. In conjunction with several agencies around the world, I landed him three one-year contracts."

"And now he has come back home," said Ainsley.

The manager nodded. "It's the twilight of his career."

Ainsley glanced at the photo again. "The people seem to love him."

"He is an Argentine icon. But right now, that is all up in the air."

"Why?"

"He won't play." Nadia thumped the pen against the table as though it were a small club. For a moment she looked angry and distant.

"Why?" said Ainsley again.

"I can't tell you that until you agree to take this job."

"I'll take it," said Ainsley. "I have nowhere else to go." That was the truth. There was no point to pretend otherwise.

"You cannot speak to anybody about this," said the manager. "It is confidential."

"I understand."

"Swear upon it."

Ainsley held up her hand. "I swear."

Nadia lowered her voice. "Someone stole his necklace."

Ainsley struggled to digest this news. She'd had jewelry stolen over the years, but she'd never let it wreck her life.

"What type of necklace was it?" said Ainsley.

"A rhodochrosite. Do you know it?"

If there was anything Ainsley Walker knew, it was

gemstones. And she knew that rhodochrosite was a pinkish stone, barely semiprecious, found almost exclusively in Argentina. It was formed by water that had dripped from manganese stalactites and subsequently bonded with carbonite. Back home, she owned a simple pair of rhodochrosite earrings; the pair had cost her less than ten bucks. She'd honestly never thought much about the stone.

"But rhodochrosite isn't valuable," Ainsley said. "Why is he so upset?"

"This necklace used to belong to his mother."

Nadia looked at her coolly, as though that fact were enough to understand everything.

"Maybe he could ask her for another one," said Ainsley.

"His mother is dead."

"Oh."

Nadia became very serious. "He never knew her. She was a victim of the dirty war."

The mood of the conversation changed. A heavy feeling flooded into the room like dark sludgewater. Even the usual small sounds of an office seemed to have died outside the door.

Ainsley cradled her head in both hands. She felt ignorant. "Nadia, please pretend that you are talking to someone who has been asleep for a century, and explain to me just what the dirty war was."

Trying to contain her irritation, Nadia began to explain. "Argentina experienced a very unpleasant period in the nineteen seventies and eighties. We were taken over by a military junta. The government squads kidnapped people out of their homes, or from the streets, and tortured them in detention centers. University students, union leaders, and subversives. A few were spared, but most were killed, about thirty thousand."

Ainsley chewed on her lip. Judging from Nadia's tone and

manner, this wasn't something you casually discussed over a game of cards.

"So he was born—"

Nadia nodded. "In the torture facility. His mother had been kidnapped when she was already pregnant."

"How terrible," Ainsley said.

"You have no idea. There are many like him today, grown up now. The children of the disappeared."

"How did he get out?"

"Ovidio says an angel brought him out. The truth is that nobody knows."

"Can't you ask his foster parents?"

"His foster parents died when he was an adolescent. They refused to tell him anything, even at the end, except that his birth mother had wanted him to have her rhodochrosite necklace. She had been wearing it on the day she was kidnapped."

Ainsley sat back. She was honestly moved. This put her own problems in humbling perspective. Her husband, the Legal Weasel, had walked out on her, and she had been manically hopping from job to job, but at least she'd gotten a good start in life. What had happened to Ovidio should've taken the wind out of his sails.

He was a strong person.

"That piece must mean a lot to him," said Ainsley.

"Ovidio wears that necklace every time he steps on the field. He says it gives him strength, knowing that his mother is somehow near to him. He won't play without it."

She had been tracing and retracing a dark box on the scratch pad. Finally the tip of the pen ripped through the page. Nadia balled up the paper and threw it into the trash can.

Ainsley felt her eyes getting moist. She knew what it was

like to lose a parent, but she couldn't imagine what it would be like to have never known one.

She looked at Ovidio's photo again. "Can't you just say that he's been injured?"

"We tried that. The paparazzi bastards with their long-range cameras found a way to photograph him in practice, exercising and playing as usual. So now there are rumors. The fans are upset and they want answers. He's even received death threats."

"But you can't reveal the truth."

"Never. The moment we announce that his necklace has been stolen, there will be ten thousand people holding up replicas, claiming a reward. Even worse, his reputation will never recover. He will appear to be a massive primadonna."

"Isn't he?"

"Of course," Nadia shot back. "He is a like a thousand needles in my ass. But the people don't know that."

Ainsley felt a bit intimidated. None of this sounded remotely like steak and tango. "How can I help you?" she said. "I don't know your country."

"You," said Nadia, "are going to be a journalist."

"I am?"

"Yes. A journalist from the States. You've come to investigate Ovidio for a profile on modern soccer. Don't worry, we have a different journalist every month. It's an easy cover story."

"Okay."

"But only three people will know the truth. You, me, and Ovidio. Here is your contract." The manager slid a sheaf of papers across the table. "Sign them and you'll get the first half of the fee."

Ainsley picked up the contract. It was in Spanish. Her language skills were intermediate and improving quickly, but she couldn't have interpreted this document even in English.

She wished that David, her lawyer back in the States, could somehow be here to back her up.

"We agreed on twenty thousand dollars," said Ainsley.

"Yes, you'll get ten thousand when you sign the forms," replied Nadia. Her voice took on a reassuring tone. "Have no fear about money. Ovidio takes care of everyone."

"I need a few hours on this," Ainsley said.

"Of course. In the meantime, you and I can go to the hotel and figure out your first move."

"You didn't have to book me a room," said Ainsley.

Nadia looked confused. "I didn't."

"Then why are we going to a hotel?"

The manager smiled. "Because you need to meet Ovidio."

# CHAPTER FIVE

As they were whisked by private car through the maddening traffic, Nadia spent most of the ride on her mobile phone, yapping in such high-speed Spanish that it made Ainsley's head hurt.

She began to think about her own history with soccer.

Ainsley had played the sport for a single season when she was eleven years old. It'd been a local youth league. True to her personality, she'd tried every position but been satisfied with none.

First she'd been assigned as a striker, but she hadn't displayed that killer instinct, that need to floss her teeth with the opponent's net. So she'd been relegated to the midfield, but the fact that she could neither turn on a dime nor run constantly for ninety minutes—both of which are job requirements for that position—had pushed her back to defense. Then her sudden growth spurt had occurred, sending her shooting up to nearly two meters in height, and quickly she'd found herself saddled with the heavy jersey and gigantic gloves of the goalkeeper. She'd allowed an average of five goals per game to pass between her gangly legs. After the final whistle of the final match blew, she'd stripped off the jersey and bid *adieu* to the world's most popular sport.

Now, almost two decades later, she was going to work for one of the world's most illustrious players.

Nadia ended her calls and stowed away her phone. "You seem sad."

"I feel like everybody has a purpose," said Ainsley. "Everybody but me."

"You have the most important purpose of all," said Nadia. She gestured to the people on the street. "In Argentina, football is a religion, not a sport. We see the suicide rates climb after the national team loses. For a lot of *porteños*, Ovidio's performance is their reason for living."

"Are you telling me that the emotional health of Argentina is depending upon me?"

Nadia paused. "You said that, not me."

The smell of diesel disappeared as the Mercedes entered a wealthy *barrio*. Immaculate landscaping and elaborate trim dominated the properties here. Ainsley rolled her window down and sniffed. There was cleaner air here, the lush scent of jasmine.

An unusual sight on her right seized her attention. There were hundreds of tiny stately roofs peeking over a long white wall.

"The Recoleta cemetery," said Nadia. "If you weren't going to be so busy, I'd tell you to go visit like all the other tourists."

"It's beautiful."

"Our pride and joy. Over there is La Biela, a famous cafe. Down that street is—" The manager stopped herself. "Enough. I am proud to call Buenos Aires my home. But we need to stay focused."

Three blocks later, the car pulled into a circular driveway and stopped beneath the opulent portico of a hotel. "This is the Alvear Palace Hotel," Nadia said. "Ovidio is living here for the moment."

"Why?"

"Because the *barra brava* have threatened his life. I'll explain more later. Right now, you need to know two things. One, don't say his name in public. If you need to refer to him, say 'my brother' instead. We all do it."

"Who is we?"

"His entourage. That's number two. I want you to investigate his friends about the theft. And he has *many* male friends. By pretending to be a journalist, you have a license to follow them around, ask them questions."

"So Ovidio suspects them too?"

Nadia nodded. "Of course."

"That's really sad."

"That's celebrity." The woman wrinkled her nose as though she'd smelled something rotten. "Just be careful around them. They're animals."

The women exited the car together. The sky had turned grayer, the wind more biting, and Ainsley pulled her coat more tightly around her body as she strode through the formal doors.

The Alvear Palace Hotel embodied the phrase red-carpet treatment. The lobby featured the plush stuff from wall to wall. There were even more down the hallways that radiated off in several directions. It felt almost like Versailles.

Ainsley followed Nadia down one of the hallways. It was lined with small pricey boutiques, mostly high-end French and Italian brands. She passed displays of creams, sprays, perfumes, furs, gowns, shoes, and all the other Eurocentric accoutrements that the well-heeled visitor could demand.

Nadia was on her phone again, yapping in high-velocity Spanish. This time, Ainsley picked out the words *el sector fitness*.

Two more corners, left, then right, and they ran into a pair of large men, dressed in black suits, standing with arms crossed. Their eyes were cold and professional. There wasn't a speck of bullshit on or near them.

"*Pasaporte*," one said.

Ainsley obeyed and handed the small booklet over. The security guard recorded her name and passport number into a leather case, then handed it back. Then he held open the door with a meaty arm.

They passed between the men into a second hallway. "Do those men work for the hotel?" Ainsley asked.

"No, they are Ovidio's private security."

"So you know them?"

Nadia looked at her oddly. "I *hired* them."

Ainsley followed, feeling chastened, still trying to wrap her head around exactly how huge a soccer player could become in South America.

They encountered an identical pair of guards stationed outside another door. This time, Nadia greeted them with a turned cheek. Both kissed her. Ainsley did the same, and felt their scruff abrade her face. She guessed that these were Ovidio's personal guards, body men assigned to his immediate space.

"This is Ainsley Walker, a journalist from the United States," she said. "No restrictions."

The men nodded impassively, but their eyes betrayed new respect. Ainsley was to be given the VIP treatment. She guessed that journalists weren't customarily given full access to soccer superstars, maybe a half-hour of supervised visits at most.

She followed Nadia between the men and through another door.

Finally Ainsley found herself standing in the hotel exercise room. At one end, a rack of dumbbells stood against a mirrored wall. In the middle, an assortment of white Nautilus equipment awaited silently, gleaming and sterile.

At the far end of the room, overlooking the gardens, was a row of elliptical trainers and other cardio equipment.

On a treadmill, in silhouetted before the window, someone was running furiously. Ainsley knew treadmills, had used them a lot. From the speed of his legs, she guessed that he'd set the machine at nine miles per hour.

The runner waved his hand; he'd spotted them. He punched a button on the face of the treadmill. It slowed down to about three miles an hour, a nice walking pace. A minute later, he punched the button again, and the machine stopped.

He stepped off and wiped his face with a towel before coming over to greet his visitor.

As he drew nearer, the lights finally illuminated his face.

It was Ovidio Angeletti.

# CHAPTER SIX

The superstar came directly in for the cheek-kiss. Ainsley anticipated this and offered it first. His masculine scent overwhelmed her. His pheromones were a hundred times more powerful than those of any other man she'd ever met.

"Nadia said you are from the United States," Ovidio said, pulling back, "but you greet like an Argentine."

"Thank you," she replied.

"How long have you been in my country?"

Ainsley noticed the first-person possessive. Not *our* country or *this* country, but *my* country.

"About two hours."

Ovidio cocked his head. He looked at Nadia. "And you hired her?"

Nadia nodded. "She came very highly recommended. You should hear what she accomplished in Uruguay."

"Uruguay." The superstar repeated the word to himself. Then he smiled and shook his head as though the country caused him some faint amusement. "We destroyed them last year in the Copa America."

"And you scored the game-winning goal in penalty kicks,"

addded Nadia. "Would you like to show her the video? So she can appreciate your talent?"

"No," he said, "she can watch for herself. But how is she supposed to help if she is a stranger here?"

Ainsley looked at Nadia for the answer. It was a legitimate complaint. "Her ignorance of our customs is beneficial," explained the manager. "She doesn't know what not to do, or where not to go. She has no boundaries."

But Ovidio had already lost attention, was barely listening. "Good, good, excellent. I need to shower. Follow me." He tossed the towel over his shoulder and swept past the women, enveloping Ainsley in the scent of his *machismo*.

She and Nadia obediently followed him out of the exercise room. The two security guards immediately snapped into action, accompanying Ovidio on both sides.

As they moved, Ainsley watched the athlete closely. Even just strolling down the hallway, he displayed a weird stride, mincing short steps, occasionally changing his pace, even checking backwards over his shoulder. Basically, this man had the energy of a five-year-old. She could sense that he would be an absolute terror on the playing field.

They entered a private elevator. One guard turned his key in a slot, and the doors slid shut. Ainsley guessed that this was the route to the penthouse.

Meanwhile, Nadia clasped her folder to her chest and looked at Ovidio. Ainsley sensed that she was gauging her client's mood, calculating the best way to communicate with him.

"I am getting restless," he said. He whipped his neck back and forth, bouncing on his toes. "I need to ... do *something*."

"You could play football," said Nadia. "They pay you to do that."

Ainsley got the sense that these two had been over this

issue many, many times. She also got the sense that discretion would be the best option here.

"No," Ovidio said, clutching his head, "no no no, I can't play. I can't play without my mother."

He was squatting on the floor of the elevator now, drumming his hands on the carpet. Ainsley scratched behind her ear. Had he just called the rhodochrosite necklace *my mother*? That would've alarmed any number of psychotherapists. Ainsley guessed that he needed some serious couch time.

The doors slid open, revealing a swank hotel suite. Ovidio sprang inside, and Ainsley followed. She scanned the room. More red carpeting, heavy swag over the French doors, gilded tables, marble fauns. It didn't feel the least bit masculine, but it wasn't Ovidio's home.

Then Ainsley heard a short squeal from the other side of the room. A petite blonde was running towards the bedroom. She was completely naked.

The soccer star was peeved. "It's one o'clock," Ovidio said. "You were supposed to leave at twelve-thirty."

"I needed to do my makeup," came the reply from behind the bedroom door.

"You are making me very unhappy, Rosa," said Ovidio. "And you are inconveniencing my guests. They had to see your ugly little butt."

"It's *Ana*," her voice shouted, "my name is *Ana*."

Nadia dropped her purse on the table as though she owned the place. "What happened to your plan?"

"What plan?" said Ovidio.

"The namecard plan."

"I don't remember."

She sighed. "At night you were going to tell the butler the name of the girl, he was going to write it down on a card, and then he was going to slip the card under your coffee cup the next morning. So you don't embarrass yourself."

Ovidio shrugged. "That only works if I find out their names." He banged with his fist on the door of the bedroom. "Rosa, there are people out here who want to talk *business*. It's time for little party girls to leave."

The muffled response: "It's *Ana*, and I'm *going*."

The blonde streaked out of the bedroom, dressed in morning-after clubwear: boots unzipped, her shirt sliding off the shoulder. She was headed straight towards Ovidio.

She was hysterical. "I need to know, this can't be the end, when can we—"

Ovidio gestured to his security guard, who had played this role countless times. He gently disengaged the girl from the athlete and steered her towards the elevator. "I left my phone number on the bed!" the girl shouted. "You call me when—"

"Thank you," Ovidio said, waving goodbye, "thank you very much, for your generous support of Argentinian football." He still hadn't looked at her. Then the elevator door closed tightly, and the girl was gone.

The athlete disappeared into the bedroom, and Ainsley heard the shower turn on.

She felt a tight ball of disgust forming in her stomach. Despite his position as her new boss, she hadn't been able to stop thinking about, whether or not, hypothetically, he might've given her a chance in the sack. After all, his charisma was undeniable.

But that was before this little display. She didn't date narcissistic peacocks.

Ainsley stood near the window, looking onto the street. "How many women does he go through?"

Nadia looked annoyed. "How many stars are in the sky? Why do you care? Just don't be one of them."

"I wasn't planning on it."

"Neither was that girl, probably. Celebrity has a strange power."

Ainsley chewed on her lip, thinking, staring out the window at the bushy tops of the green trees, waving in the gray spring afternoon.

The elevator opened again. An elegant butler wheeled a metal cart into the room, an old-fashioned number with a shiny silver dome.

"You can leave it there," said Nadia, pointing near the door. "Did you see Horacio in the lobby?"

The butler shook his head.

Nadia glanced at her watch. "That *flaco* is always late."

"Who is Horacio?"

Nadia glanced up. "Horacio is the official taster."

# CHAPTER SEVEN

Ainsley cocked her head. She wasn't sure if she'd heard that right.

"Taster?"

"Yes."

Absorbed in her phone, Nadia was acting like this was the most natural occupation in the world. Doctor, lawyer, fireman, teacher, ... and taster.

"Is he that picky about his food?"

"Not about flavor. Just about poison." Nadia put away her phone. "Ovidio thinks he's going to be poisoned."

"Really." Ainsley felt a smile curling the corner of her mouth.

Nadia saw her skepticism and explained further. "You don't understand yet how angry the people are at him. There are many who are losing money every day, legally and illegally, because of his refusal to play. Ovidio talks a lot about what happened to Escobar after the World Cup."

Ainsley remembered the story. In the nineties, during a World Cup match against the United States, a Colombian defender had scored on his own team, which subsequently caused their elimination. Three weeks later, in Medellín, he had been shot twelve times by assassins, who were rumored to have been hired by a drug lord who lost a lot of money on the match. They had shouted the word *goal* with each blast.

The elevator doors opened again. A thin man with a brush cut sashayed into the room, wearing a tight sky-blue t-shirt with an orange scarf. A touch of makeup put the exclamation point on his outfit.

"Horacio!" Nadia cried out. She stood up to exchange air kisses.

Then he noticed Ainsley. She noticed his eyeliner as he tracked her from head down to her boots, then back up to her head.

"Why is this one dressed?" he said to Nadia.

The manager shushed him with a finger to his lips. "She's not one of them. She's a journalist."

He paused. "Oh. Sorry."

"Go, go," said Nadia, slapping him across the shoulders, "make my client feel safe."

Horacio walked over to the room-service tray and lifted the lid. Underneath the dome was a single dinner plate with a *milanesa*, fries, and a salad. His nose twitched. He bent down and sniffed the food.

Then the taster pulled on a latex glove, lifted a single french fry, and laid it on his tongue. He waited for several seconds. He removed the spud and tossed it into the trash, as though it were a used tongue depressor.

Then he pulled a package of silverware from his pocket, cut off a section of the *milanesa*, and did the same routine. That was followed by a forkful of salad.

By the end, he had swallowed none of the food.

"All good," he said.

"I will let the baby know," said Nadia, flipping through a magazine.

Horacio turned to Ainsley. "I love your hair. But you are too skinny."

Nadia laughed. "You are telling her this?"

"It takes one to know one."

Ainsley blew him an air kiss, and he caught it against his cheek and twirled. This guy seemed like a lot of fun. Not to mention the fact that he had one of the easiest jobs in the world.

Ovidio came out of the bedroom, buttoning up a pair of gray slacks. He was shirtless. Ainsley discreetly admired his torso. Though not muscular, he boasted single-digit percent body fat.

"Keep looking and you'll turn to stone," the star joked.

Ainsley felt herself blushing. He'd noticed her noticing him. *Of course* he had. He was designed for admiration, wanted it, needed it. Surely he'd been missing the applause of the crowd.

"Girls come to his matches just to watch him rip off his jersey afterwards," said Nadia.

"And some boys too," added Horacio. "But we all know he'll rip it off for anybody."

"No, she has to be smiling," Ovidio said. "It's my only requirement. Besides, Pele gave away more jerseys than I have. He gave them away like candies. Ten thousand."

"You're no Pelé," answered Horacio.

The superstar rose to his feet, clearly piqued. "Who wants to be Pele?" he said. "For me, it's only Maradona, Maradona, *Maradona*." He accented each word with a hard chop to his hand. "Diego was a hero to this country."

Then Ovidio dropped onto a chair again, mouth open, shaking his head. He looked gray, almost stricken, as though the true weight of that player's accomplishment had only now been revealed to him.

His drama wasn't unfounded. Maradona had left a very big pair of cleats to fill.

Ainsley knew about Diego Maradona; nearly everybody in the world did. He'd been the best Argentinian soccer player of the twentieth century, many say the best player, period. The "little hairy one" who'd scored two famous goals against England in the 1986 World Cup, which was widely seen as revenge for Argentina's devastating loss in the Falklands War.

Later, Maradona became a punchline, a national shame, having survived a nasty cocaine habit, a hundred-pound weight gain, subsequent bariatric surgery, and mountains of unpaid palimony. But in his heyday, the masses had worshipped him, seen him as a natural leader. Ainsley thought she saw in Ovidio the signs of similar ambitions.

"So we need to talk," said Nadia. "Take yourself away, *Horacita*."

The skinny taster pouted. "Fine. See you at eleven." He turned and flounced towards the elevator. Then he turned back: "Ovidio, where do you think you'll be?"

"I don't know yet," said the athlete, exchanging glances with his manager. "Watch your phone. We'll let you know."

# CHAPTER EIGHT

The remaining three assembled in the living room.

Ovidio sat on the edge of a chair, leaning forward, white cup of coffee in his hand. The heels of his bare feet bounced against the carpet, as though he were waiting for a starting gun to fire.

Nadia and Ainsley sat down on the couch together. "I've already told her the history of your necklace," said Nadia. "We just need her to know how you lost it."

The athlete's face crinkled into an annoyed smile. "If I knew that, you wouldn't have to hire her, and I would be playing right now."

"Just tell us."

He blew an exasperated breath. "It disappeared from a hotel room, three weeks ago. El Hotel Perdido."

"Was it your hotel room or someone else's?" said Ainsley.

"Mine. The girls always come to me. Always."

"I understand."

"It was in a box, the same box I have kept it in since childhood. Not a fancy box with decorations." He shaped an imaginary rectangle with his hands. "Just a simple cigar box."

Ainsley carried on with the basic questions. "Who could've gotten in?"

"The maid."

Ainsley hadn't heard about that. Nadia explained further. "The maid hasn't shown up to work since the day after the theft."

"Then she seems a logical place to start."

"Exactly," said Ovidio. "That's what I'm saying. But this one..." He pointed at Nadia and clucked his tongue.

The manager ignored him. Ainsley guessed that she'd had years of practice doing this. "My theory," she said, "is that it was a targeted theft, since nothing else was stolen. So my opinion is that you should investigate his friends instead."

Ovidio threw one arm over his head. It was an expression of disgust.

"But it's true!" said the manager. "Your friends are lowlifes!"

"I'm not disputing that," he said. "But they are *my* lowlifes. They wouldn't betray *me*."

"Lalo did."

Ovidio became agitated. Ainsley was noticing how visibly all of his emotions passed across his body.

"Remember?" Nadia said, pressing further. "You caught Lalo selling stories about you to the tabloids."

"Of course," the superstar explained. "But it's Lalo. You know? That's something Lalo would do. He's an asshole."

"You are too generous."

"It's only money, I can forgive that." He wagged a finger at both women. "I can tell you this. Lalo wouldn't steal my mother's necklace. Nobody I know would do that. It's not possible."

Nadia kept her composure. "I think Ainsley should talk to them anyways."

The superstar bolted to his feet, upset. "But the maid is so obvious. We know she lives in Villa 27, we just need to go—"

"That's why it's wrong," said Nadia. "It's *too* obvious. She would've taken your jewelry, your gold, everything." She turned to Ainsley. "Forget the maid. Start with his friends."

Ovidio pulled a toffet in front of Ainsley and sat on it. He placed his hands on her shoulders and looked her in the eyes. The brown irises were flecked with green. Ainsley felt herself hypnotized by him.

"Listen to me," he said. "You should forget my friends. Start with the maid."

Both people, the athlete and manager, were looking at her. Ainsley realized that she had the responsibility of casting the deciding vote.

"You both have valid points," said Ainsley, "but I'm going to agree with Nadia."

The superstar stood up, aggravated. He waved Ainsley away with his hand. "Gemstone detective, bah. You don't know my country. You don't know my life. You probably don't even know jewelry."

That got Ainsley's goat. She fought down her anger and followed him over to the window, approaching him from the side. She had learned to do that with certain men when they were upset, so as to not seem confrontational.

"*Señor* Angeletti," she said, "there is not much that I am able to do well. I have quit or been fired from almost every job in my life. But this, this I can do. I'm *good* at this one thing. You know what it feels like to have a calling. Don't you?"

He nodded.

"You play football. And I find gemstones. I will get your mother's necklace back. And you will play again. Just let me *try*."

He turned slightly towards her. Ainsley noticed that there

were tears in his eyes. His voice cracked as he spoke. "Everybody thinks I am so powerful. I'm not powerful. That necklace, my mother ... it gives me everything that people expect to see."

"Then let me help."

Ainsley waited for an answer. She saw Ovidio's heavy eyebrows crinkle in suspicion as he looked out the window. "Who is that man?" he said.

"What man?"

"That one." His forefinger stabbed the windowpane. Ainsley looked down to the street. At a bus stop was an ordinary guy wearing a gray hoodie and a pair of headphones.

"The one waiting for a bus?"

"He's been there five minutes."

"Yes, he's waiting for a bus."

Ovidio's eyes narrowed. "I think he's monitoring me."

Ainsley tried not to roll her eyes. "No, you're okay. Don't worry."

He rubbed his palm on his cheek. "I don't like how he looks." Agitated, Ovidio turned to his manager. "Nadia, I need to change hotels. They're watching me—"

Nadia answered before he'd even finished. "It might be a long-distance bus. If he's still there in ten minutes, we'll investigate."

Ovidio walked to the other side of the suite. He stared at the floor, deep concern etched in his face. His mood had changed yet again.

"So Ainsley's going to start with your friends, okay?" said Nadia.

Distracted, Ovidio mumbled a noncommittal repsonse. Ainsley was impressed with the way that Nadia had waited for the perfect moment to tell him how things would be. She handled her client the same way women have handled difficult men everywhere in the world. Timing was crucial.

"You're good," Ainsley whispered. "Like a mother, almost."

"It's true," Nadia whispered, "I coddle him the way his mother never did." Then she raised her voice. "Now, are you ready to meet his entourage?"

"You bet."

Nadia lifted a finger. "In this way. You'll go to the *puerta cerrada* tonight. Ovidio will be there with all of them. Meet us at this address." She handed Ainsley a scrap of paper with an address scribbled on it. "The host will be expecting you. His name is Facundo. Remember, you're a journalist."

"Yes I am." Ainsley turned to the athlete. "Ovidio, it was nice meeting you."

He was crouched in the corner now, still shirtless, his gray slacks strained against his powerful hamstrings. His lips had worked themselves into a frustrated little ball. He looked like an orangutan.

Nadia cut in. "Did you hear her, *mono*? She's going to help you."

He lifted a finger in response. That could mean anything.

She exchanged knowing glances with Nadia. The superstar's mood had changed yet again.

Ainsley slipped into the elevator, and as the doors closed, she closed her eyes and exhaled loudly. She suddenly felt grateful for many things in her life.

Most especially for the fact that she didn't have Nadia's job.

# CHAPTER NINE

In the lobby, Ainsley sauntered past the expensive shops again. Then she heard the distant sound of tinkling glassware and the murmur of conversation. She followed the sounds. She had nothing else to do for several hours.

Turning a corner, she came upon an enormous tearoom. White-linened tables quartered by high-backed wicker chairs. Gleaming silver pots and lacquered porcelain teacups. The far end of the room was a glass wall laced with black wrought iron. Green ferns hung in globes from the ceiling.

It was like a giant birdcage. For very rich pigeons.

The maître d', a woman in a starched shirt, looked up from her podium. "Can I help you?"

"I'm just admiring," said Ainsley. "It's enchanting."

She could see the Anglophile foodstuffs, the scones, the jams, the pots of cream, the watercress sandwiches. And the tables were packed with the predictable clientele: wealthy old women, hair feathered and plumage up.

Except for one. A thin man, wearing a sky-blue shirt, orange scarf, and a touch of makeup. He was waving at her.

Horacio.

He wanted her to come over. Ainsley decided to ride the wave. She entered the tearoom and wound her way through the tables.

"There's my girl," Horacio shouted, as though they were old friends. "How did your meeting with my brother go?"

Ainsley remembered the code. "He's got a lot of problems," she said.

He was sitting with three old women who were crusted in blingy jewelry. They looked like living museum pieces. They didn't wear much makeup, but their overwhelming floral perfume assaulted Ainsley's nose. It was fragrance abuse, pure and simple.

"These are the ladies who lunch," he said.

"Nice to meet all of you."

The women nodded at her. She could feel their eyes scrolling up and down her body.

"What are you doing this afternoon?" he said.

"I don't know," Ainsley replied. "I've never been to this city before."

Horacio tossed down his napkin and stood up. "Ainsley, you're going out for *parrilla*. For a real Argentine steak."

"With who?" she said.

He looked offended. "With *me*. I can't bear to think of you eating some cold empanada all alone in an ugly cafe because you don't know any better."

That was generous, but Ainsley didn't want to step on anybody's toes. "Only if these women will let you go."

"Them?" he said. "They would take you out themselves, if they knew the right places. Right dears?"

The elderly waxworks were impassive. Ainsley knew the type. They were the type of wealthy old people upon whom nothing seems to register, who have drowned their personalities inside their pools of money. They become like heavy luxury automobiles, laden with decoration, that never feel any bumps in the road.

She watched the taster zip up his leather jacket and kiss each of the three women on both sides of their faces. He made small talk with each. To Ainsley, it sounded and seemed very much like open flattery.

"Come on, skinny," he finally said to her, "let's plump you up so these women don't have you murdered."

He left the tearoom, Ainsley following, striding past the stone pillars of the lobby, and out the front door onto the sidewalk.

Outside, she struggled to catch up. "You don't have to do this for me," she said. "I don't want to interrupt a perfectly nice lunch—"

He waved the comment off. "Those old hags. They're always on me to come to tea because I entertain them. They see me like a little goat that brays and stands on its back legs and makes them laugh." He scrunched up his face. "I'm glad to get away."

The air was as brisk as Horacio's pace, and Ainsley struggled to keep up. "So where are you taking me?"

"La Cumparasita."

"It'd better be good. You're a taster."

"Trust me," he said, "the steak I'm showing you is so good, you'll be writing about it for years. What magazine do you work for?"

Ainsley felt her throat go dry. She'd forgotten to fabricate a cover story.

Thinking quickly, she said, "*Laddie*."

"*Laddie* magazine?"

"Yes."

"Who reads it?"

Ainsley's eyes darted around. "You know, lads. Boys."

"I get it," said Horacio. "It's one of *those* magazines. Wet women in bikinis on the cover. Why did they send a woman to meet our brother?"

"Magazines always use female writers for these assignments," she said. "We girls know how to talk to men."

The traffic had been rushing along the street past them, each car ignoring the lane markers as it jockeyed for position. Then a Mercedes slowed to a stop along the curb.

The back window, tinted nearly black, rolled down. It was Ovidio.

"Ladies," he said, "I can't decide which one of you has the nicer ass."

Ainsley was annoyed. Her new boss didn't respect her boundaries.

"Keep talking like that," Horacio replied, "and I'll forget what arsenic tastes like."

Ainsley could see Nadia on the other side of the backseat. She looked pissed, probably because Ovidio was showing his face in public. She tugged on the superstar's sleeve and whispered something.

Ovidio looked at the taster. "Friend, can you cross the street for a minute? I need to speak to Ainsley alone."

"Fine," Horacio said. He tapped on his phone as he walked proudly into oncoming traffic. A single car blew its horn as it careened around him.

"*Sin vergüenza,*" said Ovidio, "*sin vergüenza.*"

Ainsley didn't understand that phrase, but she guessed that it was respectful. Then she felt Ovidio's forceful hand catch her own. Urgency came into his eyes.

"The necklace," he said, "I forgot to tell you something important about the necklace."

"Tell me."

"It has a special mark. A distinguishing characteristic."

"What is it?"

Ovidio gestured to Nadia. She handed him a piece of paper and a pen. "It has a Z," he said.

"The letter Z."

"Yes. Like this."

He used the pen to draw a wobbly but legible Z. It was kind of adorable, Ainsley thought, the effort he was putting into making sure that she knew what a Z looked like.

He handed her the paper. "It's called a Zorro rhodochrosite. It's very rare."

"I appreciate it," she said. "See you tonight. Right?"

The superstar smiled mysteriously at her as the window rolled up. As Ainsley watched the Mercedes accelerate into traffic, she finally understood something important.

Ovidio wasn't just a nice guy, or a mean guy, or a happy guy, or a frightened guy, or a pensive guy, or a crazy guy.

He was *all* of those guys.

# CHAPTER TEN

Ainsley was swabbing her crusty piece of baguette around the plate, soaking up the herby green *chimichurri* sauce, when the meat arrived.

The process required two people: One waiter to clear space in the center of their table, and the other waiter to carry and hoist the *brasero*.

As the grill landed before her, Ainsley's jaw nearly hit the tablecloth. There were fourteen different meats on the grill, both sausages and cuts of steak. The waiter turned each one over, as a courtesy, before wishing them a good meal.

This was the *parrilla*.

Ainsley had only been in Argentina for less than six hours, and already she was about to gorge herself on more cow meat than she'd usually eat in a year.

Horacio had guided her to this place, La Cumparasita, an out-of-the-way restaurant in a nearby barrio, that he claimed was the best place for steak in the entire city of ten million. Ainsley was inclined to believe him. Plus she was hungry, and had absolutely nowhere else to be for several hours.

It was a simple place, with wooden tables and wooden

chairs. A television hung in the corner, playing a talk show. A table of several businessmen were eating nearby. The place felt rough, manly, solid.

She and Horacio were the only exceptions. He was looking at her. "How did you get so skinny?"

"My husband left me," she said. "What about you?"

"I never really eat anything," Horacio replied. "I only taste. Let me give you a quick tour of the blessings." He poked at a sausage. "This is *longaniza*. It's a good one to start with. Or this one, the *biraldo*." Ainsley sampled both; they were delicious.

Then her dining partner poked at a third sausage, a plump purple tube. "This is the *morcilla*. A special taste. Not for me. Do you want some?"

Ainsley nodded. She was game for almost anything. Horacio moved it to a separate small plate and handed it to her. As she cut into the sausage, a heavy reddish-purple liquid spurted out and pooled on one side of the plate.

She suddenly recognized it. "Is this blood sausage?" she said.

"You don't like it?"

Ainsley scooped some of the liquid into her mouth. The tang of iron hit her tongue. She made a face and pushed the plate away. "Ugh. I'm with you."

"Who isn't? Try this one instead." He lifted a thick brownish-orange coil from the grill, with a beige condiment squirting out of one end. As she wondered what it could be, her imagination gripped her, disgusting images passing through her mind—

—until she realized her imagination was, this time, absolutely correct. That was an *intestine*, a real one, nicely stuffed and grilled, but a poop chute nonetheless.

"No, thank you," she said.

Horacio was already sampling it. "Every time I come here I have to taste this. It's amazing."

As lunch went on, he described how this restaurant raised its own cattle on its own *estancia* in southern provinces. How it was better to think of this place not so much as a restaurant, but instead as a huge ranch that happened to serve a few scraps of its meat in the city.

He explained each of the pieces to her, the *asado de tira*, the *vacio*, the *entraña*. He explained how this *asador* was the best in Buenos Aires because of the heat of his grill, which had been measured at nearly six hundred degrees Farenheit. He described the salt rub that coated the meat. Ainsley learned to appreciate how the charred, crunchy exterior complemented the soft pink interior.

As she sampled cut after cut, Ainsley had a revelation: She could never commit to vegetarianism. She knew all the moral objections that animal rights groups had postulated. She knew about the environmental effect that cattle grazing had upon the earth. It didn't matter. There were certain times— not often, but occasionally—when she just needed a huge piece of red meat on her plate. It was as simple as that.

Still, she kept waiting for other food to be brought to the table, some vegetables, mushrooms, pasta. But there was nothing else. Lunch was really that simple: a piece of bread, a glass of wine, and about four pounds of meat.

If only her mission were equally simple. Horacio was on his third glass of wine, so she began shifting the conversation back towards the issue.

"When did you start working for my brother?" Ainsley said.

"When he started getting death threats."

"Do you like it?"

"Sure. It's not dangerous, he's just paranoid. If somebody wanted to kill him, they'd find an easier way. He's not that hard to find." The taster put down his knife. "How are you going to write your profile?"

She thought quickly. "You know, why the superstar refuses to play. The people's outrage."

"Do you *know* why he won't play?" Horacio was watching her with sharp eyes.

"No," she lied. "Maybe you could tell me?"

"I really don't know myself," he said casually, yawning. "It might have something to do with his politics."

Ainsley's ears pricked up. "What do you mean?"

"Nadia didn't tell you?"

"No."

"Ovidio is preparing to run for president."

"The president of what?"

He looked out the window, into the distance. "The president of Argentina."

Ainsley lowered her fork. Neither said anything for several seconds. The more she thought about that, somehow, the more upset she felt.

"That's ludicrous," she said. "I mean, he's just an athlete."

"Schwarzenegger was just a movie star," said Horacio, "and he became governor of California."

"But Ovidio isn't fit to lead a country." Her voice had risen. The table of men nearby turned and looked at her.

"You mean our brother," Horacio reminded her.

"Our brother," she said, "couldn't lead a starving cat to a bowl of food."

"It doesn't matter," said the taster.

"And he's the *moodiest* man I've ever met."

Horacio lifted his palms. "I agree with you, but none of it matters. The people have always loved him. He knows it."

Ainsley thought of Nadia, how she hadn't mentioned any of this. She must not have wanted the *yanqui* to step into those waters.

"But he refuses to play," Ainsley said. "It doesn't make any sense."

"Every game that he doesn't play makes the people angrier. They are beginning to turn against him." Horacio paused, listening. He twisted around in his seat and looked at the television. "They're joking about it on the program. Go watch."

Ainsley stood up and walked to the television. A group of three beautiful people, the talk show hosts, were chatting on a couch. A picture of Ovidio had popped up on the screen, underneath which was a survey. *El Mono returns next week/next month/it doesn't matter, I'll never vote for that bastard.*

She returned to the table. "He's shooting himself in the foot."

Horacio laughed. "That's a good description. Here we say that he's letting the turtle get away from him."

"But why?" she said. "Why is he doing this to himself?"

She was testing Horacio, to see if he knew about the theft of the necklace, but he didn't take the bait. "Oh, I think he's just playing hard-to-get. To see how much the people miss him. Or maybe he's going to time the announcement of his presidency with his return."

"What an ego," Ainsley said.

"That's Argentina," said Horacio. "Every man here is that way. We all need to be coddled." He looked disgusted with his own countrymen. "Dessert would make me feel better."

"What do you recommend?"

He looked at Ainsley like she was stupid. "The classic."

The waiter brought a flan coated with what appeared to be caramel. It was the sweetest thing Ainsley had ever tasted. Horacio watched her. "*Dulce de leche.* Condensed milk and sugar. Browned until it's thick. Our national pride. We put it on everything." He shrugged. "Not much to it, really."

"I have a question."

"You're a journalist. If you didn't, you would be fired."

"Why did that program call our brother El Mono?"

"Because that's his nickname."

"How did he get it?"

"He scored a goal and swung from the bar, screaming. The announcer said he was the best monkey in the league. The name stuck." Horacio paused. "Don't say it to him. He gets upset."

Ainsley imagined how bad "upset" could be. She noticed Horacio regarding her coolly. "You really didn't sleep with him?" he asked.

"Are you kidding?" she said. "I just met him."

"That's how it usually works."

"No," she said, "I absolutely did not."

"Hm." Horacio looked confused. "He usually loves *periodistas*. And they always love him."

Ainsley shrugged. "I'm not that kind of girl."

He regarded her so closely that Ainsley began to feel like an insect under a microscope. "I wonder what kind of girl you really are."

The waiter brought the bill and placed it in front of Horacio. He passed it over to Ainsley. She looked at him with shock.

"What is this?" she said. "You asked me to lunch."

Horacio smirked. "Don't journalists always pay? So you can remain 'objective'? Just put it on your charge account. You must have one."

She didn't like his insinuations, or his tone. This lunch had taken a real nosedive. The flamboyant bastard was putting her through a shit test. And she'd have to play along to keep her cover.

Ainsley pulled her only personal credit card from her purse. She kept the face of it turned away from Horacio. She hopefully had enough open credit to cover the bill.

He toyed with his phone, pretending to text, while they waited for the waiter to return with the receipt. When he did, Ainsley signed quickly, put the card back in her wallet, and zipped up the purse.

Outside the restaurant, she and Horacio separated with barely a goodbye. As Ainsley hailed another taxi, she thought about two things.

One, she didn't like being used for a free lunch. Two, she didn't like the sleazy vibe she was getting from some of the people in Ovidio's camp.

But she couldn't complain. She was just the temporary hired help.

And she had the feeling that things were going to get even sleazier tonight.

# CHAPTER ELEVEN

Ainsley guessed that there would be plenty of hotels in the Microcentro, the business district, so she cabbed over to the obelisk, paid the fare, and began walking.

The *porteños* rushed past her, wrapped in dark coats and colorful scarves, their intense gazes focused past their aquiline noses. Many were talking on phones. Several male heads swivelled as she walked by, but there was no *piropo*, no shouted comments, no kissyface, no quick patter of footsteps.

Ainsley suddenly understood Buenos Aires. This was New York City, except in Spanish, and in the other half of the world.

She walked past two hotels without stopping. A third looked slightly more promising, except for the doorman dressed in Regency regalia stationed outside. That wouldn't do. Ainsley had never felt comfortable with costumed people holding doors for her.

Then she noticed a simple door marked with beautiful woodwork. A discreet brass sign embedded in the wall read Gran Hotel Hispano.

A healthy-looking couple stepped out of the doors, love in their eyes. They didn't look Argentinian, didn't own that peculiar intensity that had been so apparent to her in just the last few short hours. She guessed that the couple were on their first trip together, stoking the flames of love.

This hotel might do.

She entered the vestibule and trekked up an old-fashioned circular staircase. A creaky cage elevator ran alongside. At the top of the stairs, she stood winded, breathing hard. A male clerk stationed behind a front desk looked up.

"Welcome," he said. "What do you need?"

"What's the cost for seven nights in a standard room?"

"Cash or credit?"

"Cash."

"Then it will be less."

His fingers danced over a calculator. He turned the device so she could see the result. The total came to just under a thousand pesos. Ainsley hesitated. That sounded like a lot. Then she did a quick check on her phone of the exchange rate.

It was 3.87 to 1. Pesos to dollars.

She refreshed the page and checked again. Yes, that was right. Nearly four-to-one. Her thousand-peso hotel was actually going to cost her a little over two hundred and fifty dollars. For a week.

This country was a wonderland of a bargain.

Ainsley paid him in cash, and he handed her the room key. "Breakfast is from seven to nine," he said, gesturing around the corner. "You will find free Internet access there too."

He was fairly attractive, and Ainsley waited for the inevitable compliment or come-on, but it never arrived. He'd merely returned to work, like a professional man would in most other countries.

As she turned away, Ainsley found herself feeling both relief and disappointment.

She turned the corner and found herself standing in a surprisingly striking atrium, its brick walls painted pink, green ferns hanging from the glass canopy above. Black wrought iron decorated the walls. Four cream chase lounges were arranged on the floor. This hotel hadn't looked this big from the street.

It dawned on her that this space looked a lot like the tearoom in the swanky hotel earlier. Ainsley was starting to get a sense of the *porteño* aesthetic.

She found her room easily. It was spare but clean. A simple queen bed, green comforter, plus a television and a floral couch. She dropped her bag.

Then she noticed the French doors. Her stomach flipped. She knew what French doors meant.

She pushed through them and found herself on a narrow balcony overlooking the street. Ainsley had always loved balconies, and now she breathed deeply, taking in the scene. The sound of rush-hour traffic rose from the cement beneath her. A bouquet of green buds at the top of a tree was within toe-reaching distance.

She was seized by that feeling of unreasonable anticipation, the sense of being in a completely different country, alone. Her heart quickened. Everything felt different yet familiar.

She coughed once, then realized that it wasn't the first time in the last hour. The diesel engine fumes were particularly strong here, in the Microcentro, with its density and commerce.

Ainsley returned inside and closed the French doors. She stripped off her clothes and showered. Then she dried her hair and wrapped the complimentary bathrobe around her.

She hadn't planned to come to Argentina. As a result,

there was a lot that she didn't know about this country. But Ainsley *did* know that if she was going to succeed in finding Ovidio's rhodochrosite necklace, then she needed to begin familiarizing herself.

She glanced at the clock. It was only five o'clock. She didn't have to be at the *puerta cerrada* until nearly ten.

In her slippers and robe, she left the room and returned to the atrium. The staff had laid out a small table of hors d'oeuvres. Ainsley poured some cheap red wine into a paper cup, then assembled a small plate of cheese, crackers, and olives. She took a seat on one of the chaise lounges and pulled out her phone.

It was time to learn about Argentina.

12

The first topic was that amazing exchange rate. Ainsley munched on a small slab of manchego cheese and crackers as she read about Argentine economic history.

Argentina had experienced a devastating market crash five days before Christmas 2001. The cause was simple: the government had unpegged the Argentinian peso from the U.S. dollar. The value of the currency plunged overnight. There was no run on the banks, since the banks had frozen everybody's accounts. People took to the streets instead. Since, inflation had raised prices, but the currency still hadn't really recovered.

And that hadn't been the only crash. Throughout the twentieth century, the Argentine economy had gone bust more times than an oil wildcatter. One analyst said that Argentines look at financial crises like seasonal floods. They plan accordingly, by stocking up on canned food and U.S. dollars. Then they wait, because there is always another coming.

Ainsley spat an olive pit out of her mouth onto the plate and nodded. Economic turmoil was something she could definitely relate to.

Then she turned to the *guerra sucia*, or dirty war. She felt embarrassed that Nadia had explained it like she was a third grader.

Five minutes of research made the history clear. A horrific military junta, led by General Videla and Admiral Massera, took control of Argentina in 1976. They kidnapped, tortured, and killed thirty thousand of their own people, spread propaganda and enormous lies, and finally started a pointless war over *Las Malvinas* (the Falkland Islands) with another government, Margaret Thatcher's Great Britain, which was in similar need of a pointless war. Argentina lost, and the junta nightmare finally ended seven years after it had begun.

But this hadn't been the first such military takeover either. Nine different military juntas had assumed control of the Argentine national government in the last century. It's as though Argentina has been dealing cards: one for democracy, one for dictatorship, one for democracy, one for dictatorship, back and forth. The Argentine people call this long history of instability "the sausage", an idiom that didn't quite translate, but whose meat imagery Ainsley thought was totally appropriate for the country.

Still, she felt a deep revulsion creeping up her body as she read the descriptions of the torture during the dirty war in the late seventies. The prisoners had been led beneath a door on which someone had written the words "The Path to Happiness." Beyond it had been a torture chamber with unbelievable torture machines. A *picana*, or cattle prod. An iron-banded bed connected to a 220-volt machine. An electrode that went up to 70 volts. Cutting instruments, puncturing instruments, bags filled with sand to beat people without leaving marks.

When the torture was finished, some of the bodies had been burned in open fields behind the "detention centers", as the torture facilities were known, their limbs awkwardly curling up in the flames until their tendons were clipped. Many others, the ones who hadn't died under torture, had been given Pentothal injections, dragged into airplanes, flown out over the Atlantic, and dumped naked into the ocean.

The junta had even used a horrific euphemism to describe such murders: the prisoners had been "transferred". As though they'd merely changed crosstown buses.

Ainsley sat back. Her arms were shaking, and her stomach was a mess. A hundred years ago, Argentina had been one of the top ten wealthiest countries in the world. She wondered how the country could devolve into something as horrendous as this.

She also thought about Ovidio's mother, a woman whom nobody had ever known.

Ainsley searched for her employer's name. She found more than four hundred thousand webpages relevant to Ovidio Angeletti, which she supposed is what happens to celebrities. Ainsley glanced through several. Most featured that famous photo from Nadia's office, *El Mono* swinging from the crossbar with his incisors bared. She suddenly understood Ovidio's frustration with his nickname. He was much more complicated than that single primitive image. But it was impossible for him to change it now. He'd already played his hand to the public.

Nadia had mentioned that Ovidio had played soccer in Europe, but hadn't divulged exactly where. Ainsley learned immediately: Ovidio had been the star striker for Arsenal, in London. That was one of the most powerful soccer clubs in the world. After his falling out with the owner, he'd bounced around to Barcelona and Bayern Munich on one-year contracts. And now he'd returned to Argentina, his homeland, to his retirement league. He was thirty-five years old, which is old for a striker, a testament to his level of fitness more than anything else.

"Ah," a voice said at her elbow, "you are interested in *El Mono?*"

Ainsley jumped, startled. Standing beside her was the front desk clerk. She realized that night had fallen, darkness pouring in from the overhead skylight.

"Yes," Ainsley said, "he's fascinating."

His eyes noticed her paper cup. "Did you serve yourself?"

"Of course. Why?"

A look of irritation flashed across his face. "That was very poor form," he said. "Only men pour wine. I will bring you more."

He brought the bottle over to the computer terminal and refilled her cup.

"Thank you," she said.

"You're welcome. I have another talent, if you would care to discover it." She looked up. His lips blew her a kiss and his hand discreetly touched his crotch.

There it was. A *piropo*. The first she'd encountered in several hours.

"Your talent is probably not as great as you think," Ainsley said.

He was unfazed. "Did I offend you? I'm sorry. But you offended me first, sitting here in"—he pointed to her bathrobe—"that garment. Don't you have anything real to wear?"

Ainsley froze. In the excitement of the day, she had completely forgotten: She'd left most of her clothing back in Uruguay. Certainly all of her nice outfits. And she needed to look her best tonight.

"What time is it?"

"Seven thirty."

Crap. She suddenly had no more time for his shenanigans. "Where can I go shopping nearby?"

"Calle Florida." The clerk jerked a thumb in its general direction. "Do you need help in the changing room?"

Ainsley was over the flirtation. "Forget it, I have a boyfriend."

"Then I should have charged you double," he said.

"Maybe you should just go back to work," she replied.

The clerk shrugged and moved on, turning on lamps in the atrium. Ainsley closed the browser and shoved her chair under the desk. It was time for a quick shopping expedition.

As she returned to her room, Ainsley admitted the embarrassing truth to herself.

She enjoyed the game of *piropo*.

But only a little.

# CHAPTER TWELVE

At ten o'clock pm, in Barrio Norte, near a main thoroughfare called Avenida Santa Fe, a *remise*, or taxicab, flew around the corner onto Paraná.

In the backseat was Ainsley, who was hurriedly applying last-minute touches to her makeup. She hadn't had any time to primp, not after spending nearly an hour and a half doing an emergency shopping session for a new outfit.

"Paraná is the street?" the cabbie asked.

"Yes," she replied.

Earlier, she'd walked from her hotel to Calle Florida, a distance of only four blocks, but the crowds announced it before the pavement did. Unknown to her, Calle Florida was the busiest pedestrian street in all of Buenos Aires. There were thousands of bodies in motion, shoppers, commuters, and tourists, most wrapped in dark coats and scarves, hunching under mops of dark hair.

She dodged the crowds and scanned the neon street. There were leather shops, pizza shops, athletic shoe shops, and book shops. Ainsley did love the prospect of shopping for Argentine leather at a 4-to-1 exchange rate, but at this moment she had only needed something fairly nice, fast.

At the end of the street she'd stumbled upon an opulent shopping mall: the Galeria Pacifico. Inside, were fluted stone columns, extravagant lighting, even an art museum on the top floor.

But Ainsley hadn't had time to dally. Instead, she'd ducked into the first boutique, bam, a pretty purple shirt on the rack nearest the door, bam, quick try in the fitting room, bam, cash to the salesgirl, bam, out the door. Seven minutes total.

Now she was arriving at the party in that very same purple top, trying to tear off the price tag with her teeth.

"What number was the house?" said the driver.

"1408."

He looked up. "That's not a house. That is Milión."

"What's Milión?"

"The best club in Buenos Aires. The owner bought it from an opthamologist for a million U.S. dollars after the economic crash. That's how it got its name."

"Why is it so special?"

"You'll see."

He stopped the cab. Ainsley paid him and popped out. She was standing in what appeared to be a rich residential neighborhood. The block was lined with enormous four-story French Renaissance mansions, all products of enormous Argentine wealth of the early twentieth century.

The most opulent was straight ahead, and on the ground floor an old-fashioned carriage door stood open. A modest bronze sign welcomed arrivals. Two men in black suits were standing just inside the door.

Ainsley approached them. The security seemed much more serious than usual, far elevated above the run-of-the-mill neighborhood dopes. Then Ainsley recognized them. These were the same guys from the Alvear Palace Hotel.

"Remember me?" she said.

"Identification."

"We met at the hotel?"

"Identification."

Miffed, she dug around in her purse. There was no sweet talking these guys. She'd have to remember that later.

She handed them her passport—again—and waited for the reply.

They looked at her picture and then back at her. She drew a circle in the air around her face. "Still the same," she said.

Didn't matter. They checked her name against a list, then handed her the passport back, and stepped aside.

Ainsley stepped between the men and found herself at the beginning of a long cobblestone hallway. Antique sconces lit the walls. This was a rich person's garage from the early twentieth-century *porteño* past.

Ainsley walked down the hallway, planting her heels carefully in the center of each cobblestone. Wooden tables and fancy chairs lined the walls, awaiting diners on some other night. She could feel her heart racing. She felt like she was stepping onstage, into a role that she had barely prepared for.

At the end of the hallway was an ornate wooden door. It was a real museum piece, chiselled in a perpendicular pattern. Iron scrollwork decorated the edges.

Ainsley adjusted her new top one last time, clutched her bag, and lifted her chin up. She knew how to impress men. And she would need to impress here, if she was going to get people to talk about Ovidio's rhodochrosite.

Her task was obvious. She needed to meet and impress as many members of Ovidio's entourage as possible, all while pretending to be a journalist.

It was a tall order. Nearly impossible, in fact. But Ainsley had to stay hopeful.

She approached the door, placed her hand on the iron scrollwork, and pushed it open.

# CHAPTER THIRTEEN

Ainsley stepped onto a patio that overlooked a small but gorgeous backyard garden. Globe lights hung from the jacaranda trees. In the gravel, tables and chairs had been planted beneath stylish white canvas umbrellas. A few people stood chatting around some tea lights on high tables.

To her left was a long stone staircase, lined with balustrades, that led to the second floor of the mansion. And coming down that staircase was a man in a suit. His hand was extended towards her.

"Welcome, welcome," he said. "I feel like I should know you."

Ainsley couldn't find the right words, the man was so impeccably turned out. Probably fifty years old, he boasted teeth whiter than the snowcapped peaks of the Andes. His hair was gelled into a conch shell. He could've made the cover of any fashion magazine. Maybe he already had.

"Ainsley Walker," she said.

"Yes, I knew it," he said. "When I saw you enter, I said to myself, that is an American."

There it was again. Ainsley wondered if someone had pinned a sign on her back announcing her nationality.

"You are the journalist who is here with Ovidio," he said.

"That's me," she said. The cover identity felt good.

"What publication do you write for?"

Ainsley had thought ahead this time and had already prepared a better explanation. "I'm doing this assignment freelance," she said. "The profile is going to be sold to the highest bidder." She turned the tables on him. "And who are you?"

"Facundo Fuentes," he said, kissing the back of her hand.

"Nadia said you were an important person."

"I'm not," he said. Then he twinkled all ten of his fingers, then intertwined them. "I just *connect* the important people. Like a grandmother weaving a sweater."

"That's what you're doing tonight."

"Yes. Everyone here wants to help Ovidio achieve his ambition."

Ainsley was still skeptical. "Is it really possible for a soccer player to run for president?"

"Anything is possible in Buenos Aires," he said, "to those with the connections."

"But is it a good idea? Is he really a politician?"

"I think so," he said, smiling. "Ovidio is charismatic, shrewd, and dedicated to his club."

"Many would disagree with that last point."

"Trust me. He's dedicated to everything he does."

"But he won't play. The people are getting angry."

Facundo patted her arm condescendingly. "Ovidio will play soon," he said. "He's not stupid."

Ainsley bore in a bit harder. "But he is emotional, isn't he?"

The man shrugged. "Yes, of course, he is a genius. That's the way geniuses are." He thought for a moment. "So I've been told to introduce you to some people who will help you understand Ovidio."

"You have?" she said.

"Yes, a little penguin came and told me."

"Was this penguin's name Nadia?"

He beckoned for her to follow. He seemed to have grown skittish from her questioning.

Ainsley followed him up the staircase, marvelling at the crisp, moonless night sky overhead. At the top Facundo leaned into a conversational group, made a quick quip, and got a huge laugh. He kept walking. This man was a social butterfly, a born schmoozer.

Then he was off again. Ainsley followed him into the second floor of the mansion, where she found herself in a small lounge with a gorgeous wooden bar beneath a classic chandelier. Facundo was busy joshing with a group of men in business suits, all nursing glasses of beer.

He returned to Ainsley. "What would you like?" he said. "No, never mind. I know what you need." He snapped his fingers towards the bartender. "Torrontés," he shouted, pointing at his guest.

The bartender quickly poured a glass of white wine and handed it over. Ainsley took the glass and sniffed it. Not too bad. Then she sipped the liquid, rolling the intoxicant around her tongue. It tasted light, floral, and complex. She tried more.

There was no doubt. Torrontés was delicious.

"It's an Argentina varietal," he explained, "from Salta." He pointed to his left, which is presumably the direction of that area, as though Ainsley were lacing up her shoes and preparing to sprint there at that very moment.

Ainsley followed Facundo through the old mansion. She swung her gaze from the wainscoting to the high ceilings down at the squeaky wooden floors. The floor lamps, the modern red furniture with its clean lines.

"This is gorgeous," she said. "I've never seen a club like it."

"You should come here when it's full," he said.

They circled up the inner staircase to the third floor, then the fourth. "This used to be the attic," he explained, breathing hard, "but now it's very different."

Ainsley stepped onto the landing. Straight ahead, through a doorframe, was a dance club. Bright green and red neon lights were flashing. A young barman in a vest stood behind the bar counter.

And in the middle of the dance floor stood a group of four guys.

The men looked scuzzy. Ainsley had had years of experience in weeding out such types. Their chests were absurdly puffed out. Their heads were turned sideways, avoiding eye contact with one another. Three of the four were muscled beyond belief, wearing tight v-neck t-shirts. They were trading shoulder punches.

Ainsley saw the problem: Too much testosterone. That was, reliably, the main cause of scuzzy men worldwide.

"Who are they?" said Ainsley.

"Those," replied Facundo, "are Ovidio's friends. Let me introduce you."

# CHAPTER FOURTEEN

The upstairs dance club was tiny, as befits an attic, no larger than Ainsley's entire apartment back in the U.S. Throw pillows had been tossed onto a pair of couches along the wall.

The scuzzy guys were the only other people in the room. Ainsley watched their eyes dismantle and remove the pieces of her outfit.

Evidently they decided that she was passable, because the group sauntered over. As they approached, Facundo placed his hand on the back of Ainsley's neck. Normally she would've knocked his hand away, but in this instance she was grateful for the protection.

"*Che locos boludos*," Facundo said. "*Ustedes molestamos?*"

"*Buenisimo,*" one replied. "*Que es vos mina?*"

They kept talking, and Ainsley kept listening, but the slangy Rioplatense was too unfamiliar and too fast. She only understood about half of the chatting.

Then Facundo gestured to the shortest man of the group. Shorter than average, he wore a skintight blue polyester shirt, a jungle of gold necklaces, and a sleazy smile.

"Let me introduce you to La Ainsley," Facundo said. "She's

a journalist from the United States. Ainsley Walker, this is Lalo."

She recognized his name: Lalo had been caught selling stories about Ovidio to the press. Nadia had called him a lowlife. Ainsley instinctually decided to avoid touching him.

Too late. Lalo had already caught her hand. Now he was coming in for her cheek like a predator. Ainsley closed her eyes and waited for it to be over.

"*Mucho gusto*," he said.

"*Igualmente*," she replied.

"You're drinking wine?" he said, looking at her glass. "Let me get you another drink."

"I'm good," she said.

"No, I insist."

Ainsley realized that she didn't have a choice. The other three guys were smirking, amused. She sensed that she had stumbled onstage and was acting a part in someone else's play. Guys like this always made her feel a couple steps behind the real story.

Lalo came back from the bar with a tall, ice-filled glass with an inch of brown liquid in the bottom. "Fernet," he said. "Pour the Coca-Cola into it. This is the taste of the real Argentina."

She set her wine glass down. She'd promised herself to solve the mystery of the disappeared rhodochrosite, and the first step in doing that was to earn trust.

With the guys watching, Ainsley popped open the can and poured the soda into the glass. When the foam had subsided, she took a spoon from the bartender and swizzled the liquid. Then she drank.

It was horribly bitter. Not even the syrupy Coca-Cola could disguise the sharp bite of Fernet Branca.

Lalo was smirking. "It's a good try, *che*," he said. "Next time you'll suck it down like a man."

The scuzzy guys laughed at his choice of verb, but Ainsley ignored it. "Does Ovidio drink this?" she said, wiping her eyes.

Lalo waved his hand dismissively. "That *pelotudo* won't touch anything," he said. "He won't even eat *bife de lomo*."

"How long have you known him?"

"What is this, an interview?"

"I'm a journalist," Ainsley reminded him.

Lalo tossed his drink down his throat, then threw the empty glass to the bartender, scattering ice all over the floor.

"Okay, *periodista*, since you didn't do your homework, I will tell you. Ovidio and I have known each other seven years."

"How did you meet?"

"Guess."

"You used to date him."

The other guys snickered. Ainsley figured she needed to show them toughness.

"This one is funny," Lalo said, smirking. "Very good. No, I was his minder."

His minder. Ainsley thought that was a weird term to use. She was getting ready to ask about that when one of the other guys broke in: "Lalo bought toilet paper and wiped Ovidio's ass."

There was general laughter, which Lalo ignored. "I was working for Adidas, before Ovidio lost the contract—"

"Fucking Japanese," said one of the others.

"—and he had just signed with Arsenal. He'd moved to London, was living in a hotel, couldn't get a phone, couldn't find a rental house. Adidas sent me to find him a house, help him adjust, be his friend."

That was interesting. Lalo had been a professional friend. Judging by his presence here tonight, he had figured that "working" for Ovidio was a better deal than working for Adidas.

One of the guys was bent over a chair now, muttering, "Lalo, a little more to the right," while the third, crouching, theatrically wiped his ass with a cocktail napkin. The fourth guy was on the couch, laughing. Ainsley guess the drinking had been going on for a couple hours now.

"*Que cabrón*," said Lalo, "*no me lo banco más.*"

"What about the time you fixed his toilet?" said the fourth.

"He asked me to," replied Lalo.

"In the middle of the night?"

"That was my job!"

"Or the time you cleaned up his house like a maid," added another.

"I couldn't let anybody see that he'd been drunk," said Lalo. "It was during the Premier League finals."

"Or the time you stole his ski boots," said a fourth.

"I didn't steal them. I hid them. He wasn't supposed to be skiing. It was in his contract."

"He's still looking for them," said the fourth.

Lalo puffed out his chest and smirked. "I hid them very well."

"Did you ever steal anything else?" said Ainsley. "Like money?"

Lalo suddenly stopped. So did the others. They stared at her. She'd apparently crossed a line. She looked around for Facundo but noticed that he had slipped away.

Ainsley tried to recover. "I mean, if I worked for a celebrity, it would be easy, I would be stealing every second of every day." She saw Lalo starting to smile, so she kept going. "I mean, you couldn't leave a jar of baby food near me. It would disappear. And the money? There's so much flying around. Like picking cherries." She mimicked plucking fruit from a high branch and dropping it into an invisible bag.

The scuzzy guys were almost back on her side, so she pulled out her newest piece of slang. "You know what I mean, right? *Sin vergüenza!*"

Hearing a woman use that phrase, in correct context, nailed it. They burst out laughing. She was proud of herself for using that idiom. She'd heard Ovidio use it earlier, and figured that it'd meant something like "bravely, without shame". From his delivery she guessed that it had a manly connotation, a show of bravura, perfect confidence.

"I like this one," said Lalo, "she has *bronca*." They toasted her.

The four grew more relaxed. Lalo finally answered the question. "Of course I steal," said Lalo. He pointed to his friends. "Just like him, and him, and him, and you. No one here is a saint."

"I heard Ovidio caught you," Ainsley said.

"No, that *hija de puta* Nadia caught me," he corrected her. "Ovidio didn't care."

"What about necklaces? Did you ever steal one of those?"

Another aggressive comment. She watched the four men's eyes. They glanced at one another. So much for just three people knowing about the stolen necklace, Ainsley thought. This was feeling more and more like an open secret.

Lalo grew serious. "Do you know what you're talking about?"

"Not really," she lied, "but I figured you might."

"How did you find out?"

"It's my secret," replied Ainsley.

"You're a good journalist," he said. "But I need to tell you something. I would never steal something like that. Especially not from Ovidio. I *want* him to play, I *want* him to succeed.

Because when he succeeds, I succeed. You can publish that in your fucking magazine."

"We're off the record. Nobody knows about the necklace."

He made a *pffffft* sound. "Everything gets out when a *boluda* like you finds out."

"The secret won't get out. I promised."

"A promise is nothing," he said. "I promise things every day. Here, watch." Lalo cleared his throat and faced Ainsley like a dutiful soldier. "I promise you that I won't try to fuck you tonight."

He assumed a look of absolute sincerity. His three buddies snickered. Ainsley realized that their mood had changed again, that there was some unseen game they were playing with her. She wondered how she could stay ahead of that.

These guys didn't even care that she was supposed to be a journalist. Maybe that made her even more of a mark. Maybe female journalists in Argentina were known as easy lays.

Regardless, Nadia had been totally right. Ovidio's friends were lowlifes.

"You won't keep that promise," she said.

"I will," he said. "It's my promise."

Facundo suddenly appeared at her side, and she quietly applauded his timing. "I think you've had enough of these gentlemen. There is somebody else I want you to meet."

# CHAPTER FIFTEEN

The host led Ainsley down the stairs to the third floor. Ainsley noticed that the mansion was filling with more people, mostly older, serious types. She glanced at her watch. It was eleven pm. It appeared that late nights were typical for this part of the world.

She followed Facundo into a small parlor. Heavy brocade wallpaper and mood lighting made it feel like a Victorian-era bedroom.

A short man with clear spectacles and a scholarly manner was sitting in a chair beneath a reading lamp. He was looking at a sheaf of documents. His legs were crossed over one another at the knee, in the European way.

"El Oido," said Facundo.

The man looked up over the top of his glasses. Ainsley had always been mildly annoyed by the mannerism. It sent the message that the other person wasn't quite important enough.

"Facundo, *como está usted*? the man said.

"*Buenisimo*. This is Ainsley Walker."

He lowered the papers, stood up, and kissed her cheek. "I

am called Nestor," he said. "*El Oido* is just my nickname." His voice was as thin as the sound of an oboe.

"He is Ovidio's psychotherapist," said Facundo.

"That's me," the man said, "an ear for rent."

"Ainsley is a journalist from the United States," Facundo explained. "She has some questions for you."

"It's usually my job to ask the questions," the psychotherapist said.

"Please," said Facundo. "For me."

The psychotherapist sighed and removed his glasses. "I'll try to please her."

Ainsley felt her stomach sink. She was no journalist, no interviewer, and certainly no psychologist. She knew that Nestor was going to lose patience with her, quickly.

He pointed to the couch. "You can sit there," he said, taking the chair again. "What do you want to know?"

Ainsley felt suddenly alone as she scrambled for an appropriate opener. "It seems like Ovidio has emotional problems," she said.

"He is experiencing an internal struggle for identity dominance," said the psychotherapist. "That makes for a compelling personality."

"What type of identities are competing?"

"One, narcissistic tendencies. Two, a need for approval. Three, a lack of family gives him no models to pattern himself upon. All of this means that his sense of self is very fluid, very mobile, whereas yours and mine are more fixed."

She thought about that for a moment. Ainsley's own identity had been in major upheaval for nearly a year now, struggling with loss of spouse, loss of job, loss of friends, loss of purpose. Maybe she was just as adrift as Ovidio.

Nestor was continuing. "And then this fluid sense of self is reinforced by the adulation of the Argentine public. They tell him that this state is acceptable and even wanted. As a result, he embraces these contradictions within himself, instead of attempting to resolve them."

"That's good insight," said Ainsley.

"It's elucidated by Lacan," he continued. "The mirror stage initiates, and aids, the process of forming and integrating a solid sense of self. But without the Other, which is typically the Mother..." He shrugged.

Ainsley felt confused by the verbiage, which she could barely follow in English, let alone Spanish. She decided to steer the conversation towards more practical matters. "Has Ovidio ever spoken about his mother?"

"Every day for the past ten years," he said.

"He comes into your office every day?"

"No, it's mostly by phone. Day or night, that telephone is always ringing. And I always pick up." The psychotherapist smiled ruefully. "Don't get me wrong. He's the ideal patient: unlimited problems and unlimited funds. But, truthfully, it's like a prison for me." He glanced at Ainsley. "That's all off the record."

"Of course."

Then he frowned. "Where is your tape recorder?"

"I lost it," she lied.

"You have no paper or pen?"

She rushed to cover her tracks. "I'm just getting background. And my memory is excellent."

Nestor shrugged. She sensed that he was getting bored with her. Ainsley decided to cut to the chase.

"Have you discussed his mother's necklace?"

Nestor paused. He looked at her significantly. "Ovidio's entire mentality is in that necklace. I've watched him hold it against his face when he cries. I've watched him, in a fit of anger, throw it out the window into a dumpster. I had to call his assistant to retrieve it, because I knew he was going to regret it."

"I heard an interesting rumor about it," said Ainsley.

"I live in Buenos Aires," he said. "I hear rumors every day."

"This rumor says that the necklace is missing," she said, "and that he won't play soccer until it's found."

The psychotherapist's nostrils widened. "That is not public knowledge," he said, "and if you publish that, you will regret having come to Buenos Aires."

"I have no intention of doing so," she said. "But do you have any thoughts?"

"I do," he said, "but I won't share them with you."

"You can trust me," she said.

"That's not been proven."

She plowed ahead anyways. "Who would've wanted to steal his rhodochrosite?"

"Who wouldn't?" he said. The psychotherapist's eyes were dancing madly behind his glasses. "Pick an opposing manager. Pick an opposing player. They're in awe of his talent, but nobody can stand his personality. Jealousy is a powerful motivator."

"So you're telling me it could've been anybody in professional Argentine soccer."

"It's possible." Then he grew very still, and when he began speaking again, the psychotherapist's voice had changed. It was deeper and heavier. "If you're at this party, then you already know that he's thinking about running for president."

Ainsley nodded. "He's been giving interviews about it."

"What do you think about that?"

"It's a bad idea. He's not fit to be president. It would probably hurt the country."

The psychotherapist nodded but said nothing. Behind the spectacles, his eyes had grown very serious, and his gaze held hers with an unnerving intensity. The air felt heavy with unspoken words. Ainsley shifted in her seat, feeling unsettled.

Finally the psychotherapist broke the silence. *"Bueno.* If there are no more problems, I hope that I have managed to please you." He offered his hand.

"Thank you for your time," she said.

Ainsley rose, exchanged cheek kisses, and left the parlor.

As she descended the staircase towards the main floor, she couldn't help feeling that El Oido knew much more of this mystery than he was willing to reveal.

# CHAPTER SIXTEEN

Downstairs, the party had swollen to at least a hundred and fifty people. Men leaned over the staircase railing, shouting to friends on floors below. Groups of men stood arranged around fireplaces in private rooms, socializing loudly, their women standing at the elbows, looking insecure.

She moved through the crowd, looking for the guest of honor, but he was nowhere to be seen.

She ordered another glass of Torrontés from the downstairs bar, admired the woodwork, the well-dressed people, the ambience, and felt her thoughts turn towards a different topic.

Love.

She was alone, again, in a foreign country, on a moonlit night, dressed to the nines, holding a drink in a beautiful old mansion now converted to a chic nightclub. All this—and not a single romantic prospect on the horizon.

This was a missed opportunity. Ainsley would regret this evening in her old age.

Then she reminded herself that this wasn't a vacation.

This was *work*. She was on assignment to find a rhodochrosite necklace.

Through the doorway, she spotted Facundo on the balcony. He was socializing with a fury. His face had turned bright red, his laughter more forced, his shoulder-squeezes more ferocious.

Ainsley guessed that she knew the reason. Ovidio hadn't arrived yet. Facundo was feeling the pressure to provide the entertainment.

She weaved through the partygoers until she was standing at Facundo's side. He noticed her immediately.

"Was *El Oído* helpful?" said the host.

"A little," she said. "Where is Ovidio?"

Facundo could barely contain his emotion. "Why bother with such silly questions?" His smile grew bigger, his stance grew straighter. "Let's all have a good time! Mix together!" He hoisted his glass violently into the air, liquid sloshing onto his sleeve.

Ainsley watched the other attendees. The other party-goers were waiting patiently, but the signs of impatience were there. They seemed like important *porteños*. They'd come to meet Ovidio, to get a picture with him; in return, they would promise their support in his run for president. Who knew how long their patience would last? This was a moody culture.

Ovidio skipping out on his own political gathering was unthinkable. Ainsley figured that he was probably planning a grand entrance later in the evening, when the time was right. And she also figured that the best place to watch his grand entrance would be from the back garden.

Ainsley descended the outside staircase with careful steps, hand touching the balustrade. She felt vaguely like a queen. She also felt eyes watching her.

Two in particular.

Standing on the ground, beneath a canvas umbrella, was a man about her age. He had stood tall, had a full head of black hair and a flat abdomen. He carried an observant air about him.

Ainsley smiled at him. That was the only trigger he needed: these Argentine men acted fast. As she neared the bottom of the staircase, he walked over and extended his hand.

"I would hate for you to trip," he said.

"Thank you," she replied.

He helped Ainsley across the gravel, which was hellish in her shoes. When she reached the paving stones a few meters away, he let go of her hand.

She turned to look at her suitor. Up close, he was even more attractive, blessed with the killer combination of blue eyes and dark hair. He wore the mandatory three days' scruff that was apparently *de rigueur* in Buenos Aires.

"Thank you," she said.

"You're here to support Ovidio?" he said.

"No. I'm just a journalist."

He seemed surprised. "You don't look like one. Also, they don't usually let journalists into events like this."

"Then I must be special," she said, with an arch of her eyebrow. She felt her old flirting muscle coming back into shape. "How did you get into this party?"

"I'm an old friend," he said.

"Of who?"

"Ovidio. We grew up together."

Ainsley cocked her head. "Really?" She moved a bit closer, both for personal and professional reasons. "Did you play soccer too?"

The man nodded. "We met on our first day at Club Ontiveros. We were eleven years old."

"What do you do now?"

"I still play professional soccer. River Plate." Ainsley recognized the name; it was one of the most famous teams in the country. Then he added humbly: "Don't be impressed, I'm just a reserve. I don't get on the field much. I'm too old." He offered his hand. "I am called Sebastian."

"And I'm Ainsley."

She took the hand, then accepted a cheek kiss. It was chaste, but lingered a second longer than usual.

Ainsley was about to follow up with more questioning, but she never got the chance. The smell of liquor announced the arrival of Lalo and his buddies, who'd abandoned the attic club upstairs.

Lalo and Sebastian greeted each other warmly. Ainsley felt her stomach drop a little. You can always judge somebody by the company they keep, and Lalo was bad company.

Sebastian gestured to Ainsley. "Did you meet the journalist?"

"Of course," Lalo said. "I made an important promise to her."

His buddies laughed again; she was feeling annoyed by him.

"Are you ready to go yet?" said Sebastian.

Lalo nodded, picking his teeth. "We've got the back room reserved at Caballo."

Sebastian thought. "Caballo? I heard that place moved."

"It's in Puerto Madero now. Don't worry, *che*, we'll drive you."

"You don't drive anybody, *cabrón*."

Ainsley interrupted. "I'm confused. Ovidio hasn't even arrived yet. Why are you all leaving?"

An expression of sadness came across Sebastian's face. He looked at Lalo. "Do we tell her?"

The scuzzy minder shrugged, rolling his toothpick around

in his mouth. Sebastian turned to her. "Ovidio isn't coming tonight."

Ainsley was completely stupified. "Why not? This is a party for him."

"He's not coming because it's Wednesday."

"So what?"

The men looked at each other. Lalo stepped in. "Ovidio doesn't do anything on Wednesdays," he said.

"Why?"

"Because it's the day that his mother was killed," said Lalo.

Ainsley was startled. She stammered, "How does he know the day that his mother was killed?"

Lalo had already turned away, so Sebastian leaned in closer and continued the story, whispering. "You know about the dirty war? How they killed the *desaparecidos*?"

"Of course," said Ainsley.

"So you know that the prisoners were dumped out of airplanes over the Atlantic?"

"Yes."

"Those planes only left on Wednesdays."

Ainsley suddenly understood. "Oh."

Sebastian had a look of absolute compassion in his eyes. "So Ovidio won't do anything on Wednesdays. He never does. It's his personal sabbath. When we were boys, he used to skip practice on that day. The coach was angry but couldn't do anything about it. It's also one of the reasons that Arsenal transferred him."

"Why?"

"He wouldn't play any games on Wednesdays. Management was furious with him. He had one bad season, and then he was gone."

"And what about tonight?"

Sebastian shook his head sadly. "Nobody told Facundo."

Ainsley scanned the balcony until she found the host in a far corner. Facundo had his phone cradled against his ear. His eyes were blazing. He looked about a minute away from a coronary.

"This could hurt Ovidio's political ambitions," said Ainsley.

"Yes it could," said Sebastian, "if Argentine politics made any sense. But they don't make sense." He smiled. "Are you coming with me?"

Ainsley didn't have any reason to say no. She doubted that Facundo would be in the mood to continue introducing her to people. And Sebastian seemed like an invaluable resource.

"Yes," she said. "I'm hungry."

Sebastian offered his arm, and she accepted. Lalo and his scuzzy entourage joined them as they left through the cobblestone garage and to the street outside.

# CHAPTER SEVENTEEN

With her nose steaming up the window, Ainsley felt her heart leap at the panorama below her.

Buenos Aires at night.

It was nearly two o'clock in the morning. She was in Caballo, one of the city's hippest dinner clubs, on the twenty-seventh floor of a brand-new skyscraper in Puerto Madera. There were several other towers lining the port, some not even finished yet. This was one part of Argentina, at least, that had recovered quite well from the economic crash—the part that exported soybeans and meat.

She was in a private room at the back of the club, a corner room, two walls of which were clean glass, affording a nearly aerial view of South America's most exciting city. She gazed down at the bits of blue light, the ribbons of red avenues.

It took her breath away.

On a table in the center of the room was a spread of beautiful grilled meats, cheeses, and olives, which was constantly being replenished by tuxedoed wait staff. Ainsley had already scarfed two small plates and was debating a third. The only thing stopping her was the presence of the women.

Ainsley had never been very catty, but even she had to admit that these women were full-on bitches.

Upon their arrival at the club, five girls were already waiting in the private room. None looked older than twenty-three. All were dressed in shimmery miniskirts and stilettos. They had been wearing severe makeup and unattractive pouts.

And then they had surrounded the men like a swarm of fish.

Ainsley had seen possessive girls back in the States. Everybody, after all, knows at least one girl so outrageously insecure that she needs to start fights with other women.

But these *chicas* had achieved another level of clinginess. Ainsley'd found herself literally shoved aside as their manicured fingers and hands had scratched all over the men's chests and backs. Soon Lalo and his friends had become cocooned inside a impermeable kittenish cuddle.

Even Sebastian had his own personal barnacle, a girl whose smoky eyes systematically cast murderous looks at every other woman in the room. Her fingers ran through his hair. The player wasn't returning the intimacies, but he wasn't discouraging them either. Ainsley imagined that it was hard to say no. It was a mystery to her how professional athletes ever maintained marriages.

Still, her belly was full, and the muted, pulsing music from the main room provided a sexy soundtrack. Soon enough, Lalo disengaged himself from the purring women and lurched over towards Ainsley. A whiskey bottle hung loose from his hand. His eyes were having trouble focusing.

"You having a good time?" he said.

"Of course."

"The night is young," he said, then nodded towards the girls. "Younger than even them."

"Are these your girlfriends?"

"Sometimes," he said. "When we want them to be."

"Lucky you."

Lalo wasn't hammered enough to miss her sarcastic tone. "It's how we are," he said. "Don't hate something you don't understand. Besides, you don't have to be here." His pudgy finger poked at her sternum. "You're only here because we *allow* you to be here."

Ainsley understood the veiled threat. He was pulling rank. And Lalo's position was stronger than even he knew, because Ovidio had full confidence in him.

"That's true," she said. She picked up her purse and coat. "I think I'll go outside for a while. I'm curious about the docks."

"It's up to you," Lalo said. "But you're safe with us. I haven't forgotten my promise." He leered at her.

Ainsley gave him a fake smile, which probably wasn't convincing, because she wasn't particularly good at them. Then she walked past him.

Sebastian was sprawled on the couch, cocktail in hand. The barnacle was now running both her hands through his hair. Ainsley made eye contact with him and nodded as she hit the door.

Outside the VIP suite, the full blast of the music assaulted her ears. The main room of Caballo was a blur of dancers and drinkers, all young, all hip. In the corner, behind an elevated booth, a DJ had his ear cocked into a pair of headphones. This could've been any nightclub in New York, and while Ainsley wasn't opposed to dancing tonight, she needed some fresh air first. The closed space of the private room had made her feel a little claustrophobic. Sealed rooms, no matter how chic, always did that to her.

She threaded her way around the floor, found the elevator, and descended to the street.

There, Ainsley stepped onto the pedestrian area. There

were four *diques*, or square-shaped bodies of water, that comprised the heart of Puerto Madero. In front of her was the second, known as Dique Dos. She walked across a small plaza to the railing, where she stared across the water, at the buildings on the other side, only two hundred meters away.

Then she heard a voice shout her name. She turned.

It was Sebastian.

Ainsley felt her heart leap in her chest. She had played the best card that a woman could play in such a circumstance: scarcity. Voluntarily leaving a professional athlete was some-times the best way to separate yourself from the pack. She'd raised her status.

"You didn't like Caballo?" he said.

"Everyone was busy there," she replied. "All those girls."

"Yeah, Lalo arranged that. He always has them waiting."

"A nice friend to have."

Sebastian studied her, not sure what the comment could mean. "It's a beautiful night," he said. "Do you want to walk with me?"

"Where?"

"Here. Along the *diques*."

He held out his arm again. Ainsley knew she shouldn't be accepting anything like this while she was on assignment, but she didn't want to regret having wasted this night.

They strolled along the railings. Ahead of them was a white pedestrian bridge, oddly shaped, with a single asym-metrical fin poking up diagonally into the air. Several cables stretched from the fin down to the footpath. It looked like a harp.

"What is that?"

"The woman's bridge."

"Really."

"Yes, it's called the Woman's Bridge. It was built by Calatrava. When boats need to pass through, those cables swing the middle portion open."

"We women are generous like that," she said.

"Sometimes," he said.

A cold wind gusted across the open water, and Ainsley wrapped her coat about herself more tightly.

"I only know Ovidio as an adult," she said. "What was he like as a child?"

Sebastian laughed. "Competitive."

"I figured that."

"Trust me, you have no idea. He was the worst bastard in the world. He was always challenging me, let's have a penalty kick competition, let's have a handstand competition, let's have a video game competition, let's have a kiss-the-girl-first competition. He used to wake me up at five in the morning, come on Sebito, let's go practice headers before morning practice. Then he would get really mad, really *bronca*, when I wouldn't want to go. One morning I told him no and he tried to physically pull me out of bed. We got into a huge fistfight, right there, destroyed everything in my room."

"And you still kept speaking?"

"Are you kidding? After that day, we were best friends."

Ainsley laughed. "You're such *men*."

"Of course. We've stayed in touch always. Even while I've watched him explode throughout the world."

Sebastian sighed. Ainsley wondered if there was a little bit of jealousy. "Not everybody can be a superstar."

The striker responded quickly, as though he'd thought a lot about that. "I wouldn't want to be one either. It makes you crazy. Of course, Ovidio was already a little bit *loco*, you know. But the fame made it worse." He sighed. "Honestly, I don't know why we're still friends."

"Maybe habit."

"I guess because everybody has screwed him except me."

Ainsley decided to get a little bolder. "Do you know who stole his necklace?"

Sebastian glanced sideways at her. "You know about that?"

She nodded. This truly was an open secret. Nadia was hopelessly behind the gossip.

"It's a horrible crime," he said. "That necklace means more than life itself to Ovidio. He cannot function without it."

"Who could've wanted to hurt him?"

Sebastian shrugged. "There are too many. It's impossible to say."

"Surely you can narrow it down."

He shook his head. "Ovidio is a polarizing public figure. He has millions of enemies, especially whenever Boca loses." Then Sebastian grew very serious. "This country knows how to keep its secrets. We do that very well. Right now, all we can hope is that someone, someday, will be courageous enough to say, yes, I saw it happen, and then point to the guilty one."

He produced a cigarette and lit it. "I don't usually smoke, but this conversation has agitated me. I am worried for his future."

Ainsley was worrying about the future for a different reason. The night had yielded no clues, zero, not a single crack into the solution to Ovidio's mystery yet. Or, if there had been one, she hadn't been astute enough to catch it.

Ainsley struggled to get perspective on her situation. She was feeling overwhelmed by the impossibility of the assignment. She was strolling at two in the morning with a South American soccer player who, at first blush, seemed both attractive and kind. And she was mildly drunk.

The rhodochrosite didn't matter. Ainsley wanted this feeling, this night, to keep going.

She heard the distant thumping of electronic dance

music. Ahead lay another nightclub, situated in what seemed to be a line of old warehouses. The queue outside the door was at least a hundred people long. It wrapped around the corrugated iron exterior of the building, out of sight.

"You look like you want to dance tonight," he said.

Ainsley felt suddenly self-conscious. "I'm really a terrible dancer."

"Me too," he replied. "I am useless, period. The coach won't let me score goals anymore. All I do is wear my warmup jersey on the bench and applaud my teammates."

"An easy job."

He looked at her askance. Then he stubbed out the cigarette under his shoe. "And I'm with you, so let's dance."

Ainsley's heart rose at the idea. Then she looked at the queue again, and her heart fell. "How long do you think it will take to get through that line?"

Sebastian waved it away. "We won't wait in line. They know me here."

Together they made towards the front door of the nightclub, and when they stumbled out, two and a half hours later, a pair of sweaty messes, Ainsley felt absolutely confident of one thing.

For the first time in ages, she'd had a lot of fun with a man.

# CHAPTER EIGHTEEN

Shortly before seven o'clock am, Ainsley woke with a start. Next to her bed, someone had just slammed the door shut.

She groped around and realized there was no pillow under her head. Then she realized there was no bed either.

Ainsley bolted up. She bumped her head on a low, padded ceiling. Her pupils tightened enough for her to scope out her surroundings.

She was in the backseat of a luxury automobile. It was parked on the dirt shoulder of a road. A convenience store was about thirty meters behind her.

And she was alone.

Ainsley looked down at her clothes. It was the same purple shirt she'd been wearing just two hours earlier, when she'd come out of the nightclub. Her makeup looked horrible, she was sure.

She groggily tried to piece together the order of events. Sebastian had offered her a ride back to her hotel. She'd accepted, maybe unwisely. She remembered getting into the front seat of his BMW. She remembered fighting to keep her eyes open.

Then she couldn't remember anything after that.

Ainsley peered into the front seat. Her purse was in the footwell. She leaned forward, grabbed it, rifled through it. Everything inside seemed intact. Then she tried to open her back door.

It was locked.

She cursed out loud. Her fingers scrambled across the inner panel of the back door, looking for the lock button. She poked it furiously. It wouldn't work. She was sealed inside this closed vehicle.

Panicked, Ainsley banged her fists against the window, screaming, thrashing the car from side to side. She was making the entire car shake.

A small click from the doors. Her tantrum paused. She pushed the sweaty hair out of her face.

The door had unlocked. She had *made* it happen with the force of her resistance.

Ainsley yanked it open, scrambled quickly out of the car ... and tripped on her shoe. She fell onto her left side into the dirt.

Pulling herself up, Ainsley wiped the dirt and twigs from her blouse. It was no matter. She would be catching a taxi straight back to the Gran Hotel Hispano.

Then she saw Sebastian.

He was walking towards her from the convenience store down the road. He was carrying two cups, one in each hand, with lids. It looked like coffee.

"Good morning, *hermosita*," he said, "you finally woke up."

"Why did you lock me in the car?"

"Because I didn't want anybody to hurt you. This is a dangerous area." He gestured back to the convenience store, then looked at her clothing. "Did you fall in the dirt?"

"No, I went rolling around in the mud like a pig to cool off," she shot back. "Of course I fell down. I was furious."

"Towards me? Why?"

"I thought you were kidnapping me."

He laughed, then set the coffee cups on the roof of the car. "I guess it's better that you don't trust anybody. Life is easier that way."

Ainsley felt herself softening a little, but she was still wary. "What happened last night?"

"Two hours ago, you fell asleep and I couldn't wake you up."

"Why didn't you take me to my hotel?"

"You fell asleep before you could tell me the name."

"How did I get in the backseat?"

"I put you there. It would be the best place to sleep." His voice softened. "Don't worry. You were safe."

She looked at Sebastian. He didn't seem to have been partying and dancing all night. He was wearing a new pair of stylish jeans and a fresh pink polo shirt. He'd even brushed his hair. Ainsley felt hideous by comparison.

He noticed her looking at him. "I carry extra clothes in my trunk," he said. Then he glanced at her own filthy outfit. "Sorry, nothing for you."

"It's all right," she said. "I just need to catch a taxi so I can get back to the hotel."

"That's not possible right now," he said, shaking his head.

"Why?"

"Because taxis don't come out to the *villas*."

"What are the *villas*?"

Sebastian was taken aback. "The *villas miserias*. You don't know them?"

"Why?"

He looked taken aback. "Nobody told you?"

"No," she said. Ainsley was feeling impatient. "Look, we had a fun time last night, but I have different plans for today. I'll find my own taxi and go back home."

It was a lie, of course. Ainsley had no plans for the day. But she was feeling ugly, and in need of real sleep in a real bed.

She started walking down the shoulder of the road, but Sebastian rushed over and caught her arm. He looked around worriedly. "I told you, this is a dangerous area, the taxis don't come out here."

"So I don't have a choice."

He nodded. "Trust me. You want to come."

"Why?"

Sebastian straightened up with pride. "Because Ovidio is announcing his candidacy for president at the *villa* this morning."

# CHAPTER NINETEEN

As Sebastian drove them further down the road, Ainsley reclined in the passenger seat, sipped at her coffee, and listened to him explain what had really happened last night.

While it was true that Ovidio had skipped out on his own party at Milión because it was Wednesday, Sebastian said, there was also another reason.

The superstar had realized that, as a people's athlete, he needed to be seen as the people's politician, not as a tool of the rich. So he'd decided to announce his political ambitions not in a fancy mansion-turned-nightclub, but surrounded instead by people's people.

In the *villas miserias*, the poorest parts of Buenos Aires.

Ainsley suddenly understood the translation: These "villages of misery" were shantytowns.

Sebastian seemed to read her mind. "You're going someplace most journalists never see. Most *porteños* don't go here either. I certainly don't."

"But what about all those people who waited for him at Milión last night?" said Ainsley. "They're going to be even more pissed off."

Sebastian shrugged. "You can never guess which way Ovidio is going to move. It's the same on and off the soccer field. He is Argentine to his very soul."

"So does this place have a name?"

"Yes. We're going to Villa 27. It's one of the most notorious. Lots of drugs."

That name sounded familiar. *Villa 27*. She remembered Nadia mentioning it back in Ovidio's hotel suite. It was where the suspect maid, the one who hadn't shown up for work since the day of the theft, supposedly lived.

But all Ainsley said was, "I presume the media is going to be there."

"Of course," said Sebastian, "in fact, I heard Nadia was alerting them late last night. That's probably why she couldn't make it to Milión." Then he squinted and angled his head, watching something. "There. Look. The beginning of the madhouse."

He pointed. Through the windshield, Ainsley could see a swarm of activity on an open field.

Sebastian parked the car a safe distance away. Then he laid a hand on her arm. "Do yourself a favor," he said. "Stay near the stage, on the side. Don't go into the neighborhood." He looked very serious.

"I won't," she said.

"It's dangerous for everybody. Especially a *turista*."

Ainsley smiled. "It's a good thing I'm not one of those."

Sebastian smiled back. They left the car and moved down the street towards the small field. As they drew closer, Ainsley realized that calling it a park was too generous. It was an expanse of dirt dotted with patches of grass. Two pairs of wooden sticks stood as goalposts. There were no trees anywhere, not even a garbage can.

At the far end of this field, a small stage had been erected, empty for the moment, surrounded by a bank of bright lights.

A long blue-and-white banner read *Mi Gente, Mi Pais, Mi Ovidio.*

Translation: My people, my homeland, my Ovidio.

A crowd of at least five hundred had already gathered around the stage, and there were more pouring in every minute. Nearby, an elevated platform stood to the rear of the crowd, on which twenty cameras were already set up, their cables running off the back of the platform to the media trucks nearby, which were parked haphazardly on the dirt.

And encircling the small field stood the most ramshackle neighborhood Ainsley had ever seen.

This was Villa 27.

The structures were one, two, even three stories tall, but they looked like do-it-yourself jobs, as though the owners had just stacked extra floors onto their homes with whatever materials were around, whenever they'd felt the urge. Ainsley knew that her perspective had been formed by the standards of construction in the United States, but there was no denying that these structures were dangerous. She guessed that no building inspector had ever set a single toe in this neighborhood. How could a supposedly developed country allow this type of construction?

Ainsley didn't have an answer to that question. She pushed other thoughts out of her mind as she followed Sebastian around the edges of the crowd.

She studied the men and women who were milling about. They looked surprisingly healthy. The children seemed well-nourished, a few even pudgy, and bore no obvious markers of severe poverty. Most of their clothing was worn, faded, but given Ainsley's own condition—oily hair, caked-on makeup, shirt stained with dirt—she had zero right to judge anybody.

Streams of people were pouring out of the villa into the field. The crowd was growing larger and larger, the party vibe growing stronger and stronger.

Sebastian maneuvered confidently through the people, despite his own status as a professional soccer player. Ainsley tugged on his sleeve. "Aren't you worried about people recognizing you?"

He shrugged. "I've sat on the bench with a warm-up hoodie over my head for two years. It doesn't happen." He gestured. "I was nowhere near this popular anyways."

Ainsley caught a definite whiff of jealousy. She'd never been friends with a superstar, but thus far, the experience appeared to be stressful for everybody involved.

An expensive black Mercedes with limo-tinted windows pulled up into the field and behind the stage. The crowd grew excited. There was a small surge as a hundred people rushed forward.

"Isn't this dangerous?" she said. "No protection?"

"Ovidio's not in that car," said Sebastian. "He knows how these things work."

The back door opened, and a couple of masculine guys in suits stood up with chests puffed out and no-bullshit expressions on their faces. It didn't take a rocket scientist to figure that these were security guards, the first of Ovidio's personal entourage.

Then a second Mercedes pulled up behind the first. Another small surge. This time, a pair of professional women stepped out, presumably office staffers.

"He's smart," said Ainsley.

"It's the principle of crowd control," Sebastian said. "In a place this vulnerable, you must keep the energy low. Disappoint them. Keep disappointing them. Then surprise them."

A third Mercedes, then a fourth followed, each with more professional people stepping out of the backseat. There was a perceptible sense of deflation from the poor residents. Ainsley could see them turning away from the stage.

Then a simple gray sedan, a Chevrolet Classic with tinted

windows, pulled up onto the field from the road. Slowly, it began to drive slowly through the crowd of people towards the stage. The people parted as it moved. There was cheering. Hands pounded on its windows.

Ainsley craned her head. "Do you think he's in that car?"

"Never," said Sebastian. "That's the decoy. I've seen him do this before." He scanned the area. "There. That's him."

He nodded backwards. On the road, behind the distracted crowd, an outrageously gorgeous black Rolls-Royce had ripped around the corner. A fleet of six security guards stood on the running boards, hands placed on their weapons.

"He looks presidential already," said Ainsley.

"Yes," said Sebastian, "but only to them."

The Rolls-Royce accelerated around the media platform and roared to a halt behind the four Mercedes, sending up a cloud of brown dust. The six security guards stepped off the sides, hands revealing their weapons. One opened the door.

Ainsley stood up on her tiptoes. She saw the familiar face of Ovidio rise out of the vehicle.

The crowd, obsessed with the decoy Chevy moving slowly through its midst, was slow to recognize his arrival. That was the point. Ovidio wasted no time. He sprinted the few short feet towards the main stage and bounded up the stairs. He was dressed in a sharp suit. Makeup covered his face.

The crowd finally saw him. They began to roar.

And that's when Ainsley saw, for the first time, just how famous Ovidio Angeletti really was in Argentina.

# CHAPTER TWENTY

The crowd had grown to nearly fifteen hundred people now, and they were all screaming. But they weren't shouting in the usual manner that Ainsley had seen at graduations and sporting events back in the United States.

These poor people were expressing themselves in a deeper way, vocalizing a sort of soul-deep longing. It wasn't from their throats. These people were screaming at Ovidio from the very bottom of their *souls*, from the pits of their shattered spirits, in the way that only the truly desperate can do.

Ainsley nodded. She knew that feeling, had briefly tasted its bitterness.

Then a song came across on the loudspeakers. It was an odd rhythm, a genre Ainsley had never heard before.

But the people of this *villa* certainly knew it. They began bouncing in synchronization, arms in the air. Then Ainsley realized why.

Onstage, Ovidio had rolled up his white sleeves, in the typical politician's style. However, unlike most politicians, he was bouncing too. His mouth was open, a smile on his cheeks. A look of sheer joy decorated his face.

And the people were reacting towards him in the exact same manner.

After a minute or two, the song was turned down, and a sober-looking man in his fifties, wearing regular work boots and jeans, slowly climbed onstage with Ovidio. He was carrying a microphone.

The man spoke a few stumbling sentences, but the volume on the microphone was turned too low, and soon the people turned impatient, and began booing him. He looked like someone who knew next to nothing about stagecraft.

"Who is that?" said Ainsley.

"I can't really hear," said Sebastian, "but I think it's the mayor of Villa 27."

"They have mayors here?"

"Why wouldn't they? It's a community."

The man continued with his plodding speech, occasionally consulting a shaky piece of paper. Ainsley guessed that the guy was politically way out of his element. He looked like he would probably be a lot more comfortable chatting at someone's rickety kitchen table about sewage pipes.

Evidently he had the sense that he was losing the crowd, because he wrapped up his talk quickly. Ainsley caught his last sentence: "...please, I beg you, welcome, to this villa, the football star, the center of the *Albiceleste*, and your next *selección* for president of Argentina, Señor Ovidio Angeletti."

Ovidio hugged him and took the microphone from his hand. There was more of that wild roaring from the poverty-trapped crowd.

Ainsley had to admit that Ovidio looked comfortable onstage, even without his uniform or a ball. She realized that she had been unconsciously dismissing professional athletes, forgetting that, in the end, they were performers too. It's just that, unlike most actors or musicians, their performances are always improvised, each and every day.

"*Che boludos!*" the soccer star shouted.

The people roared even harder, hearing the slang.

"I want to be direct," he said. "Our homeland is a *cagada*. For too long we have watched those *boludos soberbios* look down their long European noses at us. For too long we have stood by while those *chamuyeros*, the ones with the levers of power, poured their vile honey down our throats. You in particular have swallowed more lies than anybody. What has been the result? What do you have?" He clutched the microphone and roared. "*What do you have, Villa 27?*"

The crowd was going off its head. By now, people had climbed on top of the Chevy, which was now parked in the middle of the crowd, waving blue-and-gold soccer jerseys.

Ovidio continued. "You may have heard of me from my little career as an athlete." There was more lusty cheering. He held up a hand to quiet the noise. "And, if I can boast for a moment, I'm not just any athlete, but one of the best football players that Argentina has ever created."

There was respectful applause now. The crowd recognized that he was paying respect to Maradona.

"Despite that, I have to announce something very important today. My career has only just *begun*!!"

A soccer ball suddenly flew out of the crowd towards the stage. Ovidio's reaction was unbelievably quick. He kicked up his left leg, stopped the ball, and dropped it, trapping it under his foot. The whole move happened in less than a second, as though he'd been expecting the pass.

"And that was in my *dress shoes*," he said into the microphone.

There was laughter, but his security force, lined up at the front of the stage, were visibly upset. Ainsley guessed that they knew how quickly crowds can turn.

Then Ainsley heard a dreadful popping sound from the

rear of the crowd. She saw at least a hundred people started scatter. Everyone was watching, even Ovidio.

"What's that?" she said.

Sebastian looked worried. "Firecrackers. It looks like somebody set them off under the crowd's feet."

Then Ainsley noticed disturbances forming in other pockets of the crowd. These were fights. People were shoving.

From other parts of the crowd came a chant that started slowly, but then gained volume.

"*Per-ón, Per-ón, Per-ón*".

Soon a thousand people were chanting that name in unison. Ainsley knew that reference. Juan Perón had been the president of Argentina in the nineteen-fifties, a populist hero whose philosophy had become muddied in following decades. Outside of Argentina, most people only know him from his marriage to the world-famous Eva, but inside the country, his name is still revered by the poorest of the poor.

Now the people were shouting his name at Ovidio. Ainsley was standing close enough to see the soccer player's face. His lips trembled as he tried to find the right words to recapture his audience.

Then a bottle flew out of the middle of the crowd.

Towards Ovidio.

# CHAPTER TWENTY-ONE

Lit by the morning sunlight, the glass object pinwheeled over the heads of the crowd, flinging sticky drips of alcohol everywhere. Everybody could see it.

Except Ovidio. He had turned his head to glance at his security people. His tiger reflexes, ordinarily so quick, were off-guard.

The bottle struck him directly in the side of the face.

It clattered to the floor of the stage, still intact. Ovidio stumbled backwards, stunned. His hand went up to his cheek. It came down with blood.

Then Ovidio turned belligerent. "Try to assassinate me, *barra brava*. I dare you. I'll catch the bullet in my *teeth* and spit it back at your *mother*."

The crowd were nearly out of control. Flags waving, people linked arm-in-arm and jumping.

"But I don't think you have the balls," said Ovidio. "None of you can *touch* me."

The security leapt onstage, surrounded the celebrity, and hustled him quickly down the steps and back towards the waiting Rolls Royce.

The crowd began to boo. Never mind that he'd just been injured. The crowd was booing everything and nothing— their frustrated lives, the society that kept them at the bottom of the ladder.

"He'll come back," said Sebastian.

"No way," said Ainsley.

"You've obviously never seen him on the field. He's going to be angry. Watch."

The angry jeering continued, growing louder now. The people weren't finished with him. And Ovidio wasn't finished with them.

A minute later, he bounded back onstage, holding a bloody towel up to the left side of his face. He strode directly to the center of the stage and took the microphone one more time.

"Whoever did that to me," he said, stabbing a finger towards the crowd, "is a son of a whore."

Some applause, but more boos.

"Why do you hurt the one person who wants to help you? The one who scores goals for you? The one who represented this *pais* in La Copa Mundial?"

The people's distaste grew more palpable. Ainsley saw hands pushing away the air, slumped backs turning to the stage. The people didn't like being lectured on their behavior. She remembered, in school, enduring the teachers who scolded an entire class after a single person had misbehaved.

Ovidio wound up for the final punchline. "Nobody cares about you, sons of whores! Not one stinking person in this country!" He punched the air. "All of you, *sons of whores!*"

That opened the floodgates. Despite their initial sympathy for his injury, the crowd had now completely turned on Ovidio. An angry surge of people pushed forward towards the stage. The security guards who lined the front of the stage pulled out their truncheons and began clubbing people with abandon. More *pop-pop-pops* sounded from the rear of the crowd.

Ovidio was hustled offstage again. This time, she could see him being shoved back into his Rolls-Royce, which then roared off the way it had arrived.

Ainsley stood there, shocked. She'd never before experienced a full-on riot, certainly never at nine-thirty in the morning.

But that's exactly what was starting to happen.

She heard the sharp crack of gunshots being fired into the air. The people closest to the sound tried to flee. Others, nearer the stage, were collapsing in clumps of tangled limbs. She saw a woman stumbling, one hand at her heart, the other up in the air, wailing.

Chaos had gripped the rally by the throat.

Ainsley felt herself being jostled and shoved. She glanced over at Sebastian, just three feet away. He wasn't there. She spotted him, already ten meters away. She tried to swim towards him, through the melee, but he was being carried further off.

She'd been caught in a riptide of humanity.

Soon Ainsley lost all sight of her guide, and the crowd thinned enough for her to push her way back to the road, and down towards his car.

When she found the parking spot, his vehicle was already gone. After warning her to stay close to him, Sebastian had abandoned her.

In the *villa miseria*.

# CHAPTER TWENTY-TWO

Ainsley Walker felt anger, rage, and panic flooding her body.

If she were the type of girl to spit in disgust, she would have done exactly that. Instead she swore loudly, letting loose a string of silky expletives.

Not a single person in Argentina could be relied upon, she felt, not one. Granted, it was only Ainsley's second day, but she was already sick of the flakiness, the broken promises, the weird push and pull of cognitive dissonance.

The sound of several sharp cracks brought her back into the moment. Those weren't firecrackers. Those were more gunshots.

She watched the flood of humanity come rushing down the street, away from the violence. The flesh flowed around Ainsley, a rush of blurred faces and guilty smiles of ecstasy, as though these residents relished the chaos.

Ainsley didn't share the feelings. She just stood there like a rock in a rushing stream, spinning around uselessly. She couldn't go back towards the stage. But she didn't dare enter the shantytown either.

Something very short stumbled onto her feet and made her forget the dilemma. The thing was about a meter high. It was wearing a baseball cap.

It was a little boy. His clothes looked stiff and well-cared for, but he was clearly alone, and starting to cry.

Ainsley glanced around for a parent. Nobody was looking for him. Nobody was frantically shouting a name. In other words, this kid hadn't just wandered a few feet too far. This child was *really* lost.

Ainsley crouched down in front of him, took his hand.

"Where's your mother?" she said.

The boy just looked at her in that inscrutable way that children sometimes have. Ainsley hadn't ever felt too maternal—it wasn't in her personality—but at this moment she experienced a wave of motherly pity engulf her heart. She picked up the boy in her arms.

"Can you show me where you live?"

The boy shook his head sadly.

"You don't know?"

That was a problem. However, Ainsley realized that holding this little boy would also be an advantage. It conferred a protective shield upon her. Nobody would mess with a woman holding a crying child.

But neither, she discovered, would they assist her. The flood of humanity continued pouring around her, into the long, towering alleys of the *villa*. Ainsley felt like a rubber stopper uncorked from the bottom of a rapidly draining bathtub.

"Chiche!" a girl's voice shouted.

Ainsley turned. A young girl, maybe eleven or twelve, was standing in the opening of the villa. She was pointing at the boy.

The boy was pointing back at her. He recognized the girl.

"Is this your brother?" Ainsley asked.

The girl nodded. Then another series of sharp cracks erupted in the air, much louder this time. The violence from the rally was drawing closer.

The little girl spun her hand towards herself: *Follow me*.

Ainsley hesitated. The villas were the most dangerous places in Argentina. But that girl was old enough to know where home was. Maybe she could lead Ainsley to temporary safety.

It was her best choice. Clutching the boy, Ainsley took a deep breath and passed through the gate.

She entered into the heart of Villa 27.

Ainsley found herself running down a narrow alley, which was perfectly straight, about fifteen feet wide, and lined on either side by the crooked shacks. They looked like piles of leftover material from construction sites.

She clutched the boy to her chest. As her feet kicked up clouds of dust, Ainsley craned her head to look at the upper stories of the tenements. The mouths of dry pipes opened directly onto the alley. Yellowed bedsheets were hung inside open windows.

A line of bright green liquid trickled down the middle of the road. Ainsley made sure not to let it touch her shoes.

The boy's sister was running about ten meters ahead. She had the long legs and coltish gallop of a girl on the brink of puberty. Others were running with them, hollering at neighbors, slapping hands stretched out from the shanty windows. Ainsley sensed that these residents were used to danger, had dealt with it all their lives.

There was another series of sharp cracks. Ainsley heard ricochets off the walls of the alleyways. She swore under her breath. It felt like these criminals were just shooting for the fun of it, for the power trip, because Ovidio had somehow signalled that pandemonium was okay. Or maybe they just enjoyed terrorizing people.

Whoever had the weapons, they were gaining ground quickly.

The boy's sister suddenly twisted left and dodged into a small doorway. Ainsley slowed down and followed her. The doorway was low enough that Ainsley had to duck her head. She screeched to a stop inside.

Ainsley found herself inside a family's home. A heavy woman was in a rickety kitchen chair, knitting at the table. She looked up.

"*Ay mi dios, Chiche*!"

The woman heaved herself up from the chair and ran over. Ainsley handed her the boy. The mother cleaned the dirt off the boy's face, kissed his forehead. Ainsley admired the way his little legs were splayed around his mother's torso.

Her daughter had already dropped to the floor and begun brushing the hair of a doll. "Who is this?" the mother said, pointing at Ainsley.

The girl shrugged.

The mother looked at her visitor. Ainsley stuck her hand out. "Ainsley Walker," she said. "From the United States."

"What are you doing in my house? With my boy?"

Ainsley explained the situation, and the woman softened up. "I should've known they would start shooting at that damned rally," she said.

"Of course." Ainsley thought about asking why she let her five-year-old boy wander with his sister unattended in such a neighborhood, but kept her mouth shut.

The woman continued. "What did that bastard say?"

"Who?"

"*El Mono*."

"Many things," Ainsley said. "It was very emotional."

The mother frowned. "I'm glad it ended badly. Everything he touches turns to shit."

The gunshots were growing even louder now. The woman gathered her children and slid them under the kitchen table. "Down, down, stay down," she said. "Don't get up."

Then she looked at Ainsley. She pointed under the table. "You too."

# CHAPTER TWENTY-THREE

The mother quickly shuffled over to the front door and flipped the deadbolt. Then she propped her chair underneath the doorknob. Ainsley could hear the loud voices passing in the alley outside, only a few meters away.

Ainsley peered out the window with a tentative eye. A gang of eight or nine young guys, barely teenagers, was swaggering down the lane. Their guns were brazenly hanging from their waistbands. They were young bucks on a tear.

She watched one kick over a rickety piece of fencing. Another took aim at a corrugated metal shed and blasted a hole through it. The others laughed. Ovidio had ignited the worst element of the crowd.

"Get down!" whispered the mother again.

Ainsley quickly crouched on the floor and willed herself to stay quiet. She shuddered to think what might happened if she, the *yanqui* dressed in morning-after club-wear, were to be discovered by those guys. It would be game over.

Chiche was looking at her through the legs of the table

and remaining chairs. The boy waved at her. She waved back at him.

The boys' loud conversation was directly outside the window. One made a big hocking sound from his throat, followed by the sound of an enormous spit. Something landed on the floor next to Ainsley.

It was a loogey. They'd spit through an open window.

The quartet waited on the concrete floor, not moving, until the voices died away, and the occasional gunshot sounded further on. Then the mother said, "Okay, it's good. They're gone."

The two kids went scooting into the small living room, giggling, as though nothing had just happened. Ainsley looked at them. They'd grown up with experiences that she had never known.

Ainsley pulled herself to her feet and looked around. The walls were made of cinder blocks. The kitchen had only a refrigerator and a hotplate. She couldn't see running water anywhere within sight. A narrow rickety staircase led upstairs. It looked like it couldn't support anything heavier than a dog.

The mother slid the chair out from the door with practiced ease. Ainsley realized that she'd rehearsed this a hundred times.

"I'm sorry," she said.

"This is life," replied the mother. "For now."

"How many children do you have?"

"Just three. I wanted more but God didn't bless me."

"Is your husband home?"

"No," she said, "he hasn't come home in a long while."

Ainsley guessed that that meant weeks or months. This woman seemed comfortable with a stranger in her home. "Do you mind if I wait here for a few minutes?" she asked. "Until the chaos dies down?"

The woman nodded and grew formal. "It's a pleasure. Let me put on the *mate*. Sweet or bitter?"

"Whatever you want," said Ainsley.

She poured water from a bottle into a kettle and placed the kettle on the hotplate. While waiting for the water to boil, Ainsley strolled through the main room. A simple green couch had been shoved against one wall. Above the cushions hung a picture of Che Guevara.

The floor was unfinished concrete except for one small patch, near the staircase. This area had been painstakingly covered with green ceramic tiles. Ainsley touched the edge of one tile with the tip of her shoe. It was at least an inch high. She imagined how many toes had been stubbed on it.

"We are going to finish the floor when we save enough money," the mother said.

"Have you been living here a long time?"

"No," she said, "only nine years. We're not staying much longer either. We'll leave when my husband comes back from Mendoza. He's working on a construction project."

"You've done well with what you could," Ainsley said.

"We never planned to stay here long," the woman repeated. "It's only temporary." She glanced around and said it again. "It's only temporary."

The woman said these words with a practiced air. As though she'd been telling herself this for a very long time.

Then she rose, opened a plastic container, and spooned some yerba leaves into the gourd. She shook it upside down, then opened the top and poured in the water. She waited a few seconds, inserted the silver *bombilla*, or straw, and sucked deeply.

She rolled the liquid around her mouth, then spit it out. "*Mate del zonza.* The second one will be better."

She refilled the gourd, waited a few seconds, then sucked on the straw again. A smile spread across her face. "In

Argentina, no matter how bad the problem, *mate* will solve it. Or at least make you forget."

She smacked her lips. Then she filled the gourd a third time, waited a few seconds, then passed it to Ainsley. "Please."

Ainsley accepted the gourd and drank. A hot, bitter tea streamed down her throat. She tried not to make a face, but this was an acquired taste, to say the least.

"Yes," she said again, "this is only temporary. When the government gives out the housing, we'll be first in line." She waved her hand in a circle. "Unlike all these immigrants."

"These people are immigrants?"

"Of course," the woman said, as if it were common knowledge. "These assholes living here are from Bolivia, Paraguay, Chile. They have no education. But my husband and I are Argentine." A proud yet wistful expression came across her face. "We used to have a house. And a yard."

Ainsley herself had neither. She guessed that this family had lost nearly everything after the economic crash.

Then the woman jerked back to the present. She looked at Ainsley holding the gourd. "It's not a microphone."

"What do you mean?"

"Finish it and pass it back."

Ainsley took another gulp from the *mate*. It tasted a little better this time. With some sugar, she might get used to it.

There was a swift knock at the door. Ainsley grew alarmed and stood up again.

The woman motioned for her to stay down. "There's no need," she said. "I know the knock. It's just my son."

# CHAPTER TWENTY-FOUR

A thin teenage boy in t-shirt and jeans entered the house. His eyes were intelligent and found the visitor immediately.

"*Bombón*," said the woman. "Were you at the rally?"

"Yes," he said.

"What happened?"

"*Una cagada. Ya fue.*" He nodded at Ainsley. "Who is this?"

"I forgot her name," said the mother. "Chiche went for a walk again, and she found him."

"Chiche, Chiche," the teenager said, picking up his little brother. "You are such a traveller."

Ainsley was surprised by the boy's maturity. Back in the United States, most kids his age were figuring out ways to cheat on math tests. But this kid was acting like a father, like the head of the household.

"Ainsley," she said, extending her hand. The teen kissed her cheek instead. "*Mucho gusto*," he replied, in the formal way. "I am called Hugo. Where are you from?"

"The moon." She was tired of answering that question.

Hugo laughed. "I'm guessing America."

He'd also seen the invisible *yanqui* sign hanging around her neck. "And you might be right. Were you at Ovidio's speech?"

Hugo shook his head. "He's a fine *fútbol* player, but he won't get to the Casa Rosada like that."

That was the nation's capitol building. Ainsley started to think about her mission again. She was here to find a rhodochrosite necklace that had been stolen. And one possible thief, the maid, was apparently living somewhere in this community.

And to Ainsley, Hugo seemed like the type of person who might be hooked into the inner workings of Villa 27. She tipped her chin higher. "Do you have any idea why he won't play?"

"I have heard rumors."

"Me too."

Hugo accepted the *mate* from his mother and sipped. "You go first."

Ainsley nodded. "Someone told me that his favorite necklace was stolen."

"Then we heard the same rumor," Hugo said.

It was laughable, Ainsley thought, the way Nadia and Ovidio had demanded that she keep the theft of the necklace secret. Two-thirds of metropolitan Buenos Aires seemed to already know.

The teenager was smiling now. So was his mother. There was a jovial feeling in the room. Ainsley decided to reveal one of her cards. "I also heard that the woman who might have stolen it lives in this villa."

"Really?"

"Yes."

His mother cut in. "How do you know that?"

"I'm a journalist. I talk to people."

Hugo handed the *mate* back to his mother. "You know, I think I might've heard that too."

Ainsley's heart skipped a beat. This could be the access she'd been hoping for. "The woman is a maid. At El Hotel Perdido."

Hugo stood in the middle of the room, his eyes scanning the wall. He was someone whom you could actually *see* thinking.

"I don't know her," he said.

"Yes you do," said the mother.

He turned around. "I do?"

His mother sat back with confidence in her kitchen chair. "Think. You have a good brain. It's going to get us out of this shithole."

Hugo shook his head. "Mama, I don't know who this woman is."

"It's Pedro's mother."

Hugo's eyes grew wide. "Pedro?"

"Yes."

"So that's why he stopped coming to the games." The teenager turned to Ainsley. "Yes, I know her son."

Ainsley pushed harder. "Can I meet her?"

The family exchanged glances. They seemed to be waffling. Ainsley recognized that there was a lot she didn't know. Maybe it was too dangerous. Maybe they didn't want to bring a journalist into the innermost parts of the *villa*. Maybe the families weren't getting along.

Nonetheless, Ainsley needed to at least try. She knew what to do next. From inside her purse, she unrolled a hundred pesos and laid it on the kitchen table. "I *really* want to meet this woman."

Hugo looked at the money but stayed calm. "One hundred? That gets you the family name."

The air had grown tense. Off-the-books negotiations always did that. And Hugo had accurately guessed that there was more bread where that had come from. So Ainsley dutifully unrolled another hundred peso bill, and laid that down too.

"That's all I have," she said.

The *bombilla* clattered from the mother's lips. Two hundred pesos was, for her, a weekly wage.

Hugo nodded. "Sure, why not." He took the bills and stuffed them into his pocket.

"No," his mother commanded. "Here. Give it to me."

"But *mama*—"

She stood up and punched her hands on her hips. A stern look spread across her face. Even Ainsley was intimidated.

Hugo lowered his head and gave his mother the money.

"Now," she said, "you take this woman to find Pedro. I'll buy you something later."

"Yes, *mama*."

The mother took Ainsley's hand. "*Es un placer*. Please come back any time. Not just for the money either." She lifted her little boy by the hand. "Say goodbye, Chiche."

"Bye," the boy said, then hid his face.

As she ducked under the doorway and went out into the street again, Ainsley felt a wave of happy camaraderie surge through her body. As poor as this family was, she felt a little more at ease here. And her own paycheck-to-paycheck existence back in the United States didn't look half bad by comparison.

She was also discovering that living in shantytowns didn't necessarily lead to an immoral or dissolute life. Ainsley felt happy to have helped the family out.

And now Hugo was going to return the favor.

# CHAPTER TWENTY-FIVE

The sun had risen to the top of the sky. Shacks cast short shadows onto the ground. Ainsley followed the teenager, still avoiding the green liquid trickling down the middle of the lane.

Hugo moved easily and lightly, nodding at passersby, whistling a simple tune. It was an accident of birth that he was here. In another life, in the United States, he would be finishing his senior year at an expensive private high school, sailing through his classes, trying to figure out whether an undergraduate degree from Duke or Georgetown would hold more cachet in the world of corporate law.

But instead he was here, in the midst of a broken-down *barrio* in Buenos Aires, merely trying to find a way out of the shantytown.

Still, the snotty comments his mother had made about their superiority to the other people in this *villa* seemed to have a ring of truth. While Hugo's family did at least have a house of cinder blocks, Ainsley noticed several structures whose walls were made of scrapped plywood. She watched a dirty woman rooting through a pushcart loaded with recyclables, sorting the useful from the useless.

Then there was a loud clattering ahead of them, and Ainsley instantly clasped her purse closer. The racket came from a group of residents who had surrounded a trailer and were striking on its metal sides with sticks. Some sort of official insignia had been stamped on its side.

Hugo stopped walking. "Oh, that's not good."

"What is that?"

"The government trailer. They keep promising us better housing but never come through."

Ainsley watched the people beating the sides of the trailer, over and over, in sheer anger. Now she understood the frustration that Ovidio had been alluding to onstage earlier that morning.

"We'll go this way instead," said Hugo, nodding to the right. "It's longer but safer."

Ainsley followed him into a very narrow lane, seven feet wide, puddles of stagnant brown water on the ground. A woman was giving a child a bath in a free-standing tub.

"Where exactly are you taking me?" she said.

"To lunch," he replied. "Are you hungry?"

"Yes, but—"

"Good, you can buy for both of us."

She had no problem doing that. "But what about your friend Pedro? I need to meet his mother."

"Oh, he eats there too. It's the best place to find him."

"Can't we just go to his house?"

"I only play soccer with him. I don't know where his house is."

They emerged from the narrow lane into another dirt street, this one quite a bit wider. It seemed to be the main shopping avenue of Villa 27. Ainsley spotted a bicycle repair shop. A woman sat under a tent selling premixed herbal remedies. There were a couple of *empanada* stands. None of the businesses seemed to be on-the-books. It was a shadow economy in a shadow community.

Hugo gestured towards a wide piece of hanging vinyl. It was blue, on which there was an image of St. Sebastian being pierced with arrows. "That's the *comedor*."

"Where we eat?"

"Yes. Don't say anything. Let me talk to them."

She followed Hugo around the vinyl hanging and found herself in a small outdoor dining area. There were eight picnic tables lined up in two neat rows of four each. An open door in a shack at one end of the area indicated the kitchen.

Ainsley felt like she'd just entered somebody's illegal backyard operation. Which it, in fact, was.

About twenty children were at the tables finishing a meal. Each one was scraping clean a metal pan with her fingers. It seemed that nobody used utensils here.

They sat down at one of the picnic tables. A woman came out from the kitchen scratching her belly. "*Cómo andás, Hugo*," she said.

"*Señora*," he said formally, "what is good today?"

"I don't know. That goddamned *mono* stirred up all the shit."

"So what do you have?"

"I can give you the kiddie menu," she said.

Ainsley looked over at the kids' plates. They were leaving the eating area now. She could see a grayish porridge of rice, potatoes, and carrots left in a couple of plates.

"No, we want the adult one," said Hugo. "We have money."

She thought about it. "I'm making a beautiful lamb's head stew. It will be nice and gelatiny in an hour, if you can wait."

"Do you have anything else?" replied Ainsley.

The woman thought for a moment. "Maybe some

*choripan.*"

"That's all?" said Hugo.

She looked annoyed. "You want steak? Go and make a million pesos and go to a *parrilla*. Then save a seat for me."

"I'm sorry, *señora—*"

"What about your *marida*? What does she want?"

Hugo blushed. The woman had just called Ainsley his wife. The *comedor* owner glanced at her visitor. "It's an honest question! She's so skinny, I don't know if she even eats."

"I'm really hungry," Ainsley said.

"Of course you are," the owner said. "It's been years since a piece of bread touched your tongue. Two *choripan* coming up. Give me a minutes"

The woman turned towards the kitchen. Hugo called after her. "Oh, did Pedro eat lunch yet?"

"Pedro?" she said. "That little bastard hasn't come here for a week."

Hugo turned back to his visitor. "I guess we wait and hope for Pedro."

She nodded. They were alone in the *comedor* now. Ainsley's stomach gurgled with hunger. She was trying to avoid the crankiness that comes with low blood sugar.

A few minutes later, the owner returned to the table with two plates. An enormous sausage sandwich lopped over the edges of each one. These sandwiches were easily a foot long. No condiments, no vegetables—just meat and bread. Food was easy in this country.

She set the plates down. "*Choripan* ... and *choripan*." Then she plunked down two cans of Coca-Cola. "And to drink."

Then she looked at Ainsley. "Where are you from?"

The question couldn't have been timed more poorly. Ainsley had just torn off a giant bite of the *choripan*. She had a mouthful of delicious, juicy pork sausage.

"She's from the moon," said Hugo. "That's what she

told me."

"Let me know if you like it, moongirl." She paused. "Or even if you don't. I know it's good anyways."

When she left, Hugo and Ainsley tucked into their sausage sandwiches. Ainsley chewed, tasting the fatty sausage. She listened to the sounds of passing trucks in the lane, people welcoming one another in the street. The sky was a perfect blue.

This may have been one of the villages of misery, but life felt comfortable to her at this moment.

Meanwhile, between bites, Hugo kept her entertained with a running commentary on life in Villa 27. How the entire settlement pirated electricity from the electrical cables near the freeway. How this *comedor* was run exclusively by women, how those women fed the children in shifts every day, at specific times, how the better food—the meat—was saved for adults or people with money. How the very existence of this *villa* was, in fact, illegal.

Ainsley made it halfway through her sandwich before she pushed it away and mopped her mouth with a napkin. They were still alone on the patio. She started to wonder if she'd been used again.

"So where's Pedro?" she said.

"You heard her," said Hugo. "She said he hasn't been coming."

"Maybe you can look for him."

Suddenly Hugo's eyes lit up. He was staring over Ainsley's right shoulder. "There he is."

Ainsley twisted her head. A group of eight little boys had entered the *comedor*, with an adult woman as chaperone. This was the next shift of children to be fed.

"I don't see him."

"In that group. The one on the far left."

Ainsley looked again. Pedro was a young child.

# CHAPTER TWENTY-SIX

The children ran to the picnic tables and began to clang the new plates that had already been laid out. They knew the drill.

"I thought Pedro was your age," Ainsley said.

"I didn't say that."

Ainsley was trying to contain herself. "He's five years old!"

"No, I think he's six," replied Hugo. "It's a significant difference, at that age."

Ainsley sighed. "Can you please take me to his *mother*? I need to talk to that *maid*."

He tried to contain his smile. "I told you, I don't know her personally. I don't even know where they live. I only know her son. This is the only way you can get to her."

Ainsley looked to the picnic table. The little boys were starting to beat each other over the heads with the aluminum plates.

"Seriously?" she said. "How am I supposed to negotiate with that?"

Hugo shrugged. "Offer him a candy or something."

Ainsley stood up from her table. This was oddly humiliating. She had experienced many things that were far outside her comfort zone on her South American adventure thus far —riots, murder, kidnapping, and more—but for some reason, the thought of negotiating with a six-year-old felt like her most outrageous and difficult task yet.

She took her half-finished *choripan* and approached the little boy. He'd taken a seat on the far end of the picnic table. A long and unruly mop of dark hair hung from his head. He wore a tiny pair of jeans, and his black sneakers were duct-taped together.

"Sweetheart," she said, "do you want some *choripan?*"

The little boy questioned her with his eyes but said nothing. The others around him scrambled to get to the sandwich.

Ainsley whipped the plate behind her back. "No, it's just for him, the handsome one. What's your name?"

He eyed her warily. "Pedro." Then his eyes flicked over to the *choripan*.

"Come this way, Pedro."

Ainsley walked across the *comedor* and placed the sandwich on the most distant table. It didn't take long. Pedro hopped down from his table, skipped across the dirt, and slid into the bench opposite Ainsley.

She used her knife and fork to slice the sausage sandwich into four pieces. She handed him the first piece. Pedro attacked it like a dog that'd been handed a fresh butcher's bone.

"My name is Ainsley," she said, watching him chew. "Your mother is a friend of mine."

This felt demoralizing. And Pedro didn't seem to care what she said, so Ainsley extended the lie.

"I need to talk to your mother, but she's not answering her phone."

The boy was chewing now. His legs were kicking. He was scooting around in his seat.

"Can I talk to your mother?"

When little Pedro finally began to speak, the words that came out sounded like gibberish. It was a mishmash of chirrups, squeals, and squawks.

"Excuse me?" Ainsley leaned forward in her seat.

He repeated himself. Another bizarre collection of sounds.

Ainsley grew frustrated. To her, trying to decipher children speaking in a foreign language was always impossible. In fact, it had been a running joke among her friends years ago. Whenever they'd watched a movie in a foreign language, they'd turn off the subtitles when a child was speaking, and then try to translate. It was always impossible.

Now this game was applied to real life, except with something very large at stake. She handed him a second piece of the sandwich, then waved to Hugo, who was chatting with the owner of the *comedor*.

He came over. "I don't want to feed anybody."

"I just need you to translate."

"But you already speak Spanish."

Ainsley shielded her mouth from the little boy. "I can't understand this fucking kid. Not one word."

Hugo laughed. "Okay, I will help." He sat down at the table. "What's happening, little macho man?"

Still chewing, Pedro pounded fists with him. Hugo tousled his hair. Then he looked up at Ainsley. "What do you want me to say?"

"Tell him that his mother won't take my phone calls."

Hugo spoke in low, rapid, slangy Rioplatense. The boy mumbled back. Hugo didn't seem to understand either. He ordered Pedro to swallow his food.

They went back and forth like this for a while. Ainsley found herself looking around impatiently, wanting to escape. Ovidio's friends had, thus far, proven to be a dead end. This assignment was a long shot to begin with, but at this moment, the mission felt particularly desperate. Ainsley felt like she was holding a fisherman by the ankles over the side of a boat while he cast his line, searching for a single minnow in a sea of millions.

But it was the only way to find this rhodochrosite. And returning to the United States held no allure for her.

Finally Hugo looked up again. "Pedro said that's because his mother isn't taking any phone calls right now. No visitors either."

"Brilliant. Can you get his address?"

"There are no addresses in this *villa*."

"A street name?"

"We have no street names either."

Ainsley laughed out of frustratation. Villa 27 was the place where the streets literally had no name.

"What about his father?" she said. "Maybe he can help."

Hugo resumed the conversation. Listening to their mumbled syllables, Ainsley began to understand just how difficult it was to become truly fluent in another language. No matter what her abilities, given her monolingual childhood, she was probably doomed to intermediate ability in second languages.

"His father is not around very much," said Hugo. "But he did say that his father likes to tango."

Inside her, the frustration had grown into an enormous tumor. "Ask him where does his father like to dance the tango? Maybe I can find this man. And maybe this man can lead me to his wife."

Hugo handed the boy a third piece of *choripan*. They conferred for another moment. Ainsley chewed her nails. It'd always been her worst habit, even worse than smoking, and not even bitter apple polish would stop her from doing it.

Then Hugo looked up. "He has no education. It's hard to understand exactly what he's saying."

"Then give me your best translation. Please."

"He dances at a Monday night *milonga* called Malevos."

Today was Monday. Ainsley wrote down the information on a napkin. "What is his father's name?"

There was another moment of conversation, and Hugo reported back. "Simón Fe. His mother is Maria Jose."

Ainsley copied the names down and stashed the napkin in her purse. "You've been very helpful, Hugo."

"It has been my pleasure. Here." Hugo handed her another napkin with a telephone number scrawled on it. "Let me know if you need more help."

Of course he would want to help her. That had been two hundred easy pesos. There weren't many opportunities for legitimate entrepreneurship for a teenager in this community.

Ainsley went to the owner of the *comedor*. She was stirring a pot of innards over a dirty stove. "This is my specialty," the woman said. "Come back for dinner?"

"No thank you. Here."

Ainsley pressed two hundred pesos into her palm. The woman gaped. "You are very generous."

Ainsley took her hand. "This is for three things. One, for both lunches. Two, for finding me a safe ride back to the city center. Three, you didn't see me talking to that boy."

The woman nodded. "My husband can drive you. I'll send a bowl of the stew along with you."

# CHAPTER TWENTY-SEVEN

The owner's husband, a meek man in his late fifties, owned a severely rusted truck. He'd driven Ainsley out of the *villa* and several miles back towards the city center.

When she'd begun to spot the familiar black-and-yellow design of passing taxis, she'd ordered the man to stop, thanked him, and stepped out. Then she'd hailed the next taxi and ordered it back to the Gran Hotel Hispano, in the Microcentro.

In the backseat, she heaved a sigh of relief. The *villa*, a place she'd never asked to go, was behind her at last. Then she reflected for a moment.

The maid's husband, Simón Fe, was a tango dancer every Monday night. Today was Monday. It was a tiny toehold in the mystery of the stolen rhodochrosite, but this was all she had at the moment.

The problem was that Ainsley didn't know much about tango, or any other dance. She was choreographically challenged, to put it nicely. But she did know that tango had its own set of rules, its own sociology. It was a separate ecosystem.

If she was going to crash a *milonga* tonight, she couldn't afford to step on any toes, either literally or figuratively. She would need a guide.

She pulled out her phone and called Nadia. The manager picked up immediately and wasted no time. "Tell me."

"I'm sorry," said Ainsley, "but his friends were useless. I talked to Lalo, I talked to some psychiatrist, and I talked to Sebastian. They didn't know anything."

She swore in Rioplatense. "They are liars. Don't believe any of them."

Ainsley put a positive spin. "But I have good news. I got dragged into Villa 27 by Sebastian this morning for his press conference."

"How is that good news? It was a disaster." Then it dawned on Nadia. "Wait, don't tell me you found the maid."

"I found her son. And he told me where to find her husband."

"Where?"

"At a *milonga* tonight. It's called"—she consulted her notes —"Malevos."

Nadia sighed. "I'm telling you, Ovidio's friends are the guilty ones."

"Even Sebastian?"

"Not Sebastian," said Nadia. "He's the only loyal one. And chasing the maid is pointless. Don't bother with her."

Ainsley had an answer prepared for this. "Please, let me follow this idea, just for tonight. If it doesn't work out, then I'll go back to his friends tomorrow."

"But you don't know anything about *milongas*."

"That's why I'm calling you. I need a guide."

Nadia was agitated. "I don't know anybody who likes the tango. It's really not that popular."

"Can't you find just one person?"

There was silence. Then she said, "It has to be a woman.

Preferably older, someone who knows the scene." Nadia thought for a moment more. "Let me call you back."

By now it was three in the afternoon, and taxi was threading its way back into the beating heart of Buenos Aires, the walls of the buildings taller, the sidewalks flooded with thousands of urban workers. Ainsley could feel a late-afternoon crash starting to hit. She needed to sleep.

After summoning the energy to drag herself up the circular stairs of her hotel, she had never been so happy to plug her room key into its lock.

She was asleep from the moment her cheek hit the fabric of her pillowcase.

# CHAPTER TWENTY-EIGHT

A distant sound pulled Ainsley back to the surface of consciousness. She realized that the sound had been occurring for some time.

She flipped the blankets from over her face. The sound was coming from her phone. A few more seconds, then the message finally sank in.

Her phone was ringing.

She sent a groggy hand towards her nightstand, which scrambled around the surface until she found the device. Then she peeled open an eye and looked at the display. The number was unfamiliar to her. It must be Nadia.

"Hello?"

A man's voice said, "It's Sebastian."

Ainsley was instantly awake. "Ah. The asshole who abandoned me in Villa 27 this morning."

"I had to go. Ovidio was calling me, crazy like a goat, out of his mind. I couldn't find you in the crowd."

"So Ovidio is more important to you than my safety is."

"Of course. He and I are like brothers. I just met you yesterday. I'm sorry, but that is the truth."

She had to admit that at least Sebastian was being honest. She propped herself up against the headboard and twirled a piece of her hair.

"So how is he?"

Sebastian sighed. "This is the first minute I have had to myself all day. Only because the baby fell asleep."

"He's that bad?"

"Inconsolable. The whining, the crying, the shouting. I'm not a violent man, and I want to slap him."

Ainsley stifled a laugh. It wasn't hard to imagine Ovidio needing a lot of attention after his disaster of a political launch.

His voice grew serious. "So did you make it out okay?"

"Yes."

The heavy silence during the pause between them. "No problems at all?"

"Nothing I couldn't figure out for myself. Don't worry about me, I'm good. Go take care of your infant."

"You sound sleepy."

"You just woke me up. And now I'm about to go back to sleep."

"I want to get together tonight."

"That won't be possible."

"Why? What are you doing?" He sounded offended.

"Going out."

"With who?"

"That's not your business." She was enjoying the flirtation, the push-and-pull. It'd been a long time since any man had wanted to win her affections.

Sebastian sighed. "I will not stop bothering you until you see me again."

"I'm sure you will. You're an Argentine man."

"*Sin vergüenza*," he said.

"Of course."

"So I will call you later, after you change your mind about tonight. Which will happen, I have no doubt."

"Why?"

"Because you're a woman."

"Goodbye, Sebastian."

"See you in a few hours—"

Ainsley hit disconnect. She glanced at the time. It was only six pm. She'd slept a little more than two hours. More was needed.

She slid down into the sheets and pulled the pillow over her head. She was nesting, trying to find her happy place. It was a mission that felt even more difficult than her current one.

What felt like an instant later, a distant sound pulled her back into consciousness. She flipped the pillow off her head.

It was her phone again.

She glanced at the clock again. Only twenty minutes had elapsed. Goddamn Sebastian. He really was a pest. She'd made it clear that she was trying to sleep, and here he was purposely trying to interrupt her.

She picked up without looking at the display. "I told you I was sleeping, I am going to rip your balls off the next time—"

A man's voice said, "It's Gabriel."

Oh Christ. Nadia's assistant. She closed her eyes in embarrassment.

"Gabriel. Please forget that comment."

His reply was serious. "My girlfriend likes my *huevos*, so I would appreciate it if you let them be."

"Let's start over. Hello?"

He played along. "Ainsley, it's Gabriel. Nadia said you need an experienced tango dancer to go out with you tonight."

"I do. Did she find one?"

"No, but I did."

"Who?"

"My mother."

A smile hit Ainsley's face. She almost dropped her phone. "Is she anything like you?"

"Nothing at all. She's attractive, informed, and responsible."

"Then I'd be enchanted to go."

"So would she. Her best friend is laid up with a bad back right now, so she's dying for company anyways."

"Let her know I can't dance."

"Neither can she."

"I don't believe you."

"Neither does she, but trust me, she can't dance." Gabriel suddenly shouted. "Ah, ah, ah, *mama*, sorry!" To Ainsley: "She's standing right here and didn't like that comment. Oh, she has one question for you."

"Go ahead."

Ainsley could hear a woman's voice speaking. "She wants to know if you have the right shoes for tango."

Ainsley thought about her closet. The only shoes she owned here were a pair of workmanlike boots and the cheap heels she'd bought last night.

"Not really. We might need to go shopping."

"That's what I thought. Okay, this means we need to move fast. It's six-thirty right now. We'll meet you at eight o'clock at the Galeria Pacifico."

"Okay," Ainsley groaned.

"What's the matter?"

"I'm never going to sleep."

"You can sleep when you're old," said Gabriel. "Right now you're on assignment for us. Eight o'clock. We'll buy you an espresso."

Ainsley ended the connection and tossed the phone towards the end of the bed. She didn't want to imagine what she looked like right now. But she could fix that, given an hour with running water and her makeup case.

What she couldn't fix so quickly was her exhaustion. She rubbed her eyes and yawned once, like a wildcat waking from a nap. Then she rose from the bed and staggered towards the bathroom.

She could sleep when she was old.

# CHAPTER TWENTY-NINE

Ainsley turned the shoes around in her hands, admiring the craftsmanship.

She was in the shoe section of a department store at the Galleria Pacifico, the same deluxe shopping mall at the end of Calle Florida that she'd visited the previous night.

This time, she had company. Gabriel stood on one side, dressed in a black suit.

On the other side was his mother, Valentina. A stout but glamorous woman with a short mane of reddish-brown hair, she had embraced Ainsley like a longlost daughter. Her suffocating perfume announced her presence for meters in every direction.

Now she was giving Ainsley a crash course in tangowear. She snatched the shoes from Ainsley's hands. "See, they're leather on the bottom," said the woman. "It's better. This brand in particular is divine. Nothing else will do."

Ainsley glanced at the price. It cost sixteen hundred pesos. That was four hundred U.S. dollars. "I don't know," Ainsley said. "I mean, this is only for one night."

"Just buy them," ordered Valentina. "You will never regret

buying an expensive shoe. You will only regret *not* buying expensive shoes."

The woman had a point. Ainsley went over to the cash register and dutifully plunked down a small stack of hundred-peso notes.

She returned with her box inside a plastic shopping bag. "Now we eat before tango," said the woman. "Always we eat before tango."

"I'm famished," said Ainsley. It'd been almost eight hours since she'd visited the *comedor* back in Villa 27.

"Tonight we enjoy pasta," announced Valentina.

"Why is it always pasta, mama?" said Gabriel.

"Because I need good pasta to dance. When your mama goes to the *milonga*, *che*, she doesn't stop." She slashed a heel in the air behind her calf, a flourish that Ainsley recognized as being very tango.

Gabriel laughed, presumably at his mother using the word *che*. The trio left the shopping mall, Valentina leading out front. Ainsley watched her make comments to passing strangers.

"How do you live with that?" said Ainsley.

"I'm quiet like a mouse," he replied. "So she doesn't see me."

Ainsley understood why he was such an effective assistant. He'd grown up under the wing of a loud woman. Working for Nadia was probably easier than staying at home. At least he was getting paid.

Valentina led them to a local Italian restaurant, where Ainsley discovered that it felt the same as local Italian restaurants did anywhere in the world.

There, over a dish of *linguini con funghi*, she listened to Gabriel's mother discuss the tango. It'd been born in the brothels of the dock district, danced initially only by men. Slowly the dance spread through the city, through the *compadres* (friends), *compraditos* (show offs), *guapos* (handsome men), *obreros* and *obreras* (laborers), and *conventillo* (squalid city homes) dwellers. It became a worldwide name once the French, those famous arbiters of taste, accepted it in the 1920s. Only then did the elite of Argentina finally accept their own homegrown dance.

Ever since then, tango's fortunes had been swinging up and down, depending on the government's attitude. Sometimes it was demonized as a subversive activity, other times it was used to draw tourists. Currently, Valentina explained, it was stylish again.

"Why?" said Ainsley.

"Because nobody has money," said Gabriel. "Tango is a cheap activity. You don't have to import it."

"But I never gave up on it," said his mother. "I have always been faithful. Thirty years ago, nobody was dancing tango except me and a few hundred horny old men. You wait long enough in this life and you eventually gain credibility."

Gabriel turned to her. "Mama, do you know this *milonga* we are going tonight? Malevos?"

"Do I know Malevos?" she said, offended. "I know it like I know my jewelry drawer. I haven't been there in twenty years, but it used to be my favorite. It was very traditional then. They used the *codigos*."

"What are those?" said Ainsley.

"The rules of a *milonga*," she said. "There are many, many rules. Even the smallest movements carry importance. For example, a single nod of the head from a woman, and the man will approach for a dance."

"The *cabaceo*," said Gabriel.

"So I need to be careful about eye contact?" said Ainsley.

Valentina nodded vigorously. "If a man gives you a *cabaceo*, you must wait at your table for him to come over and collect you. Sometimes we misinterpret and steal another woman's *cabaceo*. But always by accident." She winked, which led Ainsley to believe that wasn't true at all.

"That's when things get ugly," said Gabriel. Then he meowed. His mother slapped his shoulder.

Valentina glanced at Ainsley's long legs. "I can already tell you that the *milongueros* will be looking at you."

"Why me?"

"Because your long legs are made for the tango. They will want to see if you can dance."

"Plus they already know the regular women," said Gabriel. "Like mama."

"Oh, I'm sure nobody remembers me there," Valentina said. "It's been twenty years. But they will know me by the time the sun rises tomorrow." She lifted her glass of wine for a toast. "To the sunrise."

The three of them clinked glasses. Ainsley realized that, if she stayed in Argentina, she wouldn't sleep when she was old either.

# CHAPTER THIRTY

Ainsley had always imagined a Buenos Aires tango salon to be stately and luxurious. Gold leaf design, rich oak decor, a crystal chandelier suspended above a parquet dance floor. Tuxedoed men with white teeth and broad shoulders slanted over slinky women in spangly red dresses. She pictured tango parlors as chic, expensive, and European.

Malevos was nothing like that.

It was a hovel.

Located in the basement of a century-old building, the *milonga* looked like it had fallen into disrepair at least ninety years ago. Once-mighty cornices had weathered, cracked, and fallen off. Green weeds sprouted from little runnels of dirt that had collected in the edges of the ornamentations.

Ainsley followed Gabriel and his mother down into the moldy basement. At the front door, Valentina handed her coat to a check girl inside a long, narrow closet.

Gabriel noticed Ainsley's hesitance. "What's the matter?"

"It's just ... dirty."

"Traditional tango halls always have been. Who do you think invented this? Thieves and criminals."

A rule that held true for most of the best dances. Ainsley checked that the pockets of her coat were empty before handing it to the check girl. Then she kept a tight grasp on her purse as they moved inside.

The interior fulfilled the squalid promise of the exterior. A small band was warming up the songs on a stage at one end of the room. The dance floor was empty, its sour-yellow wooden planks scuffed from decades of dragged shoes. Around the dance floor was a motley collection of fifteen or so mismatched tables. Very few people had arrived yet.

Ainsley felt her eyes begin to water. The *milonga* had barely begun, and the room was already suffocated with a blue-gray smell of tobacco. Nearly a century of cigarette smoking had seeped into the walls.

Valentina swept through the tables, her arms out. It was a regal entrance to an empty room.

The woman chose a table near the stage, prime property, and Gabriel pulled out a chair. With a swish of her skirt, she lowered herself to the seat and fussed with her clothing, much like a hen fluffing its feathers before bedding down.

Then Gabriel pulled out a chair for Ainsley. The seat looked sticky. She used her handkerchief to wipe it down first.

A waiter came by and brought three Coca-Colas. The *milonga* was not even halfway filled yet. Ainsley looked at the other people, careful to keep her eyes glancing quickly. She found her foot tapping to the infectious swing of the band.

"It's still early," said Valentina. "Now is a good time for Ainsley to practice."

Gabriel sipped his soda. He pretended not to hear.

"Gabriel," his mother said.

"No, please, don't ask me to give lessons," he said. "I'm not that good. And if I dance with her they will think she is mine."

His mother made a *pffft* sound. "Nobody is here yet. Just give her one dance so that she doesn't embarrass herself with this man if he comes."

He set the Coca-Cola down. "Fine," he said. Then he turned to Ainsley. "You and I will now dance for the entertainment of my mother."

"I do appreciate it," said Ainsley.

Gabriel stood up and offered her a hand. She accepted, and he led her to the dance floor. "I'm no expert," he said, "but one thing I know is that the man is supposed to lead."

"Okay."

"The man is everything. If the man doesn't know what he is doing, the dance ends. Now, take my hand here and here."

He guided Ainsley's hands to the appropriate places: one on his hand, the other on his shoulder.

"Is that right?" she said.

"I don't know. Maybe. What does my mother say?"

Ainsley looked over at Valentina questioningly. The woman nodded at her.

"She says it's fine."

"Okay. Now watch my feet. I know this part." She focused on following his rhythm. Step one, step two: tango close. Step one, step two: tango close.

Ainsley screwed up her lips in concentration. The movements were harder than they seemed. Raised on a steady diet of American blues-rock, she had developed an ear that was used to steady, on-the-nose beats. But this tango rhythm was something else entirely, more like the off-kilter push-and-pull of a *mazurka*.

"Now," said Gabriel, "we always walk around the center of the floor, to the left. Don't hit anybody else. Don't do anything flashy, no *boleos*, no *adornos*, no *enrosque*. Just keep the rhythm... and walk."

Ainsley could keep it simple. As for those other moves,

she didn't even know them, much less have the desire to attempt them.

By now, the band had picked up its pace. The small accordion, which Ainsley remembered was called a *bandoneon*, was being squeezed more quickly, the bass plucked more loudly, the piano keys struck more forcefully. There were no drums. In tango, you don't need them.

Now more couples were trickling onto the creaky dance floor. Above their heads, a set of battered stagelights with colored gels reluctantly snapped on. Rings of red, blue, and green circles made slow kaleidoscopes around the dance floor. To Ainsley, it felt old-fashioned. These people partied like it was 1959.

Gabriel had been watching her closely. "You walk well," he said. "That's the most important part of tango."

"That's good to know."

He nodded. "And another thing to know is that if you accept a dance from a man, you don't dance only one song."

"Why not?"

"It's tradition. You have to dance three or four songs."

"You're kidding."

"No. It's called a *tanda*. You'll know when the *tanda* is over because the band will play something impossible to dance to."

Ainsley wasn't sure that she could trust her own judgment about that. The floor had become more crowded now. Gabriel fluidly moved her around another slower couple, and then the song ended.

"That's how you do it," he said, shaking her hand. "An excellent start."

"Thank you," said Ainsley. "So now what?"

"You return to the table and wait for another man to ask you to dance."

"You're not coming?"

Gabriel shook his head. "If a man sees me at your table,

they will assume we're together, and you'll never get asked. That would defeat the purpose, wouldn't it?"

"Yes."

"One more thing. What is this man's name?"

"Simón Fe. He's from Villa 27."

Gabriel pursed his lips, thinking. "If he is from a *villa*, you may need to be careful."

"Will you be my lookout?"

"Of course. Why do you think I'm here tonight?"

"Because your mother told you to come," said Ainsley. Then she playfully punched him in the shoulder. Something about Gabriel made him feel like the brother she'd never had.

He brushed off his shoulder. "Go back to the table. I'll circulate and try to find him. Wait and watch for my signal."

# CHAPTER THIRTY-ONE

Ainsley returned to the table and plopped down in the seat. Gabriel's mother was watching her with a mixture of shrewdness and jealousy.

"You walk well," said Valentina.

"Thank you."

"Gabriel doesn't," she said. "He never had the passion."

"Well, it doesn't matter, because he won't be back to the table tonight."

"I know," said Valentina. "But he'll give me a courtesy dance. He always does that. Otherwise he won't eat dinner this week."

Ainsley smiled and sipped from her glass of Coca-Cola. This *milonga* really felt like it was from another era, like a high school spring formal from half a century ago. There were many similarities. The men-will-be-men attitude, the hard-to-get women, the formal skirts, the square suits, the old lighting rig, the creaky floor, the feeling of a just-good-enough neighborhood place.

It wasn't uncharming, but neither was it glamorous.

Valentina however, was feeling a bit more strongly. "This place is shit," she announced.

"Why?"

"Look at those old men."

The mother nodded at a table of elderly men. All were dressed respectfully, ice cubes melting in their untouched glasses of soda on the table.

Ainsley was confused. "What's wrong with them?"

"One of them should've sent me a *cabaceo* by now."

"Maybe they're not interested."

"No, those men are waiting for a young *turista*." Her nose twitched. "I should have known this would happen here."

"Well, I'm having a good time," said Ainsley.

"Of course you are, it's all new to you." Then Valentina nodded towards a far corner. "Look over there carefully," she said. "Look at those four men."

Ainsley casually glanced behind her. A crew of older guys was kicking around in the shadows, smoking cigarettes. They wore the shifty facial expressions of those who've been marginalized. The most puzzling thing about them was their formal suits. They looked like the impeccably dressed criminals of old studio gangster movies.

"What about them?" said Ainsley.

"They are scum."

"I don't understand."

Valentina sighed, as if explaining this phenomenon was a chore. "They're taxi dancers."

Ainsley had heard the phrase but didn't know the meaning. "What's a taxi dancer?"

Valentina leaned across the table. Her cleavage made a deep canyon below her wattled chin. "A taxi dancer has one purpose in life: to hook a *turista*. Dance with her. Sweep her off her feet. Make her fall in love. Make her come to Buenos Aires every month. Then..."

"Then what?"

"She helps him get a visa. To get out of Argentina."

"So this happens a lot?"

Valentina nodded. "It has been going on for decades. The *turistas* don't change. Our Argentine men cast a spell on foreign women." She wagged a stern finger. "But it doesn't work on us."

Ainsley understood her message. She'd definitely felt the tractor-beam allure from Ovidio, but had chalked it up to his celebrity. Maybe that charisma didn't come from his money or fame, but from the *machismo* culture itself.

"Of course," said Valentina, "the taxi dancer's nightmare is that she decides to move to Buenos Aires to be with him. Because the *turista* doesn't know that she is just one of many fishes on his hook."

Ainsley finished her Coca-Cola and set down her empty glass. The dance floor was saturated with bodies now, a colorful swirl of black fabrics and red cheeks circling in a counterclockwise pattern.

But nobody had asked Ainsley to dance. Gabriel was chatting with a couple of men, but he hadn't given her any signs yet. She wondered if she ought to check out the goods, so to speak, while waiting for Gabriel's signal.

That question resolved itself quickly. Her roving eye had landed upon a young man in a suit. And he was staring into her eyes.

Quickly she glanced away, but not quickly enough. Her suitor was moving through the bodies, across the room.

"Oh no," said Ainsley.

"It was going to happen sooner or later," said Valentina. "Did you look away?"

"Of course."

She clucked. "These new assholes. Okay, listen—just say yes to him. He'll be good practice."

The young man arrived and stood before Ainsley. His feet were planted wide, his pants a couple of sizes too big for him. He had a broad southern Italian nose with wide flared nostrils.

Ainsley folded her hands and kept her head down. She could hear him clearing his throat. Then the words finally came.

"Would you like to dance?" Her suitor's voice was high and trembling.

"You're the first *turista* he's probably ever approached," said Valentina.

"He can hear you," said Ainsley.

"I don't care if he hears me." Valentina rolled a toothpick around her mouth and let her eyes work its way up and down the young man. "I'd like to give him the number of a good tailor when you're finished with him."

"Yes, *señora*," he said. He was respectful. Then he repeated the question to Ainsley. "Would you like to dance?"

Ainsley felt as though she were fifteen years old again. "Yes," she said.

He took her hand as she rose from her chair, then guided her to the dance floor. His hand settled onto her waist. It felt soft and beefy.

They began the simple tango walk. She moved lightly alongside him. He was staring into her eyes as though he was trying to read a message burned into the back of her skull. She couldn't meet his gaze and stared at her feet instead.

They flew around the dance floor like that, in silence, Ainsley feeling his body twist slightly beneath his jacket, watching his knees constantly bent.

The music ended, and an audio skit came on the speakers. Ainsley knew that this was the end of the *tanda*. It had been quick.

"Thank you," she said.

"You're welcome," he replied.

As Ainsley returned to her seat, she knew she'd passed the test. She could feel the stares of the other men in the *milonga*. They'd been sussing her out, watching her to see if she could dance. Now the verdict had been delivered: she wasn't an embarrassment. She was a low intermediate, right off the bat.

That meant it was open season on the *turista*.

She sat down, slightly breathless. "You have the motion and the look," said Valentina. "Fresh meat. They'll want to teach you. Keep your eyes on me."

Ainsley faced her. In her peripheral vision, she could see several men jostling for position within eyeshot. It was flattering. This never would happen back home. She could understand how a foreign woman, especially a middle-aged divorcee carrying a lifetime of romantic disappointment, could get hooked on this scene.

It was alluring to Ainsley too, but she reminded herself that she was here for a different purpose: to find Ovidio's rhodochrosite necklace.

"Where is Gabriel?" asked Ainsley.

"He's around somewhere," said his mother. "He's always been a good talker. People like him."

Ainsley quickly surveyed the room. Pairs of dark eyes beneath darker eyebrows tried to grab her gaze. It felt like she was being pinned down by hundreds of optic lasers.

"I don't see him," she said.

"There," said Valentina. "He's pointing towards a man. Your man. That's your Simón Fe. Turn and look, quickly."

Ainsley swiveled in her chair. Gabriel was watching her. He was standing with the gang of four black-suited men in the corner, the impeccably dressed criminal types that Valentina had spotted earlier.

And he was discreetly pointing, with four knuckles, to the man on his left.

The target swiveled and gazed towards the dance floor. He was tall and shaped like a snowman, with a large round gut and a smaller but equally round head. Two beady eyes were poked into the tanned skin of his face like raisins into cookie dough.

That was Simón Fe.

He caught Ainsley's eyes. He nodded once. Ainsley found herself nodding back.

Then Simón Fe began walking across the floor.

Towards her.

# CHAPTER THIRTY-TWO

Ainsley watched Simón Fe's slow progress through the chairs. He moved with an odd grace, lumbering but fluid, like a walrus in the surf.

As he approached, she could see that Simón Fe was as ugly as a sack of rancid butter. Ainsley figured out her approach. She would choke back her disgust, dance with the man for the remainder of the *tanda*, then push away and try to maneuver off the floor to a place where they could talk. At a greater personal distance.

When he arrived at the table, however, he ignored Ainsley. Instead, he took Valentina's hand and kissed it.

"That is for being beautiful," he said, "and for loving tango."

"Are you asking me to dance?" said Valentina.

"You look very talented," he said, "and I would only disappoint you. So, no."

"You're a charmer," said Valentina.

"With a face like this, I'd better be," he quipped. Then he turned to Ainsley. "Lovely, I would caution you to avoid the street. A face like yours will cause a thousand automobile crashes."

That was slick. "Thank you," she said.

"Would you like to dance? I can teach you some new moves."

"Yes."

The hand was proferred, Ainsley accepted it, and a moment later she had followed Simón Fe to the dance floor.

She assumed the proper position. His hands found their way to her waist and hand. He smelled like a cologne bath, which made her choke a little.

But as they began to move, Ainsley could feel just how powerful a lead Simón Fe was. Following him was extraordinarily easy. It was as though someone had replaced her clumsy feet with agile ones. And he wasn't speaking, or even making any special movements. Just the right touch on her hand, or at her waist.

Then Ainsley felt herself falling, his hand supporting the small of her back. She felt her arm arch out dramatically. Then she was yanked up to a standing position.

Wordlessly, Simón Fe had just dipped her. She hadn't even thought about it. It'd just happened.

Ainsley was breathless. She had never felt something like this before.

She didn't know how long the tango lasted, but she did know that when another prerecorded skit came on the speakers signalling the end of the *tanda*, she felt disappointed. Simón Fe was living proof that she should never judge a book by its cover.

"Thank you," she said.

Her amazement must've shown. He quickly replied, "I think we should talk somewhere else."

"Absolutely. But first I need to know your name."

"Simón Fe. And yours?"

There it was: a positive ID.

"Not yet," she said.

She followed him off the dance floor and wended her way through the crowd towards her table. She took her purse from her chair, then leaned over towards Valentina. "I've got my man. We're going to leave."

"Be careful that he doesn't get you," said Valentina.

"Only on the dance floor." She kissed the older woman on the cheek. "Thank you for your help."

"Don't agree to take any lessons," she said. "The taxi dancers are all the same. But if I don't get a *cabaceo* soon, I may have to order some whiskey."

Ainsley chuckled. She retrieved her coat from the check girl and followed Simón Fe out onto the sidewalk.

He was waiting for her. He took her hand and kissed it theatrically. "Lovely, are you sure this is new to you?"

"Yes."

"You dance like a natural Argentine."

She smirked. He'd probably used this line hundreds of times on hundreds of *turistas*. But part of Ainsley was hoping that it was the truth.

"I can say that you are honestly the best dancer I've ever been with in my life," she replied. "How long have you been coming to *milongas*?"

"My whole life," he said. "This is more than just my home. This is me. It's my identity."

There was the opening.

"I would love to see where a dancer such as yourself rests," she said. "You must get your energy from somewhere."

He waved it off. "Let's go have coffee."

Simón Fe offered her the crook of his arm. Ainsley accepted it, and they began to move down the street. She struggled to keep a smile on her face. His dance skills aside, she didn't know which was more repulsive: his appearance or his disregard of marriage.

But she needed to follow this lead to the bitter end.

It was three o'clock in the morning now, and he led her to a late-night cafe nearby. Simón Fe chose a discreet table in a corner. He ordered an ice cream with two spoons.

"Tell me where you come from," he said.

"The United States."

"Which part?"

"It doesn't matter," she said. "I'm kind of travelling right now."

"You're a free spirit," he said.

"I don't know," she replied. "Maybe I'm just kind of lost. But tell me more about you."

"I teach tango to women who deserve it," he said. "You are one of those women. Your legs are so long. You move naturally for this dance."

"I'm usually terrible," she said.

"It's true," he said, "I can't imagine you dancing salsa. Only the women with the big hips do that."

She laughed. "Are you saying I have unattractive hips?"

"Not at all," he said. "In fact, I would love to get a closer look between them tonight."

Ainsley blanched at the come-on. That was pretty bold. She thought that he'd been merely angling for tango lessons.

The server arrived and placed the ice cream sundae between them, a gorgeous pile of swirled cream and sugar, with *dulce de leche* crisscrossing its slopes. The adults-only conversation had just received a children's prop.

"I'm sure that I would be more open to that idea," she said, "with better jewelry."

"Most women are," he said.

She decided to launch another trial balloon over his head. "In fact, I've been looking for a rhodochrosite necklace."

The man's doughy face betrayed nothing. "Those are worth very little. Maybe I should teach you about gemstones too."

Then he took a spoon, dug it into the ice cream, and moved the scoop towards Ainsley's face. "Nothing is sweeter than you, but taste this anyways."

She rolled her eyes but opened her mouth. He was spoon-feeding her. That had never happened to her on a first date before. It had probably worked for him with many foreign women in the past. Maybe she was just the latest data point in a decades-long experiment investigating the exact combination of behaviors that led *turistas* to open their wallets and legs for him.

"It's delicious," she said, feeling like she was playing a part.

He scooted his chair around the table. "If you agree to my earlier suggestion, we can go around the corner. There is a place called a *telo*. You will see that the tango isn't my only talent."

His beefy hand landed on the inside of her upper thigh. Ainsley felt her blood suddenly turn to ice water. She had zero interest in learning what a *telo* was.

She felt all the murky lies evaporate from her mind, leaving nothing but the dry powder of truth.

"I know your son," Ainsley suddenly blurted.

The man removed his hand. His nostrils flared out, and his beady eyes became suspicious.

"His name is Pedro," she continued. "I met him today in your *villa*."

Now Simón Fe was staring at her, aghast. "*Puta madre*," he said. He began to scoot away.

"Don't be angry," Ainsley said. "Pedro is a wonderful boy. He said I could find you at this place."

Most of the color had drained from the taxi dancer's face. He was becoming aware that the tables had turned, that the predator had become the prey. He didn't react well to this realization.

Ainsley knew she'd better make her offer quickly. She reached into her purse and unrolled two hundred pesos. She laid them on the table and moved the ice cream sundae on top of the money.

"That's for taking me to meet your wife." It was her turn to pin her gaze upon him. "You know why. We don't have to say it."

Simón Fe pursed his lips. He had the twitchiness of someone caught in an offer for which there was no good answer. He couldn't say yes, but he couldn't say no.

"I want two hundred more," he said.

She'd expected this. "You'll get two hundred more when we arrive at your house. Then you'll get another hundred when you return me to the city center. That's five hundred total." She paused. "It's easier than giving tango lessons. Right?"

Simón Fe threw his hands into the air. "Sure, why not."

"Good," Ainsley said. "Let me call my friend."

"Why?"

"So we can leave."

"We're going right now?"

"Right now," she said. She saw him reach for his phone and quickly took it from him. "Don't call your wife either. This is going to be a surprise."

He sat back with a miserable expression on his face. On her own phone, Ainsley dialed Gabriel's number. She felt an excited tingle zip through her body.

She was one step closer to accomplishing her mission.

# CHAPTER THIRTY-THREE

They took Gabriel's car, a small, worn Peugeot. The assistant sat behind the wheel and Ainsley beside him in the passenger seat. In the back, like a felon being transported by law enforcement, sat Simón Fe.

"So what is your job?" said Gabriel.

"You must be simple," came the reply. "I'm a tango teacher."

Gabriel shook his head. "No, what is your *real* job?"

"Tango teacher. That is all."

Ainsley knew what Gabriel was getting at. Simón Fe was wearing several gold chains and a gold watch, a little more bling than you might expect from someone scamming tourists. Neither of them pushed the question any further.

Ainsley switched topics. "Tell me about your wife. Her name is Maria?"

Simón Fe sighed. "She is a good wife," he said. "She is excellent at laundry and cooking."

"You have just the one son? Pedro?"

"No, we have four."

"That's why she works at the hotel."

"Yes. She's only been there for a few months."

Ainsley chose her next words carefully. "There are people who think that she stole something."

"Are you working for these people?" he said.

"No."

"Then who do you work for?"

"Don't worry about it." Ainsley peeked at her notes. "The hotel says that she's been absent from work for two weeks."

"She's been very sick."

"With what?"

"Bronchitis. It's impossible for her to change sheets. Because of the coughing."

"Isn't she afraid that she'll be fired?"

"There are other hotels. And she's dependable. Like I said, she's a good wife. She's good at laundry and cooking."

Ainsley couldn't tell from his voice if he was lying. "Some people think that she's scared to report to work."

"Maria is very scared," he said. "Because she knows that there has been a misunderstanding."

So, according to her husband, innocent Maria the maid was going to play turtle, wait for everything to blow over, then meekly go back to work. That story may be true. But this strategy ignored the fact that she was a prime suspect in the mind of the victim, a victim with a lot of resources, and that he would use those resources to hire people like Ainsley to actively search for her.

The car was travelling down a darkened two-lane road. A long wall stretched on the left. Ainsley recognized the area: this is where she had parked the car with Sebastian yesterday morning. Or was it this morning? She was so tired that she was getting the days confused.

Gabriel cleared his throat. "Villa 27 is up ahead, but I don't know where to go exactly."

Simón Fe pointed towards the left. "That gate."

Ainsley recognized it, even in the dark. It was where she'd been sucked into the *villa* with little Chiche.

Gabriel turned left. Instantly they were in the same lane that Ainsley had run down that morning away from the mob, the little boy clinging to her body. It was totally dark, there being no public streetlamps, no legal electricity even. She rolled down the window and looked at the vague shapes, the broken walls and windows of the hovels, whizzing past in the darkness. Somewhere along this street was Pedro's house. It was almost impossible to spot the home in the dark.

Simón Fe gave directions: left here, right there, then a quick hairpin left, go straight. As they continued through the twisty streets, the structures grew taller, the lanes narrower. They were plunging even deeper into the community than she had gone before.

Then the lanes shrank to mere alleyways, wide enough to accommodate only one car at a time. The sound of the Peugeot's engine doubled off the walls of the dwellings, amplifying itself. "It's up ahead," said Simón Fe.

"How far?"

But there was no answer from the backseat. Ainsley glanced back at their passenger. He had edged forward on the seat and was peering at something.

Ainsley followed his gaze. Ahead, three cars had turned their headlights onto a home. A mass of people were milling around in the white beams, their legs and waists illuminated.

"That's my house," he said. "That's my house!"

Ainsley grew suspicious. "I told you not to tell anybody we were coming."

"I didn't. Stop the car. Please."

Gabriel pulled over and killed the engine. The three opened the doors and stepped out. They were mere inches from a nameless family's window.

Someone ahead noticed Simón Fe and shouted his name.

The tango teacher broke out into a run towards the small crowd. Ainsley traded glances with Gabriel. They both trotted after him.

The faces that greeted Simón Fe outside his home were mournful and empathetic. Arms and hands tried to comfort him, but he was having none of it, and pushed his way through the people. Whatever had happened, it was bad news.

"We couldn't stop them, Simón—"

"They had guns—"

"They were so fast, those *cabrónes*—"

Ainsley paused outside the circle of headlights. She glanced at Gabriel again. He nodded.

She stepped into the crowd. She didn't object when Gabriel cast a protective arm across her shoulder. At times it helped to have a man on your side, especially during what felt like a volatile situation in an alley of a pitch-dark shantytown.

They quietly followed Simón Fe through the small group of people. Nobody paid too much attention. It was easy for Ainsley to thread her way through the few clumps of people towards the door and into the home.

The interior was similar to Hugo's home that afternoon: unfinished flooring, no running water, threadbare furniture, picture of Che Guevara above the couch.

The difference was that this home had been shredded by what appeared to be a team of commandos. The cushions had been torn open, the drawers cast across the floor. Plates, dishes, cups had been flung onto the floor. The intruders had clearly been looking for something.

Maybe a necklace.

"What happened?" said Ainsley.

Gabriel was eavesdropping. "They're saying that Maria Jose was taken from her home this evening. Four men in a truck, with guns."

Ainsley noticed children crying near the stairs, four in total. These were Simon Fé's kids. Several adult women were circled around them, trying to comfort. Ainsley heard the word *mama* over and over.

The smallest one was Pedro. His eyes were frozen into perfect circles of terror. His gaze had fallen upon Ainsley, but he didn't seem to remember her. She could see the dissociation happening. He was out of his body.

She couldn't imagine what it must feel like to see his parent ripped away.

"Maria Jose was kidnapped?" she said.

"Yes," said Gabriel, "but keep your voice down."

Ainsley shushed herself, but she was still baffled. "Does this happen a lot? Just sometimes?"

"Almost never," said Gabriel. "The neighbors are saying that this was so clean, it had to be the military."

Ainsley felt the unspoken being passed around the room: The techniques of the dirty war were still here, thirty years later, in this very room.

She looked at Simón Fe. He was walking around the room, wailing, his hands theatrically clapped over his eyes. A gaggle of neighbors followed him, touching him, consoling him.

He may be a shitty husband, Ainsley thought, but nobody deserves this.

Her own mission had just ended. The rhodochrosite necklace wasn't here, not anymore. Not if a team of professional criminals had just ransacked the house, presumably looking for the same object. And now that someone had taken Maria Jose, Ainsley had no one to interview.

There was only one thing left to do.

Ainsley reached into her purse and unrolled a thousand pesos. She scanned the room and saw that Simón Fe had thrown his overcoat onto the kitchen table.

She slipped the bills into the inside pocket. She put his phone in there too.

Then she motioned to Gabriel with a sideways nod of her head. *Let's go.*

He nodded back and followed her out of the house.

# CHAPTER THIRTY-FOUR

Nine o'clock am.

Slumped in her chair at Nadia's office, Ainsley tried to stifle a yawn.

There was a mirror to her left, but she kept her eyes averted. Ainsley knew what she would see there. It would look like something that had been tied to an anchor, tossed overboard, and dragged across a hundred kilometers of coral reef.

Gabriel sat in the next chair. He hadn't slept a wink either, but he had showered, changed into a different suit, and cheerfully acted as though he'd just enjoyed eight hours of uninterrupted beauty sleep. Ainsley was flabbergasted. These Argentines were unreal in the way they could disregard their body clocks.

Across the desk from both of them sat Nadia. She was drumming her pen against the desk again.

"That's a very disturbing story," she said.

"We never even met the woman," said Ainsley. "But there was no doubt she was kidnapped."

"Maybe it was staged."

"Impossible. Nobody knew we were coming. I had Simón Fe's phone. There wasn't even time for him to arrange anything anyways."

"It was real," said Gabriel. "Those people were scared."

Nadia blew air out of her mouth. "This is beyond our concern. It's a tragedy, but now we forget the maid. We actually have an even bigger problem."

Ainsley waited. She didn't know what could be worse.

"Ovidio's disaster of a political rally yesterday has caused major changes. He wants his necklace. Immediately."

Both Gabriel and Nadia looked at her. Ainsley felt hemmed in. "What? I'm not superwoman."

"I know that," replied the manager. "But Ovidio is a child. And the child has decided that he wants to play in the sandbox again. It's the best way to salvage his political reputation. To remind the Argentine people why they like him in the first place."

Ainsley grew annoyed. "Tell him that I need more time."

"We don't have more time. There is an important match tonight. Boca is facing relegation to the second division. He's demanding that you find the necklace by kickoff."

Ainsley burst out laughing. This was utterly ludicrous, an act of monumental self-absorption. But she was surprised to see that Gabriel and Nadia were sharing none of her amusement. They looked mortified.

Then she realized that such an unreasonable demand was a joke to her, because she could walk away from the assignment, go back to her life in the United States. To them, however, failure carried serious consequences. They could lose their jobs.

"That's a big request," Ainsley said, "but I'm out of ideas."

Nadia sat back in her chair, oddly composed. "I'm not. There is one more option."

"What's that?"

"Bring him a Zorro rhodochrosite necklace."

"But I can't find it in twelve hours—"

Nadia shook her head. "Not *the* Zorro rhodochrosite necklace. Just *a* necklace."

Ainsley understood. "You want me to find a replacement?"

She nodded. Gabriel shifted uncomfortably.

"You disagree?" said his boss.

"Ovidio will see the difference," he said. "He knows that stone like he knows his own feet."

Nadia spun around in her chair. "What else can we do? We only have two choices: total failure, or failure with a slight chance of hope. Which way would you choose?"

The three of them grew quiet. Then Nadia broke the silence. "We would need to find a perfect replica. We would need to find a gemstone expert to vouch for it. That expert would need to be nearby, because we need it quickly. Mostly, we need that person to be able to keep a secret."

Ainsley sucked the inside of her cheek. She caught Nadia's eyes. "Are you thinking what I'm thinking?"

"You say it first."

"It's only a three-hour-ride on the Buquebus."

Nadia smiled. They did have the same idea.

"Who should call him?" said Nadia.

"I will," said Ainsley.

Nadia tossed the headset towards her. Ainsley fumbled to put it on, while the woman tapped at her laptop, then dialed a number.

A moment later, a familiar voice came on the line. "Hello?"

"Bernabé, it's Ainsley."

Ainsley was calling Bernabé Gradin, the rotund gemologist in Uruguay who'd helped her find the amethyst treasure, El Árbol Negro, on her last adventure. He was funny, cranky, clever, and a world-class flirt.

"I thought I had gotten rid of you, *Señorita* Walker," he said.

"Likewise," she retorted.

"Let me guess. You hate Argentina, and you're coming back to Uruguay to be with me."

At this moment, that didn't sound half-bad. "No, but I really need your help. It's an emergency."

"Talk to me."

She outlined the situation for him: Ovidio, the theft of his necklace, his political ambitions, and the game tonight.

"So Nadia wants you to find a replacement."

"Yes."

"I recommended that when Nadia first called me. But she resisted. She is too ethical. She wanted to find the real rhodochrosite for her client. So I suggested you as an investigator."

"I bet you're regretting that."

"Cheer up. It sounds like you've been doing as well as you possibly can in a country of forty million assholes."

Ainsley tried not to laugh. Bernabé was unapologetically provincial, a Uruguay booster. "So," she said, "can you help us?"

She could hear him rustling around, the sounds of cabinetry opening, drawers sliding. "I am looking in my storehouse. Any rhodochrosite will do?"

"It has an unusual marking."

"Tell me."

"It has a Z."

There was a heavy pause. "The Zorro rhodochrosite?"

"Yes."

"Hold on a moment."

She could hear him talking to somebody, probably Hector, his droopy-faced silent assistant. Then Bernabé returned. "I have one. It's quite old. They were suddenly taken out of circulation."

Ainsley sighed with relief. She nodded to Nadia, who thumped her pen on the desk with satisfaction and sat back in her chair.

"So how can we get that piece here?"

"I can courier it."

"Courier?" Ainsley looked up. Nadia was shaking her head no. She pointed to the phone and made a movement with her hand, like a ship floating on the water.

Oh. She wanted it personally delivered.

"Nadia says no," she said. "Maybe Hector can bring it?"

The old man scoffed. "Hector couldn't find his own ass in a hallway of mirrors. No, I will bring it personally."

"Today?"

"On the next boat, if that's what you want."

Ainsley covered the phone. "He'll be on the next boat."

"Excellent," said Nadia.

"I want you to know," said Bernabé, "how great a sacrifice this is. I haven't put a toe in that filthy city in almost twenty years."

"Your sacrifice will be greatly rewarded," said Ainsley.

"It had better be," he said. "The air is so bad, I'm going to have to bring an oxygen tank."

"I'll be waiting for you at the Buquebus terminal," she said.

"Of course you will," he said. "And tell Nadia hello. I remember selling pieces to her grandmother decades ago. She was a great lover of jewelry."

"I will."

They disconnected. Ainsley exhaled and dropped her head into her chest.

It appeared that the mystery of the missing rhodochrosite would be coming to an artificial end.

If Ovidio fell for the trick.

# CHAPTER THIRTY-FIVE

Ainsley was flat on her back, staring at the ceiling. She could feel her limbs trembling.

By her calculation, she'd slept three hours in the last sixty. That was about the same amount as what Navy SEALS are allowed during their hell week.

But she wasn't training to be an elite warrior. It was simply impossible to sleep, with daylight glowing through her tightly-drawn curtains, and her circadian rhythms at their highest point.

She didn't need to be at the Buquebus terminal for almost seven hours. A quick web search had revealed that the next hydrofoil didn't depart Montevideo until four pm, so after another quick phone call to Bernabé, she had left Nadia's office and come back here, to her hotel.

To wait.

She felt as though she were in purgatory. As though she were a few hours from stepping up to St. Ovidio, who would accept her gift, peer into his big book of souls, and render judgment.

Hopefully Bernabé would bring a gemstone that would

fool the soccer star. She didn't know how observant Ovidio was. He was clearly very aware of body positioning on the field, but regarding details of jewelry, she just didn't know.

She lifted one leg into the air and pointed her toe at the overhead light fixture. It was three glass clam shells, a bulb nestled in each. Quite a lovely design. Ainsley had become quite an expert on ceiling lights, having spent countless sleepless hours with eyes wide open, just the way she was now, while The Legal Weasel, her erstwhile husband, had begun pulling away from her.

Then one day she'd come home, dropped her purse on the table, and seen it. A note on the counter. The hairs had pricked on the back of her neck. She knew what that note had said before she'd even picked it up. She'd read through it once, twice, then balled up the note and hurled it into the kitchen garbage.

The next morning, a hangover drilling inside her skull like a demonic construction worker, she'd pawed through the trash, fished out the paper, unfolded it, then sat at the kitchen table and read it a third time.

He hadn't offered many details, just the broadest outline. He'd been unhappy, had felt too pursued by Ainsley, had needed more "space". Beyond that, there wasn't much, just some vague non-explanations, comments that had demonstrated, to Ainsley, just how unreflective he'd truly been.

Ainsley had pursued the relationship. That much was true. She had cared about the marriage more than he had.

Maybe that was her fault.

There'd been a few lost months after that, during which time Ainsley had struggled to erase him from her mind, but the memories had kept rising to the front of her mind, like a bloated corpse surfacing on a river.

Deep down, however, she knew that these memories would disappear. She just needed more layers of new experience, which is precisely what these gemstone assignments were offering.

In other words, if life was a shit sandwich, Ainsley was trying to slice the bread as thickly as possible.

She nodded to herself. That was a good metaphor. Slicing thick hunks of lifebread, that's what she was doing on this madcap mission here in Argentina. So that she wouldn't ever have to suffer the shitty taste of hopelessness again.

Ainsley was still thinking about that when exhaustion finally overtook her.

# CHAPTER THIRTY-SIX

She heard the horn signaling the arrival of the hydrofoil and shot up from her chair.

It was evening now, and Ainsley was in the bar at the arrivals area of the Buquebus terminal, the same room in which she had arrived only two and a half days ago. She stood on her tiptoes and peered out the bottom edge of the high window. She could just make out the dockhands tossing thick ropes onto the ship and lassoing them around the anvil-like cleats.

Bernabé had gotten on the four o'clock boat from Montevideo. Her watch read seven o'clock now. The gemologist was arriving.

She went back to her small table, swirled her rum cocktail, and glanced around the bar. The decor was modern. Yellow walls, clear fiberglass tables, weird podlike chairs. Suspended above her table was a single globe lamp; there were several matching ones suspended in the adjoining lobby.

Ainsley knew that the disembarking process would take a few minutes, as would getting through customs. She could add a few more minutes for Bernabé because he walked slower than most. He was eighty-four years old.

She had big plans for him tonight, however. After the business of the rhodochrosite was concluded, after Ovidio was satisfied with his necklace, she was going to take the old jeweler out to dinner at Las Lilias. That restaurant had been mentioned by Gabriel as the best *parrilla* in Buenos Aires. It was also the most expensive. She could expect to drop four hundred pesos, minimum, per person.

But Bernabé was worth it. She owed him for his recommendation. Plus, she really liked the amiable old gemologist. Ainsley's life had been chronically short of decent male company, and she appreciated all worthwhile men, no matter what their age.

He appeared on the ramp sooner than she'd thought. Ainsley couldn't help smiling. Bernabé was wearing his usual porkpie hat and long fur-trimmed coat. Behind him trailed his droopy-faced assistant, Hector, carrying a brown leather satchel.

"Bernabé," she shouted, waving.

Hector caught his arm and pointed at Ainsley. Bernabé nodded. The pair came across the lobby.

"You look the same," he said, exchanging cheek kisses with Ainsley.

She noticed that his face was drawn and tight. "You look upset."

He looked around uncomfortably. "What do you think? I'm in Argentina."

Ainsley couldn't help laughing. "Come over here."

They followed her back to her table at the bar. The old man glanced around skeptically at the mod decor. "It looks like a child decorated this place."

Ainsley signaled for three cocktails, and the bartender brought them over quickly.

"I didn't order this," said Bernabé.

"I thought we could have a social drink."

He shook his head and pushed it across the table towards her. "You can have it. I'm not putting anything to my lips in this damned city."

She had to stifle another laugh. "Then I guess we should get down to business."

"Oh no," he said loudly, "please, by all means, let's waste my few remaining months of life sitting in a nation of drama queens and financial disasters."

The other patrons were staring daggers at him now. Bernabé was straddling the line between being a funny character and being a misanthrope. She guessed that he suffered from plantation syndrome, the intense anxiety some people feel when away from home, something that grows stronger with age. She had trouble understanding that mentality, seeing as how it was basically the opposite of her own compulsive wanderlust.

"Well, Nadia is paying you," she said, "so it's not a total waste of your time."

"I don't need money at this point in my life," he said. "I'm here because you asked me for help."

"You're very sweet."

Magnified behind his lenses, his eyes were dancing with playfulness. "Don't tell anybody. They won't believe you anyways."

He nodded to Hector, who opened the leather satchel and withdrew a small box that was wrapped in newspapers. He slid it across the table.

"The rhodochrosite," said the jeweler.

"May I?" said Ainsley.

He nodded.

She unwrapped the newspaper and opened the box. A bezel-set rhodochrosite cabochon was resting on a bed of black velvet. A simple black cord was looped through the setting.

She peered more closely. A distinct Z could be seen among the swirls and squiggles of the cabochon.

"I think the velvet is worth more than the stone," he said.

"It looks pretty to me."

The Uruguayan laughed. "Did you ever really think about that? Argentina's most identifiable gemstone is nearly worthless. How appropriate."

"I hope it fools Ovidio," she said.

"Of course it will. He couldn't pour piss out of a boot with directions on the heel."

"Can I ask you something?" she asked.

"Of course."

"How did you happen to have a Zorro rhodochrosite?"

Bernabé looked at Hector. He stabbed a finger towards Ainsley. "What did I tell you? Always curious, this one."

The glum-faced assistant sipped his drink and stared straight ahead. Nothing could move him.

"See, I knew you would ask that," said the gemologist. "So I made some phone calls this afternoon."

"And?"

He took off his glasses, serious now, and massaged the bridge of his nose. "Most rhodochrosite is from Capillitas. It's unremarkable. But there was one mine that was very small, but unique, because the entire vein was shot through with the same Z formation. I don't know the geology of the site well enough to explain more, but that's where this stone came from."

"And so did Ovidio's?"

"Almost definitely."

Ainsley set down her drink and studied the stone. That was interesting.

Bernabé continued: "Most importantly, I know the person

who owned that particular mine. We used to be professional acquaintances. Until today, I hadn't thought of him for a long, long time."

"Who is he?"

"Marcelo Carrazo. He's retired in Patagonia now. I don't know why, but he got out of the mining business very suddenly. He might be able to help you find out what happened to the original." Bernabé paused. "If you're still going to pursue the case."

He nodded to Hector, who produced a piece of paper from the brown leather satchel and handed it to Ainsley.

"This is his contact information. I had to search through all my old telephone records."

Ainsley was grateful but didn't know what to do with this information. She certainly wasn't planning to contact the original miner. She failed to see how it would help her mission.

Bernabé saw the confusion in her eyes. "Trust me. Just keep it. A gemstone detective needs all the information she can find."

That was true. "Thank you," she said, then stuffed the paper and the rhodochrosite necklace into her purse.

The old jeweler checked his watch. "Only ten minutes. We have to catch the last boat."

Ainsley was confused. "To where?"

"Back to Montevideo."

She grew agitated. "But you just *got* here."

"Yes, and now we're leaving."

"Please, stay. I was going to ask you to a *parrilla*."

Bernabé patted her hand. "You are sweeter than kitten milk, but you should know something about me." He looked serious for a moment. "I would rather grill one of my own children than eat the crap they serve here."

Ainsley laughed, despite her disappointment. The old

man stood and stretched out his arms in a rock-star Christ pose. Hector slipped his full-length coat onto the old man's frame, then placed the porkpie hat onto his head.

"You've been a great help," said Ainsley.

"I know," he said. "That's how I like people to remember me." He kissed her on the cheek. "And that's for your persistence. It's the best quality any person can have."

He caught her eye to make sure that she knew that he meant it. Then Hector picked up the bag, the pair turned around, and left.

Ainsley watched them trudge back up the ramp towards the same hydrofoil. She suddenly felt abandoned again. But that feeling didn't last long.

She had less than an hour to get to the stadium.

# CHAPTER THIRTY-SEVEN

Even though she was inside a taxicab, Ainsley knew from the whooping and shouting on the sidewalks that this wasn't going to be any ordinary game.

She was approaching the outskirts of La Boca, a colorful neighborhood whose homes traditionally were painted a garish display of bright blues, greens, reds, oranges, and yellows. The tradition reached back to the Genoese tradition of decorating homes with leftover paint from ships.

But today, on either side of the cars, a flood of soccer supporters, bouncing and chanting, were flooding down the sidewalk.

All wore blue and gold jerseys.

She looked down at her own clothing. She was dressed in neutrals today. Hopefully the other team wouldn't be similarly clothed.

Three minutes passed, and the taxicab inched forward. Ainsley leaned out of her window, much like a dog sniffing the wind, and peered ahead. She saw nothing but a long line of red brakelights stretched ahead.

It was game night in La Boca.

The driver shrugged at her. "Okay, this is good," she said, handing him a twenty-peso note, and stepping out of the cab.

The air was electric with anticipation. She twitched her nose as the sharp stench of pollution hit her nostrils. It was coming from her left, where an ugly iron bridge crossed a shit-brown inlet of the river. This was the old port, the original site where the Italian and Spanish immigrants had first stepped into South America, where the tango had been invented, where millions of people had come and gone, lived and died, and nobody had ever remembered their names.

But Ainsley wasn't going to be forgotten.

The difference was the secret inside her purse. The simple necklace that could release Ovidio from his neurotic dilemma, send him back onto the field. And potentially turn her into a hero, if anyone were to find out.

None of that was guaranteed, however. If Ovidio recognized it as a fake, any number of consequences could follow. She blocked those things out of her mind.

Ainsley slipped into the flood of fans moving down the sidewalks, wedged herself tightly behind a group of men who were linked shoulder-to-shoulder. She could smell their booze, their sweat, their body odor.

She was carried by the river of fans down the street towards an abandoned railroad track. Ainsley guessed this was a relic of La Boca's industrial days.

And that's when, over the heads of the crowd, she finally glimpsed the stadium.

It was a blue-and-gold behemoth sitting like a mirage at the far end of the railroad track. The pride of Argentina soccer, its formal name is the Estadio Alberto J. Armando. Around the world, however, it's known by another name.

La Bombonera.

Translation: the Chocolate Box. The legendary home of

the legendary soccer club Boca Juniors, whose players included the legendary Diego Maradona, among others.

When the fans around Ainsley caught sight of the blue-and-gold ramparts of their beloved stadium, they started to sing.

Loudly.

It was a fight song, bellowed with such gusto that Ainsley even felt stirred herself.

She was carried along by the flood of people towards the bright lights of the entrance. The first thing she saw were the police officers in full riot gear, arranged in long, intimidating lines. The second thing she noticed were the signs directing Boca fans to one entrance and visitor fans to a different entrance. They would presumably be separated for the whole game. Their fandom was that intense.

Ainsley pulled out the handwritten directions that Nadia had given her. She was to circle La Bombonera until she found the secret VIP entrance, near the loading dock, behind the hurricane fence.

She walked on the old cobblestones in the shadow of the structure, navigating the sea of fans rushing into the various entrances. Overhead, hundreds of oblong security cameras watched the crowd like curious shoeboxes.

Standing near an alleyway, a heavy man wearing a dirty Boca jacket grabbed her arm. "You need a ticket."

"I don't."

"You don't have to lie. I can read you. You're not wearing any colors, walking around like a lost sheep."

"I'm looking for the VIP entrance."

He chuckled and jerked a finger over his shoulder. "It's that way, but nobody gets in that way." He lifted his hand far above his head to illustrate. "You come back here when you need a ticket. This is where the real fans come." He pounded his chest proudly.

Ainsley kept walking. She was sure that she wouldn't be needing his help.

A few minutes later, around the flat back end of the stadium, she finally spotted the loading dock. Next to it was a piece of green fencing, behind which stood a door and a few imposing security guards.

She approached them and went through the usual routine: name, passport, clipboard, check. They waved her through.

Ainsley stepped into a long, dark tunnel. At the far end was a small circle of spotlit grass. As she walked, she could hear the crowd above her. She could feel the people jumping, their shoes literally shaking the concrete all around her.

These Boca fans were *loud*.

The disk of spotlit grass ahead had grown larger. Ainsley caught the scent of rank humanity. She was approaching the end of the tunnel. Ainsley drew a deep breath and clenched her hands.

She stepped out onto a small terrace and found herself in the middle of thousands of people. To the left, to the right, forward, behind, across the field—La Bombonera was a human carpet, thousands of heads covered in shaggy mops of hair.

And the human carpet was moving.

The green field was flush up against the sides of the stands; there was no distance between the fans and the players. A pair of white tunnels extended out onto the pitch from the sides of the stands.

Proud fight music burst out of the speakers. A fleet of soccer players burst out of one end of the tunnel, each running like mad, each wearing the blue-and-gold strip of Boca Juniors.

Total chaos erupted around her. The human carpet let loose with all of its props—blue confetti, gold streamers, air horns, noisemakers, waving flags, whirled jackets. She watched a grown man thrust his fists into the air, throw his head backwards, and openly cry.

Then a vast movement across the stadium caught her attention. An enormous blue-and-gold banner, forty meters across and twenty meters long, had been unfurled across the heads of the people sitting behind the far goal. It bore the famous Boca Juniors shield and words *No. 12*.

Number twelve. She was clueless about its meaning.

Then Ainsley noticed something else. On the field, a man dressed as a king was parading around, wearing a blue cape with the number 12 on the back. He was followed by a team of female dancers clad in blue wigs, short gold skirts, and glittery heels.

Ainsley had never seen anything like this. These people were utterly mad. There was no sporting event in the United States whose supporters could even begin to compare with these maniacs. She clutched her purse and shrank back inside the opening of the tunnel.

Then she collected herself. Nadia had told her to find executive suite 47, so Ainsley circled the terraces, towards the flat side of the arena. She walked quickly.

It didn't take long. She found Nadia standing outside the door to the suite, her face drawn as tightly as drumhead.

"I'm sorry," said Ainsley, "but Bernabé didn't arrive until seven. I came as quickly as possible."

Nadia seemed distraught. "They're booing him," she said. "Every time he comes on camera, they boo him."

The manager gestured behind her. At that moment, a picture of Ovidio filled the video screen. He was sitting on the bench, wrapped in his warmup gear, arms crossed. He wasn't even watching his team. He was just staring at nothing, his lower lip jutting out stubbornly. He looked even more like a chimpanzee than he had before.

The booing immediately erupted. A shower of trash rained down upon the canopy over his head.

Ainsley nodded. "He has a serious public relations problem."

"I accepted the job of managing this asshole," said Nadia. "I mean, I could've said no. But I thought that I would be the one to rehabilitate him." She spat on the ground. "He is uncontrollable."

Ainsley understood. This wasn't the first time that a woman had tried to rescue a man from himself. Except in this case, the relationship was professional, not romantic.

Then Nadia suddenly seemed to return to her senses. She noticed Ainsley, almost for the first time.

"So you have the necklace?"

"I do."

"Good. Let me see if we can meet him in the locker room at halftime. Just wait in the suite until I come get you."

She gestured towards the executive suite. A guard was standing at the entrance. Nadia pointed to her visitor and nodded.

The guard stepped aside, and Ainsley entered.

# CHAPTER THIRTY-EIGHT

Thirty people were inside, all pressed against the glass wall that looked out over the field. They spoke in excited voices, pointing fingers at the action on the turf, voicing loud opinions about the coaching, the players' strengths and weaknesses.

A waiter appeared at Ainsley's side and accepted her coat.

"Will you be having anything to drink?" he asked.

"White wine," she said.

"And to eat?"

"There's a kitchen?" she said.

He pointed towards a swinging door. Through the porthole, Ainsley could see a cook and the bright lights of a kitchen. It was tempting, but she was too nervous to eat.

"No, thank you, just the drink."

The waiter disappeared. Ainsley tossed her hair and waited for one of the Argentine men to make his move.

It didn't take long. One man peeled himself away from the window to introduce himself; he was the owner of a leather retail chain. Then a second man joined the conversation: the vice-president of a bank. A third butted in; he was a well-known restauranteur from the local neighborhood.

For her part, Ainsley played the part of a bubbly *periodista*. She laughed, flattered, flirted, even played dumb. Soon she had gathered a group of male admirers. She had become Scarlett O'Hara in the southern hemisphere.

The men were more than happy to explain to the journalist the inner workings of La Bombonera. They started with the ubiquitous number twelve.

That, Ainsley learned, was the symbol of the Boca fans themselves. Famous for their intensity, and their ability to intimidate the opposing team, the Boca Juniors crowd literally influenced the outcome of the games. And they knew it. Since there were eleven players on a team, they had christened themselves La Doce, or "the twelfth player".

The most rabid fans, Ainsley learned, were corralled behind the far goal. She could see the fence at that end of the field was almost eighty feet high, with spiraled razor wire at the top. This was the *barra brava*, the organized crime syndicate that controlled much ticket distribution and influenced the election of club presidents. They had grown in importance to the point that television news programs showed the *barra brava* arriving at home games alongside the team itself.

Furthermore, after the three long whistles that signalled the end of each game, the *barra brava* were locked into their section. Literally. For forty-five minutes, they weren't allowed to leave the stadium, not until the opposing team's fans had left first, and dispersed throughout the city.

The waiter brought Ainsley a glass of white wine. It was sweet. It tasted even sweeter after she learned that alcohol was strictly forbidden in the stadium. On game days, you couldn't even get a drink in the surrounding neighborhood.

Such were the perks of the executive suite.

At one point she mentioned Ovidio's refusal to play. Her

admirers offered several rumors. Ovidio had become mentally ill. Ovidio had been diagnosed with a tumor. Ovidio was part of a satanic cult.

None of them mentioned his rhodochrosite necklace.

Two drinks later, Ainsley was feeling completely comfortable. She glided through the suite, chatting easily, touching men's forearms. Maybe she was being too friendly. She didn't care.

She found a piece of open window and looked out upon the game. Under the floodlights, on the green grass, the twenty-two players were feinting, dodging, sprinting, leaping, and colliding. Ainsley was impressed with the physicality of the game. Anyone who thought that soccer was boring hadn't ever seen it played like this.

"These guys are spectacular," she said.

"Actually they're not playing so well today," said the man standing to her side. She looked over. He was sixtyish, blonde, handsome. He was wearing a crisp military uniform.

"Why is that?"

"One, they played three days ago and are still tired. Two, Ovidio isn't on the field."

"You're still a fan of his?"

He looked at her sternly. "I have been a supporter of Ovidio since I saw him play on the Bahia Blanca youth team at age twelve."

Ainsley noticed an odd twitch in the man's left eye. It was one of those weird quirks, especially on a handsome person, that she had to force herself to ignore.

"And you've followed him all this time," she said.

"He is very special," the man said. "I have attended every game, except for the ones when he was playing out of the country. It's almost like the pride of a father."

"Good for you."

The man nodded. "He is an absolutely superior human. One of the fruits of our civilization."

This guy sounded heavy, but she decided to continue the conversation anyways. "I'm Ainsley," she said, "a journalist from the United States."

He suddenly adopted a very formal tone. "And your family name?"

"Walker."

"Ainsley Walker." The military man repeated the name to himself, as if committing it to memory. "I am Lieutenant Colonel Ortiz." They shared a firm handshake. "This is my wife, Maria Libertad."

On his other side, a thin woman glanced down at her shoes. She was well turned out, pantsuit, gold earrings, heels. Around her head floated a brittle shell of dyed blonde hair. It looked like she used it to protect herself from new ideas. Sometimes Ainsley had intuitions about people. Here, those intuitions told her that Maria Libertad was an empty vessel.

She really couldn't stand women like that. Devolving into a plus-one was Ainsley's greatest fear, but this woman looked like she had aspired to the position. Maybe life as an integer was better than life as a fraction.

Lieutenant Colonel Ortiz placed a hand on the back of his wife's neck. "We have been married for thirty-five years."

He announced this with obvious pride. Maria Libertad didn't react in any way. She stood there like a pretty silk handkerchief stuffed into her husband's shirt pocket.

"Congratulations," said Ainsley.

The waiter came over. Ortiz shooed him away. His hand never left Maria Libertad's neck.

"What magazine do you write for, Miss Walker?"

"I'm freelance," she answered, well-versed in the lie now. "I'm doing a piece on Ovidio that I hope to sell when I get back."

"Listen to me. I know the man very well. I helped him early on, when his parents were dying, and when he was very poor. If you need any background, let me know."

"I will, thank you."

"What part of his life in particular are you focusing on?"

Ainsley hesitated. She didn't know if she could trust this man, but she was just tipsy enough to plunge in.

"I've heard rumors about a rhodochrosite necklace," she said, "a sentimental object to him. I might focus on that, if he ever finds it."

The lieutenant colonel fixed his eyes upon hers. Ortiz had a strong gaze and it wasn't easy for Ainsley to return it. "I haven't heard about that necklace," he said. "I wonder why Ovidio never mentioned it to me."

Ainsley shrugged. "Maybe he didn't trust you."

The man's nostrils flared. She suddenly realized that the wine had gotten the better of her. She was annoying one of the superstar's oldest benefactors.

Then she felt someone grab her elbow. It was Nadia. The manager looked very upset. "Let's go," she said.

She hauled Ainsley across the floor and pushed her out of the executive suite.

When they were on the concourse, Nadia faced her square on. "What were you doing talking to that man?"

"That guy? He introduced himself to me."

Nadia shook her head. "No, no, no. Listen to me. You don't talk to the *milicos*."

"Why?"

"You just *don't*. Nobody does. It's dangerous. They are not with us." Nadia emphasized the concept by pushing her hands apart from each other. "They are *separate*. Understand?"

Ainsley shrugged. "Sure."

But Nadia still looked agitated. "Now, about my client.

We have been given permission to enter the locker room at halftime."

"We have?"

"This is very unusual, but the Boca Juniors manager has made an exception. He knows what is at stake."

Ainsley nodded. "I'm ready."

There was no middle ground here. This stunt was going to be either an explosive success or a mind-boggling disaster.

"Then let's go," said Nadia. "We have five minutes until halftime."

# CHAPTER THIRTY-NINE

Ainsley followed Nadia around the terraces, down two sets of stairs, past three checkpoints, and into the basement tunnels, the very bowels, of La Bombonera. She could still hear the rumbling, roaring, and cheering of the thousands of people above her. It evoked all sorts of thoughts about the madness of crowds.

But she pushed such philosophy out of her mind as they arrived at a heavy blue-and-gold door. A tall man in a business suit, flanked by several assistants, was deep in concentrated conversation. He carried an unmistakable air of authority.

"Patricio is the team manager," she whispered. "Don't say anything."

The manager glanced up at Nadia. "You know," he said, "I was thinking about it, and it's really not a good idea. Your presence would disrupt the players. Plus we're making progress with Ovidio anyways."

"He's my client," answered Nadia. "I have the right to see him."

Patricio patted her arm condescendingly. "We're feeding the baby his bottle. I think he'll stop crying for his mother soon." He turned away to discuss something with an assistant.

His callousness shocked Ainsley. To her surprise, Nadia clapped her hands three times directly in the manager's left ear. His shoulders jumped. He whirled on her.

"I wasn't finished talking to you," she said.

Ainsley tried to hide her smile. Patricio was steaming mad, but now at least he was listening.

Nadia continued: "If you let us into the locker room, I guarantee that Ovidio will play in the second half tonight. And for the rest of the season."

That was gutsy. Patricio struggled with the question. His eyes bounced around, searching for the best way out.

Finally he succumbed. "Okay. But we're getting close, even without"—he pointed a thumb at Ainsley—"your tricks."

"Trust me."

"I trust nobody," he said. "Go on."

The men standing guard on either side of the locker room pulled the door open and gestured for Ainsley and Nadia to enter.

The smell assaulted the two women as they stepped inside the men's locker room. It was a deep man-stink, blooming with the sweat, the hair, the dirt, and the blood of a group of very healthy male specimens who spent their most of their waking hours exercising their bodies.

It made Ainsley's head spin. Even Nadia seemed a little cowed, and she'd been here before.

The floor of the locker room was bare linoleum; the walls were average plaster. Overhead fluorescent lights lent a ghastly look to the scene. Several icons of the Virgin Mary were affixed to lockers. Of course, the room didn't need to be much. Ainsley had learned from someone in the executive suite that the Boca Juniors spent most of their time at a plush practice facility elsewhere.

The most interesting aspect of the room were the thirty players, all standing around in various states of undress. Some were splayed across benches, others leaned against pillars. A couple were getting their legs rubbed down by trainers. One was sitting in a bubbling therapy tub with his hands across his eyes, grimacing in pain.

Ainsley noticed something else too. Up close, almost every one of these men was attractive. Not gorgeous to die for, but definitely enough to cause heart-fluttering amongst girly-girls.

A girly-girl, however, Ainsley certainly was not. She put on her game face and steeled herself for major *piropo*. Sure enough, as she and Nadia walked through the locker room, the players started to notice their female visitors. There were a couple of catcalls, a kissyface or two. Those were probably the substitutes with nothing better to do. Most of the others—the sweaty ones —were too focused on each other, and their own bodies, to care.

"Where is Ovidio?" she said.

"In the back," said Nadia. "He has his own changing room."

Of course, Ainsley thought. Why would Ovidio *not* drive an unnecessary wedge between himself and his teammates by demanding special treatment? It was totally in keeping with his character.

Nadia approached a blue door and rapped on it firmly. "It's Nadia," she said. "Let us in."

Ainsley heard a muffled moan inside. Nadia traded glances with her and pushed through.

The private room was about the size of a bedroom. There was a table holding lotions and bandages, a freestanding closet, a small refrigerator, and photos of himself wearing various team jerseys posted proudly on the walls. Ainsley noticed that he had been given the number 9 throughout his entire career. The *El Mono* photo was conspicuously absent.

The superstar himself was stretched out on a padded massage table near the wall. A trainer was hunched over his foot, kneading Ovidio's big toe.

"Does that hurt?" said the trainer.

"Like a dragon breathing fire," said Ovidio.

Then he noticed the visitors. "It's a disaster, Nadia. Look at my toe."

Nadia had the air of someone who'd been through this routine many times before. "It looks fine."

"It's not. Something is wrong with it."

He leaped off the table and paced the room. "See, I can't walk right."

"You're walking perfectly," she said.

"No, there is something wrong with me."

"You're good for the moment," said the trainer.

Ovidio lifted a finger. "But there *will* be something wrong soon. I can tell. I am not at my peak of health."

Nadia had zero patience for this. "You imagine an injury almost every week."

"No," the celebbrity protested, "this time it's for real."

She carried onwards. "We have news for you."

"What kind of news?"

"Big news."

The trainer, sensing the climate of the room, zipped his bag shut, and slipped out the door.

# CHAPTER FORTY

Quick as a thunderclap, Ovidio's spirits had changed. He hopped back onto the massage table. He looked at the two women, his eyes bright and lively. "Is it good news? I can never tell with you women."

Ainsley felt her heart racing. This was the moment. She decided to let Nadia do the talking.

"Someone in this room," Nadia said, "has found your necklace."

Ovidio's mouth opened slightly as he regarded his American visitor. His eyes roved up and down Ainsley's entire person, almost as though he was making sure that she wasn't an apparition.

"How?"

Ainsley had rehearsed this in advance with Nadia. "I found the maid. She'd stolen it."

He clapped his hands, rolled onto his back, and kicked his feet in the air. Then he leaped off the table and kissed Nadia. "You see what this means?" he said. "It means, don't ever doubt me. I know my friends."

Then Ovidio grabbed his manager's face and kissed both cheeks. Nadia tolerated it.

"Say I'm sorry," he ordered.

She rolled her eyes. "I'm sorry."

"Say I'm sorry for ever doubting you."

"I am sorry for ever doubting you," she repeated, "your majesty."

He didn't seem to notice the sarcasm. Ainsley admired Nadia's pretended humility. She didn't think she could've pulled that off, but that's why she wasn't a celebrity manager.

Ovidio turned to Ainsley, his chest up and proud: "Okay, *yanqui*. Let's see it."

Ainsley fumbled in her purse with trembling fingers until she found it. She handed the box to Ovidio. Her stomach was in knots. Her breaths were coming quicker.

"That's pretty," he said. "It didn't come in a box the first time."

"Ainsley is an amazing detective," said Nadia. "I knew from the moment I saw her."

Ovidio had opened the box. He pulled the rhodochrosite necklace from the black velvet backing and draped it across his fingers. His eyes were narrow with concentration as he studied the necklace.

"We changed the chain," said Nadia.

Ovidio looked at her. "I see. Do you know what else you changed?"

"What?"

"The stone."

Ainsley wanted to form words. She really did. But they wouldn't come out of her mouth. She'd been struck mute.

Nadia quickly explained. "Ovidio, it's your stone. We found it in the maid's house. In Villa 27. Ainsley found it."

But the superstar's eyes were burning into Ainsley over his manager's shoulder. "This isn't my rhodochrosite."

Ainsley sunk her head. She was trying not to let her body language betray her, but there was no denying it. She'd been caught lying.

But Nadia was still pushing for it. "No, Ovidio, it's your stone, believe me, I know the Z too—"

"This Z is different," he said. He picked up the rhodochrosite and pointed at its delicate veining. "Here. See those lines? Not like mine. And see those? Not mine either. Believe me, I have looked at this necklace for my entire life."

"That's nonsense," Nadia said, "you just—"

"That's enough," said Ainsley. They both turned to her. "Ovidio is right. It's not the real necklace."

Ovidio drew himself up to his full height, which was still three inches less than Ainsley's own. "Why would you lie to me?" he said.

"Because you demanded the necklace and I wasn't any closer to finding it."

A tyrannical darkness settled over his eyes. Ainsley supposed that it was useless to look for sympathy from him, especially at this moment.

Nadia had retreated to the corner of the room. The panic was plain on her face. Ovidio was her best and only client. She couldn't afford to anger him this badly. They'd taken a gamble, and lost.

Ovidio rubbed his hands together. "Now I need to ask a question. What do you do when someone lies to you?"

Ainsley shrugged. Nadia tried to interject: "Ovidio, please—"

He held up a hand. "No, I am addressing *Señorita* Walker."

Ovidio approached Ainsley. His nose was almost touching herx. His eyes bore into her own. She'd never stood this close to a man without kissing him.

"I know what to do," he said. "The situation is well-known to me."

"Tell me," Ainsley said.

He shaped his hand into a gun. Then pointed it at Ainsley's head.

"You're fired," he said.

# CHAPTER FORTY-ONE

The small room was dancing with negative electricity. Nadia looked stricken. Ovidio looked like a raging bull.

And Ainsley looked for a way out.

Her mind raced through all the possible scripts. She could say that the maid must've given her a fake rhodochrosite, but then there would be more lies to invent, more investigation, more backtracking, more coverups. Ainsley had too much pride for that.

Another possibility was to pin the blame on Nadia. After all, the trick had been the manager's idea. But Ainsley wouldn't turn on anybody like that, not someone who had trusted her, who had hired her with almost zero experience. That would kill future recommendations, which were the lifeblood of small agencies. After all, it had been slowly dawning on Ainsley that a becoming a self-employed gemstone detective was not a total impossibility.

No, she would fall on her sword. It was the right thing to do. It was the only thing to do.

"You're right," said Ainsley. "I deserve it for trying to trick you."

Ovidio thrust the necklace at her. "With this piece of shit, you erase my only connection to my biological parents. It's horrible. What you did is like *murder*." He paused, seized with a better word. "No, it's even *worse* than murder."

Ainsley wasn't sure what exactly could be worse than murder. But she was sure of something else: The cliché of the passionate Latin male was alive and well, living right here, in this room. As his tirade grew longer, he became more victimized and embittered. He blamed her for everything short of the Incan genocide and continental drift.

She stood there and calmly took his ranting. She agreed with him at every turn, you're right, Ovidio, absolutely right.

Of course, Ovidio was justified in his anger. Ainsley *had* stabbed him in the back. But it was basically by his own request.

When he had finished, Ainsley swept up the shards of her dignity and dumped them into her purse. "Should I leave now?"

"Go."

Ainsley turned towards the door, and Nadia started to follow. "But not you," he commanded.

Nadia nodded to her.

Outside the room, Ainsley saw all thirty members of the Boca Juniors soccer team staring at her. They'd been listening to his ranting through the door. It would've been impossible not to.

"He's very angry," she said.

"He's always angry," said one player. "What was it this time?"

"A broken shoelace," said a second.

"A papercut," cracked a third.

Ainsley smiled. Their sympathy was helping her feel a little less miserable. But she wasn't sure what to do next. So she moved towards a bench to wait for Nadia.

The players cleared some space for her, kicking aside jockstraps and wet towels. One handed her a paper cup with Gatorade. She caught a glimpse of her own face in a mirror opposite. It looked ashen.

She kept quiet, huddled on the bench, while the players slowly returned to their stretching and chatting. There were a thousand thoughts scurrying through her mind.

At last Ovidio's door opened, and the superstar himself came swaggering out. She noted how the temperature of the locker room changed, how his teammates paused their conversations, how they stepped aside for him.

He waltzed past Ainsley as though she didn't exist. She was expecting that. Then he tipped his chin to Patricio.

"So?" Patricio said.

"Not yet," Ovidio replied.

"Keep this up," said the team manager, "and ownership is going to end your contract next month."

"I'm thirty-five. This is the end anyways."

"Is this how you want to go out? Like a scoundrel?"

The superstar shrugged. "People can watch the video of my better seasons."

"But all of Argentina wants you to play."

"Argentina can fuck itself."

Then Ovidio flipped up the hood on his warmup jacket, stuffed his hands into his pockets, and turned away.

Seething with frustration, the manager turned away. Then he banged his clipboard against his thigh and called a team meeting.

Ainsley watched the Boca Juniors gather around. He delivered, in rapid Spanish, a quick outline of the strategy for the second half, along with potential substitutions. Then the players kneeled on the floor for a quick benediction from a priest. Lastly, they ran out of the locker room and back towards the field.

Left in the nearly empty locker room, Ainsley heard the thundering of the crowd as the team reappeared on field. Only then did Nadia emerge from Ovidio's private room. She was wiping hey eyes with a tissue.

"We gave the baby the wrong toy," she said, "and he didn't like it."

"I'm sorry."

The manager clutched her head. "That was the worst professional move of my entire life."

"Did he fire you too?"

"No. But he's going to talk to my company, and they probably will."

The two women sat side-by-side on the bench. The locker room was empty now, except for a janitor hurriedly cleaning the floors and benches before the players returned in forty-five minutes.

"And there's something else," she said.

"What."

"I can't pay you."

Ainsley felt alarm race up the back of her legs. "But the first half—"

"You didn't return the contract to me. And Ovidio is forbidding it."

"He can't do that."

"Without a signed contract, he can do whatever he wants." She took Ainsley's hand. "It's not my decision. I would like to honor our agreement."

Ainsley swore to herself. That would teach her not to drag her heels on getting contracts back to people. Now it was going to cost her thousands of dollars.

"So what do we do now?"

Nadia shrugged. "There isn't anything left to do. My career is finished."

Ainsley suddenly felt very vulnerable. "But what should I do?"

Nadia looked at her in the eyes.

"Go home," she said.

# CHAPTER FORTY-TWO

Ainsley Walker thumbed through the money in her purse.

She was sitting at an outdoor cafe on Avenida Libertador, the remains of a cappuccino with perfect foam before her. It was a warm spring morning in the Southern Hemisphere. She was not yet thirty, fairly attractive, and free as a bird. And, by her count, she was carrying six thousand pesos in her purse, which, at four-to-one, translated to about fifteen hundred dollars.

So why did she feel so miserable?

One reason could be found in the small ashtray on her table. Seven cigarette butts lay inside, freshly stubbed out. She'd sworn off this habit more times than she could remember. The problem lay in the nature of nicotine. It really did relieve stress.

Ainsley pulled out her latest purchase. A pack of Nicorette chewing gum. She'd bought it this morning, along with the cigarettes themselves. The clerk had snickered at her. That was all right. She didn't have to always make sense.

The other reason for her mood was more abstract. Ainsley had no purpose. Some people thrived on this feeling.

Ainsley had always secretly admired people like that, those free spirits in peasant dresses and sandals and no makeup, the ones who flitted from place to place, thought to thought, man to man. The girls who lived happily on a diet of whim and impulse.

But Ainsley couldn't live like that. She was too goal-oriented. She was built for constant, purposeful, forward motion.

And now her only remaining objective—to find a rhodochrosite necklace—had been yanked away. Ovidio had fired her. It stung a little, but not too much. After all, she'd been fired several times already. She'd walked this path before, knew the road well.

She reflected on her dilemma. The idea of returning to the United States tasted like soggy cardboard. After all, she knew what awaited her there: an empty apartment, an empty savings account, an empty workday. The nagging feeling of missing the boat, of watching others build conventionally successful lives. That task was getting harder and harder to do anyways.

Not that Argentina was much better. There was proof right on this street. Ainsley could see it from her chair.

She peered down to the corner, where a lovely, three-story mansion stood on an expanse of pine-dotted lawn. It was white with a terracotta roof. The portico had four columns. A large, official Argentina seal hung prominently over the front door.

This was the Navy Mechanics School. She had recognized the name on the sign from her afternoon of Internet research back at the hotel a few days earlier.

Its history wasn't nearly as pretty as the setting.

The Navy Mechanics School was the detention center where, during the dirty war, an estimated five thousand prisoners had been stored before being ultimately "transferred".

Prisoners had slept in the attic when they weren't being tortured in the basement. The goods that had been stolen from their homes— books, televisions, mattresses, washing machines, paintings, furniture, clothing, jewelry, tango records—were kept in The Hold, a chamber near the officers' quarters on the first and second floors.

There had been many, many other detention centers too, all across the country. Most of them had been destroyed, others converted. To erase the memory of the disappeared.

But Ainsley wasn't disappeared. She was right here, with three more nights of prepaid hotel, and she needed to feel useful. Her thoughts turned back to the rhodochrosite necklace.

She remembered how quickly Bernabé had recognized the Zorro vein of rhodochrosite, as he'd called it. He'd told Ainsley about the man who had mined it, Marcelo Carrazo. He'd given her the contact information too. Talking to that gentleman might prove worthwhile, even if she wasn't being paid any more.

Would that be considered overstepping her bounds? Continuing to work, for no money, on a task from which she'd been fired?

Probably. It was also a little crazy. Ainsley needed to think about that.

She downed the rest of her cappuccino and put a ten-peso note on the table. She needed to use the bathroom. Making the decision to continue the mission, in defiance of Ovidio, would require a clear head.

Ainsley stood up and walked inside the café. "Restroom?" she asked. A nervous-looking waiter with darting eyes nodded towards the rear of the establishment.

She found the women's toilet and locked the door behind her. She stared at herself in the mirror, thinking about her next step.

She decided what she would do. Nothing.

She would head over to Parque Lezama and check out San Telmo, the historic *barrio* popular with tourists, before doing anything else. In other words, Ainsley would relax, just for one afternoon, and try to enjoy herself, like a normal goddamn person. Then, maybe, if she felt like it, she would call this Marcelo Carrazo to see if he knew anything at all.

There was no rush. She was out of danger. It felt like volunteer work now. She had as much time as she wanted in this country, and a little bit of money to carry her over. Maybe she'd even call Sebastian back.

Ainsley splashed water on her face. She used a paper towel to dab it dry. Then she unlocked the bathroom door and opened it.

Three men dressed in black paramilitary garb were blocking the door. Their faces were covered except for their eyes. They were carrying guns.

And the guns were pointed directly at her.

# CHAPTER FORTY-THREE

Ainsley stopped in midstride. Her mouth dropped open. She was having trouble registering their presence.

"What the hell is this?" she said.

The men said nothing. She sensed that they were trying to identify her. One nodded. Another stepped forward and put his hand roughly on her shoulder. She slapped it away using the classic windmilling arm technique she'd learned in self-defense class. The first guy attempted it on the other side, but she knocked him away too.

Ainsley fell backwards into the bathroom and tried to kick the door shut, but the assailants had already entered. There was no hope of overpowering them.

In the small space, the men surrounded her, turned her around against the wall. She felt the cold metal of a weapon pressed sideways across her shoulder blades, pinning her to the wall. She felt her purse being slipped off her left arm.

She felt panic mixed with infuriation. In her peripheral vision, she could see that the men had unzipped her purse and had found her passport. One of them held it up to her face. To compare.

That satisfied the men. She was yanked roughly from the wall and her hands were bound. The plastic bit into her wrists. A hand on her neck pushed her out of the bathroom.

That's when Ainsley realized that this wasn't a robbery.

This was a kidnapping.

The cafe had been emptied. Ainsley glimpsed the waiter and the cook on the sidewalk, being detained by another man in paramilitary garb.

But they didn't push her towards the front door. Instead, they pushed her into the kitchen, past the stoves, the walk-in freezer, the bags of flour and sacks of vegetables, out the back door and into the alley.

In the alley was a green Ford Falcon. With heavily tinted windows.

Ainsley felt her stomach pitch. That was the same type of car that the government had used in the dirty war to "disappear" political prisoners. To snatch them off the streets and, apparently, even out of café bathrooms.

She tried to bolt, but the men had anticipated this—maybe this wasn't their first kidnapping—and had already surrounded her. Six rough hands stopped her instantly.

She began screaming until she felt a hand cover her mouth. Her face grimacing, her body writhing, she twisted and turned like a temperamental four-year-old being dragged off to bed. Ainsley had always been able to make a stink when she wanted to.

But it wasn't enough. They dragged her towards the Ford Falcon. A fourth man had opened the back door. She felt hands pushing down on her head, other hands clamped on her shoulders, arms, and before she knew it—

—she found herself thrust into the backseat.

The door slammed shut behind her. Ainsley sat down on her butt, arranged her legs, looked around the compartment. A thick plexiglass divider separated her from the front seat.

There were no handles, no window cranks, nothing but smooth surfaces.

Breathing heavily, Ainsley considered her options. It didn't take long.

She had no options.

Two of the men entered the front seat. One started the car and floored the accelerator. They peeled out of the alley and turned onto Avenida Libertador.

She pounded on the divider with her shoe. "What's happening to me?"

They didn't respond.

Ainsley saw the Navy Mechanics School coming up on the left. She could feel her heart thumping faster. The dirty war had ended thirty years ago, but if it had happened once, it could happen twice. After all, they'd already disappeared the hotel maid from Villa 27. What if she were next?

She raced through the problem in her mind. Who in the United States would be willing to look for her? What kind of diplomatic rescue could she expect? She hadn't told anybody back home that she was going to Argentina. The cavalry would never be on its way.

She was truly, undisputably *alone*.

The Navy Mechanics School drew closer. Every muscle in Ainsley's body drew tightly.

Then the car passed by, and the men didn't even turn their heads. She let out a small breath of relief.

Two minutes later, the Falcon drove up to an elevated freeway, joining the flood of vehicles headed away from the city center, towards the outskirts of Buenos Aires.

This kidnapping could be going anywhere.

Ainsley looked at the people in the cars next to her, working men in garbage trucks, ordinary office workers in beat-up jalopies. They had no idea about the horrendous event that was occurring behind these tinted windows. She felt a sudden overwhelming love for these strangers, a need to talk to them. She'd never felt like this before.

Ahead, a sign above the freeway read *Aeropuerto Internacional Ministro Pistarini: ½ km*.

The driver put on the right-turn blinker and shifted into the exit lane. Ainsley gripped the upholstery.

The car exited the freeway and followed the curve. Ainsley saw ads for car-rental agencies, hotels, parking, airlines.

She was being taken to an airport. Ainsley couldn't make sense of this.

The driver avoided the arrivals and departures circle, instead turning onto a small gravel road. It ran parallel with the fence that surrounded the tarmac.

Soon they came to a gate. A guard was smoking outside the security booth, his hand resting casually on the mechanical arm. When his eyes landed on the green Falcon, he flicked the cigarette away and headed into his booth. The mechanical arm quickly lifted.

No ID check.

Then they were on the tarmac, roaring back the way they had just driven, the fence passing by on her left.

Ahead was the terminal. A large commercial airplane, the usual Boeing 737, was parked with its nose in the loading dock. She could see the luggage trucking up the conveyor belt to the luggage hold.

That's when the terrible realization hit her. Of what they were about to do.

The Falcon roared up under the belly of the plane. A door opened on the terminal and a customs official walked down the stairs. His bearing seemed serious.

He approached the Falcon. The driver rolled down the window and handed him something. Ainsley recognized it.

Her passport.

The customs official disappeared into the airport. Ainsley closed her eyes. Her stomach had dropped. They could be doing anything with the document. She wondered if she would ever see it again.

She watched the last of the baggage being thrown into the hold, the luggage truck pulling away. She watched a worker disconnect the fuel hose, and then the fuel truck pulled away too.

At last the customs official reappeared, her passport in hand. He moved across the asphalt and silently handed it back to the driver.

Just before the customs official turned away for good, he glanced at Ainsley in the backseat. There was a brief flash of a smirk on his face. Then he was gone.

The door on her left was suddenly yanked open. A pair of men stood there, dressed in military uniforms. She hadn't seen them approach.

Then the door on her right opened too. She felt rough hands pulling her by the upper arm across the upholstery.

"Ainsley," said one of the military uniforms on her left. She turned her head to look at him.

Then she felt a prick on her right shoulder. Ouch. She looked to her right. The needle was already being withdrawn from her skin. Another military man held the needle. He quickly disposed of it in a small case and stowed it in his pocket.

"Stand up," a voice said.

Ainsley obeyed. She was feeling woozy. She felt her plastic snipped off her wrists. Then she felt a man on either side of her. One arm snaked around her shoulders, another across her lower back, both directing her towards the staircase that led to the airplane.

"Move your legs," the voice said. "Keep walking."

She was having trouble focusing her eyes, but she could

still follow the orders. They directed her towards the staircase.

"Go up the stairs," the voice said.

She obeyed. The metal steps beneath her shoes, ordinarily so hard, felt squishy and soft.

Then she felt herself being guided inside the accordion gangplank. The walls were rippling oddly. Her thighs had started to feel rubbery. Her mouth was dry. Her head hurt.

Then she was passed into the airplane. She saw the distinctive black rubber floor beneath her shoes. She couldn't lift her head; it felt extraordinarily heavy. She watched her shoes shuffle down the aisle. She felt herself being guided into a seat. She felt a seatbelt click across her waist. She felt the side of her head thump against the window.

And then, for many hours, Ainsley didn't feel anything at all.

# CHAPTER FORTY-FOUR

Ainsley Walker had never seen a child fall facefirst into a birthday cake before, but there was a first time for everything.

She was standing against the wall, a camera in her hand. She was in the living room of her friend Deirdre, whose son, Justin, was celebrating his second birthday. There were about ten mothers here, and twice as many children.

Ainsley, being single, was the assigned photographer.

She'd watched the kid toddle around. The mothers had applauded. He'd teetered, twirled, and finally tipped over into his own vanilla sheet cake. He'd wandered around the living room, his arms out, frosting smeared across his entire body. He looked like a tiny mummy.

Ainsley had snapped several frames before Deirdre had grabbed the kid and swept him away to the bathroom for cleanup.

Now the laughter was dying down. Ainsley poured herself a Sprite into a red plastic cup and walked into Deirdre's kitchen. She surveyed the cutesy ladybug refrigerator magnets, the cartoonish boxes of breakfast cereal, the Bed Bath & Beyond coupons on the counter.

Then she looked at the ceiling, inhaled deeply, and exhaled a long breath.

This was the United States. She had returned home.

But not by choice.

The entire episode had felt like a dream. She'd woken up on the airplane to the pilot's announcement that they were an hour from landing at New York's JFK airport.

On the plane, she'd been beyond confused. She hadn't even been able to talk. And the flight attendants had treated her like any other passenger. Maybe they hadn't known. Maybe they'd assumed that Ainsley was just tired. Maybe they'd known.

That was unthinkable.

But there was no doubt that her kidnappers had acted with absolute professionalism. She'd found her purse tucked safely under her arm. Nothing inside had been touched, not even the cash. Her passport had been given an Argentina exit stamp. She hadn't even had to pay for the seat.

In retrospect, Ainsley had to hand it to them. It had been a very smooth operation.

After landing, she'd walked mutely down the gangplank, waited in line for customs. She didn't say a word. Who would have believed her? She had answered the questions, watched her passport stamped, and re-entered the United States.

Spit out into the concourse of New York City's JFK terminal, Ainsley had wandered towards the ticket counters. She paid cash for another flight, back to her home city. There was nothing else she could do. It was an automatic decision. As though someone were still controlling her from halfway around the world.

That had been four days ago. Upon her return, she'd slept

for thirty-six straight hours, with an occasional break to drink water. She hadn't said a word to anybody about her return, or her kidnapping. Again, who would believe her?

She'd left voicemails for both Nadia and Gabriel. Neither had returned her calls. She'd tried emailing them. Nothing. Maybe they were truly finished with her. Maybe somebody had gotten to them.

Maybe the Argentine military.

A woman wearing baggy mom jeans waddled into the kitchen. She was bent over a toddler stumbling between her legs. Her hair obscured her face. Only when she looked up did Ainsley recognize her: Deirdre, the host of the party. She and Ainsley had been party girls, years ago, back in the days of flirting and free cocktails.

Those days were gone forever. The only parties Deirdre was throwing now were the ones where all the guests were two feet high and drank from plastic sippy cups.

"Very good," she was saying to the boy, "... now careful ... watch out ... you don't want to hurt yourself."

Ainsley sipped her soda and smiled. In some ways, it felt good to be back, here in middle-class America, where nobody was ever kidnapped or disappeared against her will. Where discovering cat vomit on the sofa was the lowest point of the week.

Deirdre looked up, smiling with a mother's delight. "So I heard that you were travelling somewhere. Like, in Central America or something."

"A bit further south."

"How exciting. I wish we had time to go travelling." She squeezed her child and turned her attention back to him. "But what would this little manly man do without me? What would he do?" She nuzzled his cheek.

"He could go with you," Ainsley said.

She looked startled by the suggestion. "Do you think so? I don't know. I think he would probably like it here better."

The little boy found his legs and stumbled back into the living room, where a small nursery had been set up.

Deirdre craned her neck to check on him. Then, satisfied, she turned back to Ainsley. "So what are you going to do now?"

"I'm kind of between jobs," said Ainsley.

Deirdre's expression hardened. "So maybe now's the time to try meet someone new and settle down."

"That's not on the menu at the moment."

"Why not?"

"I've got a lot of things going on," Ainsley lied.

"If you really need a job, Matt can see if there's anything open at his credit union," Deirdre offered. "They have PPO coverage."

Ainsley hemmed. "I'm not sure that would be the right place for me."

But her friend wouldn't be deterred. "You should think about it," she said. "There's not a lot of time left, you know. We're getting older."

Ainsley excused herself and wandered out of the kitchen. She didn't need the extra pressure right now. She was barely holding herself together anyways.

It didn't get any better in the living room. One by one, the mothers approached Ainsley, introduced themselves, and asked about her travels. Word had leaked out somehow, as it always does, and Ainsley realized that she'd probably been the topic of several coffee klatches.

She mouthed the usual explanations. Yes, she had an amazing time abroad. No, she wasn't posting the pictures on social media. Yes, the travelling was finished for now. No, another job wasn't out of the question.

But their questions kept piling on, and soon Ainsley felt the pressure building behind her eyeballs. She excused herself, ran upstairs into the spare bathroom, and locked it behind her.

# CHAPTER FORTY-FIVE

There, Ainsley tripped over the kiddie toilet on the floor. She cursed the thing and kicked it aside.

Then she turned on the faucet, planted her hands on either side of the sink, and looked at herself in the mirror.

She couldn't fault these mothers. They were sweet and supportive, every one of them, almost to a fault. But they had a narrow viewpoint. And that viewpoint would become Ainsley's present and future, if she stayed here.

That thought made her head feel even worse.

She opened her purse, looking for her ibuprofen. She noticed an unfamiliar piece of paper, folded into quarters, at the bottom of her purse.

As she unfolded it, she recognized it. It was the slip of paper that Bernabé had handed her just before he'd returned to Uruguay.

She read the name again. *Marcelo Carrazo*. The owner of the Zorro vein of rhodochrosite. Bernabé had included the man's phone number and address.

He lived in Patagonia.

The phone call happened as though someone else were

acting through her. Ainsley watched her fingers fly across the numbers of her keypad, first the international country code, then the area code, then the number itself. She felt the phone pressed against her ear.

A deep male voice answered. "*Hola?*"

She paused. Her Spanish had deserted her. Then something shifted in her mind, and she found her second tongue. "Is this Marcelo Carrazo?"

"It is. Who is calling?"

"My name is Ainsley Walker."

Outside the door, a child started to bang fiercely against the bathroom door. Annoyed, Ainsley climbed into the bathtub and slid shut the translucent door.

"Why are you calling?" the man said.

The banging on the bathroom door grew stronger. Ainsley plugged her finger into her other ear. "Someone told me," she explained, "that you are the owner of the Zorro rhodochrosite mine."

"No, I'm just a poor rancher."

"No, that's not what I was told."

"Who did you talk to?"

"Bernabé Gradin."

There was another silence. "So you are the girl working for *El Mono*."

"I am," she said, then corrected herself. "Actually, I used to. Not anymore."

The man sighed. "I was wondering if you would call me."

Ainsley's heart leapt against her shirt. She plunged on. "Do you know about Ovidio's necklace? The one from his mother?"

There was yet another silence. Ainsley wondered if the connection had failed. Then the man's spoke hestitantly: "Yes, I do."

"It was taken from your mine."

"I know."

There was another silence. Ainsley sensed that he was clamming up. Then it just came blurting out. "I feel like there is something you want to tell me, *Señor* Carrazo."

When Marcelo replied, his enunciation had become very precise. "Listen to me," he said. "I am going to tell you something very, very important."

"I am all ears," she said.

"They lied to him."

Ainsley lifted an eyebrow. "Who's they?"

"I can't tell you that over the telephone."

Ainsley jerked her head back, as if she'd been physically smacked. She could still hear the toddler banging on the door.

"You're joking."

"I'm not."

"Tell me more," she begged.

"I can't. I don't trust this instrument. There are too many ears listening."

She started to panic. "Marcelo, you are the person I have been looking for. How can we talk?"

"Come down here, and we can talk. Did Bernabé give you my address?"

He had. Ainsley looked at the piece of paper. Marcelo lived in Patagonia. The rugged, southern province of Argentina, where only the hardiest souls could travel.

"He did," she said, "but that's going to be difficult for a lot of reasons."

"Yes, and by design. I don't need those *porteño* assholes killing my peace."

"I'm in North America right now."

She could almost hear the shrug. "If you show up, I will be here."

"I'll try to make it. But it's a long journey."

"I will welcome you, and we will talk about many things."

"But—"

"If you can't get here, then I will be here anyways, living my life. Good luck."

The line disconnected. Ainsley was completely still, in a state of shock. Her eyes looked straight ahead without seeing anything.

She was thinking.

From a practical perspective, returning to Argentina made zero sense. She'd been fired from her only job in the country and been paid nothing for the trouble. Nobody in Buenos Aires was returning her calls. And the journey wasn't safe, since the military had already forced her out of the country, presumably for sticking her nose into a place where it didn't belong.

But from an emotional perspective, returning to Argentina made perfect sense. It would give Ainsley an excuse to postpone her return to an American life. She could keep searching for Ovidio's necklace. If she were lucky, she could possibly even find it, and redeem herself in his eyes. And most of all, she would feel a sense of completion. She hated leaving tasks unfinished, especially when it hadn't been her decision to abandon them.

She pondered the choices. It was going to be tough to ignore her emotions.

Ainsley climbed out of the bathtub and opened the bathroom door. Deirdre was standing there with her little boy. He streaked past her to the kiddie toilet.

"I'm sorry he was being so loud," Deirdre said, "but Matthew has to go really bad."

Ainsley zipped her purse shut and slung it over her shoulder. She looked her friend in the eyes.

"So do I," she said.

PATAGONIA

# CHAPTER FORTY-SIX

With the television volume loud enough to rattle her seat, Ainsley couldn't believe that anybody on this bus was sleeping.

She was staring at a flatscreen that had been mounted at the front of the coach, just above the windshield. Onscreen, a martial arts star from the nineties was delivering a round-house kick to a quartet of enemies. Every strike sounded as loud as a gunshot.

Ainsley was back in Argentina.

A week and a half after being expelled, she was heading to Patagonia on an overnight bus. The return hadn't been easy.

There had been two major concerns: money and immigration officials. In short, she needed more of the first, less of the second.

She still had two thousand dollars left, but the flight cost fifteen hundred. That left her with five hundred dollars in her wallet.

To solve this problem, Ainsley had hit upon the solution of flying to Uruguay first. In that country, she still had a plastic bag of thousands of pesos that she'd dropped into an outhouse toilet during a stressful moment on her previous adventure. If she could recover that money, she'd be set.

And that's exactly what had happened. Another long flight, a quick rental car in Montevideo, a five-hour drive up to Artigas, a return to Guarasquil, and an afternoon socializing with the village.

Before she had left that country, she'd instructed the people of the village to haul the money out of the toilet, clean it, and repackage it. They'd done so. Ainsley had counted every peso, and nothing had been missing. They loved her. She had seen that their stolen treasure, El Árbol Negro, was returned to them.

The second reason for going to Uruguay was more bureaucratic. Ainsley suspected that officials at Ezeiza airport in Buenos Aires would be on the lookout for her return. The worst-case scenario was that her passport would be flagged, if the military wielded that type of influence.

But she discovered something else: the Argentine national immigration system was very, very uncoordinated. Quick research had shown her many people, mostly American and British expatriates, posting long screeds online about how inefficient the country's computer systems were, how the provincial offices had poor access to central records in the capital.

And so that's why she'd taken the Buquebus—again—across the Rio de la Plata. To arrive by sea increased her chances of slipping through the net. She'd walked down the plank, held her breath, and handed her passport to the lady official at the immigration desk.

"Welcome back to Argentina," the woman had said, stamping it.

Ainsley had practically sprinted across the lobby with the hanging bulbous lamps, past the spot where Nadia's driver had held up a sign, past the bar where she'd met Bernabé and Hector, outside to the taxi stand.

Back again. Victorious.

She'd zipped across Buenos Aires to the Retiro bus station, where she'd purchased a ticket on an overnight bus to Patagonia. It was a twenty-three-hour-long journey.

And that's where she was now, on the seventeenth hour of the haul, trying in vain to get some shuteye.

She pushed earplugs into her ears, cranked her seat back to an almost full recline, and yanked the curtain around her makeshift bed. It was a sleeper seat. This bus was remarkably well equipped, especially when a ticket only cost a hundred and thirty dollars, which included three meals with alcohol.

But sleep wasn't coming. Ainsley became more and more convinced that the Argentine government had sprinkled caffeine into the national water supply.

She cranked her seat back up to a sitting position, clicked on the light, and pulled out her e-reader.

Before she left America, Ainsley had loaded up on books about the dirty war. After all, she'd had lots of empty transportation time, first on the plane, then on the boat, now on the bus.

What she read gave her the shivers.

The Argentine navy considered itself the protector of civilization. And as such, the navy was—and is—proud that they gave the prisoners Pentothal before tossing them out of airplanes. That was the civilized way to kill someone, they argued.

She looked up from the screen, alarmed. Maybe that's what they'd injected her with. And they'd even loaded her onto an airplane too. Fortunately, they'd skipped the last step.

Ainsley went back to the text. The Argentine navy often boasts of its European roots, and most of the officers speak more than one European language. It's consistent with the myth that Argentines have created about themselves: that an accident of geography has placed these Italian, Spanish, and British people, all white-skinned, in the middle of what they perceive as a sea of barbarism. Ainsley learned that they even deride their Peruvian and Brazilian neighbors, those of indigenous or African heritage, as *cabecitas negras*, or "little black heads".

"Coffee, coffee," said a voice. Ainsley looked up. A steward was walking down the aisle with a tray of paper cups and an aluminum thermos. Ainsley took one with cream and sugar.

She returned to the text. During the dirty war, the navy's treatment of the prisoners veered from abusive to friendly. Some prisoners broke during torture, and subsequently went out into the street with the guards to point out and turn in their *compañeros*. Some of the prisoners even stayed in the navy for years afterwards, adopted the rigid mindset, forgot their subversive past, and rose through the ranks of one of the most reactionary organizations in modern memory.

Ainsley was especially curious about the female prisoners. She was surprised to learn that rape wasn't common. Even more surprising was the fact that the female prisoners had been sometimes asked out to dinner by the guards, who had used the opportunity to vent, over plates of pasta and glasses of wine, that their relationships with women had been destroyed by the demands of the *junta*.

How absurd.

Furthermore, the guards and officers had secretly admired the female prisoners. These prisoners were usually members of the *Montoneras*, the urban Peronist guerilla group. They were free-thinkers, often university students, and could discuss books, travel, movies, politics. The officers' wives, on the other hand, were usually from other navy families, had been raised decoratively, and often didn't know how to talk about anything at all.

Once in a while, Ainsley learned, after a few such dinners with a handsome officer, a female prisoner sometimes ended up falling in love.

Ainsley tried to imagine how those dates must have ended, back at the prison. A romantic kiss at the door of the cell, a blindfold slipped sensually across her eyes, handcuffs clicked onto her wrists, and the cell door closed gently behind her. The torturer's gentle farewell: *Good night, my dear, let's meet again Tuesday, no, wait, I'm scheduled to electrocute your cellmate that night...*

Marriages had even occurred this way, which seemed utterly ludicrous.

Ainsley was still thinking about that as the sun began to rise at the far edge of the horizon, and the bus began to slow down.

# CHAPTER FORTY-SEVEN

*Holy mother of God*, Ainsley thought.

The wind.

It howled around her like the screams of the spirits of the dead. She pulled her knitted wool hat lower over her ears. It was a new addition to her wardrobe back in the States, a cutesy blue and green number. She'd thought it would be perfect.

She couldn't have been more wrong. Loosely-knitted fabric was useless in the face of wind like this.

The bus had stopped, and Ainsley stepped out onto a plain. It wasn't a typical plain, the type that ended in a row of hills, or a line of trees, or an ocean, or a developed subdivision.

This plain didn't end.

She squinted her eyes and spun around. The land stretched out to the horizon, in every direction, seemingly forever. It was carpeted in a gray-green vegetation, no more than a few centimeters high.

This was Patagonia.

The temperature was typical of a spring day, but that bastard wind made it feel nearer to freezing.

She was standing on Route 40, the main thoroughfare through southern Argentina. The bus had stopped in front of a small tavern. It was the only structure within sight for a hundred miles. A single gasoline pump was stationed outside of it.

Tucking her chin into her coat, Ainsley headed across the pebbles towards the door.

Inside, she stamped her feet, ripped off the hat, and shook off the wind. Then she studied the room.

A long copper bar stretched along one wall. A ceramic penguin filled with peanuts sat forlornly on its countertop. A photo of Martín Fierro hung on the wall. There were a few wooden tables arranged on the other side of the room.

In the middle stood an empty salad bar. An unplugged electric cord lay coiled on the floor next to it. The scooped-out plastic containers that once held soft vegetables now held bolts, washers, electrical cords. Someone's dream of serving fresh salads had bitten the dust. It seemed that there were higher priorities down here, at the far end of the world.

A middle-aged man with a moustache like a turn-of-the-century Frenchman waved to Ainsley. He was standing behind the bar, filing a fingernail.

"Do you have the piece?" he said.

Ainsley drew a blank. "I don't know what you're talking about."

"You came on the bus?"

"Yes."

"The catalytic converter? I ordered it from Buenos Aires a week ago."

"How am I supposed to know?" Ainsley said.

"Did you see anybody put it into the luggage compartment?"

This man was practical. Ainsley immediately sensed that everybody was expected to pitch in here.

"No, I didn't. Do you want me to check?"

"Never mind," he said, "I'll do it myself."

He rapped on the bartop with determined knuckles. Then he went outside. A gust of wind blew through the room until the door swung closed behind him.

Ainsley was alone in the small tavern now. She could hear the wind howling, the bus idling outside. Apparently nobody else was getting off at this stop.

She needed to call Marcelo. She pulled out her phone and turned it on. There was no service. She didn't know if it was because she'd failed to convert the phone back to Argentina's standards, or because there just weren't any cell phone towers.

Then she heard a heavy clunk against the wall. Alarmed, Ainsley went outside.

A huge automotive part was leaning against the outside of the tavern. It hadn't been there a minute ago. The tavern owner was shaking out his arms as though he'd just dropped a huge stack of weights.

Behind him, the bus driver was closing the luggage compartment on the bus.

"That's the piece," he said.

"Can I use your phone?" Ainsley said.

"Of course. It's on the—" The tavern owner trailed off. He was studying the piece, his head cocked. "They sent the wrong one."

He turned around and ran towards the bus. The driver had just closed the door on the coach.

Ainsley went inside, leaned over the bar to retrieve the phone, and dialed Marcelo's number. The line rang several times before someone picked up.

"Hello," said the voice.

"I'm here," she said.

"Who is this?"

"Ainsley Walker."

"You're in Patagonia?"

"Yes. I just got off the bus."

He paused. "Are you at the tavern?"

"Yes."

"Don't go anywhere. I'll come pick you up."

*Don't go anywhere*: that was funny. Ainsley hung up the phone and parked herself at a table and stared out the window at the dreamy landscape. The only trees in sight—a row of seven poplars near the window—were bent at a thirty-degree angle. The wind had kicked up a brown dust cloud in the fields. But she felt warm and protected.

Ainsley heard the bus pull away. The owner returned from the outside. He washed his hands in the sink.

"Goddamn them," he said. "In Patagonia we help each other. That *porteño* bastard wouldn't even put the piece back inside. Now I have to pay someone else to ship it back."

He shut the water off with a forceful twist. Ainsley shrugged. Maybe life down here, at the end of the world, wasn't that much different from life anywhere else.

"Maté?" he said.

"Sure," said Ainsley. This place was making her feel oddly safe. Certain rooms did that. Maybe it was the harshness of the weather outside.

"Sweet or bitter?"

"However you like it."

He boiled the water, went through the steps of the ritual, then came out from behind the bar. She took the first drink. The owner seemed to like it bitter. When she was done, he filled the *calabash* a second time and drank.

Neither said anything. Ainsley decided to wait for him to

open the next part of the conversation. Country people never like chatterboxes.

It took three refills before he started talking again. "I can't get Volkswagen parts anywhere down here," he said, "and the order from Buenos Aires takes a week to ten days to arrive."

"That's too bad."

He nodded, wiped his face. "My brother offered me his Renault 12, but I didn't want to take it. Maybe that was a mistake."

Ainsley said nothing. She checked her watch and wondered how long it would be before Marcelo arrived.

"So what are you here for?"

"Adventure travel," she said. It was adjacent to the truth, and it was plausible. Most foreigners came to Patagonia for mountain-climbing or skiing.

"This time of year?"

"Sure."

"But the winds..."

Ainsley thought fast. "I got a discounted deal on the trip." Then she drank the maté a little too fast and coughed.

He waited until she'd recovered.

The man changed subjects. "You should try to listen to the whales."

"Where?"

"At the coast. You can camp just a few meters from the water. The whales come right up to the beach and sing."

"Beautiful."

An hour passed like this, the man recommending activities for Ainsley. He brought out some *alfajores*, Argentina's favorite cookies, two pieces of thin shortbread pressed together with *dulce de leche* and dusted with powdered sugar. They went through three pots of water and even more trips to the bathroom. Nobody entered the tavern.

Two hours later, Ainsley heard the sound of an engine motoring up. Then it turned off, and the door slammed.

The tavern owner had cocked an ear. "I don't know the sound of that door."

A burst of wind announced that the motorist had entered the tavern. He was about sixty years old but carried himself like a man half that age. A shock of white hair curled out from beneath his jaunty black beret. He wore a red corduroy jacket, a heavy gray sweater, another shirt, and a bright yellow ascot. His skin was tanned and his face was lined.

"Ainsley Walker?" he said.

"Marcelo," replied the tavern owner, standing. "*Macanudo*. You dog."

"Don't bother me now," said Marcelo. "My life can't tolerate another problem."

"Is your herd still living?"

"Yes, and it's a miracle. I'm thinking of getting out of this game."

"You should, while you're still young," said the owner.

Marcelo didn't laugh. "You're a comedian. Now I know why I don't come here." He turned to Ainsley. "Are you ready to go?"

She looked at the tavern owner. "What do I owe you?"

He waved it away. "It's nothing. You're leaving with a legend of Patagonia. I owe him many favors."

Ainley didn't know how to take that. The comment was straddling on the line between sincerity and sarcasm. She thanked him anyways, picked up her purse, and followed Marcelo outside.

As they drove away, the tavern owner watched Ainsley through the window with curious eyes.

# CHAPTER FORTY-EIGHT

Ainsley sat in the passenger seat of Marcelo's Toyota Hilux 4 x 4, a practical vehicle for these parts.

He accelerated quickly up to freeway speeds, despite the fact that they were riding on a rough gravel road. Marcelo kept a firm grip on the steering wheel, adjusting to every small change in the gravel below.

Ainsley stared outside the window. The landscape was both romantic and terrifying. The entire Patagonian steppe was covered in a thin layer of shingle. It was comprised mostly of pebbles known as *rodados patagonicas*. She could hear them being kicked up against the undercarriage of the truck. They were the reminders of the awesome crushing power of glaciers.

Her ears detected music playing at a low level from the speakers. "You get stations out here?"

"Satellite radio," said Marcelo. "It's the only option."

That made Ainsley feel miserable for a moment. She couldn't afford satellite radio back in the United States.

Then she wondered if it was too soon to thank Marcelo

for his hospitality. But then she guessed that everybody was hospitable out in the boondocks.

Ainsley cleared her throat. "So can we talk?"

Marcelo shook his head. "Not yet. There will be time later. For now, just watch."

He pointed ahead. Ahead lay a hill, as gray and wrinkled as the dome of an elephant's head. The road spun up and over it, and Marcelo seemed to accelerate around its bends. He was clearly comfortable on these roads.

As they crested the hill, Ainsley saw that they had risen to the next plateau. This one was a ragged patchwork of red, yellow, ochre. Stripes of pink, yellow, and brown were splashed across rocks that had been pushed up out of the earth.

And overseeing everything was a majestic mountain range.

It rose from the land like Poseidon out of the sea. The peaks were serrated, like vicious sawteeth; the flanks were streaked with white snow and gray-brown boulders, the lower slopes covered in smaller foothills. She had the dizzying sense that it affected the weather.

"*La cordillera*," he said.

Then it finally hit her. These were the Andes, the so-called "spine" of South America. Turning her head, she watched the mountains stretch out forever in either direction.

They inspired something within, an excitement deep in her soul. It was the first time she'd been affected like this by anything in nature.

Marcelo must've known, because he said nothing. He was letting Ainsley have the moment.

"I'm just... it's ..." she stuttered, before lapsing into stunned silence. Her eyes drank in the textured slopes. Her ears listened to the sound of the bits of gravel flinging under the car, her stomach felt the gentle rise and fall in the road.

"Do you still feel like this?" she finally said. "After living here for years?"

"Every day. It keeps me young."

"It looks like I could reach out and touch them."

"They are seventy kilometers away."

Ainsley stared again. She would've estimated less than a quarter of that. She guessed that the visibility was due to the clean air. With zero pollution, the world could be seen in crisp, pristine detail.

The Toyota tore across the plateau, up and over several more hills, moving ever closer to the mountains. Ainsley could feel the atmosphere change. It felt somehow more electric, more dangerous.

Then Marcelo cranked the wheel to the left and pulled past a wire gate into a driveway. A hundred meters down, in a small bowl nestled between the bare scrubby hills, was a small ranch.

"My home," said Marcelo.

He pulled up to the house, which was made of concrete blocks. The roof looked like it had been cobbled together with spare parts. It had probably been constructed by hand.

She stepped out of the car and observed the ranch. There wasn't much to it. An open field behind the house looked like it was used for grazing. An empty corral lay nearby. There were hoofprints in the moistened dirt near the trough, evidence of recent activity.

One thing was missing. She didn't see any cows.

"Where are your cattle?" Ainsley asked.

Marcello approached a horse had been tied to the fence. He patted its flank and checked its shoes. "My *gauchos* took them up to summer pastures four days ago," he said. "I'm heading up there now to check on them."

"On horseback?"

He shook his head. "I'm too old for that now. You and I will drive. We can talk there." He glanced at her. "There is someone I want you to meet too."

Ainsley felt relief for two reasons. One, that she would finally learn the secrets of Ovidio's rhodochrosite. Two, that she wouldn't be forced into a saddle. Horses had held no romance for her, not since she'd been bucked at summer camp in middle school and shattered her left arm.

"Just let me clean up a few things first," he said.

"Do you need any help?"

"No, please," he said, "you're a guest."

She watched Marcelo move around the ranch, washing out buckets, hoisting bales of hay. It was hard to believe that he was considered a senior citizen. Ainsley realized that a life of physical labor either broke you or made you stronger.

Then Ainsley heard a car pull up behind her. She turned. It was another Toyota HiLux. A man climbed out from behind the wheel. He was dressed in a blue denim shirt, patched purple trousers, and an English bowler hat. He was the kind of guy who made Ainsley smile just by looking at him. She imagined that Patagonia was packed with such eccentrics. You had to be, to want to live in such an environment.

Marcelo saw the man and shook his head. "No."

"Please," said the visitor.

"*No.*"

"But my sheep have already arrived."

Marcelo picked up several shovels from the muck and arranged them in his tool shed. "We shared a ride last year," he explained, "and you made me wait two extra days while you tried to learn how to fix a fence. I can't afford to waste that time again."

The visitor betrayed a guilty smile. "I have no skills. Please wait for me."

"The answer is no," said Marcelo again. Then he gestured to Ainsley. "Say hello to my guest from the United States."

The eccentric nodded at her. There were no kissed greetings down here at the end of the world.

"Who are you?" asked Ainsley.

"I am the Englishman," he said.

"Is that all?"

He cracked a wide grin. He was missing several front teeth. "My grandfather built the railroad."

"And he won't stop reminding people about it," said Marcelo.

The Englishman reached into his pocket and pulled out a small bird. It had a broken wing. "This is my new friend. I found her yesterday. Her name is Maria." He lifted the bird up to his face, then turned it to face Ainsley. "Say hello to the beautiful *yanqui*."

The bird flapped its one remaining wing in a valiant effort to escape. The Englishman gently stuffed the bird back into his pocket.

"I care for all living things," he said sadly, "but living things don't care for me."

"Including your sheep," said Marcelo.

"I only lost four this winter," the Englishman replied. "It was a good year. Maybe I'm going to get rich after all."

These guys had known each other a long time, and their comedic jousting had been developed over a lot of years. Out here, they probably had to put in extra effort to be good neighbors. It was all too easy for people to turn reclusive and lose their minds.

"Are you ready to go?" said Marcelo to Ainsley.

"I'm in your hands," she said.

"Please," said the Englishman, "just wait until tomorrow." He was following Marcelo across the yard like a puppy. "I can be ready by the morning."

"Why don't you do me a favor for once?" said Marcelo. "I'm always doing things for you."

"Like what?"

"Two years ago, I repaired your fence when you were sick with pneumonia."

The Englishman giggled. "Yes, that's true."

"The year before that, I shot the puma that was eating your sheep. It took me two days of hunting."

"Oh yes, I forgot about that."

"And ten years ago I chased down that *peon* who stole your equipment."

"Okay," said the Englishman. "It's true. I owe you."

Marcelo slung a couple of duffle bags into the back of his Toyota. "We're going now. You can hang around if you want, but don't go inside my house."

"But I like your sofa," said the Englishman.

"Then make one for yourself."

"It's too much work. When will you be back?"

"Tomorrow. Don't go inside for any reason. Understand?"

The Englishman nodded.

Ainsley climbed into the passenger seat again. As Marcelo pulled away from his own property, the Englishman was waving goodbye.

"He is a lunatic," said Marcelo, "and a very bad shepherd."

"But he has a good heart," Ainsley said.

"True. That's why I let him hang around my ranch. But he loves to look through my house." Marcelo thought for a minute. "Honestly, I'm surprised that he's survived as long as he has."

A simple door lock could solve this problem, Ainsley

thought, but apparently such a device was unheard of in Patagonia.

"Anyways," he said, "buckle your seat belt. This isn't an easy ride."

# CHAPTER FORTY-NINE

Ainsley stared at the puddle of yellow gruel on the ground. It had issued from her own mouth just a few seconds earlier. The bitter taste of stomach acid was still on her tongue.

She was on her hands and knees, at the edge of a road dug into the side of the Andes, at more than two thousand meters altitude.

Ainsley had been able to tolerate the drive for a while, with Marcelo wheeling the steering column left, then right, then left, then right, up the endless switchbacks towards the higher reaches of the *cordillera*. But after an hour, Ainsley began to feel queasy, and then she'd mumbled something.

He'd stopped fast, nearly pushed her out. And now she was kneeling at the rim of the road, looking out over the Patagonian steppe, one of the grandest vistas in South America, with a thin trail of vomit decorating the outside of her cheek.

She watched an ugly black dot circle far below her. She squinted harder. It was a condor. Then she felt the wind kick up.

"The altitude does it to everybody," called Marcelo from inside the car. The engine was still running.

"Yeah," she said.

"Why don't you come back inside? We're almost there."

She stood up, wiped off her cheek on her sleeve, and returned to the car. He continued the winding drive but took the turns more slowly. "You'll feel better when we reach Lago de Miel," he said.

"What is that?"

"The place we are going. Where my cows spend their summers. It's green and watered. No frost. It's beautiful."

"How many cows do you have have?"

"One hundred and seventeen. Not many. Just a small *criancero*. They're weak and ugly. I don't even know how much longer I'll keep doing this. My son wants me to move in with him in Bahía Blanca."

Ainsley craned her head, gazing at the escarpments, the mountain walls. She tried to imagine herself pushing a hundred and seventeen cows up the steep trails on the flanks of this mountain range. She couldn't. It was unimaginable.

Marcelo was more amiable now, speaking openly of life on the Patagonian steppe. It was harsh, he said, but one that he had chosen over twenty-five years ago, so he had no reason to regret anything. The soil was thin, making it a difficult place to raise livestock. He was especially grateful for rainfall; when it didn't occur, he had to buy imported hay to feed the cattle, which was expensive.

"What about the wind?" Ainsley said. "How do you deal with it?"

"It doesn't blow like this all the time," he said. "In fact, it's supposed to end very soon."

Eventually they pulled out of the switchbacks, and Ainsley heaved a sigh of relief. No sooner had the road levelled out, however, than Marcelo cranked the Toyota onto an unmarked sideroad and into a field of boulders. The truck hurtled down a twisty but level path. It was nothing more than a barely marked cat track.

Ainsley admired the giant chunks of schist, each plopped there like a demented sculpture by a demented deity. Then she clutched the handle and shut her eyes. Her stomach was feeling queasy again. She didn't want to make Marcelo stop a second time.

Then the car stopped. "We're here," he said. "You can open your eyes."

She did.

They were parked in an enormous natural bowl, its gentle flanks covered in a carpet of lush green grass. A crystal-blue lagoon lay before her, as serene as a yogi.

It was beautiful.

Ainsley stepped out of the vehicle and drank in the scenery. The wind had stopped for the moment, and the air was fragrant with lavender. A few hundred meters to the left, at the edge of the lake, were a herd of skinny black cows, their heads bent to the earth, mouths working hungrily.

"They are so happy here," said the cattleman, watching them. "Pitiful but happy." He sighed, then smiled. "Lago de Miel."

"It's amazing," she replied.

"We spend four months a year here. I wish it could be more."

Then Marcelo began walking towards his herd, whistling loudly. Another whistle sounded in response.

Ainsley spotted the source of the response. Two *gauchos* were on horseback in the middle of the herd. They were dressed in checked shirts, berets, and *bombachos*, the classic short balloon pants of the region.

As he drew closer, Marcelo and the men exchanged some

information in fast ranch hand Spanish, half of which Ainsley couldn't begin to understand. Then Marcelo returned to her.

"The drive went well," he said. "We only lost two."

"The men couldn't find them?"

He walked two fingers over an imaginary cliff and dropped them, whistling. "They're gone."

Ainsley noticed the *gauchos* staring at her. Marcelo shouted at them, "She is not for you, bastards."

The two men cackled grotesquely, their toothless mouths spread open. They were pure country spirits.

"No living Christian would love them," muttered Marcelo. "That's why they live with cows instead."

Ainsley stared at the *gauchos* wheeling their steeds through the grass, applying a touch of heel here, a clipped syllable there. Watching a real equestrian wheel his bay around an open field was one of the more compelling sights on earth. The horses responded to every direction willingly. It looked as though the men had been poured into their saddles.

"They're really good," she said.

"That's what I pay them for."

"Can you ride like that?" she said.

"Never," said Marcelo, shaking his head. "You have to be born on a horse. No, I'm just the owner. You?"

"Beginner, basically."

He nodded. "This territory is a bad place to start. It's good that you don't have to ride."

"That's true," she agreed. Ainsley didn't know what she would do if she were asked to mount a horse.

Marcelo gazed at his herd, his hands on his hips. Satisfied, he grunted, clapped his hands once, then turned to his guest. "Now, *Señorita* Walker, are you ready to talk to me?"

"I literally flew halfway around the world to talk to you," she replied.

"I'm flattered. It will be worth your effort."

"Oh, it had better be."

He crooked a finger. "Follow me. I want you to meet somebody."

# CHAPTER FIFTY

They strode across the grass, through the bellowing cattle. The smell of clover nearly suffocated Ainsley. She admired the white wisps of clouds scudding across the sky. They seemed almost within arm's reach. It felt like heaven on earth.

"I have not always been a rancher," said Marcelo, "as you know."

"Indeed," she said.

"I used to own a mine in Capillas. It never did very well."

"The Zorro mine," she said.

"Yes. Because we found that single vein of the rhodochrosite with a distinctive Z."

"Bernabé told me."

"People think I was sitting on a lot of that rhodochrosite. I wasn't. We only found enough to make about six or seven hundred pieces. And they didn't even sell very well."

"They were a curiosity," offered Ainsley.

"Exactly," he said. "So then I marketed them in the catalogs as Zorro stones. The name was my invention. I thought it was sexy, would make them sell more quickly."

"Did they?"

"No. A year later, I had sold only a few. I thought the vein was a failure."

Marcelo was overcome with sadness for a moment. He stared off at the peaks. Then he recovered himself.

"Then, one day, I received an interesting call. It was from a man who had seen the Zorro advertisement in one of the catalogs. He wanted to know how many were available. I asked him how many he wanted. He said that he was looking for three hundred. I said yes, we have three hundred, and gave him the quote. He agreed, said it was a reasonable price."

"And?"

"And when I asked for his name or address, he refused to give them to me. He said that he didn't want them to be shipped, that it wasn't safe. He wanted to pick them up personally."

"Really."

"So we agreed upon a day and time that he would come by the office in Capillas. I didn't think he would come."

"Did he?"

"Yes, at that precise minute. He was about my age, maybe thirty, blonde hair, dressed in a casual sweater and pants, but looking very uncomfortable. We greeted one another. I introduced myself by name. He said he was pleased to meet me but didn't offer his own name. He was handsome and seemed a little arrogant. He didn't want to waste any time. In my office, we made the exchange. He gave me the pesos, and I gave him the box of stones. He examined them, and I could tell that he was thinking about many things. Then he asked me an interesting question."

"What was it?" said Ainsley.

"The man said, 'If you knew you were going to die, would you give this distinctive rhodochrosite to your children?'"

Ainsley's stomach plunged into her shoes. She sensed that she was standing on the edge of something that was much, much bigger than just Ovidio. She felt like a poor fisherman in the boat glimpsing the dim outline of a battleship as it emerged out of a fog.

"That's exactly what Ovidio's mother did," she said, gasping. "It was her favorite necklace before she disappeared."

"I know that story," he said. "Now look."

Marcelo had led her up the grassy slope to the lip of the bowl. As they crested the rise, she felt her breath being sucked away, again. On the other side was a tremendous panorama, a vista of peaks, valleys, blue-green lakes, and far below, the flat gray Patagonian steppe spread out like a matte background.

Then she spotted something else. A tiny cabin. It was down the slope, just a hundred meters away. It had been built out of oil cans and plywood.

"What is that?" she asked.

"My summer resort," Marcelo said. "I'm joking. The gauchos sleep there. They used to camp during the summers, but not anymore. They're spoiled now."

Ainsley didn't see the point yet. "So why are we going there?"

"Because inside is someone I want you to meet."

He led Ainsley to the door and pushed it open.

The hut was primitive at best. There was a table, two chairs, and a cot. The sour scent of men's sleeping quarters assailed Ainsley's nostrils.

Sitting on the edge of cot was a third *gaucho*, stropping a knife against a piece of leather. He had a heavy beard, but beneath it, his face betrayed his relative youth. He was probably only in his mid-thirties. A flick of his eyes was his only acknowledgment of his visitors.

"This is Cristiano," said Marcelo. "He has worked for me

for almost fifteen years. He stays up here in the summer watching the cattle. Don't try to speak to him. He is a mute."

Ainsley tried to catch his eye, but he stayed resolutely down, on the stropping.

"Cristiano lost his mother in the dirty war too," said Marcelo, "just like Ovidio. He never met her, just like Ovidio. And he has one thing to remember her by: her favorite necklace. It was given to his adoptive parents."

Ainsley felt a heat coming over her face, the white-hot knowledge of everything, of what she was about to see, of what Marcelo's next words would be, of the truth about this fascinating but horrible chapter of Argentine history.

Marcelo placed one hand on the man's shoulder. His other hand went to the man's chest, reached inside his shirt, and produced a necklace.

"Look," he said.

"No," said Ainsley.

"Look," he commanded. "You need to see this."

She knelt down before Cristiano and took his necklace in her hand. She already knew what she was going to see.

Around his neck hung a Zorro rhodochrosite.

# CHAPTER FIFTY-ONE

Ainsley held the cabochon in her hand, her eyes staring through it. She listened to her heartbeat quickening. She was mere inches from Cristiano's face. She could smell his clothing, his musky animal scent. He kept his eyes down.

She stayed there for what felt like minutes. She was obsessed with a single thought that kept pinging around her brain.

Marcelo seemed to read her mind. "It was a shock for me too," he said, "when I learned about Ovidio."

"Somebody lied to both of them."

Marcelo nodded. "And there are more."

"How many?" Ainsley said. Her voice was a raggedy whisper.

"Fourteen, so far."

Fourteen. So it was a system of lies. Ainsley stuffed the necklace back into the gaucho's shirt. Then she stood up. "Who have you told?"

"Nobody," said Marcelo.

"Not one person?"

"You are the first."

"And you don't know who that mysterious buyer was?"

"I have no idea. But today I realize that he must've been part of the junta."

Outside the cabin, somebody whistled, piercing the alpine solitude. Marcelo cocked an ear. It sounded like one of the other *gauchos*.

Marcelo stepped outside. Ainsley followed him. She didn't want to be alone in a remote cabin with a bearded mute sharpening a knife.

One of the other *gauchos* was outside, astride his horse. The animal was short-legged but powerful, its coat a glossy chestnut.

"What is it?" said Marcelo.

The *gaucho* was looking back anxiously at something.

"The Englishman is here," he said. "He wants to speak to you."

"Now?"

"He says it's important."

Marcelo seemed confused. "This is very strange. I didn't think he was driving up today." He turned to Ainsley. "Do you want to walk with me?"

"Absolutely," Ainsley said. She was glued to his side. She could feel the *gauchos* looking at her as though she were a side of roast beef. That's what years without women can do. She wasn't going to be the one to break their dry spells either.

She and the rancher trekked back over the lip, descended the gentle slope of the grassy bowl back to Lago de Miel. Then they followed the shore of the lake back to the Toyota.

As they drew closer, Ainsley could see that the Englishman's Toyota was parked next to theirs. The Englishman himself was wandering around the grass, bandy-legged, his purple patched pants and ridiculous bowler hat looking even more out of place in this windswept alpine valley.

"What's happening, *loco*?" said Marcelo.

"I have news, news, news," said the Englishman. His hands were nervously picking at stray threads on his pants.

"Tell me."

"I did something bad."

Marcelo rolled his eyes. "You went inside. I *knew* it."

"But I love your sofa."

"Build your own sofa!" said Marcelo. "That's *my* sofa. You really drove up here to tell me *that*?"

"Your phone was ringing," the Englishman said.

"And?"

"I answered your phone."

"That's *my* phone," said Marcelo. "Do you know the difference between *mine* and *yours*?"

The Englishman pulled the bird out off his pocket and began stroking it furiously with his thumb. Ainsley sensed just how much of a lunatic he really was.

Marcelo summoned all his patience. "Okay, my friend," he said, "someone was on the phone."

"Yes," said the lunatic.

"Who was it?"

"A man."

"Which man?"

"The man who runs the tavern."

Ainsley's heart skipped a beat. She'd just spent the morning drinking *mate* and getting tourist recommendations from him.

"What did the tavern owner say?"

"He wanted to know if the American was still with you."

"She is."

Shielding his eyes from the sun, the lunatic shepherd peered up at Ainsley. His squinty eyes creased his craggy face.

"Hello, American," he said.

"Hello," she replied.

Marcelo was losing patience. "Why did the tavern owner want to know about the American?"

The Englishman's nose twitched. "He said that there were some men asking about her." He grew serious. "They were *milicos*."

Ainsley felt her stomach drop to her shoes again. It had been doing that a lot today.

So the military had found her. Maybe through immigration. Maybe through the bus company. Maybe through Marcelo. She would never know how, and it didn't matter anyways. They had caught up with her.

Marcelo's face had turned white. "They were *milicos*. What did the tavern owner tell them?"

"That you had picked her up."

Marcelo grew very still. "Is there anything else the tavern owner told you?" he said. His voice was resolutely monotone.

The Englishman's thumb stopped stroking the bird. The insanity disappeared and his eyes seemed clear, intelligent, and very sad.

"They are coming up the road," he said, "to find both of you."

# CHAPTER FIFTY-TWO

Ainsley felt hot flashes of panic in her innards. She felt regret for everything. What was she doing back in Argentina? Why had she been stupid enough to return? She'd been selfish, pursuing her own desires.

Then she had an epiphany. She was like a poisonous invasive species. Anybody who touched her was going to get chased, pursued, disappeared. The government had even tried to eliminate the poisonous invader by inoculating her, then shipping her out.

Marcelo had softened. "You drove all this way to tell me that."

The Englishman's thumb was stroking the bird again. He had lapsed back into incoherence. There would be nothing more from him.

"I don't know how they found me," Ainsley said. "I was really careful."

"I had a feeling that from the moment I took your call that this would happen."

"What do you mean?"

"I think they've been watching me for a long time. Ever

since Ovidio became famous, when people began to talk about his necklace."

"Then we're both bad news," she said.

Marcelo's face grew ashen. He nodded. "The *milicos* don't drive up into the mountains just to chat."

He was right. Ainsley had already become acquainted with their tactics.

They both turned to face the Lago de Miel. For the first time, Ainsley could feel the frigidity of its waters on her face.

Marcelo was pondering the distant peaks beyond. "So maybe the bad news should leave for a while," he said.

"Where to?"

He pointed to the mountains. "There." He chewed on his lip. "In the worst-case scenario, they will be here in an hour. So we need to leave immediately."

"But how?"

Marcelo whistled to the *gauchos*. All three came galloping over, the first two on separate horses, and Cristiano on a third.

Marcelo addressed his three employees. "This is an emergency. We need to disappear into the mountains."

"Have a good time," said one.

"Don't take my matambre," said the other.

Marcelo drew a finger across his throat. "No, *all* of us must leave."

Suddenly the *gauchos* realized that he was serious. The smiles and ribald jokes were suddenly gone, replaced by silence and alarmed eyes.

"The American and I will take one horse. You two will double up. Cristiano keeps the third."

The two *gauchos* looked at each other. Then one dismounted and handed the reins to Marcelo.

"It's better for all of us to split up," he continued. "Whatever happens, do not return for at least two days."

"But the cattle," said one.

"Not important," said Marcelo. "We'll find them later. Now, we leave. Any questions?"

The three men stared at him in silence.

Marcelo clapped his hands. "Then go."

The *gaucho* helped the other onto his horse. Cristiano had already wheeled around and was cantering across the field.

"What about him?" said Ainsley. She was pointing at the Englishman. He was on his hands and knees, sniffing in the grass.

Marcelo sighed. "I don't know. We can't take three."

"But you can't leave him here."

"I know." Marcelo walked over to the Englishman. "*Loco*, you have to hide." The rancher tapped him on the back. "Get in your car and drive over there, in the rocks. Hide yourself."

The Englishman twitched his nose. "Have I told you about my father?"

Marcelo was running out of patience. He lifted the Englishman by the armpits, got his feet beneath him, then pushed him along back towards the field of schist. "Go back into those rocks and hide your car."

But the lunatic just stood there, petting his little bird.

Cursing under his breath, Marcelo handed Ainsley the horse's reins. "Wait here."

The rancher grabbed the Englishman by the arm and propelled him across the grass towards the Englishman's Toyota. They got into the vehicle, started the engine, and disappeared back into the field of rocks.

Ainsley stood there, holding the horse dumbly, listening to the wind whistling through the grass around her. This was all happening too quickly. She was having trouble processing it.

Ten minutes later, Marcelo reappeared on foot. "I just hope he stays there."

"Why?"

"That asshole keeps saying that he's a sheep, and he needs grass." He rolled his eyes. "I told you, it's a miracle that he's survived this long."

"Does he have any family?"

"None."

"What about your car?"

Marcelo looked pensive. "Just leave it. We've wasted enough time already." He managed a half-smile. "So are you ready to share a horse with me?"

"Where are we going?"

"I know someone. It's about three hours' ride away." The rancher gauged the sun. "We have just enough light left, if we leave now."

Marcelo hoisted himself easily onto the horse. He was still athletic for a sixtyish man. Then he leaned over and offered his hand. "Up here, *señorita*."

Ainsley swung her purse as far onto her back as possible. Then she took his hand, stuck her shoe into the stirrup, and pushed herself up.

A moment later, she found herself clinging to Marcelo, astride the steed's broad back.

"This is my best horse," he said.

"What's his name?"

"He doesn't have one."

Marcelo turned the horse around, kicked it in the flank. They took off, galloping across the grass. Ainsley saw the old rancher lift his hand towards his herd as they galloped out of the bowl—

—and further into the Andes.

# CHAPTER FIFTY-THREE

As they picked their way across the landscape, Ainsley held onto the rancher's corduroy jacket.

They had been riding for more than an hour. They'd splashed through shallow mountain creeks, the droplets of water backlit by the setting sun. They'd maneuvered around *calafate* bushes, whose sharp thorns had reached out and clawed at her jeans and boots.

Now they were moving through a sparse pine forest. Ainsley watched small basalt rocks skitter and roll under the horse's shoes.

Marcelo hadn't said a word. He was focused on the ride. Though he was skilled, Ainsley could sense that being in a saddle wasn't one hundred percent natural to him, the way it was to the *gauchos*.

Finally she hazarded a bit of conversation. "Where are we going exactly?"

"To a *puestero*," he said.

"What is that?"

"A hermit who lives up above the tree line."

"Is he a friend?"

"He is a hermit. He has no friends. I have only seen him from a distance, a hundred meters. That was three or four years ago. He might even be dead now."

"You're betting that the military doesn't follow us out here," she said.

"They won't," he said. "They can't follow us without a horse, and nobody could get a horse trailer up that road. The lack of hoofprints on the hard ground and multiple stream crossings would make it almost impossible to track us even if they did have one." He sighed. "We're safe as long as we stay out here."

That was true. Ainsley softened a little, knowing that their lives weren't entirely lost yet. But part of her wondered if the lunatic Englishman hadn't imagined the telephone call, if nobody at all were coming up the road to find them. If that were true, they were all going on an unnecessary sleepover out in the bush.

"You love it up here in the summers," said Ainsley.

"Yes, I do," said the rancher. "We call spending the season here the *veranada*. Anyone who doesn't love it must be dead inside. Unless the wind is blowing. Then it's a different story. The Mapuche thought it was our punishment from the *cordillera* for humanity's presence in the mountains."

"Do you believe that?"

"On the worst days, yes. It can be unbelievable."

Suddenly Marcelo pulled the horse up short. Dead ahead was a wide blue creek, swollen with the springtime snowmelt. Ainsley could feel its icy temperature even here, on the bank. And the current looked incredibly strong.

"Do we have to cross that?" she said.

"It's only about fifteen meters wide," he replied.

"Have you done this before?"

"No." Marcelo thought. "But I think we can do it in less than thirty seconds."

"I don't know, my boots—"

Ignoring her, Marcelo spurred the horse forward. It trotted gamely into the river, and the water reached the horse's chest. Ainsley gasped as the river water poured over the tops of her good boots, the ice-cold snowmelt filling the insides of her socks. Her feet froze quickly.

She closed her eyes and clung to Marcelo's corduroy jacket. She could feel the water rise to her knees, her thighs, her waist. She gasped, her eyes flying open. Her lungs started to convulse inside her chest.

Meanwhile, Marcelo was trying to push the horse forward. The creature's head was kicking up and down, its haunches straining against the swiftly moving current. This river was no joke. Here in the middle, its force was threatening to push them over.

Then Ainsley felt the force of the water grow gradually weaker. The water level began to drop, down to her knees, then to her feet. She relaxed her abdominal muscles. A moment later the horse pulled them safely onto the shore on the other side of the river.

Marcelo let out a very uncharacteristic whoop. "Break time," he said.

Ainsley swung off the horse and landed on the rocks. Her feet were chunks of ice. She could barely feel the ground beneath her boots.

The rancher stamped around on the rocks. He pulled a canteen from his saddle and drank from it. "That was good," he said. "That was professional. It makes me think maybe I should keep at this. I mean, I would really miss those cows." He smiled. "I'm happy out here."

They both breathed in, the scented pine air filling their lungs. Marcelo looked pleased. Ainsley thought that he looked like a man who was exactly where he should be.

Then a distant crack echoed across the mountain. It came from the bowl.

"That didn't sound natural," said Ainsley.

"It wasn't," he said. "That was a rifle."

"The *gauchos*?"

"No, they wouldn't use it. I told them we needed silence."

Another crack sounded. Then a third. Followed by a fourth, a fifth, a sixth, a seventh. Ainsley stopped counting as the volley of pops continued. If that was the military, she didn't know why they would be using that many shots.

Then the answer hit her.

She looked at Marcelo. His mouth had dropped open. Evidently the same conclusion had occurred to him.

"Is that..." Ainsley said.

He nodded.

The military was shooting his cows.

They stood there dumbly, unable to act, or even to move. Ainsley's wet clothing suddenly felt heavier, the cold fabric even more oppressive.

The shooting went on for several minutes, well over a hundred shots fired, until at last the final crack echoed across the landscape. Then there was a terrible silence.

"I'm sorry," she said.

Marcelo didn't respond. His jaw was set tightly against his skull. He simply climbed back up into the saddle. Ainsley took his hand, swung up behind him again, and held on as he pointed the horse further into the Andes.

# CHAPTER FIFTY-FOUR

At four thousand meters altitude the horse carried its riders across the treeline, the height beyond which no more vegetation grows. Almost immediately the landscape changed. The birds disappeared, the trees disappeared, the ubiquitous *jarilla* brush disappeared.

Ainsley found herself in a field of bare gray rocks.

Despite the spring weather, piles of snow were still crammed into crevices and beneath boulders, all the nooks and crannies untouched by the new sunlight.

The horse picked its way carefully across the scree. The sound of rocks skittering across the slope followed behind them.

Marcelo hadn't uttered a word since the long volley of rifle shots. Ainsley knew he was upset.

"It's my fault," she said.

"It's not you," he replied. "I'm cursed."

"No, you're not."

"I'm not meant to have a productive life."

"You'll survive. You have to."

His hand slapped his thigh. "Everything I do ends prematurely. The mine. The cows."

"We don't know that for sure yet."

He harumphed. "Do you know who brought this upon me? That bastard who bought the Zorro rhodochrosites. Everything has gone wrong ever since."

"Why?"

"None of the wholesalers would buy my stones after he visited. I had to sell the mine."

"Was it a coincidence?"

"I don't think so." He sounded bitter. "I think someone scared them."

Ainsley really felt bad for Marcelo. "It would be nice to know his name."

The rancher had tensed. "That arrogant bastard had everything planned out. He was getting ready to steal babies from the mothers of the disappeared, and then sell them."

Ainsley sucked the inside of her cheek. "Can't you remember anything else about him?"

"I've tried, but it's been so long. Let me think."

Marcelo lapsed into thoughtful silence while guiding the horse up a series of steep switchbacks. They didn't speak for a long while. Ainsley inhaled deeply; it was a clean, cold smell. The emptiness of the primeval mountain wilderness.

"There it is," he said. "The *puestero*."

He pointed ahead. Ainsley didn't see anything but a field of gray stones. Over it, the dome of blue sky.

"Where?" she said.

"There."

She squinted and looked harder, following his pointed finger. A rock hut materialized out of the scene. It had four walls made of boulders on the bottom and meticulously stacked rocks above. There was even a rock roof. It blended beautifully into the landscape.

"Is that roof safe?"

"Absolutely. This hermit used to be a doctor. He gave it all up years ago to live here alone." Marcelo tapped the side of his head. "He isn't quite right in the brain."

Ainsley didn't say anything to that. There seemed to be many such people in Patagonia.

They dismounted the horse and approached the hut. She was surprised to see an actual door, a wooden piece that had been shaved and shaped to fit snugly into the opening of the rocks.

Marcelo knocked loudly on the wood. The sound immediately died into the air. Ainsley listened to the wind whistling. She could feel the skin on her face getting chapped. She pulled her coat more tightly around herself and wiggled her toes. Sensation was finally starting to return.

"He's not here," said Marcelo.

"Maybe he's coming back?"

The rancher gazed around the landscape. Then his eyes landed upon something.

"No, he's not."

Marcelo walked over to a pile of rocks on the ground. From a distance, it looked indistinguishable from all the other random piles of gray basalt on this lunarlike landscape.

Then Ainsley saw the cross. It was crude, just two sticks roped together with twine.

Marcelo took his hat off and folded his hands. He looked at the grave and said nothing for a moment. Then he put his hat back on and turned back to Ainsley.

"Death is always sad."

"Who could've buried him?"

Marcelo shrugged. "It's a mystery. But you know, he lived the way that he wanted to."

Ainsley chewed on that one for a while. Though embarking on forced sleepovers in remote Andean huts wasn't her idea of a party, playing at international gemstone travel had sparked something in her soul that nothing ever had before. The game was a high-wire act for sure. But she was intoxicated by her own life at last; she was living according to her own rules.

Just the way this dead hermit had lived his life.

Marcelo went over to the hut and used his shoulder to push open the door. Ainsley followed him inside.

The single room had a dirt floor. There was a simple wooden table with a single stool. A rusted hurricane lamp sat in a corner. Nearby, a green wool blanket was unrolled on the ground, which Ainsley guessed had served as the bed. A pile of weathered books was stacked neatly in one corner. They looked like they'd been read many times.

Then Ainsley saw the bag.

It was burlap and was resting on the ground. She looked inside. There were strips of dried meat tied together with a piece of twine. It looked like beef jerky. Underneath were two potatoes and a few carrots.

Ainsley rolled the potatoes in her hand. Something was odd about them. Then she realized what.

The skin of the potatoes was smooth. Unless this hermit had died in the last three days, there should be the telltale sprouts.

"These potatoes are new," she said. "Look."

Marcelo glanced at them. Then he froze.

"What is that sound?" he said.

"I don't hear anything."

"Listen."

Ainsley froze, concentrating on her audio senses. There it was. A rhythmic crunch, outside the hut, and it was growing louder.

"It sounds like footsteps," she said.

Both she and Marcelo sprang out the door. They whirled twisted, scanning the field of scree.

"There," said Marcelo.

He was pointing towards an approaching figure. The person was dressed in brown rags. It carried a staff and walked with an odd sideways shuffle. A heavy hood covered its face.

"Who's that?"

"The hermit," said Marcelo.

Ainsley glanced at the crude memorial. "So who's in the grave?"

"I don't know," said the rancher, embarrassed. "Maybe it was his dog. I told you I have never met this man before, only seen him at a distance."

Marcelo whistled loudly. The hermit suddenly stopped walking. He didn't lift his hood, but he was listening.

"Friend," said Marcelo, "we humbly ask to spend the night. I am Marcelo Carrazo."

The hermit slowly looked up. Ainsley glimpsed long, stringy, grayish black hair tumbling out from beneath his hood. The hand gripping the staff, while gnarled, was delicate.

"Will you permit us?" asked Marcelo.

The hermit slowly reached up and drew back the hood, revealing its face. Ainsley drew back in horror. It was a haunted face, with sunken cheeks, piercing eyes, strange shape to the lips.

But then Ainsley noticed that the cheeks were delicate, the eyes had long lashes, and the lips were oddly small.

The creature cleared its throat, then slowly spoke a single word:

"*Bueno*."

It was a high voice, without any lower register, any masculine timbre. It left Ainsley with no doubt whatsoever.

This hermit wasn't a man at all.

# CHAPTER FIFTY-FIVE

The sun had sunk behind the Andes, sending fingers of pink and orange overhead, through the gaps between the peaks, across the empty grayish-green plain below. The rocks were suffused with such soft light that they seemed to be glowing.

The hermit walked past the visitors towards her hut. She didn't offer anything, didn't even look at them.

Marcelo turned to her with apologetic eyes. "How was I supposed to know? I never saw him up close."

"You can stop saying *him*," said Ainsley.

The rancher was disturbed. "It doesn't make sense. What kind of woman lives up here alone?"

"One who doesn't want to worry about rapists following her out to her car."

Marcelo wasn't in the mood for humor. "Let's go make some conversation."

They entered the hut again. The hermit had removed some of the brown rags from her body and folded them carefully and laid them on the floor. She was sitting crosslegged on the green wool blanket.

Ainsley sat down near the woman. The hermit was utterly unconcerned with her visitors. She reached into the burlap bag and removed a carrot. Her teeth nibbled on the root vegetable, leaving tiny bite marks, the way a small animal would.

Up close, Ainsley could make out her face a little better. She had been a plain woman, with a narrow chin and brown eyes. Now her skin was blistered and sagged, presumably from the ultraviolet radiation, which was surely stronger at this elevation. Plus there was apparently a giant hole in the ozone layer over Patagonia anyways. Ainsley had read that in one of her books on the plane.

The hermit put the gnawed carrot back in the bag and wrapped it. She looked straight ahead. Her narrow shoulders were slumped forward.

At last the hermit turned to Ainsley. "Did you bring anything to read?"

"No," Ainsley said.

"I'm starved for a good book," she said. "The rocks all say the same things after a while."

Ainsley wasn't sure if the rocks spoke to her literally or metaphorically. "My name is Ainsley Walker," she said, "and I am from the United States."

The hermit didn't respond to that. She was excellent at blocking out unwanted static, like *yanqui* voices.

"I am called Marcelo," he said, "and—"

"Are you a rancher?" asked the hermit. She glanced at his clothes.

He nodded. "My herd is at Lago de Miel."

"It was."

He grew very sad. "You heard the gunshots too."

"Yes, so I went to see."

"They're dead?"

"They are."

Marcelo dropped his head into his chest. Then he looked up. "If I ever find that man."

"Someone is trying to destroy you," said the hermit.

"Yes, it's absolutely true."

The three of them sat in silence, digesting this fact. Ainsley was burning with curiosity. "So what's your story?" she said.

"I live alone," the woman replied.

"Have you always lived alone?"

"No."

"What were you before?"

"I used to be a nurse."

"Someone said you had been a doctor," said Marcelo.

"No. I was in obstetrics. I was a nurse in obstetrics."

Ainsley had never given birth, but she had been told that the obstetrics nurses often knew as much as the doctors did, and sometimes even more. So this woman had probably been an invaluable resource at one time.

"You were probably very good."

The hermit's eyes grew wide. "Oh, I was excellent. I birthed two thousand one hundred and seven babies."

"So why did you leave?"

The hermit stood up unsteadily. "I would offer you some tea, but the fuel is very difficult to get up here."

"We have some water," Marcelo said. "We also have some *matambre*. Can we share with you?"

The hermit nodded sadly. Ainsley sensed that she was growing tired of her self-imposed loner lifestyle.

Marcelo unwrapped their food and spread everything out on the wax paper on the floor of the hut. Then he cut the slab of rolled flank steak into several slices with his knife. He offered the woman the first slice.

Ainsley accepted the next one. Inside the rolled meat

were minced vegetables, eggs, and herbs. It was savory and delicious, even cold.

The three people ate in silence for a few minutes. Ainsley could hear the sound of her own chewing, her own swallowing. She'd forgotten how hungry she was.

When they were finished, Marcelo closed up the wax paper and put it back in his pack.

The hermit woman seemed more at ease now. "I left nursing because I saw some bad things."

She had something she wanted to get off her chest. Ainsley gently nudged her to continue. "Like what?"

The hermit sized her up with a saucerish eye. "Babies taken from their mothers."

Ainsley felt her stomach take another maddening drop. It was a roller coaster for her digestive tract today. "The children of *desaparecidos*?" she said.

"You don't have to speak about this," said Marcelo.

"It doesn't matter," said the hermit. "You don't know my name. I've even forgotten my name." She cackled.

"Where were you a nurse?"

"Tucumán."

A deep sound of sadness issued from the back of Marcelo's throat. "That was the center of the dirty war," he said, looking at Ainsley. "Near to my mine. There were more detention centers and informants there than any place else."

"That's right," said the hermit. "The reward for turning in somebody was a state job."

"It was a smart move in a bad economy," added Marcelo.

Ainsley tried to stay diplomatic. "So what did you see?"

The woman was almost in a trance now. "Blindfolded pregnant women brought in secret doors. Locked delivery rooms. One doctor did all the deliveries. He asked me ... he asked me ..."

She began to falter.

"He asked you what?" said Ainsley.

The hermit sounded fainter now. "He asked me to assist him."

"Did you?"

She dropped her head. "I couldn't say no to a doctor."

Marcelo interrupted. "This story is well known. The public trials brought everything out."

"Not everything," the hermit said, alert now. "Not everything. Those trials are why I ran away. I found marks of abuse on the woman. Torture."

Ainsley didn't say anything. Outside the hut, the wind was starting to grow more violent.

"After the delivery, the doctor took the baby. Immediately." She smacked her hands together to emphasize the point. "The mother was wheeled out of the room. I never heard from her again."

"It was a national tragedy," said Marcelo.

"And he kept asking me to assist. Over and over. Always, the babies disappeared immediately. And that doctor was respected too. He was a lecturer at the medical school."

"You didn't have to follow his orders," said Ainsley.

The hermit was agitated now. Her hands were twisting the green wool blanket into tiny little knots. "We couldn't say no. We all had to do what he said. He was a *doctor*. Besides, he was taking orders himself."

"From who?"

"The military."

Ainsley and Marcelo exchanged glances. Then the rancher cleared his throat. "I have my own history too."

Ainsley listened as Marcelo explained his own past, his Zorro rhodochrosite mine, his mysterious customer, and the adopted children who'd surfaced in later years with those very necklaces.

The hermit sat very still, listening. Ainsley guessed that she valued the spoken word. At this altitude, it was in even shorter supply than oxygen.

When he had finished, the former obstetrics nurse was silent for many seconds. Then she spoke. "So you know what it feels like. We were all part of the conspiracy, whether we wanted to be or not."

"It's true," said the rancher. "But what I have been trying to learn for years is the name of the military man who your doctor was taking orders from."

"Why?"

Marcelo grew intense. "It may have been the same one who destroyed my life. Why do you think I moved here?"

"I don't know if I can remember the name," said the hermit. "It's been so long."

"What did he look like?"

"I only saw the man once, for just a few seconds, and he wasn't dressed in his military clothes. But he was tall, handsome. Very blonde. He was attractive."

Ainsley perked up. That matched Marcelo's description.

Then the hermit stared off into the distance. "But he had something else." The hermit's finger went up towards her eye. "His eye. It wasn't healthy. There was a ... a twitch."

Ainsley felt her head starting to spin. She thought back to the executive club at La Bombonera. She remembered talking to the military man in his dress whites, feeling pity for his empty shell of a wife.

It all made sense. In fact, it had been at the back of her head ever since her own subsequent kidnapping and ejection from the country. And now she guessed what was coming next.

The hermit was still deliberating. "I think ... his name was—"

"—Ortiz," said Ainsley, interrupting her. "Lieutenant Colonel Ortiz."

The hermit nodded. "Yes, that was him. I thought I'd forgotten."

Marcelo looked at her, amazed. "How did you know that?"

"Because I've met him too," Ainsley said.

# CHAPTER FIFTY-SIX

The windstorm arrived that night. Even inside the relative safety of the hut, it was one of the fiercest weather events that Ainsley had experienced.

The wind played a horrible symphony on the primitive stone hut, like an orchestra tuning up before a performance. The treble was played on the small finger-like crags. The roar of the wind across the land occupied the midrange. And the heavy bass—that was the sound of large stones bouncing down the scree slope. It was enough to rattle Ainsley's teeth.

It was an enormous racket.

Marcelo was the only one sleeping. He was on the hermit's green woolen blanket. The recluse had offered it first to the American, but Ainsley knew she wasn't going to be sleeping—it wasn't in the cards in this country—and opted to sit upright instead, against the stone wall of the hut. She felt the wind blowing onto her back through the miniscule gaps between the stones. It felt as though she were reclining against a wall of plastic straws.

The hermit was perched on the stool at the table. She'd lit the rusted hurricane lamp, which was somehow still functional. Under the lamp was a fashion magazine that Ainsley had stowed in her purse. The woman was poring over every single word and photo on the page.

But the truth was, Ainsley barely noticed anything outside her own head. She was preoccupied by the revelation of a couple hours before.

Of the thousands of military personnel in this country, she had encountered, by chance, one of the most lethal. Lieutenant Colonel Ortiz had been a hidden architect of the dirty war.

Before he'd fallen asleep, Marcelo had told her that Ortiz was a well-known name, but that he had seemed to have escaped national discussion for the last few years. He'd also escaped prosecution during the public trials of the perpetrators of the dirty war, a painful process that had been chugging along for several years.

All of which meant one thing: Lieutenant Colonel Ortiz was very clever indeed.

She thought about her mission. She'd been assigned to simply find a necklace. That was all.

Now, through a combination of luck, idiocy, and sheer doggedness, Ainsley had ended up discovering a much larger secret: part of the hidden history of tens, hundreds, maybe even thousands, of grown children.

She wondered what other secrets the future held in store.

The hermit woman turned a page. Her finger followed each line, and her lips formed each word silently.

"What is 'www'?" she said. "I see it before many words without spaces."

"That's a website address," said Ainsley.

"What is a website?"

"It's on the Internet."

"What is the Internet?"

"It's an electronic resource. Like a second world. You go there on a computer, which is—"

"Oh, I know what a computer is," snapped the hermit. "I haven't been out here *that* long."

Ainsley smiled to herself. Then her stomach growled. She was starting to get hunger pains. Now was the time of night she might wake up to head to the fridge to swallow a few slices of salami, or to swipe a few crackers into some hummus. But those were just fantasies out here. The *matambre* was gone. There was nothing left to gnaw on but rocks and blasts of gale-force wind.

"What do you do when you get hungry?" she said.

"I don't get hungry anymore," the recluse said. "That was only the first couple of years."

That was an intimidating answer. This hermit had mastered her bodily desires. Ainsley knew she could never be such an ascetic. She'd rather end her own life than give up fresh *burrata*.

She decided to change the topic. "If somebody could find this man, Lieutenant Ortiz, and eventually put him on trial, would you be willing to give your testimony? About the doctor who cooperated with him?"

This would be an enormous act of will for her. To come down from the mountains, clean herself up, learn how to interact with people again.

"Would I be safe?" the recluse said. "People warned me never to speak. My life was in danger."

"You would be safe."

"Then I would consider it."

Ainsley nodded. They didn't say anything else for several hours, not until the first pink rays of sunlight shot through the stone walls of the hut.

Marcelo sat up. His hair was completely flat on one side.

"Good morning," Ainsley said. She felt worse than a heap of wet garbage but was determined not to let it show.

"What's good about it?" he answered. "My cattle are shot dead and I'm broke. And the wind is howling."

"Because today we can start planning revenge on the man who did this to you," she said.

He thought about that for a moment. "That's good motivation. I think we should leave."

"Even in the wind?"

"It won't be a fun ride, but that's life in Patagonia."

They gathered their belongings. The hermit was still absorbed in the fashion magazine, shaking her head.

"What is it?"

"Mascara," she said. "I haven't worn it in years. But now that I have seen these glamorous women, I can't stop thinking about it."

"Look, we will come get you when the time is right," said Ainsley. "You're important."

"I will be here," she said, "unless I die first."

"Then please stay alive," Marcelo said. He kissed the woman on the top of her head. Ainsley recoiled at the thought of pressing her lips to the woman's scalp, but Marcelo was a generous spirit.

"Take care," Ainsley said.

But the recluse didn't hear her. She had withdrawn into herself.

Outside, Marcelo untied his horse from a boulder. He removed a roll of dried meat from his pouch and left it outside the woman's door before they left.

# CHAPTER FIFTY-SEVEN

As they started the return to Lago de Miel, Ainsley saw a bird fly backwards.

It wasn't flying in reverse. It was facing forwards, the usual way, and flapping its wings in the usual way too. But the wind was so powerful that it was being blown straight backwards. It had lost all aerodynamics.

Ainsley couldn't imagine what might happen to an airplane trying to land in such weather.

The wind obliterated everything. It made her eyes water, froze her nostrils, blistered her cheeks, and ended the possibility of conversation. She held onto Marcelo's jacket and kept her face hidden inside her coat.

The horse carried them back below the treeline, and when they forded the swollen river, which hadn't subsided at all overnight, they emerged equally wet but doubly cold on the other side.

A few minutes later, Marcelo steered them towards a small cave formed in the overhang of a boulder. It was almost completely protected from the wind. They dismounted, and he quickly gathered some wood and started a small fire.

Ainsley watched him work. "You're really fast," she said.

"I learned from my *gauchos*," he said. "They're the experts."

"I wonder how they're doing."

"Those cockroaches are doing fine. They'll survive the end of the world, if they don't kill each other first."

The two of them stripped off some of their outer clothes and held them over the fire. As Marcelo's wool sweater dried, the heavy odor of wet sheep floated into Ainsley's nostrils. The smell was oddly reassuring in this dry landscape.

"Ortiz," he said, then shook his head. "It's difficult for me to believe that I sold three hundred gemstones to one of the designers of the dirty war. I helped him accomplish his mission."

"He was the bad man," Ainsley said, "not you."

"I hope he gets his day in court," said the rancher. He chewed on his lower lip, suddenly pensive. "There is something else that I remembered on the ride."

"What is it?"

"A rumor I heard about Ortiz. A friend told me. I can't remember who, exactly."

Ainsley could see him physically trying to remember, the squinted eyes, the jaw working itself, the stuttered sentences.

She waited patiently. Marcelo had a way of circling around his points. But the points so far had been worth the wait.

"Go on," she said.

"It was about his wife."

"I met her," Ainsley said. "She was an empty vessel."

"What do you mean?"

"She had no personality."

Marcelo nodded. "My friend said that she herself had been a *desaparacido*."

Ainsley sat there gaping at him over this miniscule campfire. She wondered how many bombshells were going to be dropped onto her in a single twenty-four-hour period.

But the rancher kept talking. "They said that she had been a prisoner. That she was pregnant when she was disappeared, along with her fiancé."

"What else?" said Ainsley weakly.

"They said that she broke under torture. She turned in all her friends, pointed out other subversives on the street. They said that she had fallen in love with her torturer." He looked at Ainsley. "Have you ever heard of anything that sick?"

It was seriously hard to breathe, and not because of the altitude. Ainsley heard herself gasp the next few words. "Do you know what happened to the baby?"

"The baby." Marcelo watched her for a moment. Then he shrugged. "I don't know. I can't imagine such a *milico* raising a subversive's child. It just wouldn't happen."

Their clothes were mostly dry now. Marcelo stood up, stamped on the small fire, offered Ainsley some water. She shook her head. There was too much confusion in her at the moment.

"Enough about that," he said. "I have to prepare to see my herd."

She could see him stuffing his emotions away. He swung onto the saddle, helped his rider up, and pointed the horse downhill again.

Ainsley sat behind him for the remainder of the time, the now-familiar feel of his corduroy jacket in her hands. She was in an almost catatonic state.

Lieutenant Colonel Ortiz's wife had been a pregnant *desaparecido*.

The whereabouts of the baby, if it had survived, were unknown.

Then she remembered that Lieutenant Colonel Ortiz had boasted about attending every one of Ovidio's soccer games.

That he had "discovered" the boy as a teen in Bahía Blanca. That he felt almost as much pride as a father would.

The crayons and the paper and the outline of the picture had all been handed to her. She just needed to color everything in.

Ainsley mused upon her next move until the horse crested the familiar lip of the grassy bowl of Lago de Miel.

She felt Marcelo's body tense. She craned her head around his body.

On the field, the carcasses of one hundred and seventeen cows lay fallen on the grass. Many were concentrated in a single group at the shore of the lake. The edge of the water had gone dark red with their blood. Other carcasses were stretched further down along the shore.

Some—the younger, more agile ones—had tried to escape up the sides of the bowl, and had been shot there, in the grass.

There were no humans anywhere in sight. The military had shot the cows and then left. To teach Marcelo a lesson.

The rancher walked the horse through the killing field. Ainsley looked down as they passed the corpse of a steer. Its black fur was matted but still fresh. It had been shot directly between the eyes. Very professional.

"I'm sorry," said Ainsley.

"I guess I'm finished," he said. "My emergency plan was sell them all for glue. Now I can't even do that."

"You'll be okay."

"No, I won't," he said. "Twice now that asshole has tried to destroy me financially." She watched his fist clench the reins tightly. "He doesn't have the right."

"No, he doesn't," she agreed.

"Oh no," said Marcelo, looking into the distance. "No no no no no..."

The rancher spurred the horse forward into a full gallop. Ainsley held tight and peered around him.

They were heading towards what seemed to be an odd pile of clothing on the grass. Purple pants. Blue denim shirt.

Then she saw the bowler hat nearby.

It was the Englishman.

# CHAPTER FIFTY-EIGHT

The lunatic shepherd was laying facedown on the grass. His arms were spread out at an uncomfortable angle. Ainsley thought that this was a weird position in which to sleep.

Then she saw the brain matter blown across the grass.

Ainsley turned her head away, disgusted, horrified, and deeply sorry. The Englishman had driven up to this lake to warn her and Marcelo. Now he was dead.

"I knew this would happen," said Marcelo. "All he needed to do was stay in his car."

"It's awful."

"I knew this would happen," he said again. "I knew it."

A movement on the grass caught Ainsley's eye. The Englishman's pet bird, the one with the broken wing, was in the grass near his body. It was flapping its wings, desperately trying to launch.

"Hold on," she said to Marcelo.

She hopped off the horse, picked up the bird, and put it gently into her purse. It was the very least she could do.

Then she tapped Marcelo, who was still on the horse, on his leg. "Do you want to help me destroy them?"

"Absolutely," he said. "I will make it my life's work. I have the *bronca*."

"Then take me to Bahía Blanca."

"Why?"

"Because I think that Ovidio's mother is Lieutenant Admiral Ortiz's wife."

Marcelo stared at her, mouth open. He'd been pelting Ainsley with new information for well over a day now. It felt good to surprise him, for once.

"How do you know this?" he said.

"I don't know, not for sure. But it's an educated guess."

"Okay."

"There's a navy base in Bahía Blanca?"

Marcelo nodded. "The biggest one. It's the very heart of the navy."

"I need to get onto that base to find her. Your son lives nearby?"

"Just a few miles away."

"Then maybe he can help me."

Marcelo swung his horse around in a circle. "All right. We have a plan."

Ainsley looked around. "Where's your car?"

"There."

She saw his Toyota, in the same place where he'd left it. The tires had been shot and the windshield destroyed. She could smell gasoline; the gas tank had evidently been punctured too.

"I expected that," said the rancher. "That's why I have these."

He produced a set of keys and jangled them.

"What are those?"

"The Englishman's. I keep a spare set because he always loses them. I'll be right back."

Marcelo galloped away. Ainsley looked down at the grass.

She could see the tracks of the vehicles that had been here. She could see how the men's bootprints had stamped down the grass. She shuddered as she thought about how close she had come to ending up like the Englishman.

Then she realized what exactly she had just committed herself to doing next. She was voluntarily going into the heart of the enemy's nest. It was either pure genius or sheer idiocy. More likely the latter.

Ten minutes later, the other Toyota Hi-Lux roared around the corner. It screeched up alongside Ainsley, and she climbed inside.

"I'm ready to nail these bastards," the rancher said. His eyes were on fire.

"Me too," said Ainsley.

She climbed into the car. Before she could even buckle her seat belt, he had floored the accelerator. Soon were tearing down the mountain road, and this time, Ainsley kept her lunch down.

Three hours later, Marcelo flew past his own ranch without even a sideways glance.

"We can stop, if you want to," said Ainsley.

He shook his head with steely resolve. "I can weep later. Now is the time for revenge."

And then they were back onto the steppe, gradually descending through the series of plateaus. The air grew warmer. Eventually Route 40 came into view, the place where Ainsley had begun her Patagonian adventure. The tavern was still there too, unchanged from the morning before.

"Should we stop and thank the owner for his phone call?" she said.

"I don't think so," said Marcelo. "He might not be happy to see you. Who knows what they did to him."

That statement depressed Ainsley. Her presence here, at the far end of the world, had attracted the worst element of the Argentine government. She had damaged too many people here.

As they drew closer, she could see that the catalytic converter was still leaning against the outside wall. The automotive part that he needed to ship back to Buenos Aires.

"Pull over for a moment," she said.

"Why? You shouldn't talk to him."

"I won't."

Marcelo pulled over and stopped. Ainsley hopped out, grabbed the catalytic converter, and dragged it across the dirt to the Toyota. She opened the trunk and heaved the thing inside.

When she got back into the passenger seat, she was breathing heavily. Marcelo was staring at her.

"What was that?" he said.

"I'm returning his favor. Just go."

The rancher nodded. He understood how favors worked.

Ainsley felt herself pressed backwards into her seat as the Toyota turned onto Route 40 and accelerated down the ruler-straight highway, beneath the dome of blue Patagonian sky.

BAHIA
BLANCA

# CHAPTER FIFTY-NINE

Ainsley sipped her pumpkin soup and tried to ignore the woman's jealous eyes upon her.

She and Marcelo were sitting at the kitchen table of his son, Luca. The jealous eyes belonged to Laura, a thin woman with a hawkish nose who had pinned Ainsley with a stare that could've woken the dead, a gaze that hadn't let up, not from the moment the young American woman had crossed into her home.

It was female dominance, pure and simple, but there wasn't any need for it. Ainsley was nobody's prize at the moment. Her wet hair was piled on top of her head from a quick shower in the upstairs bathroom and she wore no makeup. She was even dressed in Laura's extra robe. Her clothing was so dirty that Laura had ordered that it be immediately washed, dried, and ironed by the family maid.

"How is the soup?" said Laura.

"It's very good, thank you," replied Ainsley.

"Do you like soup?"

"Yes."

"You can have more soup, if you want. I can give you more soup."

"That would be nice."

The woman lifted her chin arrogantly. "I made the soup myself. With ingredients from my garden. Do you make soup from your garden?"

"No," Ainsley answered, "I don't."

That was the right answer. Laura nodded smugly, crossed her arms, and sat back.

It was eight o'clock in the morning, and Ainsley and Marcelo had driven through the night, more than twelve hours, nearly fifteen hundred kilometers, back up to the rich grasses of the pampas. Now they were in this modest home on the northwestern outskirts of Bahía Blanca, a modest-sized town known mostly for its proximity to the naval base.

Luca was watching her too, but with much more friendliness in his eyes. "So what are you doing hanging around with my old man?"

"Fighting evil," Ainsley replied.

That wasn't really a joke, but Luca chuckled. It ended with a glance from his wife.

Marcelo set down his spoon. "She is here to investigate a missing gemstone."

"Which one?"

"It's better not to discuss."

The couple accepted that. Luca addressed his father. "So then why are you helping her, *papá*?"

"Because the military just slaughtered my cows."

Luca slapped his hand against his forehead. "How is that possible? Why?"

"You know my history."

"But the cows are everything you have!"

Marcelo shrugged. Ainsley concentrated on spooning the soup into her mouth. It was a difficult situation to explain without betraying the reason for her mission. She listened to Marcelo doing a halfway decent job of dancing around the questions.

Then she heard Luca say, "Then what do you need? Why are you here?"

Ainsley set her spoon down with a bit more force than necessary. The sharp clunk caught everyone's attention. "We're here because I need to get onto the navy base."

"Puerto Belgrano?" said Luca.

"Yes."

Ainsley waited for the inevitable reply: you're crazy, it's impossible, never, forget it. She put her face down into her bowl and prepared for the worst.

All Luca said was, "Okay." As though she had suggested picking up an extra carton of eggs at the store.

Ainsley looked up. She was confused. "We're talking about the navy base. Isn't it difficult to get inside?"

Luca shook his head. "No, not really."

"Aren't there guards?"

He shrugged. "If you're a familiar face, it doesn't matter."

Laura agreed. "Our friend Tico goes there every day to drop off and pick up laundry. Sometimes he takes his children, sometimes his wife. The guards don't really care."

Ainsley pushed even further. "Do you think I could go with him?"

Laura fixed her with that irritating stare. "If he decides that he likes you, then maybe."

It finally dawned on Ainsley why this woman was so antagonistic. Laura thought Ainsley was angling her way into their family. Maybe she assumed that Ainsley was a black widow who ensnared old men like Marcelo and sucked them dry of their riches.

That was ridiculous. One, all of Marcelo's riches were rotting in a high-altitude pasture with bullets between their eyes. Two, Ainsley wasn't into relationships of exploitation. She'd already played the pursuer-distancer game with the Legal Weasel, her missing husband. They'd played it so well, and for so long, that he'd distanced himself right out of their marriage.

But Laura didn't know any of this, and probably wouldn't have cared anyways. She had just been seized by that primitive desire to scare away any potential females that would disrupt her nest.

"I can pay him," said Ainsley. "Here."

She reached into her purse and laid down a hundred pesos. She hated greasing the rails in this way, but sometimes it had to be done.

Laura nodded at her husband. "I'm sure he would appreciate that," he said. "Where's the phone?"

In the other room, he found the receiver, dialed, and had a quick conversation. It was friendly in nature, judging from his body language. When he hung up, he turned to Ainsley.

"Tico will be here in ten minutes."

That was good. Ainsley wiped her mouth. She stood up from the table and went into the living room. She listened to Luca and Laura trying to persuade Marcelo to move in with them.

Then the front door burst open. He was a stocky man with a barrel chest, a short haircut, and a wild pair of eyes. He was dressed in a navy blue jumpsuit and work boots.

"*Cómo andás, che*," said Luca. The men slapped each other on the backs and kissed each other's cheeks.

"Is this the one?" said Tico, looking at Ainsley.

She offered her cheek for the kiss. "Nice to meet you, I'm—"

But Tico gently pushed her face aside. "It is killing me to say this to such a beautiful woman, but I don't want to know your name."

"Why?"

"In case you get into trouble. We never met."

Ainsley pulled back. Once again, she felt like a poisonous flower, like Rappaccini's daughter.

"Look, all I need is to get inside the base," she said. "Can you do that?"

Tico puffed out his chest at being asked to perform something. "A baby could crawl onto that base. But not through the main gate." He winked. "The guards put on a good show for the tourists there. The work gate for the civilian personnel, that's where I go in. They don't give a shit, especially when it's busy."

"When are you leaving?" she said.

He looked at his watch. "Right now. I have to be at the barracks in an hour."

"Let's do it."

"So what do I get?"

Ainsley peeled off two hundred pesos and handed it to him. "You never saw me."

"You never saw me either."

Ainsley went over to Marcelo and exchanged cheek kisses with him. "You've been such a help."

The rancher looked up at her peacefully. "Find that bastard's wife," said the rancher, "and nail him."

The maid brought Ainsley her clothing. She gathered her purse and started to walk towards the bathroom to change. Then she felt a hand on her shoulder.

"*Mi corazon*, you need to wear this," said Tico. He was holding a navy blue jumpsuit.

"That?"

"Yes. You're substituting for my wife today. She's sick."

"Really sick?"

"No," he grinned, "she's *agreed* to feel sick."

Ainsley smiled. She took the jumpsuit and went into the

bathroom and closed the door. The garment was about four sizes too small and had green splotches down the front. It could be chimichurri sauce. Apparently Tico's wife couldn't handle her condiments.

She undressed and put on the jumpsuit and buttoned up the front. When she was finished, she looked in the mirror.

The sleeves only extended halfway down her forearms. The pants didn't even reach the tops of her boots. And she couldn't close the two buttons across her chest, leaving the tops of her girls peeking out. The effect was unsettling. She looked like a deranged washerwoman whore.

Ainsley put on her coat and opened the bathroom door. Laura was outside, waiting. She handed Ainsley her clothing, neatly pressed and folded, inside a plastic bag.

"Thank you so much for your hospitality," said Ainsley.

But the woman wasn't nearly as cordial. "So what about us? You just use me and my husband? We give you what you need and you leave?"

Ainsley peeled off two hundred more pesos. "Here," she said.

"No," said Laura, pushing it away, "I don't want money."

"Then how can I repay you?"

The woman's eyes flicked down to the clothes in Ainsley's hands. "Where do you go shopping?" she asked.

Ainsley was flabbergasted. "I don't know. Many places."

"I want to go with you. I need to improve my wardrobe, but I don't know how."

Ainsley looked down at her ridiculous outfit and stifled a laugh. "You have a deal," she said. "As soon as this is done, we'll go shopping."

Laura stood up on her tiptoes and exchanged cheek kisses. The tougher the outside, the softer the inside.

# CHAPTER SIXTY

As the laundry truck edged forward in the long traffic queue, Ainsley drummed the fingers of her right hand on her knee.

She was five minutes away from the base, and she was nervous.

On the drive, Tico had entertained her with stories. The navy, he assured her, wasn't as powerful as it had been a generation earlier. The loss of the Falklands and the dirty war had sullied its reputation, and fewer people were considering the military as a career.

In fact, his union, the Government Workers' Union, had gone on strike a few years earlier, an event that essentially closed down the base until its demands were met. The civilians kept the place running now, and most of them lived in a nearby neighborhood called Punta Alta, including himself.

Ainsley didn't disagree. But the military was still influential enough to disappear a nameless maid from her villa. And to kidnap and deport Ainsley herself. And to chase her up into the mountains. And to kill one hundred and seventeen cattle—and one innocent shepherd—just to intimidate.

Or, more likely, it was just one man in the military, one

well-placed man, who was ordering these things. And now she was sneaking into the very belly of that beast to find that man's wife.

Maria Libertad Ortiz.

What Ainsley would do when she found this woman, she wasn't quite sure. Ask her questions? Pretend friendship? Ainsley had survived this long living by her wits, and she would improvise. It had been working so far.

"So where on the base are you going?" said Tico.

"I don't know," she said.

"You're just going to wander around?" he said, shocked. "It's thousands of hectares. Gigantic."

"I'm looking for the wife of a lieutenant colonel."

"Oh, she's one of the big fish." Tico thought about it. "I know exactly where you should go."

"Where?"

"The polo field. That's where the fancy wives hang out. They like to watch the players."

The truck lurched forward. They were almost at the gate now. A naval officer was inside the small hut, chatting with each driver, almost all of whom seemed to be civilian laborers going to work. A no-nonsense metal sign reading *Base Naval Puerto Belgrano* was planted in the soil.

Through the gate, Ainsley could see an open expanse of field, with trees and brick structures in the far distance. She was entering a different world, where the normal rules didn't apply. She felt sweat erupting from her armpits.

"Relax, act casual," said Tico. "Here."

He handed Ainsley a newspaper. She pretended to read, but the thin paper was quivering in her hands.

Tico took the paper away from her. "Never mind," he said. "Just look ahead. I'll talk. This guy is my favorite."

They pulled up to the guard, who looked about twenty-five and made of action-hero musculature. His triceps bulged against the sleeves of his crisp shirt as he hooked one hand on the roof of the cab and peered inside the truck.

"Tico, *cabrón*! Your wife put too much starch on this collar! It hurts!"

"That's too bad," said Tico. "We want you to look professional, you know?"

The guard looked at the passenger side of the cab and his face hardened. He had noticed Ainsley.

"Maria's sick," said Tico. "This is her cousin visiting from Buenos Aires. She's helping me for the day."

The guard peered at her. He seemed to buy the story. After all, Ainsley had chopped her hair recently, in the current *porteño* fashion, and she was wearing the washerwoman's outfit.

"I have to sign her in," said the guard.

Ainsley's heart leapt in her throat.

"She's my cousin," said Tico. "Please, I'm late. Let me check her in when I leave."

"You won't remember," said the guard.

"Please," begged Tico.

The guard hesitated.

Tico lowered his voice. "I'll put in less starch. Tomorrow morning. Just for you."

The guard thought about it. Then he straightened up and pounded a fist on the roof of the truck.

Translation: Move along.

As they pulled forward through the gate, Ainsley finally exhaled. The butterflies in her stomach were performing lunatic pirouettes. Every limb in her body was trembling.

"You are the *best*," she said.

Tico smiled. "Welcome to the home of the Argentine navy."

The truck lumbered across the open field that lay just inside the Puerto Belgrano gate. Tico held his hand up to the right side of his face as Ainsley stripped off the jumpsuit and pulled on her own clothing. She wasn't wearing that uniform one second longer than she had to. Then she adjusted her makeup in the flipdown mirror.

"I'll drop you off near the polo field," said Tico. "It's too far to walk."

"Thank you," she said.

Ainsley looked out the window. This base seemed about as militaristic as a piece of cherry cheesecake. Lush pine trees lined the sides of the streets. Tico gunned the engine at a stop sign and flushed a covey of birds out of an acacia. The scent of lavender floated everywhere.

She watched the officers' residences glide by, lovely examples of brick construction, the landscaping vibrant.

They passed an elementary school, a hospital, a grocery store, a golf course. Ainsley checked her watch. They'd been driving for a while. She guessed that this base was at least the size of her own town back in the United States.

Then a long fence appeared on the right, with an open field of grass beyond. Tico immediately pulled over.

"This is the polo field," he said. "If you walk up there, you'll see the club where the fancy ladies flock like birds."

"Thank you," said Ainsley. "Here is your jumpsuit. What time are you leaving today?"

"About two o'clock."

"Can I catch a ride out?"

"If you tell me where you'll be."

"I don't know where I'll be," she said.

He scratched his face. "If you are standing at the corner of that main commercial street, in front of the grocery store, you'll see me pass by at two o'clock. If not, adios."

She exited the truck and closed the door. "Hey," said Tico, leaning over, "I can't resist asking something."

"What is it?"

"Which officer's wife are you looking for?"

Ainsley paused. "Lieutenant Colonel Ortiz," she said.

She wasn't prepared for his reaction. The color drained from Tico's face immediately. His mouth clamped shut. He quickly rolled up his window, popped the truck into gear, and pulled away from her.

Ainsley watched him go. Apparently she'd said the wrong thing.

Her confidence was shaken. Ainsley suddenly felt way outside her comfort zone. She'd been hired to find a necklace, but the job had now expanded to also include finding the identity of her employer's birth mother. Never mind the fact that she'd been fired from the first, and therefore had no right to be pursuing the second. Or that, truth be told, she felt unqualified to be doing either.

But she couldn't turn back. For better or worse, Ainsley pursued everything in her life to the end. The follow-through was the thing, money be damned. She trusted that that would be enough upon which to build her reputation as an international gemstone tracker.

She turned towards the polo field. The first thing that impressed her was its sheer enormity. It was the size of five soccer fields. She could barely see the other side.

She followed the fence, passed the concrete seating area, and finally spotted the club. The path to the entryway was marked by two rows of blue-and-white pennants.

Ainsley strode proudly down the sidewalk. She was melting on the inside but tough on the outside. Fake it until you make it.

The front door was decorated with a pair of crossed mallets. The sign said Puerto Belgrano Polo Club.

She pushed the door open and entered.

# CHAPTER SIXTY-ONE

It was almost eleven in the morning, and the room was filled with round wooden tables, surrounded by rattan scoop chairs. Pools of light shot down from recessed lights in the ceiling. An empty bar ran along one side of the carpeted room.

Beyond the tables, the entire far wall was made of glass, through which guests could see the expanse of green lawn.

Tico had been right about the fancy ladies. The tables were filled with women. Each one was made up as if they were ready to step out to a show: pantsuits, dresses, blouses, skirts, gaudy jewelry, bracelets, heavy makeup. Two-thirds of the hair in the room was lemon yellow, the type that came from a bottle.

Her eyes scanned the room. There was one table, nearest to the window, around which five well-manicured older women were sitting. Tall highball glasses of clear soda with lemon wedges sat on the table before them.

One of the women had an especially big nimbus of blonde hair, sprayed and laquered. Her frame, however, was frail, and she slumped forward in her seat. Even from across the room, Ainsley recognized her.

Maria Libertad Ortiz.

"Welcome," said a voice.

Ainsley turned. She was startled to see a fortyish woman with a no-nonsense black bob approaching. Possibly she was a manager. She had the brisk walk of a person in charge.

"I'd like to have a drink," said Ainsley.

"But are you a member?"

"No."

The woman betrayed no emotion. "This room is for members only."

"Is there an exception? I'm waiting for my husband to arrive."

"Is he an officer?"

"No," said Ainsley, "but he's the manager of a polo team."

That was a pretty big whopper, but it worked. The woman grew more interested. "From where?"

"The United States. He's here taking a meeting with members of your team."

The woman tilted her head. "I didn't know there were meetings with Americans today."

"It wasn't announced. The men said I should wait here until they were finished. They always have business to do."

That comment struck a chord. "Of course," the woman said, then picked up a menu from behind the empty podium. "Follow me."

Ainsley trailed her through the room. She could feel the women's eyes upon her. She was the stranger in town. These women were probably tired of looking at the same faces every morning.

The manager led her to the only available table, next to Maria Libertad.

Ainsley tried to appear as cool and glamorous as possible. She asked for a gin and tonic without looking at the menu. It seemed like the perfect drink to have at a polo club, even if it was ten-thirty in the morning.

Then she angled her seat so she could study Maria Libertad. The lieutenant colonel's wife was dressed, as before, in a cream-colored pantsuit, trimmed in gold jewelry. A white pearl necklace lay draped upon her bony chest. Lipstick had been applied as carefully to her lips as an undertaker would to a corpse's.

The wives sat in silence, wet rings soaking the tablecloth beneath their highball glasses. They were staring out the window blankly. Ainsley followed their stares.

The polo game was visible from here. At either end of the field was a pair of tall red-and-white striped wicker cones. Between them, Ainsley could see the riders streaking around on their brown horses, their saddle blankets all featuring the same military pattern. They were swinging their mallets in wide, looping arcs. There was a rhythm to the play that she could feel but not quite understand.

The wives couldn't have cared less. It was a weekday morning. From her lifetime of reading fashion magazines, Ainsley sensed that most polo fans attended the matches for the scene, drinking splits of Moët & Chandon, yanking up Manolos that had sunk into the grass, maybe scheming ways to seduce the newest player on the squad.

"We like your choices," said a woman's voice.

Ainsley looked over. One of the women at Maria Libertad's table was leaning towards her and pointing towards her boots.

"Thank you," said Ainsley, "they're my favorite."

"My daughter has some just like them," the woman said.

"It's funny, I was admiring your friend's pearls," said Ainsley, nodding towards Maria Libertad. "They're beautiful."

"We all have pearls," said the woman, "but hers are the biggest."

"There's nothing as classy as a pearl necklace."

The other woman had been listening now and jumped in. "Are you alone?"

"No, my husband is meeting with some of the managers of the polo team today," said Ainsley. "We're putting together a team ourselves."

The women grew quite interested. "What is your husband's name?"

Ainsley scrambled for an answer. "Oh, he doesn't want to be known."

"There are only twenty-five people in the United States who can mount a team," said another woman.

"I wish I could go to the United States," said another. "I would go to Hollywood."

"Why bother?" Ainsley said. "Just go to Buenos Aires instead. It's better than Hollywood."

The navy wife laughed. "Ricardo would never allow it. Me? The wife of an admiral? Out alone?"

Ainsley smiled. "I was out in Buenos Aires recently. I had an *amazing* time."

"Come and tell us what you did," said one.

That was exactly the invitation Ainsley had been hoping for. She pulled her chair up to their table and began describing her night at Malevos, dancing tango with Simón Fe.

The women listened, enraptured. "Nobody here dances anymore," said a woman. "Our husbands don't like it."

"You don't need your husbands," said Ainsley. "Just go by yourselves. Or with each other."

While the women chewed over this, Ainsley turned to her right. There sat Maria Libertad Ortiz.

She wore the waxen expression of the severely medicated. Ainsley touched her hand gently. Maria's face swung around a second or two later. Her eyes were dilated. Ainsley wasn't worried about her being recognized from La Bombonera. This creature was barely sentient.

"You look tired," said Ainsley.

"I'm always tired," she responded.

Maria reached into her purse and pulled out a cigarette case. She lit a cigarette with shaky fingers.

"I've tried to quit many times," she said.

"Me too," Maria replied. "I'm not strong enough."

"Have you tried Nicorette?"

"No," she said, "the drug store here doesn't carry it."

Ainsley realized how small the woman's world truly was. If the local drug store on the base didn't carry it, then Maria Libertad couldn't have it.

The other women were lighting up now too. Orange flames flicked out of from expensive lighters. One woman piped up from behind a freshly-lit cigarette: "She's an addict. We all are."

Clouds of smoke soon curled in the beams of light. Someone handed Ainsley one of the devil's sticks. She found herself joining in, and hated herself for it.

"Tell us about the United States," said the woman. "How are the men?"

"Assholes," said Ainsley, puffing away.

That got some chuckles. "Not like the assholes we grow here," said one.

"They're double-sized," said another.

"Especially my husband," said a third. "I call him the fourteenth."

"Why?" said Ainsley.

"His name is Louis."

Maria Libertad puffed silently, contributing nothing to the conversation. Ainsley sensed that these women were her support group, her nurses, her counselors. They didn't expect much from her. She was the village reclamation project.

"So where is your man?" said one woman. She'd finished her drink and was slurring a little.

Ainsley shrugged. "He said he would be finished soon."

"Oh," said another, "these meetings go on forever. He probably won't be back before one in the morning."

"Then I guess I'd better get some lunch," said Ainsley. She reached for a menu.

"No," said a wife, "put that away."

"Why?"

"This club makes terrible food. We only come here for the drinks."

"We always eat lunch at home," added another.

"Where are we today?" said the third. "At Maria's house?"

"Yes," said the first, "her maid is making chicken divan."

"You should come along," one said to Ainsley. "Otherwise you'll be sitting here alone all day, eating bad sausage."

Ainsley was thrilled, but she had one very important concern. "Is her husband home?"

Everybody looked to Maria, who shrugged. She clearly had no idea of her husband's whereabouts.

"It's not an imposition?" said Ainsley.

"No, it's nothing," said the women.

Standing up, Ainsley tossed her coat over her shoulders and followed the navy wives out of the polo club.

She was driving further into the belly of the beast.

# CHAPTER SIXTY-TWO

Ainsley pushed the chicken, rice, and sauce around her plate, pretending to eat, but she couldn't jam anything down her throat.

The reason: The five-foot-high oil portrait of Lieutenant Colonel Ortiz on the wall.

She was in his living room.

It was the home of a Francophile. There were gilded edges on the furniture, Impressionist canvases of lily ponds. The floor was made of limestone that looked as if it had been pulled from an old chateau. And there was a delicious Burgundy wine in Ainsley's glass.

But she swallowed the liquid without tasting it. Every nerve in her body was tensed. She didn't think that a busy navy officer would stop home at midday, but more surprising things had happened.

The maid silently moved around the table, collecting the women's porcelain dishes. The wives began to light up again. Ainsley took another cigarette and joined in.

The women asked Ainsley many more questions about America, mostly about Hollywood celebrity culture. Ainsley managed a few weak comments on the latest starlets before silence had swallowed the table again. She began to understand that these women just didn't have very much in their mental tanks.

And that, of course, was exactly why they'd been selected to be military wives.

Soon Ainsley was left with nothing but her Burgundy and her thoughts. Most of which were centered upon the differences between American military wives and Argentine military wives. In America, the officers' women were generally strong. They could and did carry entire households on their backs during their husbands' deployments.

These women, however, didn't seem like they could carry a loaf of bread.

Ainsley forced herself back to the task at hand. Through cunning and luck, she'd managed to penetrate all the way into this man's living room. Now she had one thing left to do.

Get proof that Maria Libertad was Ovidio's mother.

The direct, bullheaded way was obvious: ask her. The problem was that this would very likely get Ainsley ejected from the home, probably arrested on base, and likely turned into fish food. And Maria Libertad didn't appear capable of answering anything at the moment. She had the look of a lobotomy patient.

Ainsley racked her brains for another way. Nothing came to her. So she would adjourn to one place where she would be guaranteed a moment of privacy.

"I need to use the bathroom," said Ainsley.

"Down the hall on the left," said one of the wives.

Ainsley pushed up from the table and walked across the carpeted living room. She could feel the women's eyes watching her. They seemed so bored. Her presence, humble as it was, was something of a feast for them.

She walked down a long, darkened hallway lined with

sconces and portraits of landscapes in Provence. The lieutenant colonel had exquisite taste for a sociopath.

On her left, Ainsley passed a door. It didn't feel like a
bathroom. Ainsley turned the doorknob and slowly
opened it.

Her eyes scoped the room. She was in a man's office. Rich
leather chairs. A cowhide stretched across the floor. Naval
artifacts were placed everywhere: an antique steering wheel, a
rudder, thick ropes. An enormous desk, four solid slabs of
mahoghany, anchored the opposite side of the room. Everything smelled of pipe tobacco.

This was Lieutenant Colonel Ortiz's study.

Ainsley's breath came out in short rasps. She really
shouldn't be here, for a multitude of reasons.

She walked through the room in wonder, touching the
fabrics, admiring the artifacts mounted on the walls. Her
hand spun a globe on its nautical stand. The small scratch of
its axle sounded like the squeak of an intrusive mouse.

Ainsley happened upon the bookshelf. She admired the
neat rows of serious tomes, many in Spanish, others in
French, German, a few in English. The lieutenant colonel was
well-read. That made her feel sad. Well-read people acting
barbarous wasn't a very good advertisement for reading.

Ainsley sat down in the high-backed chair behind the
desk. She drummed her fingers upon its edge, feeling its heav-
iness, its power. She fingered the heavy ballpoint pens that
were perched at forty-five-degree angles in their holders. She
studied the small battleship paperweight. She noticed the
image of the Virgin Mary embossed in the wood.

For the first time, Ainsley was feeling like an honest-to-
God intruder here. One with good motive, but an intruder
nonetheless.

If she was going to break the law, she may as well go all
the way.

She yanked open a desk drawer and began to rummage. In one she found an exquisite antique pistol, with a hand-tailored ball-and-hammer. Ainsley hated weapons, but she always admired artistry.

In another drawer she found a sheaf of old pictures, black and white, of military commanders from other eras. Several looked Argentine, serious men with gelled hair and cold pebbles for eyes. Some were of French officers, standing in exotic north African rooms. One was of a Brazilian officer in full regalia aboard a gleaming white frigate. There were even a few SS officers with grim looks on their faces.

She shut that drawer. She should really be moving along to the bathroom before someone noticed her.

But there was one more drawer, at the very bottom. She tugged on the handle. It was locked. Ainsley had never liked being denied entry to anything. Cabinets, doors, rooms—she'd always had a lifelong need for access.

She reached into her pocket and pulled out a plastic credit card. This was the easiest trick in the book, one she'd learned from an ex-boyfriend of dubious morality.

Ainsley slipped the card into the crack, felt around for the top of the mechanism, and wiggled the card back and forth.

It didn't work. Ainsley guessed that the trick only worked on doors. Then an even simpler solution occurred to her.

She pulled out the drawer above—the one with the photos—and removed it from its track.

It was true. Sometimes designers could really be that stupid.

Ainsley looked down into the supposedly locked drawer. And what she saw at the bottom came was both surprising and entirely expected.

It was a Zorro rhodochrosite necklace.

# CHAPTER SIXTY-THREE

Ainsley sat there at the lieutenant colonel's desk, her hands on her knees, staring at the necklace.

It looked like the right one. The chain was made of brown leather, and it had that shiny quality that leather acquires after years of sweat and weather has beaten it to a high gloss. She imagined the thousands of soccer matches that this piece of jewelry had experienced. The number of times Ovidio had plowed it into the grass after a flying header.

She picked up the cabochon, balancing its heft in her hand. It felt surprisingly heavy, though maybe that was just her imagination.

Was this truly the rhodochrosite necklace she'd been assigned to find? She couldn't be sure. She didn't know the precise pattern of the veins on the cabochon. And, according to Marcelo, the lieutenant colonel had purchased three hundred such gemstones. This could be any of them.

Only one person knew for sure, and that was Ovidio himself.

She looked down. Under the necklace was a scrap of paper

with a pair of telephone numbers scrawled on them. There were no names. Those could be important.

Ainsley was confronted with an ethical dilemma. Until now, she'd been wandering in a moral gray zone: sneaking onto a military base, lying about an imaginary polo team, wangling an invitation to lunch at the Ortiz home. All while hiding her true agenda. Things that weren't quite right—but weren't quite wrong either.

If she were to take this necklace, however, she would finally cross the line. She would become an out-and-out thief.

Then again, stealing something that had been stolen itself made the situation even more complicated, and threw into the air the entire question of what, exactly, constituted private property.

It didn't matter. Ainsley knew her own mind. She stuffed the rhodochrosite necklace and the telephone numbers into her purse. She had no problem stealing from a murderer.

Then she noticed a vertical file at the back of the drawer, in the darkness. She had missed them a minute ago.

Ainsley pulled out the file. It was filled with several papers, official-looking documents. She flipped through them.

They were hospital records. One looked to be a medical exam. Another seemed to be a medical discharge form. A third one was a birth certificate from 1977. The mother's name was listed as Maria Libertad Pieres.

And the line containing the child's name was blank.

Ainsley was holding Ovidio's birth certificate.

This was almost, but not quite, the evidence she needed. Even if Ovidio's name wasn't on the birth certificate, she doubted that Maria Libertad had given birth to any other children in the detention center that year.

Ainsley stuffed the documents into her purse. Then she

replaced the drawer and quickly left the lieutenant colonel's office.

She beelined for the bathroom. It was only a little further down the hall. Once inside, she locked the door behind her, turned the sink to full blast, and sank down into a crouch on the floor. She reviewed her options.

Ainsley knew that she should leave. She'd committed a theft, and the lieutenant colonel may or may not be coming home sometime soon.

But there was something else.

Ainsley hated leaving things undone. She'd always been one to stick things out to the bitter end. And she couldn't leave this house, having been so close to Maria Libertad Ortiz, without trying to get *something* that could prove that she had been Ovidio's birth mother. The birth certificate was blank, so it wasn't quite the smoking gun.

Ainsley thought hard. How did people prove maternity? She knew that a blood test was the only absolute way, but how could she steal Maria Libertad's blood? Ask her to chop some onions, then viciously knock the knife onto her fingers? It would never work.

Then Ainsley remembered participating in a genetic database project. To submit the test, she'd had to do a buccal swab on herself. That is, she'd scraped the inside of her cheek with a special pad, sealed it in an envelope, and mailed it off.

Ainsley guessed that the same test could be used to establish probable maternity as well. But again, how could she find an excuse to stick her fingers inside this woman's mouth? There wasn't any feasible way.

Then it struck her. She didn't need to stick her own fingers in Maria Libertad's mouth. She just needed something that *had been* in Maria Libertad's mouth. Something that a laboratory would accept for analysis.

She racked her brains. What items do people routinely put in their mouths, then take out, without swallowing?

Plastic straws. But Ainsley hadn't seen any straws in the house. These women wouldn't use them anyways.

Toothpicks. She hadn't seen any of those either: too manly.

Maybe gum.

Chewing gum.

*Nicorettes.*

The plan was absurdly simple. Ainsley felt excited. She pawed through her purse until she found the pack of smoking cessation squares. There they were, unused. Ainsley's failed attempt to stop a nicotine relapse would finally be put to good use.

She flushed the toilet without using it, in case anybody was listening, and washed her hands. Then she left the bathroom.

The wives had moved to the living room. They were sitting on the heavy furniture. The air was thick with bluish-gray cigarette smoke.

Ainsley coughed twice. "It's so smoky in here," she said.

"We can't stop," said one.

"Completely addicted," said another. "*C'est la vie.*"

"Have another one," said a third.

"I'd like to offer all of you something else instead," Ainsley said.

She held up the package of Nicorette. The women looked at the package as if it were a dead frog. "We don't have that at our drug store," said one.

Ainsley tried not to roll her eyes. "Yes, I know. That is why I am offering you my own. Consider it my thank you for a lovely lunch."

She opened the package and passed it around the group. "You have to try it one time, before you dismiss it."

The wives shrugged and accepted the gum. They put the pieces into their mouths and began to chew.

"It tastes awful," said one.

"This isn't worth it," said another. "I'd rather smoke."

Ainsley watched Maria Libertad chewing. There was no expression on the woman's face. Any passion she had once possessed for life had been drained out by her future husband on the torturer's rack.

"If you're finished, I can take it for you," said Ainsley.

"Let the maid do that," said one.

"No, please, allow me." Ainsley stood directly in front of Maria Libertad and held out a paper napkin.

The woman looked up. She made eye contact with Ainsley for the first time, as if she somehow knew what the next move would mean down the road.

Maria Libertad spit the gum into the napkin and closed it. Then she handed the wad back to Ainsley.

As her hand closed around it, Ainsley felt an artery throb once, violently, inside her temple. She had gotten the gum. She had gotten the necklace.

Now she just had to get the hell off this base.

Ainsley passed around another paper napkin. The women delicately placed their Nicorettes inside it.

Then the thunk of a car door slamming shut came from the driveway. All the women looked up.

"Who is that?" said Ainsley.

"Lieutenant Colonel Ortiz," said one.

# CHAPTER SIXTY-FOUR

The sensation of pure adrenaline is a powerful drug, equal to heroin. For Ainsley, it felt as though someone had tipped the needle into her arm and pushed the plunger down.

"I need to throw this out in the kitchen," she said.

She slipped out of the living room, walked swiftly through the dining room, and ducked into the kitchen. The maid looked up from scrubbing dishes in the kitchen sink.

"Which way is the exit?" said Ainsley.

The maid gestured towards the front door. "That way."

"No," said Ainsley, "I need a different exit. Quickly."

The maid pointed down a small service corridor off the kitchen, to a laundry room at the end. A door leading outside was visible. "That one," she said, "but—"

Ainsley didn't wait to hear the rest. She was already down the hall and at the door. She opened it and stepped outside.

She was standing on a concrete slab in the lieutenant colonel's backyard. High black fencing encircled her. Two aluminum bowls were at her feet.

Then an ominous growl sounded to her left.

She saw the dog two seconds before it sprang, a Rottweiler, with a jaw strong enough to break steel.

Ainsley immediately stepped backwards and shut the door. She felt the dog's body slam into the door.

She stood in the laundry room, breathing heavily. Life wasn't like the movies, she thought. Sometimes, we are truly, irremediably screwed.

With terror in her heart, Ainsley turned back to the service corridor and returned to the kitchen.

The maid seemed amused. "I was trying to tell you that there is a dog outside that door."

"I found that out," said Ainsley. "Is there another exit?"

"No, only the front door."

At that moment, the door opened and slammed shut. The sound of keys landed in a dish. "Maria," a male voice bellowed, "are you ready to go?"

Ainsley drew back into the laundry room. She could hear Maria Libertad answer. "Where are you taking me?"

"The capital," said the lieutenant colonel. "La Boca plays tonight. Our flight leaves at four o'clock. Hello, ladies."

Ainsley heard the other wives murmuring.

"Do you want to meet the visitor?" said one.

Ainsley's heart skipped a beat.

"What visitor?" said Lieutenant Colonel Ortiz.

"I forgot her name. She is from America, with a polo team. We met her in the club."

There was an ominous pause. The moment seemed to last an eternity. Ainsley crouched behind the washer, bowed her head, and prayed. No atheists in foxholes. For a moment, she even understood why warriors committed suicide rather than be captured by an enemy.

"No, I need to use the bathroom first," said the lieutenant colonel. "Tell her to wait."

Ainsley heard his footsteps disappear down the hallway on the other side of the house.

In a flash, she sprang out of the laundry room. She streaked through the kitchen, through the dining room, into the living room. The wives saw her coming and went slack-jawed. Their guest had transformed into a world-class sprinter.

There was time for one quick excuse. "My boyfriend called," said Ainsley, not breaking stride, "he needs me immediately, thank you all for lunch, you've been wonderful."

She knew that she looked like a freak, pushing Nicorette on them, then dashing out without warning. It broke all laws of decorum. She didn't care. Ainsley flew into the foyer, yanked open the front door, and dashed out of the house.

Running down the driveway, Ainsley glanced backwards over her shoulder. The navy wives were piling out of the house onto the porch, watching her, mouths agape.

On the street, she turned left, got out of eyeshot, and glanced around. It looked like classic suburbia. Two neat rows of houses on each side of the street, lovely acacia trees, and not a soul in sight. Good.

She looked at her watch. It was five minutes to two. The grocery store was several blocks away. Tico was her best ticket out of the military base.

Ainsley took a deep breath ... and started to run.

She still remembered sprinting techniques from her high school years, honed by innumerable hours she'd spent on the track. Lean forward for the takeoff, then pull more vertical midway through. Her arms and hands aggressively hammered the air. Her head was aligned with her neck and trunk, her mouth slightly open.

Thirty seconds and two hundred meters later, she slowed to a walk. She laced her fingers behind her head, taking huge gulps of air. She shouldn't feel this winded. When this was all over, Ainsley vowed, she would really get back into shape.

A car turned down the street, heading towards her. It was a military vehicle. She quickly darted behind a hedge and waited until it passed.

She decided to switch streets, in case the lieutenant colonel decided to follow. Ainsley crossed the residential yards onto the next street. Then she sprinted another two hundred meters. She walked for a minute, then did a third sprint.

That put her within sight of the commercial center of the base. Ainsley committed to walking so as not to attract further attention. She kept her head down, her stride tight, her eyes level. She passed several people, some military, a lot more civilians.

The grocery store finally appeared, the women leaving the exit with paper bags in their arms. Ainsley stood on the corner and checked her watch. It was fifteen minutes after two. Tico's truck was nowhere in sight.

She'd missed him.

But she remembered the way out. Directly up this street, maybe two kilometers away, stood the gate from which she'd entered. She could just walk up the road, across the empty field, and out the gate. Couldn't she? There was no law against leaving a military base on foot. It wasn't unthinkable.

But it sure as hell wasn't ideal. She would prefer to ride out of this base in a vehicle, like a civilized person.

She tried to imagine the conversation that happening in Lieutenant Colonel Ortiz's house. She wondered how long it would be before he noticed the necklace was gone. It wasn't advisable to stick around and find out.

Ainsley continued walking briskly down the sidewalk. In a few minutes, she had passed the last commercial business and passed into the open field. She reached the back end of a line of vehicles. She guessed they were backed up at the gate, which looked to be at least four hundred meters away.

There were hundreds of cars, trucks, and vans. She thought it was odd that a rush hour was occurring at one o'clock.

Her stomach in knots, Ainsley strode quickly along the right side of the vehicles. She could feel the eyes of the commuters upon her. She heard some men making *piropo* as she passed. It didn't matter. She was moving faster than the commuters locked in their cars.

Two hundred meters before the gate, Ainsley spotted a military officer up ahead. He was on the left side of the cars, moving from vehicle to vehicle, asking questions.

She panicked. She knew that she looked suspicious. This officer would ask for her visitors' pass. And she would have nothing to give him.

Panic flooded her body. Her thighs locked up. She couldn't move. She was rooted to the ground.

Then Ainsley spotted a familiar truck. Up ahead. A picture of a woman washing laundry decorated the back.

It was Tico's truck.

Ainsley felt her legs unlock. In two blinks of an eye, she'd sprinted alongside the vehicle, opened the passenger door, and jumped inside.

Tico had a sandwich lifted to his mouth. When he saw her, his eyebrows arched above his forehead like a pair of parentheses.

"No," he said.

"I'm going to be arrested by the fucking military if you don't let me stay in this truck," she hissed.

"I don't want any part of your trouble," he said.

Ainsley sighed and slapped a hundred pesos onto the dashboard. She was going to bankrupt herself buying favors here. "Can I ride in the back?"

He couldn't refuse that. "Fine, go," he said, "but you have to get inside the laundry bin. Hide under the clothes. And if they search me, I'll deny knowing you to my own mother."

Ainsley was already opening the door again. "Do they search cars often?"

"Sometimes."

So it wasn't as easy to get on base as Luca and Laura had made it sound. But then again, they had never had anything to hide.

Ainsley could see the officer drawing closer. She slid out of the right side of the vehicle, ran around the back, threw open the door, climbed inside, then rolled it down again.

The back of the laundry truck was completely pitch black. She decided to stow herself as far from the entrance as possible. She climbed on her hands and knees over piles of clothes until she reached a large canvas bin filled with dirty clothing, up against the cab.

She fell into the bin. The oily stench of dirty fabric was overpowering. These were officers' uniforms. She could feel a thick braid against her hand, fringe tickling her cheek, epaulets under her butt.

Ainsley burrowed deeper into the bin, curled into a fetal position at the bottom, and waited. She felt the heavy pressure of fabric upon her back. She felt the slow-and-go of the vehicle.

Then a small movement inside her pocket startled her. She reached inside. It was the Englishman's helpless bird. She'd forgotten about the small creature. It was a survivor. She cupped it in her hands and prayed silently.

She felt the truck stop again. She heard a muffled voice speaking, and Tico's voice answer. Then the truck accelerated again.

Soon she felt the truck work its way up to a decent speed.

The road was humming beneath them. And this time, it didn't stop.

Ainsley heaved a sigh of relief. She had escaped the Puerto Belgrano Naval Base.

Now she only had one thing left to do.

BUENOS
AIRES

# CHAPTER SIXTY-FIVE

Six hours later, Ainsley was in another traffic jam, this time on the outskirts of the nation's capital.

After Tico had dropped her at Laura and Luca's house, she'd shown Marcelo the necklace, told him the story. The old rancher had volunteered to immediately drive her down to Buenos Aires. He'd looked delighted.

Ainsley knew that, for him, revenge was sweet. He wanted to begin the process of exposing the true identity of the monster who had stolen newborn babies out of their mothers' arms.

They'd flown down the two-lane road that afternoon. On either side of the car, the tall grass of the pampas had flattened itself, as if bowing before the passage of the gemstone that throbbed like a secret inside Ainsley's purse.

Now the Toyota was crawling down the freeway, the engine of the Englishman's truck sputtering. It backfired suddenly, belching a cloud of exhaust into the windshield of the poor vehicle behind them.

Ainsley wouldn't speak ill of the dead, but she would definitely speak ill of the dead's choice of transportation. This

Toyota, unlike Marcelo's, was a rolling barrel of donkey crap. The stuffing was popping out of the seats. Not a single gauge on the dashboard was functioning. And the suspension simply didn't exist. Ainsley was stunned that they had travelled this far—half the length of Argentina—without incident.

Tonight was game night at La Bombonera. She'd heard the lieutenant colonel say it, and Luca and Laura had confirmed it. Not just any game either, but the biggest of the year.

The *Superclásico*. Boca Juniors vs. River Plate.

It was Ovidio's team against Sebastian's team. Of course, neither would see any playing time. Ainsley wondered for a moment what it felt like to face a good friend on the field.

She fingered the rhodochrosite. Then she looked at the phone numbers on the paper that she'd filched along with it.

Should she call? From her own cell phone?

Ainsley threw caution to the wind. It had been flying out of her fingers easily for quite some time anyways.

She dialed the first number. Four rings, and then the voicemail picked up. She recognized the voice immediately.

It was Horacio. The flamboyant taster who'd taken her out to a *parrilla*, and then made her pay for it.

Quickly she ended the connection. She chewed on her lip. Lieutenant Colonel Ortiz had that little rat's phone number.

Had *he* stolen the gemstone?

She looked at the second number. She was afraid to dial it. Afraid of who might be on the other end if she did.

She watched her fingers dance across the pad. Heard the ringing in her ear.

"Hello?" said a man's voice.

"Hello, who's this?" she said.

"Ainsley?"

Her heart climbed into her throat as she recognized him.

It was Sebastian. Ovidio's best friend from their youth. The substitute striker for River Plate—and the only friend who hadn't betrayed the superstar.

Lieutenant Colonel Ortiz had his phone number too.

Ainsley tried to speak, but her throat had gone dry. She gasped like a fish.

"Are you in Argentina?" asked Sebastian.

"Yes," she said.

He lowered his voice to a whisper. "But the rumors said the military took you—"

"I came back," she said. "I needed to get the story."

There was an unfriendly silence. "I know you're not a journalist, Ainsley."

That was a relief. "Then what am I, Sebastian?"

"You were working for Ovidio. And he fired you. Is that right?"

"Maybe," she said. "I'll tell you, if you can help me."

"What do you need?"

"Get me into La Bombonera tonight," she said. "The VIP entrance."

"Why?"

"Because I have something Ovidio needs."

She didn't want to reveal that it was the necklace. It could be information. It could be a new slutty girlfriend. Sebastian didn't need to know.

Sebastian hesitated. "What do you have?"

"I can't tell you."

He hesitated again. "I will talk to security. Give them your name. They will take care of you."

"Thank you. Have fun on the bench."

"The coach said he might substitute me. We will see."

She hung up the phone. Something about him sounded different. Ainsley always knew when somebody was hiding something, and Sebastian's tone of voice had set her on edge.

Mostly, however, she couldn't get around the fact that he was apparently communicating with Ortiz. She couldn't trust Sebastian.

Marcelo cleared his throat and spoke. "How do people live like this?"

"How?"

"Like this." His hand swept around at the freeway traffic.

She looked over at the man. He was a rancher, before that a mine owner. He probably hadn't seen traffic like this in decades.

"When was the last time you were in Buenos Aires?" she asked.

"I lived here forty-two years ago."

"Much has changed?"

"No, it looks the same. Actually, I'm more concerned about this truck right now."

"Why?"

"I don't think it's going to last much longer."

Ainsley shrugged. "Just get me as close as possible to La Bombonera."

He shook his head and tightened his grip on the steering wheel. "I don't know why people even go to soccer matches. It's too easy to get stabbed by the *barra brava*."

Half an hour passed. The Toyota was still stuck in traffic, but this time on Avenida Defensa, in San Telmo, three kilometers from the stadium. Ainsley gazed out the window towards Plaza Dorrego, famous for its antiques market on Sunday mornings. She'd been planning to go there just before she'd been kidnapped. Maybe she would still get there someday. She wanted to play tourist at some point.

"At this rate, I don't think you're going to make it," said Marcelo.

"Be patient," she replied. "It's the biggest game of the year."

"Maybe you should get out and run."

"I'll wait until we get a little closer."

"That may not happen."

Then Ainsley heard the engine suddenly make three weird coughs, followed by a long, slow death rattle. Then it puttered out.

Marcelo turned the key in the ignition, gunned the motor. Then he pounded the dashboard with the flat side of his palm. "The last gift of the Englishman."

"I guess I'm walking," she said. "Thank you for everything."

He nodded solemnly. "It was my honor to help you on this mission."

She opened the door and climbed out of the car. Then Marcelo leaned over and grabbed her hand. The skin felt rough but the shape of the hand was friendly. "Listen to me," he said. "I want you to destroy that *milico* bastard."

Ainsley nodded and closed the passenger-side door. She checked her watch. It was seven o'clock.

She only had half an hour to find her way inside La Bombonera.

# CHAPTER SIXTY-SIX

Ainsley ran down the sidewalk, dodging the bouncing, dancing fans who were pouring once again towards the stadium.

On her side of the street was a sea of blue-and-gold Boca jerseys; on the other side of the street, the red-and-white shirts of River Plate. The two sides were singing obscene songs at one another.

Then Ainsley found the railroad tracks, turned, and sprinted towards the stadium. There were twice as many policemen in riot gear patrolling the crowd. These security measures were tight. They'd probably learned the hard way.

She lined up along the barricades and waited for the patdown. The police officer who looked through her purse either missed or ignored the rhodochrosite necklace.

Inside the perimeter now, Ainsley made a quick decision. She wouldn't try to enter through the VIP entrance. She didn't trust Sebastian. For all she knew, he could have told security to escort her to the local Navy office.

No, she would try to buy a ticket, like a normal fan.

She checked her wallet. She had one thousand pesos remaining. That was about two hundred and fifty dollars.

Ainsley glanced around and saw exactly who she was looking for. The fat ticket scalper was standing in the same place, just inside the alley, wearing the same Boca jacket.

He saw Ainsley approaching. "Ah, the lost sheep. You've been wandering outside the stadium for two weeks."

"No, the VIP won't let me in this time," she said.

"So you need something from me?"

"A ticket would be nice."

"The box office has some. You can check there."

His chin tipped saucily to the side. His eyes danced with good humor. Ainsley stuffed a roll of four hundred pesos into his hand. He looked down at the money.

"I need two hundred more," he said.

Ainsley was shoving it into his palm before the sentence was already out. She'd known this was coming and had it ready. All together, it was approximately one hundred and fifty dollars. For a ticket to a soccer game.

The scalper gestured for her to come into the alley. He pulled a single ticket from his inner coat pocket and handed it to her.

Then he pointed at her chest. "Keep that covered."

She looked down at her modest endowment. "What are you talking about?"

"That."

His pudgy fingers pinched the fabric of her red sweater. "Don't let anyone see that." The ticket scalper pantomimed buttoning up his coat.

That was good advice. As she approached the sheer walls of La Bombonera and followed the instructions to her gate, she understood why.

The gate on her ticket simply read La Boca. She'd just bought a ticket to the supporters' section.

The *barra brava*.

She handed the ticket over for scanning, then found herself pushed into a horde of screaming, bouncing men dressed in blue. They pushed her up a short tunnel into the stadium.

And just like that, Ainsley found herself entering one of the most famous sporting events in the entire world.

The Argentine *Superclásico*.

The field opened up before her, a carpet of green. White tickertape already decorated the outside edges of the grass. She looked at the now-familiar white tunnels and dancing Boca girls.

But this time, Ainsley was behind the eighty-foot-high razor-wire fence. Somehow, it reduced her. She felt less like a human, more like an animal.

There was a reason for that. All around the supporters' section, thousands of fans were singing at the top of their lungs. Some were tossing cans into the air. Others were brawling. A few were attempting to dismantle their bench seats. Three adventurous fans had even decided to scale the eighty-foot fence, until the police officers on the other side had started beating the men's fingers with long billyclubs.

Ainsley knew she couldn't stay in this section. It wasn't safe.

She whipped out her cell phone. She scrolled through the contacts until she found Nadia's number. Quickly her fingers tapped out a text message.

*It's Ainsley Walker. I'm in La Bombonera right now. I have Ovidio's necklace and other news. Come rescue me from the barra brava.*

Ainsley hit send. She waited an interminable minute. She watched the executive suite across the stadium. Then her phone beeped.

*On our way.*

Ainsley danced a little jig and stowed her phone away. On the field, the Boca players had burst out of the white tunnel and were doing warmup kicks on the field. She could see Ovidio warming up with them. He was avoiding his teammates. He especially kept his back turned on the *barra brava*.

Five minutes later, a small commotion near the edge of the tunnel caught Ainsley's attention. A flying wedge of seven security guards had bulldozed their way into the supporters' section. No-bullshit expressions were etched upon their faces as if they were made of concrete.

In the middle of the flying wedge was Nadia. She was glancing around anxiously.

Ainsley threaded her way through the bleachers. Nadia spotted her coming, pointed at her to the security. The seven men surrounded Ainsley and Nadia like a bubble and quickly pulled them back towards the tunnel.

"Where have you been?" Nadia said.

"Where have *you* been?" Ainsley answered. "I tried calling you."

"I couldn't answer. I thought maybe they took your phone and it was a trick."

"So you didn't abandon me?" said Ainsley.

"Never," she said. "I'm not like that."

So Nadia had just been afraid to tangle with the military. "I got deported," said Ainsley. "The morning after the game."

"I heard they took somebody from a cafe."

Ainsley nodded. "That was me. They drugged me and put me on a plane."

The women were moving quickly down the tunnel, the roar of the crowd at their backs.

Nadia seemed to be deeply pained. "I'm so sorry. Why the military picked you for such treatment—"

Ainsley interrupted. "I know exactly why," she said. "Listen and I will tell you."

As they circled the stadium, Ainsley told the manager everything. Her kidnapping. Her empty life in the United States. Her need to finish the assignment. Her phone call to Marcelo. Her adventure in Patagonia. Her sneaky infiltration of the naval base. Her theft of the necklace from Lieutenant Colonel Ortiz's desk. Her discovery of Sebastian's number under the necklace.

By the time she had finished, Nadia was rolling the rhodochrosite around in her hand. "Ortiz was working with Sebastian. That is a surprise."

"But you were right," Ainsley said. "It wasn't the maid. It was his friend."

"Just not the one I expected."

"And his employee."

"I never trusted that little taster," said Nadia. "He's an actor, you know."

"He seems like one."

"Last year he lost his job as an understudy when the director caught him stealing money from the lead's purse while she was onstage. I just found out."

That didn't surprise Ainsley. He'd basically stolen a lunch from her. "You're better off without him."

Then Nadia looked at her admiringly. "You did all of this in two weeks."

"Yes."

The manager threw an arm across Ainsley's shoulders.

"I need to tell you something," she said.

"Okay."

"I have never liked an American before. Your people have egos almost like we do. But I like *you*."

Ainsley grinned.

"Now let's go tell the baby the news."

# CHAPTER SIXTY-SEVEN

Nadia led them into the bowels of La Bombonera again. Ainsley waited outside the door of the locker room while Nadia argued with Patricio, the Boca manager, nearby.

"I can't take Ovidio off the field right now," said Patricio.

"Why not?"

"Because he's part of the team."

"But he's not playing. He's on the bench."

Patricio shook his head. "Ovidio needs to be with the team."

Nadia grew exasperated. "Why? So people can throw more trash at him? It's only for a few minutes anyways."

"No."

She beckoned to Ainsley. "But we have something that will interest you."

Ainsley produced the Zorro rhodochrosite necklace.

Patricio took it, held it up to the light. He seemed faintly amused. "You already lied to Ovidio once. Think carefully before you do that again."

"No, that was stupid," said Nadia. "This necklace is for real."

The manager looked skeptical.

Ainsley decided to pipe up. "If you bring him back here," she said, "you will have Ovidio on the field in the second half."

"I've heard that before."

"We didn't really mean it before. Now we do."

Nadia got on the train too. She began to paint an imaginary picture for the manager. "This is the Superclásico. Imagine the story. Ovidio's second half return leads Boca to victory in the biggest game on the schedule."

The manager hung his head, a smile slowly creeping across his face. Nadia had just touched his secret desire. "Okay," he said.

He looked at an assistant and gestured to the field, nodding. The assistant immediately took off running down the hall.

"You can wait inside," said Patricio.

The two women entered the empty locker room. Ainsley stood in the middle of the benches, tapping her toe on the floor. She noticed that a few more posters of the Virgin Mary had made their way onto the lockers.

A minute later, the door opened and Ovidio burst into the locker room. He was still wearing his blue warm ups. Up close, his face seemed drawn and haggard.

His eyes lighted upon Ainsley. "I fired you. In this room."

"You did," she said.

"Nadia said that you—"

"Ovidio, shut up," Ainsley said, cutting him off. "I found it."

She held up the rhodochrosite necklace. Ovidio's face went from stunned to doubly stunned. He ran across the floor and took it from her hand. He turned his back on both women as he inspected it closely.

Then he turned back to the women. His eyes danced back and forth between them.

"This is my necklace," he said. He regarding Ainsley with open shock, as though she were an angel that had been lowered down to earth.

Ainsley played it humble. "I know."

"Where did you find it?"

She hedged. "You might not like the answer to that question."

"But I want to know. You must tell me."

Ainsley took a deep breath. "Lieutenant Colonel Ortiz had it. In his desk. At home."

Now Ovidio was triply stunned. "You know Ortiz?"

Nadia had stepped back. She was letting Ainsley have her moment in the spotlight.

"Unfortunately," said Ainsley. "I think Ortiz ordered me deported. It happened the morning after I met him."

"And still you came back to Argentina?"

Ainsley shrugged. "I had no choice. I needed to finish the job. Even though I was fired."

He blew air out of the circle of his lips. "That bastard."

"That bastard is here tonight," said Nadia. "I saw him in the executive club."

Ovidio shot up from his bench. "You're right. He always comes to see me play." He turned towards the door. "I am going to ask him if this is true."

Nadia stepped between him and the exit. "That is not a good idea."

"I don't care. I need to talk to him. Which suite is it?"

Nadia lowered her head. She didn't have the authority to deny him much of anything. "Forty-seven," she said. "Please don't go. You'll make a scene."

But Ovidio was already gone. Nadia and Ainsley caught each other's eyes.

"You like running?" said Ainsley.

"I hate it," said Nadia.

They took off together. The two women ran up three flights of stairs to La Bombonera's main concourse. They went streaking down the concrete, past the concession stands, the vendors, the bathrooms.

Ovidio was already far ahead of them. Ainsley tried to imagine the fans' faces as *El Mono* himself sprinted past them in warm-up gear. Word would be spreading quickly, but Ovidio probably didn't care. He could outrun the entire stadium anyways.

In any event, it was stupid to think that either Ainsley or Nadia could keep up with one of the world's elite athletes. By the time they reached the suite, they were severely winded. They stopped to catch their breath.

The roar of the crowd encircled them like a wall of endless noise. They had to yell in each other's ears to be heard.

"I don't want to go in there," said Ainsley, gasping.

"Neither do I," replied Nadia. "But he's my client."

"Ortiz will try to kill me if he sees me."

"He wouldn't try anything here. Not in front of so many people."

"But his wife could identify me."

"So what? You don't intend to stay in Argentina, do you?"

Nadia pulled back and looked at her questioningly. Ainsley thought about that. From the little that she'd seen, Argentina really was an astonishing nation, unmatched in a multitude of ways. But one man's wicked agenda would make it impossible for her to stay.

"No, I don't," said Ainsley.

"Then let's go inside and make sure the baby doesn't get spanked."

# CHAPTER SIXTY-EIGHT

The thirty members of the executive suite weren't standing at the windows, as usual. They had arranged themselves in a circle in the middle of the room.

In the middle of the circle stood two people: Ovidio and Lieutenant Colonel Ortiz. They were facing one another, like two men in a duel.

The military man was in his customarily crisp military uniform. He was listening very closely, a serious look on his face. His right hand was hooked around the neck of his wife, Maria Libertad. She was looking at Ovidio with the usual blankness in her eyes.

Ainsley's breath caught in her throat. If she really was his mother, was this the first time that she had ever met her son? It was very likely. And it was also likely that neither of them knew it.

She crept into the room behind Nadia. At the outside of the circle, Ainsley peered over her shoulder.

"So this American," Ovidio was saying, "she is called Ainsley Walker—she says that she took this from your house. This afternoon." He lifted up his necklace. "It's my necklace."

"Is it?" said the navy officer.

"Yes, it's my necklace. You know it well. You've known me for decades."

"I don't think she's being truthful."

"She said that Sebastian's number was underneath it."

The navy officer shrugged off the accusation. "She can say whatever she wants."

"But I believe her."

Ainsley could see the *milico* keeping steely control of his emotions. "I've always supported you, Ovidio. I was there when you were nobody."

"But this woman has a very compelling story."

Lieutenant Colonel Ortiz grew more impatient. "If Miss Walker is here, she can speak for herself. Like a civilized Christian."

Ovidio looked around the circle. Ainsley shrank back, but his eyes found her. "There she is. Come out, necklace detective. Talk."

Nadia leaned into her ear and whispered, "Ortiz can't hurt you here."

Ainsley sincerely hoped that was true. She took a deep breath and stepped into the circle. Ovidio's arm went around her shoulders. She appreciated the gesture of support.

"Maria, do you remember me?" she said.

Maria Libertad's eyes searched Ainsley's face. "You were in my house today. Why are you here?"

"Your husband can explain."

It was taking every drop of Ainsley's willpower to ignore Lieutenant Colonel Ortiz, who was a mere three steps away. She felt his reptilian stare burning into her skull.

Ainsley waited for a reply, but that single comment seemed to have depleted Maria's entire mental reserve. She felt sorry for the woman. The torture, all those decades ago, had really done a number on her.

But the lieutenant colonel took over. "How is anyone going to believe you that this necklace was in my house?"

"Because your wife invited me, and that is where I found it."

He sneered. "Nobody believes her. She's just a woman. She has no education." The acid in his voice blistered her ears. "And you ... you're not even from Argentina."

Ainsley placed her hands on her hips. "You need to believe me when I say that I was in your house today. Remember the wives talking about the American visitor?"

"No, I don't," he said. "They talk so much nonsense anyways."

Now he was lying. The situation was ludicrous. Ainsley was actively trying to convince someone of her criminality.

But she was determined to win this fight, so she began ticking off a list of descriptions. "Your house has a French-style decor. Your Rottweiler is kept in a concrete yard off the laundry room. Your maid makes an amazing chicken divan. Your wife and her friends smoke constantly. And the necklace was in the bottom drawer of your desk in your study. Which was supposedly locked." She paused. "You should get a better desk."

There were some chuckles among the observers. She was glad that the members of this executive suit, these upper-class *porteños*, heard every word.

The lieutenant colonel's face began to blanch as he understood that he was on the losing side of the argument. His eye began that odd twitch. He was the only one denying reality. Like a good tactician, he knew that it was time to disengage.

With calm precision, Ortiz collected his overcoat from a chair and took Maria's hand.

"We're leaving," he said.

"No, I have more questions for you," said Ovidio.

The *milico*'s response was cold and brisk. "Another time.

Remember who supported you all those years. Don't ever forget."

Then the navy officer walked his wife across the room. At the door, Maria Libertad turned and stared at the athlete.

"Ovidio," she said.

An odd sound caught in his throat. "Don't go."

"Ovidio," Maria Libertad said again. It was mostly to herself, as though she were remembering something from long ago.

Then the moment was over. Lieutenant Colonel Ortiz hooked her by the neck again and pulled her out of the executive suite.

Ainsley breathed a sigh of relief. Ovidio seemed dazed. The thirty members of the club immediately enclosed him.

She could hear the athlete talking to himself. "Why is he lying to me? Why did he want my necklace? He's only done good things for me."

Nadia took Ainsley's arm. "You have to tell him. The sooner, the better."

Ainsley nodded. It had to be done.

"Do you want me to be there?"

Ainsley nodded again.

The manager slipped into the group and took Ovidio by the elbow. "Ainsley has more news for you," she said.

"What is it?" he said.

Ainsley said, "It's private." She didn't think that he would want the members of the executive club hearing what she had to say.

"Okay," said the athlete. "Where can we go?"

Ainsley had something in mind. She gestured towards a swinging door in the corner of the club. "The kitchen."

Ovidio nodded. She and Nadia followed him as he pushed through the door.

Inside, two cooks were slicing a carcass on an island countertop made of stainless steel. The knives were paused halfway through the cuts as the men stared at their celebrity visitor. Their mouths were hanging open.

"*El Mono*," one said, then made a sign of the cross.

The athlete grimaced. "Please, I hate that name."

When one of the cooks reached into his pocket, Ovidio went over and put an arm across him. "Brother, you can take a photo later. My friends and I need to use the kitchen for a private conversation."

The cooks nodded dumbly. They moved the meat to a large pan and began to clean the cutting counter.

"No, please, just go," said Ovidio. "We only need a minute."

The cooks left. The door swung shut. Ainsley and Nadia stood there facing the soccer star.

"I'm ready," he said. "Speak to me."

Ainsley took another deep breath. The next words were quite difficult to say, but with an act of willpower she forced herself to utter them.

"Ovidio," she said, "your mother isn't dead."

# CHAPTER SIXTY-NINE

The soccer star didn't respond. His eyes were looking over her shoulder. He hadn't processed the news. So Ainsley repeated it.

"Your mother isn't dead, Ovidio. Your mother is alive."

"No," said Ovidio, "she's dead. I'm sure of it."

"How do you know?"

"Because they told me."

"Who told you?"

"The people who raised me."

"How did they know?"

"Because the angel who brought me to them said so."

"Do you know who that angel was?"

"No."

"It was Lieutenant Colonel Ortiz."

He stepped backwards. Ainsley felt horrible. It was no fun being the bearer of such news. She imagined how he must be feeling.

"Are you sure?" he said.

"Ninety-nine percent. This is why." She handed him the sheaf of documents from Ortiz's desk.

He looked through the documents, a confused expression on his face. "What about my mother?"

Ainsley swallowed hard. "Based on these documents, and from what I've read and learned about the dirty war, it seems like Maria Libertad Ortiz is your mother."

He stood completely still.

"Ortiz took you from a young woman in a torture facility. She fell in love with him around the time of your birth. They were married. They're still married. It's right there."

Ovidio staggered back against the island countertop. His knees started to buckle. Nadia ran to his side and caught him.

Then Ovidio did a surprising thing. He lifted his legs, swiveled sideways, and laid himself down on the stainless steel island counter. Stretched out in the animal blood. He didn't care.

"Tell me everything you know," he finally said, "from the beginning."

Ainsley could do that. She leaned against the sink and began to patiently explain every move that she had made since the last time they'd seen each other. Nadia posted herself near the door in case anybody tried to enter.

Ovidio listened intently. He stared into the overhead light without blinking.

The story took almost ten minutes. When she was done, Ovidio exhaled loudly. "Sebastian was in my room the night it was stolen. I never even considered him."

"I'm sorry."

"He was the only one of my friends who didn't try to screw me. We were almost like brothers."

"Maybe Ortiz paid him."

The soccer player groaned as he sat up. His hair and back were speckled in blood. "Yes, Ortiz supported him too, back in the early days." He thought for a moment. "You know, I always wondered why I went to the Bahía Blanca under-fourteen team. My stepmother made me to go to those tryouts. It never made any sense."

Ainsley nodded. "Maybe Ortiz felt bad about making his wife put you up for adoption. Maybe he was trying to make up for it by taking care of you."

"So he could act like a father," said Ovidio. The light dawned in his eyes. Then he shook his head. "It's all too much. I don't believe it."

"You can believe it," Ainsley said. She fished out the tissue paper with the Nicorette wrapped inside.

"What is this?"

"A piece of chewing gum. Maria Libertad had it in her mouth this afternoon."

"So what?"

"It can be used for a DNA test. Take it to a lab. They'll let you know if Maria Libertad could be your mother. If so, you can pursue her for a full blood test, if you want."

He looked at the tissue. "I cannot believe you have done all this."

"I'm a full-service agency," Ainsley wisecracked. "I even keep working after I've been fired."

The soccer star smirked at her. The point had been made.

The door swung open. Ainsley watched Lalo and the rest of his sleazy entourage came sliming into the kitchen. Nadia couldn't stop them.

Ovidio smiled broadly when he saw his friends. He held up the rhodochrosite necklace. "Look," he said.

"For real?" said Lalo.

"It's no joke."

The entourage roared. "*Que groso!*" shouted Lalo. He pulled the lit cigarette out of his mouth and flicked it across the room in celebration.

"Which bastard stole it?" he said.

Ovidio pointed at Ainsley. "She says it was Sebastian."

"I never liked that asshole. He's too smooth." The professional minder looked at Ainsley with new eyes. "I remember you."

"And I remember you," she said.

"I'm still keeping my promise."

"You'd better be."

One of the entourage piped up. "Ovidio, Sebastian is on the field."

The soccer player looked up. "Impossible. He's one step from the glue factory."

"River Plate just substituted him in. It's almost halftime."

Ovidio slid off the bloody table and wobbled on his feet. "So now I have my necklace. And Sebastian is on the field."

"Kill him," said one of his friends.

Ovidio fastened the rhodochrosite around his neck. A wistful expression came over his face. "It's curious, Ainsley. Even though I know that this is bullshit, I still can't play without it."

"I would feel the same way," she said.

"Come here."

He brought Ainsley in a tight embrace. Then he kissed her cheek. "Thank you," he said. "You've given me a lot to think about."

"It's my job."

"Let's talk later tonight." He turned to his boys. "I need to get to the locker room. Who wants to be security?"

The entourage roared, and Ovidio led everybody out of the kitchen.

Nadia threw her arm around Ainsley. "Do you want a drink?"

"Yes."

"You can't have one in this suite." Then she sprung the punchline: "You must have at least *two*."

Laughing to the point of tears, the women stepped out of the kitchen, back into the executive club.

Twenty minutes later, drink in hand, Ainsley stood at the window of the executive suite, watching the second half begin. When Ovidio ripped off his warmup jacket and jogged into the center of the grassy field, the roar of the fans nearly tore apart the stadium. It felt like La Bombonera was about to split the ground open and fall into the earth.

"They really love him," said Ainsley.

"Watch the players," said Nadia. "They're up to something."

Ainsley watched. The Boca Juniors did something odd: they had split into three small groups. Now, each group crowded a different referee. They seemed to be complaining mightily about something.

Meanwhile, with the authorities distracted, but the fans watching his every move, Ovidio ran directly to Sebastian, arms open. Sebastian returned the gesture.

But instead of an embrace, Ovidio drove his right cleat into Sebastian's foot. The traitor dropped to the grass.

The crowd roared even harder, thinking about the rivalry. Nobody knew the reason behind the violence except for Ainsley and Nadia. And the referees had missed it entirely.

"He planned that, didn't he?" said Ainsley.

"Ovidio doesn't know politics," said Nadia, "but he knows this sport, both clean and dirty."

Limping, Sebastian took his place for the second-half kickoff. The whistle blew; play began. A Boca midfielder immediately chipped the ball to Ovidio. The crowd roared. Ovidio bolted sideways with the ball, turned on a dime, then ran at a diagonal in the other direction. Then he whirled again, and ran back parallel with the first sprint. He fired off a long shot, twenty meters, and it slipped through the hands of the goalkeeper.

His first goal. It took less than two minutes.

The crowd thundered. Nadia leaned over to Ainsley. "Did you notice anything about the way he ran?"

"No."

"Watch. I bet he's going to do it again."

Three minutes later, there was another pass to Ovidio. Again, he bolted sideways, lost the defender, turned on a dime, ran at a diagonal the other way, then turned again and sprinted parallel to the first line he'd run.

It was the same as the first attempt. And it ended in a second goal.

"Don't you get it?" said Nadia.

"No," said Ainsley.

She smiled. "He's making a Z. It's his signature play. Didn't I tell you about this?"

"No," she said, "you didn't."

Ainsley was aghast. He really was an artist, someone who applied his inner passions to his craft.

For the rest of the half, Ovidio played like a man on fire. She watched him score two more goals using the same play. No living defender could keep up with his ferocious speed and deft turns.

When the final whistle blew, Ainsley watched the Boca Juniors hoist him high onto their shoulders in victory. She watched him throw his fists into the air. She felt the walls shake with the thunderous sounds of La Doce. It had been the best game of his career, according to Nadia.

In the end, it didn't really matter whether the necklace had really come from his biological mother or not.

The Argentina rhodochrosite didn't just define Ovidio's life.

It *gave* him life.

# CHAPTER SEVENTY

When the shopowner closed and locked the door behind her, Ainsley Walker understood what life as a celebrity was like.

She had just entered the Louis Vuitton shop on the ground floor of the Alvear Palace Hotel. Two black-suited private security guards had followed her from store to store. Now they were posted outside the door.

They were protecting *her*. They had been for the past week.

Since the *Superclásico*, Ovidio had become a changed man. The laboratory results from the chewing gum had signalled the strong possibility that Maria Libertad was in fact his mother.

Nadia had alerted the celebrity of the danger that Ainsley was potentially in. After all, she had infiltrated Lieutenant Colonel Ortiz's home. The navy officer's theft had been revealed. His dignity had been publicly injured. He was most likely going to try to retaliate.

That's why, for the last seven days, Ovidio had stashed Ainsley in a room at the Alvear Palace Hotel. She'd been free to move around within the hotel, but stepping outside was prohibited. She wasn't the only one under lock and key, either. Marcelo, Laura, Luca, and even Nadia herself had been brought here for temporary protection. They all shared a warren of adjoining rooms in a private hallway.

Through the store window, Ainsley glanced at the men, their arms crossed, stances wide. She knew that there were even more men posted around the hotel. Having this level of personal protection, the same given to most rich South Americans, made her feel much safer. But she also felt cooped up.

She wasn't alone. Laura was annoyed at being yanked from her home. So Ainsley had suggested that a little bit of shopping downstairs would do them both some good. Besides, she had promised.

"Do you like these?" said Laura, modeling a pair of five-inch platform pumps.

"They cost three thousand pesos," said Ainsley. That was about seven hundred dollars.

Laura tried to hide her surprise. Then she picked up a purse. Ainsley waited for the sticker shock. Laura looked at the price tag and blanched.

Laura wrinkled her nose and put the shoe and the purse back on their displays. "Can we go back up to the room? I don't like shopping as much as I thought I would."

The shopkeeper unlocked the door, and the two women slipped out into the grand, red-carpeted hallways.

"I don't know how people afford to look this good," said Laura.

"Most people can't."

Laura thought for a moment. "When do you think we will be able to leave?"

Ainsley shrugged. "Nadia said that Ovidio was putting something together. Maybe tomorrow."

The private security guards followed the women into the

elevator and pressed the buttons for them. They stepped out first when the doors opened. Ainsley thought it was very chivalrous.

The women walked down the hall towards their rooms. Ainsley slid the keycard in the slot. The green light beeped. She stepped inside.

She leaped back, startled. A man was sitting on her bed. He was silhouetted against the light from the window.

Then the man stood up. It was Ovidio.

"The manager let me in," he said. "I can't just stand around the lobby waiting. People harass me."

"It's fine," she said. "You're the one paying."

"In more ways than one," he replied. He handed her a brown package. She peered inside. There was a stack of American dollars.

"It's twenty thousand," he said. "Your price."

"I didn't think you would do it," said Ainsley.

He looked offended. "You've given me what I asked for, and even more. You've changed my life."

"Thank you," she said.

"Now there is something you have to do," he said.

Ainsley shook her head and waited for the other shoe to fall. She had been through enough already.

"You have to leave Argentina today."

"Why?"

He stood at the window. "The only way to guarantee your safety is to bring everything out into the open. Just like during the trials. So Nadia is preparing the media rollout for this afternoon. We want to present you in a press conference at the airport. You'll give public testimony about your kidnapping, the maid's kidnapping, Marcelo's cattle, everything you know. All the newspapers and magazines are going to be there. Your name will become spread all across the world."

"And then—"

"You'll turn and walk with me through immigration and onto your airplane. The cameras will be following. In that spotlight, with your knowledge, they'll have to let you leave. No tricks from them."

Ainsley admitted that it sounded like a good idea. "But what about your political plans?"

The athlete shook his head. "I'm giving that up. The presidency isn't for me. How can I tell other people what to do when I'm still trying to find out who I am?"

He sat back, confounded by the mystery of his own identity. Ainsley was impressed by the change. Ovidio was in the process of discovering himself.

"Besides," he continued, "I think they stole my necklace for political reasons."

"What do you mean?"

A cynical look came onto his face. "The military knows that they can't control me. And that's what the history of this country is. Military control of the president. It's either hidden or open, but it's always the same."

Ainsley didn't know enough whether to agree or disagree. "So you think Ortiz was taking orders from someone higher?"

The athlete nodded. "They knew how important the necklace was to me. Stealing it was a good way to neutralize my popularity. To use my own neuroses against me."

Ainsley was stunned. Nadia had been right when she had said that Ovidio was an intelligent man. He had just been too overwhelmed by his own emotional issues to show it.

"That's very wise," she said.

Ovidio smiled ruefully. "El Oido helped me discover that yesterday."

Ainsley thought back to the psychotherapist. Her suspicion had been right. He'd figured out a lot more of the situation than he had revealed.

"And Horacio?" she said.

"I fired him. That *maricón* was helping Ortiz. Him and Sebastian. Both crooks." He moped. "I can't trust anybody."

"I know how you feel," said Ainsley.

Then Ovidio brushed off the melancholy. "So it's all good?" he said, clapping his hands.

"It's all good," she said. "When do we leave?"

"Right now. The conference starts in an hour. Your plane to the States leaves after that."

Ainsley thought for a moment. "Can I do something first?"

"Of course."

She picked up the payment money and went out into the hallway and knocked on another door. Laura opened it. "No more shopping," the woman said.

"I'm leaving," said Ainsley, "and I need to see Marcelo."

She welcomed the American into the room. The rancher was sitting stiffly in a chair near the window. He seemed ill at ease in an environment of luxury.

"I have to leave," she said.

Marcelo nodded. He seemed very dejected.

"What are you going to do?" she said.

"I don't know. Luca and Laura still want me to move in with them."

"I'd like to help."

"How?"

She reached into the package and counted off five thousand dollars. Then she put the money into his hand.

"I couldn't have found the necklace without you," she explained, "so you shouldn't be the only one who suffers."

He stood up. A single spasm of emotion seized his face. "Come here and say goodbye."

They embraced. Then Ainsley hugged Laura goodbye. She went back to her room, assembled her clothing into a bag, and took the elevator downstairs.

As the red-coated doormen welcomed her through the heavy doors, she saw Ovidio waiting in his Mercedes. She slid into the backseat next to him. He clasped her hand. She clasped it back.

"To think I fired you," he said, shaking his head.

"And to think I came back," she replied.

"We're both a little *loco*."

"Agreed."

He nodded to his driver, and the Mercedes tore off towards the airport.

# EPILOGUE

In the next seat, the heavy woman in the floral t-shirt was staring at Ainsley. She had been quietly staring at Ainsley for almost nine hours already, practically since the plane had lifted off. It was a relief when she broke the ice.

"You're that girl from the airport," the woman said. She had an American accent.

"I am," said Ainsley.

"You were the one in front of all those cameras and reporters."

Ainsley nodded. "Mm-hm."

The woman felt emboldened to speak even further. "If you don't mind me saying, you speak Spanish really good. I thought you were Argentinian!"

"Thank you."

"I only understand a little bit of it. But hey." She grew interested. "Did you really get drugged and deported? The first time you came here?"

"Yes. I don't recommend it."

"Heavens, no." The woman clucked. "But I wouldn't mind

a bit of unconsciousness right now." She fanned her face. "I feel just *terrible*."

The flight from Buenos Aires was headed towards Miami, at which point Ainsley would book a different flight to her home city. She wasn't relishing the thought. She had a nice stack of money, true, but the idea of decomposing on the sad couch in her sad apartment, unemployed again, held no attraction whatsoever.

"So you're a gemstone detective?" the woman said. "Is that what you said up there on the stage?"

"Yes."

"How did you get *that* job?" The woman was staring at her in amazement. Her face was extremely flushed.

"It doesn't matter," said Ainsley, "since it seems to be finished anyways."

"No more work?" She looked sad. Ainsley sensed that the heavy woman had latched onto her. "Well," she said, "I lost an earring last week in my hotel room. Want me to hire you?"

Ainsley's seatmate began to laugh. Soon it had transformed into a deep coughing fit. Her chest was heaving. Ainsley shifted as far away as she could move in her seat.

"Oh my God, I feel just horrible," the woman complained.

"Do you want me to get a flight attendant?" Ainsley asked.

"No, no, I can get over it ... just let me be for a minute ..." The heavy woman laid her head against the window shade.

Ainsley returned to her e-reader, but her thoughts flitted back to the news conference. She had done extremely well. Ovidio had announced that he would not be seeking the presidency. Then he'd explained the theft of the necklace. Finally, he and Nadia had introduced Ainsley. They'd stood by her side while she explained into the microphone, in her best Spanish, everything she'd discovered. They hadn't allowed any questions afterwards.

Then, just as promised, she'd stepped off the stage, and

Ovidio had escorted her through immigration, an arm around her shoulders. No problems.

Now her name and accomplishment were circulating through Latin American news media. And she was here, forty thousand feet over the Atlantic. Or possibly the Caribbean. She wasn't sure exactly which route the pilot had chosen.

Ainsley glanced down at her seatmate's left hand. It had stiffened into a weird birdlike claw. That was odd. Then Ainsley looked at the woman's face. Her mouth was open, her eyes had rolled backwards into her skull, and her breath was coming in short rasps. Her skin had turned a sickly yellowish-gray.

This wasn't airsickness. It looked like a heart attack.

Ainsley quickly punched the flight attendant button. Then she unbuckled her seatbelt and stood up. She didn't know what to do. She knew nothing about any health procedure more complicated than swallowing an ibuprofen.

The flight attendant arrived. "What's the problem?"

Ainsley pointed to the woman.

"Oh my God," said the attendant. She motioned to another member of the crew. Soon two other flight attendants had arrived and were tending to the stricken woman.

Five minutes later, a flight attendant went running to the galley. She grabbed the intercom and tried to mask the urgency in her voice: "Ladies and gentlemen, if there are any health professionals on board, the crew is requesting that you please come to the rear of the aircraft immediately."

Ainsley stood in the aisle, feeling useless. "Ma'am, would you mind choosing another seat?" one flight attendant asked. "There's a few available in first class."

"No problem," said Ainsley. "Let me know if I can help."

"We will," she said.

At that moment, the woman's body jerked. A bizarre moan issued from her lips. Unnerved, Ainsley collected her items and walked to the front of the plane, into the first-class section. She sank into an empty leather seat.

A beautiful woman with dark lustrous hair was reading a magazine next to her. They looked to be about the same age.

"My seatmate is very sick," said Ainsley. "They told me to come up here."

The woman looked up. "It's no problem. I'm sorry for her." She spoke with a sexy musical accent, like a cooing love-bird. It was very different from the Rioplatense accent that Ainsley's ear had become accustomed to recently.

"I hope she makes it to Miami."

"Oh, me too."

Ainsley twisted her fingers together. A few minutes later, the intercom snapped on.

"Ladies and gentlemen, this is your pilot speaking. Due to a passenger medical emergency, we are unfortunately going to have to make a unscheduled stop."

The dark-haired woman perked up. "Where do you think it will be?"

Ainsley shrugged. "I don't know."

"I think we're close to my home," she said. "Maybe we will land there."

The pilot continued: "According to our charts, the nearest airport is San Juan International. Problem is, a little weather system called Hurricane Hannah is about one hour from making landfall, but we're gonna scoot in just before they lock it down. Please note that the fasten-your-seatbelt sign has been lit. Flight attendants, cross check the doors for landing."

Ainsley's seatmate was almost glistening with happiness. "That's my home! Have you been to my island before?"

"No," said Ainsley.

"Then let me welcome you to Puerto Rico."

## PLOTWORKS PUBLISHING

If you enjoyed this story, please leave a review at the place where you purchased it.

Then visit Plotworks Publishing to follow Ainsley Walker on her next exciting gemstone travel mystery!

Turn the page for a sneak peek—

# THE
# PUERTO RICO
# PEARL

## AN AINSLEY WALKER
## GEMSTONE TRAVEL MYSTERY

# J.A. JERNAY

# THE PUERTO RICO PEARL

Two hours later, as the sun drowned below the waves, Ainsley stood on a beach holding a kayak upright in the sand.

Ainsley had travelled to the other side of the island, having bounced across the mountains in her tout's military-issue jeep. His name was Edwin. It sounded vaguely nerdy, which wasn't totally inaccurate. His nervous darting eyes betrayed his discomfort with the tall gringa client.

Ainsley, meanwhile, felt equally uncomfortable. One reason was the new floral bikini that she was wearing. It didn't feel right to be wearing this little at night, even though the soft Caribbean breeze was sliding around her hips and purring at her.

In her left hand, the edge of the fiberglass kayak felt hard and unforgiving. Its nose was buried deep in the sand. She ran her fingers along its ribbed footwells, its sleek bottle nose.

Before her lay the calm surface of Mosquito Bay.

The name was deceptive. Maybe there were mosquitoes, but a quick flip through Edwin's three-ring binder had told her this bay was famous for a different type of tiny creature: a tiny dinoflagellate. When it was agitated, it emitted a blue glow. This was called bioluminescence. And this was why this bay had become one of Puerto Rico's main tourist draws.

Tonight, though, the lagoon was empty. Edwin stood next to Ainsley, holding his kayak. "Very beautiful. We launch soon."

"When?"

He glanced over his shoulder. "One more coming. We have to wait."

Ainsley stood patiently and watched darkness blot out the last streaks of light until a black dome had fallen atop the island.

Then Edwin perked up. "He comes now."

She turned. A large musclehead had come down from the palms that fringed the beach. He was carrying the kayak on his shoulder as casually as a small duffel bag. Ainsley hadn't even been able to lift hers.

He drew closer. The orange tip of a lit cigarette dangled menacingly from his lips. His eyes were a pair of knife-slits in his face.

"You ready?" said Edwin.

The musclehead grunted, then effortlessly tossed the kayak into the water. It made a gigantic splash, ripples moving across the water.

She tried to catch the eye of her kayaking partner, but he wouldn't look at her. This tour was feeling more than a little weird. Lunkheads like him didn't usually make special night-time trips to splash in sparkly water.

Edwin turned to Ainsley. "Let's go."

"I'm ready," she said. Then she spotted another person, much further down the beach, a heavy figure. He was coming their way. "Who's that?"

Edwin turned and looked. His eyes narrowed. "Looks like a bandit."

"A bandit?"

He nodded. "Vieques has many beach bandits. We have to go." He pointed at Ainsley's bag. "Don't leave nothing. Keep that in your kayak."

Ainsley didn't argue. She would dive to the bottom of the bay to retrieve it, if necessary.

Edwin helped her lower the kayak into the water. Then Ainsley slipped the life vest around her neck, buckled it, and hopped into the seat. He handed her the purse, which she stowed between her feet, then gave her the double-ended paddle.

The group of three began moving out to the center of Mosquito Bay. Ainsley hadn't ever kayaked before, but she took to it easily. The motion was even easier than walking, especially on such a tranquil night.

The waxing moon rose above the horizon, casting white shimmers on the black surface of the water.

Ainsley dipped her oars into and out of the water, watching it cascade off the flat blade. "So how do the little things work? The dinoflagellates?"

"I don't know," Edwin said.

"What about the tides? Do they affect the biolumi-nescence?"

"I don't know."

Ainsley crinkled her forehead. "I thought you were supposed to be a tour guide."

He shrugged. "I just paddle."

So much for conversation. The musclehead behind them hadn't spoken either. She wondered if he had had his mouth sewn shut. Ainsley was feeling as though she'd let herself be carried into a bad situation.

"Here," said Edwin, dipping a paddle, "look."

His paddle was glowing blue. Ainsley trailed a finger in the water. It felt warm and clean, but even more surpris-ingly, it glowed. A sheath of purple luminescence surrounded her finger and left a trail in the water as she glided by.

Her mouth dropped open. "That's beautiful."

"We'll go further out, so you can swim," said Edwin. "It's against the rules, but who cares, huh?"

In her peripheral vision, Ainsley glimpsed a figure. It was a dark figure in a kayak, paddling towards them.

The bandit.

"Look," she whispered.

Edwin glanced their pursuer and frowned. "He make trouble, we have problem. Go faster."

He doubled his pace, and Ainsley followed. The leisurely paddle had become a pursuit. The sounds of splashing echoed across the surface of the bay. Her shoulders began to ache. She wondered where on earth Edwin could possibly be leading her.

She twisted around. She could hear the furious dipping of the bandit's paddle behind them. What would he do if he caught up to them? Pull out a gun? Strap a knife on the end of his paddle? Ainsley had heard of carjacking, but she'd never heard of kayakjacking.

"He's fast," said Edwin.

"What should we do?"

Edwin's arms stopped moving. He drifted to a halt and put his paddle across his lap. "We fight."

Ainsley stopped paddling. The musclehead came up alongside the other side of Edwin. They exchanged a few low words. She assumed they were planning the defense.

Ainsley watched them uneasily. She wished that she had never entered this situation. What was supposed to have been a dreamy excursion into an aquatic wonderland was about to become a low-tech robbery.

She turned the kayak around. The bandit was

approaching quickly. She could see a swirling puddle of glowing blue with each dip of his paddle, left, right, left, right.

"What should I do?" she said.

Edwin's eyelids had lowered oddly. "You don't have to do anything."

That was a strange answer. Then she heard the bandit shout something at them. She listened. He had a deep voice. It sounded familiar.

He was shouting her name.

Ainsley peered across the water. The waxing moon, while not yet full, was strong enough to illuminate faces. And as the bandit came closer, she saw the outline of a heavy man.

The stranger shouted her name again.

She glanced at Edwin. A strange reptilian look had fallen across his face. She realized that the musclehead had disappeared.

Then she felt something crush into the back of her head with enormous force. A sheet of white light blinked across her field of vision.

The last thing Ainsley remembered was pitching over the side of her kayak into the water.

## PLOTWORKS PUBLISHING

Visit Plotworks Publishing to follow Ainsley Walker on her next exciting gemstone travel mystery!

Then explore a new series by J.A. Jernay—the Cosmo Bennett Mapping Thrillers!

Turn the page for a sneak peek—

# J.A. JERNAY

## BOUNDARY

A COSMO BENNETT MAPPING THRILLER

FROM THE AUTHOR OF THE AINSLEY WALKER GEMSTONE TRAVEL MYSTERY SERIES

# BOUNDARY

Cosmo Bennett and his assistant Noah shuffled down the dirt shoulder of the boulevard in the midday heat, sweating and miserable.

Each was lost in his own thoughts. Cosmo dreamed of hitting a heavy punching bag at his gymnasium. Noah dreamed of passing level nineteen of Operation Earlobe, an obscure RPG he'd abandoned last semester.

The morning's meeting had been a complete bust.

"I don't think we should continue," said Cosmo finally.

Noah didn't respond, but Cosmo took no notice. He continued: "I don't think anybody here takes our task seriously. I don't think this propaganda map was as influential as they say. I don't think this map has driven the civil unrest. I think social media and centuries of tribal warfare are more to blame for the unrest than anything else."

He looked over at Noah, waiting for a response. "What about you?"

The graduate assistant came back from his reverie. "Huh?"

"Did you hear anything I said?"

"No."

"I was just saying this is pointless and we should go home."

"I don't have a problem with that."

They arrived at Vida e Caffe. It was a chain café, with hundreds of similar franchises scattered across the southern part of the African continent. The branding was modern and inviting. A hundred people sat beneath umbrellas at small tables on the large outdoor patio.

An arm was waving at them. It was Christopher, their fixer, a cup of tea on a ceramic saucer in front of him. Two other cups awaited them.

"Hello sirs," he said. "I ordered us all a rooibos. It's a vanilla tea that is extraordinary."

Cosmo and Noah pulled out the chairs and sat down. The driver quickly sussed out that something was wrong.

"It was a bad meeting?" he said quietly.

"Yes," said Cosmo, "there was no progress made."

"I'm very sorry."

Cosmo sighed. "I think we have to leave."

The fixer looked confused. "But you just sat down—"

"The country," he clarified. "We have to leave Fabajouti. We can't seem to do any good here."

Christopher looked crestfallen. "I do understand your frustration."

Noah said, "If it's okay with you, we'd probably like to just get in the car and go back to the hotel."

The fixer rediscovered his manners. "Of course, as you wish—"

"But we'd love to try the tea first—" added Cosmo.

"You two enjoy the rooibos," said Christopher, "while I fetch the car. The parking lot is very jammed and it will take quite a while to remove. I've already paid the bill."

Before they could object, the driver had shot to his feet.

He clapped Cosmo on the shoulder and left the patio. They watched him cross the boulevard to an off-street parking area that was crammed tightly with vehicles. On his approach, the attendant began shifting other cars.

Noah sipped the tea. "This does taste really good. I don't drink enough tea."

"I like tea," said Cosmo. He sipped from the cup. "This one is good."

"What's your favorite?" asked Noah.

"Maybe pu'er."

"That one's bitter, right?"

"Yeah. It's fermented."

"What about Earl Grey?"

"A cliché."

"I think I'm more of a fruity tea guy," said Noah.

Cosmo nodded. "Yeah, they have their charms."

"You ever try chamomile?"

"It's good for sleeping," said Cosmo, "but otherwise it's—"

His comment was cut short by a massive fireball that erupted from the parking lot across the street.

———

In a split second, Cosmo and Noah instinctively rolled off their chairs and onto the ground beneath their table. Their eyes met. Each was filled with terror.

Then the shock of the overpressure hit. Cosmo felt the force of the blast wave hit the left side of his body. The highly compressed air rattled the left side of his skull. It even sent his lips and cheeks flapping to the right.

The initial sound of the explosion was deafening, but that was soon replaced by a symphony of falling destruction. A thousand pieces of metal, plastic, glass, and upholstery rained down upon the boulevard, the grass, the other cars.

A shower of tiny shrapnel hit on the patio of the cafe. One hit Noah in the hand and sizzled his flesh. He shook it off.

They waited another few seconds for the shrapnel rain to end. Then Cosmo and Noah lifted their heads.

The patio of the café was transformed into pandemonium. The patrons started to pull themselves up from the ground and flee out to the street and in the opposite direction. The street itself was coming alive with panicked people running in every direction.

"What the actual—" said Noah.

"Christopher!" interrupted Cosmo. "What about Christopher?"

He scrambled up to his feet. Without waiting for Noah, he sprinted out of the café and across the boulevard, weaving through the stopped cars. The air was acrid with chemicals and the heat had somehow intensified even further.

The parking lot was a field of wreckage. The bomb had exploded in the middle of the space, shredding every vehicle and person within twenty meters. Pieces of concrete and metal and glass had been blown across the scene.

"Christopher!" he shouted again. "Christopher! Don't do this!"

He saw a shoe with a foot still in it. He saw a red string of guts entangled in a hubcap. A wave of nausea gripped his stomach. He covered his nose with his t-shirt and backed away.

He tripped backwards over a piece of metal, stumbled, and fell to the ground.

That's when he saw it.

A long strip of shredded fabric. A yellow-and-green printed tropical shirt.

It was bloody and torn.

Cosmo turned his head and retched onto the asphalt. All the tea he'd just drank came out.

He somehow pulled himself to his feet and staggered back to the café. Noah was waiting at the far corner, on the sidewalk, pacing frantically.

"So?"

"I found him," said Cosmo. He forced the next words out. "A little bit."

Noah's face went white. "Oh my God."

Cosmo didn't say anything. He just gripped Noah by the upper arm. "Walk with me. And don't look back."

———

The pair moved briskly down the boulevard, away from the scene. People were running past them, mouths open, eyes full of fear, but Cosmo maintained a steady pace. His face betrayed an intense desire to appear as normal as possible.

"So we're just going to leave the scene?" said Noah.

"Yep."

"Why?"

"Don't make me answer that, Noah."

"I think we should talk to the police, cooperate, tell them everything—"

"In a different country," Cosmo replied, "in a different scenario, you'd be right. But not here, not now."

Noah looked back over his shoulder at the scene.

"Look straight ahead," Cosmo said through his teeth, "and listen to me. Our Mercedes is gone. Christopher is ... gone."

"Shit—"

"And I'm going to suggest something else that could blow your mind."

"What?"

"It's possible that we were the intended target."

"That's insane."

"Is it?"

"How do you know?"

"I don't. But it's a possibility. Here's another one. It's possible that we are going to be used as scapegoats. We were the last people seen eating with Christopher. Do you want to be put in a Fabajouti jail on suspicion of a crime?"

They walked for another half minute in silence. Behind them, the chaos grew distant.

"Where are we going?" Noah said finally.

"Back to the hotel."

"And then?"

"We're leaving, like we planned."

"We're not going home, are we?" said Noah.

Cosmo's mouth grew hard and his jaw jutted out. He stared straight forward at an invisible point on the horizon. "No, we're not."